Two Seasons

by

David Wilson

ISBN: 979-8-218-15460-8

DEDICATION

To Mary Jean Igoe. Your son has been my lifelong friend.
Thank you for having him.

CONTENTS

PROLOGUE

The stories contained within the chapters of this book are, in part, variations of tales that my father spoke of throughout his life of personal experiences that he'd either witnessed or been a part of at one time or another. Included within these are tales based on adventures that my father and I shared, all set to the fictitious characters and setting within this book.

My father was a storyteller, and my overall inspiration for writing this particular novel. Dad enjoyed telling his tales to anyone who cared to listen, or even didn't care to. However, by virtue of the fact they were present and enjoying his company, they were subject to a story that he chose to reminisce about. My father had a unique way of beginning his stories, as he would always preface with, "If I've told you this story before, stop me," which, of course, I never did, and I also never interrupted him by reminding him that he'd told me the story before. Even my personal friends who knew my father well would get a chuckle out of the fact that Dad seemed to never have the ability to recall if he'd already told them the story. Now, I realize that it's certainly not uncommon for anyone, especially someone with some age behind them, to begin a story, "If I've told you this story before, please stop me." In fact, it's very common. What made my father's tales unique was what he'd say next. Every time, and I'm being quite serious when I say that every single one of his stories continued with the next line, "I had a friend once, he's dead now," and then he'd continue with his tale.

I often wondered, if my father told his other friends stories about me when I wasn't around to hear them, how he may have begun each one given the fact that I wasn't dead and all. The way in which my father began his stories became something of an anecdote between myself and my circle of friends to the point that one evening we had a good belly laugh over it at my father's expense.

It was during the late 1990s when one of my lifelong chums, a man by the name of James, was along on a camping trip with my father and me on Sysladobsis Lake in Lakeville Plantation, Maine. My father and I had built the camp on "Dobsy" Lake off the East Shore Road where Dad had leased land from the Dead River Company in the late 1960s and had placed a tag-along camper trailer on the lot, and he declared it to be, "camp." Throughout the 1970s he expanded on the trailer and ultimately Dad purchased the lot when much of the land surrounding the eastern portion of the lake was provided to the Passamaquoddy Indigenous People during a 1980 Maine Indian Land

Claims Settlement, and my father was given the opportunity to purchase our spot on the lake and finally had the ability to begin to complete the cabin, comfortable in the fact that he now owned the land that it was sitting on.

And by the way, when I say that my father and I built the camp, what I mean by this is that Dad built it, entirely by hand, with no power tools, no chainsaw, and almost entirely by himself. I was only about six years old during the initial construction in the early 1970s when I held the boards for him while he hand-cut each one, and occasionally he'd allow me to swing a hammer to finish off a nail or two. As I got older, I'd have the ability to work alongside my dad, and it would be in the 1990s that he'd finally consider it completed. Most would have you believe this is when Dad started enjoying the camp. However, I'd come to realize that my father was never happier than the times he and I were working on the building projects at the cottage on Dobsy Lake prior to its completion.

Anyway, on the first evening of the weekend trip, my father, James, and I were enjoying the sunset, being that the camp pointed out of a cove facing directly west, which provided us with an indescribable view of the day's closing from across the lake. Each clear evening the sun would reflect off the water as the last of the burning star disappeared behind the tree line of Big Island, leaving the clear sky to be filled with billions of shining planets. The three of us were enjoying a toddy, watching the scene from the camp's front picture windows when my father prepared to go into a story. He began as always, "If I've told you this story before, please stop me. I had a friend once…" to which James immediately leaned to my father and chimed in before his sentence could be completed, saying in an emotionless, monotone voice, "I bet he's dead now." Both James and I burst into laughter to my dad's bewilderment as, up to that point, he'd simply never realized how he'd historically begun all of his tales and he was forced to puzzle on how James not only knew what he was about to say but somehow knew that my father's friend, whose name he'd yet to mention, had passed since the telling of the tale.

These moments, along with the stories my father told are the inspiration for this book. Among the familiar tales, well, at least familiar to me, will be stories that I've created to add to the character and setting of the novel.

The main character of "Ma" Farnsworth was born using characteristics and eccentricities of many people that I've known throughout the years. I've put a little bit of everyone within her persona and physical description. Ma's a bit of a person that we all know, and please take my word when I say that you may just know her too, or may recognize someone that you know within her. Ma's an older woman in her later sixties; she's short, stocky, and brash, but at the same time caring in her own way, even though she'd never intentionally let on to be so. She's rough around the edges, and her vocabulary can be harsh, vulgar, and, frankly, in your face with her distinctly opinionated ways which she's always prepared to offer. More so than anything else, and above all, she's a true Mainer at heart and very protective of *her* town and the people that live there.

In the pages ahead, I'll also introduce you to other primary characters, all of whom again have characteristics based on people that I've known. As you read through the chapters my hope is that you may recognize someone you've known in the uniqueness of each of them.

The setting for the story, while obviously fictitious, looks like any other small, unorganized township within the northernmost points of Maine before you cross over the Canadian border. Far up in "the county," where many sparsely populated villages are commonly referred to by numbers like 'T2-R8' rather than formal names. Where instead of formally named roads, you may find numbered "fire lanes," which is simply describing where one needs to send the volunteer fire department if there's an emergency. Many of these villages are sparsely populated, and more often than not are resided in by townsfolk that are closely related to one another, and are certainly tight-knit.

More on Ma, the town, and the setting of this book to come in the pages ahead. And to be fair, I'd like to mention that the stories won't necessarily be in any chronological order. My preferred style is to convey the stories as if we're all sitting around a campfire telling random tales. So, the stories contained here in this book won't be in the order that they may have occurred, or that you might expect them to be. Please picture yourself sitting at the cottage around that campfire with me over a few summer evenings and listening to tales about our characters and the unique little town they live in. Each evening that we sit around that warm, cozy fire, another tale from another season will be told.

I hope you enjoy the stories you're about to read and get a good chuckle from some of them anyway, which is something we all need nowadays, to smile and laugh. I'd like to start by saying that if after beginning a chapter you feel you've already heard the particular story before, well, try reading it again. You might just find something new that you hadn't heard before, because in the re-telling of any good story, like many tall tales, they've had a few extra details added to them each time.

I'd also like to say once again in reference to the many endearing stories that were handed down to me over the years by my father that I, in fact, had a friend once. However, he's gone now.

And I dearly miss him.

Harold Winslow Wilson
"The Storyteller"
Photo taken during the continued construction
of the camp on Dobsy Lake, circa 1980-something.

Chapter 1

The Town of East Puddleduck

Let's begin with a bit of history, shall we? We need to begin somewhere, and rather than break off in the middle of the book for a brief history lesson, let's just get it out of the way right here. And yes, I realize that sometimes history lessons aren't the most popular or interesting things to read about for some who may not be history buffs. But I suppose if you're going to be reading about our particular little town which, along with the character of Ma, is really a centerpiece of the book, it might be helpful if you know just how that town came to be. It might help you understand how individual and eccentric, in other words, how entirely "nuts" the residents are if you know the backstory of where a few of them came from. So, in these first two chapters I'd like to take a few moments to set the scene and paint the characters for you.

◆ ◆ ◆

It was 1846 and many families were seeking a better, more abundant life and were headed to the western portions of the United States from their various central or midwestern roots. They were known as pioneers. One very such group, the Farnsworths, were an extended family of thirty or so men, women, and children who were seeking their fortune somewhere other than Missouri, where they were originally from. Along with the Farnsworths were several other closely related families which rounded out the seventy or so apprehensive but excited adventurers. Jedediah Farnsworth, the patriarch of the family, and his wife, Rosemary, were leading the charge and others were eager to follow, trusting in their promises of a better and more prosperous future. Each homesteader had arranged to settle what was left of their failing farmlands and planned to collectively purchase several covered wagons, horses, cattle, and ample supplies. They well prepared themselves to leave in the spring of the following year.

Now, you'd think that all would have started out well, having planned and prepared well in advance. However, the evening before their journey was to begin, the Farnsworth kinfolks had partaken in a huge festive meal to discuss their journey along with another group that they were due to partner and head out with the following morning. The second group being primarily led by two other local families by the name of the Donners and the Reeds.

You may have heard of them.

During the evening get-together, and while performing their last-minute preparations, the Farnworths and their group consumed a good deal of beverages of the alcoholic kind, while the Donner party and the Reeds decided to remain primarily sober. By the next morning when it was time to strike out on their adventure, both Jedediah and Rosemary, along with their followers, were still a bit inebriated and the skies were overcast, making directional determinations a bit difficult by looking at the sky. You see, Jedediah had chosen to trust his mapping skills on a more primitive system by looking at the sky and the stars, not that he could see very clearly, to begin with that faithful morning, which he certainly couldn't. The result was that Jedediah chose an easterly direction to point the wagons, instead of west. Not to help the situation, Rosemary, who was somewhat known as a boisterous, aka "mouthy," woman who was quite dedicated to her husband, agreed that the east looked very similar to the west and that's where they were heading, much to the argument of the Donners and Reeds, who were using a compass, maps, and other more modern methods for their directional determinations. Jedediah and Rosemary proceeded to "poo-poo" their fancy tools and led their group in the opposite direction where they truly felt west to be.

Additionally, and unfortunately for the Farnsworths and their followers, a slow-moving front caused the weather beneath them to remain foul for twenty-eight days straight, and to which Jedediah and Rosey remained boozed-up for at least twenty-three of those twenty-eight days. By the time the sky had cleared, not to mention Jedediah sobering up to the point that he'd realized his mistake, it was too far into their journey to turn back. And due to the fact that everyone included in the Farnsworth group had been juiced on that last evening before departing Missouri, and not one of them in their hungover states had initially noticed they were going in the wrong direction, no one dared to speak up during this time and offer their opinion that they believed they were traveling east and not west.

As a side note and as the story goes, it's been said that Jedediah and Rosemary are believed to have given up alcohol on the twenty-seventh day and after realizing their terrible mistake. Depending on who tells the story, it's also been said this just happened to be the day that the group's alcohol simply ran out.

About the time the Farnsworth group neared the New Hampshire and Maine border, they were met on the trail by several Indigenous Peoples who were seemingly friendly and willing to provide assistance to the weary travelers. The leader of the small group introduced himself as the chief of the Black Bear Tribe. Now Jedediah, not being familiar with any of the Indigenous Peoples nor the individual tribal names in the east, took them for their word and was basically pleased they were courteous and friendly, and that they spoke enough English so that he could understand and carry on a conversation with them. Jedediah believed what the chief had to say, knowing the Indigenous People had traditions in the Americas that went far beyond his base of knowledge. Not to mention the Farnsworths were superstitious by nature and felt any guidance that the Indigenous People offered should be taken at their word or bad things might just occur that could hamper their success, and the group certainly didn't need any additional odds to be against them as they were pretty much screwed as it was.

The chief told Jedediah that his group was nearing their journey's end. To be certain of where they were to settle, they must take his wisdom if they were to be successful and prosperous in the growing seasons to come. He told them they must capture a duck. No species in particular, just a duck, and they must keep the duck alive, feed it well, and keep it healthy and safe for fifteen days. Upon the fifteenth day, they must stop on the trail and take the duck from its enclosure. Holding the duck up high above his head, Jedediah must then let the duck go into the air. The chief was specific in telling Jedediah not to *throw* the duck, just let it go. If the duck were to take flight from his hands, their journey is not over and they must find the duck again, capture it, keep it safe and healthy for five more days, and then let the duck go again in the same manner. The chief told Jedediah he must continue this ritual until the day that the duck falls to the ground when released. If the duck falls to the ground instead of taking flight, they have arrived at their destination, and at that point their travels are to cease, they are to stake their claim and name their new settlement.

The group took the chief's words as wisdom and truly believed this would be the answer to the question of how far to travel before settling in their new eastern location. Jedediah expressed his sincere appreciation to the chief and his fellow tribesmen, provided them with what the group could spare from their supplies in thanks, and continued on their journey with their first order to be in finding a duck.

The group soon realized it wasn't easy catching a duck in a manner as to not harm the animal, not to mention their warm clothing quickly became soggy and soiled in the numerous attempts as ducks are primarily found in the water. But ultimately they had their duck. The group believed the species of their new friend to be a Bufflehead, not that it matters for the purpose of the story. For the next fifteen days they fed, watered, and kept the duck safe and healthy. One of the children in the family even named the duck "Puddles." Puddles the Duck lived large in its small wicker environment within the lead wagon.

On the fifteenth day, about midday, the wagon train stopped along the trail. In actuality, with Jedediah's poor sense of direction, he'd strayed off the beaten trail that eventually led to Canada and was at the edge of a field with barely a goat path ahead of them. It was just dumb luck that it was the fifteenth day, as there was no apparent way to continue on without backtracking a bit and locating the trail they'd strayed from.

Puddles was removed from its cage by Jedediah who stood tall in the middle of the goat path, holding the duck high above his head as he was instructed to do, and he let it go. Now, the feathered animal was quite capable of flying. The problem was, after fifteen days in the cramped wicker basket, Puddles was a bit stiff in the wings. The duck dropped, beak first, to the ground, letting out a loud "*squawk!*" as it did so. The duck landed, wobbled back to its feet, shook its wings, and turned back towards Jedediah. The portly feathered animal waddled past Jedediah to a small pond off to one side of the field. Puddles, at the edge of the pond, shook its wings again, along with its head and tailfeathers, and jumped into the pond, seemingly quite content to be there. The pioneers all took this as a sign; this was to be their new home.

The new township, settled in the year 1847, sits far in the northern region of Maine somewhere between St. Francis and Fort Kent and was named after its finder, Puddles, and because they were traveling east, it was formally named East Puddlesduck, or East Puddleduck for short. To this day, there is no West, South, or North Puddleduck, just East.

Have I mentioned yet that Jedediah was a moron? Or as we say in Maine, "number than a pounded thumb?" Hence the poor direction of travel to begin with, let alone the fact that back in Missouri the reason the Farnsworth farms had failed just might have had something to do with the fact that they were attempting to grow an orange crop. After several seasons of frozen, dead oranges they finally gave up and began their trek east, believing it was west.

Oh, and the whole duck thing. Yeah, that was bogus too. It seems the "chief" of the Indigenous Peoples that the group had encountered who had provided them the wisdom of the whole duck thing turned out to be the son of one of the elders of the Wabanaki Indigenous Peoples, and the whole "Black Bear" tribe was made up. The Wabanakis consisted of four tribes, and none of them were known as Black Bear. It seems the tribes had a running bet on who would have the ability to use the ruse first to any group of foolish pioneers who happened to be traveling east and seeking to settle nearby them. When they'd arrived back at their reservation later that same faithful day and they conveyed the tale of the Farnsworth settlers, they all had a huge laugh over it and many had to pay up on their individual wagers.

Oh, and Puddles the 'duck' that had discovered their newfound home? Well, Puddles in actually has been rumored to have been a loon. Go figure. I think there's a statute erected to Puddles in the Town of Lincoln on the banks of the Mattanawcook Lake. You might want to check on that if you get the chance.

There's a similar story on how the neighboring town of Skunksquirt, which will be referred to many times in the pages to come, was named. However, it's far too disgusting to even mention, so I won't.

Legend would have it that about a year after heading out completely in the wrong direction and settling in northern Maine, Jedediah would be quoted as saying in his own defense, "Well, at least we didn't have to eat each other at the end of the trip." So, in reality, as far as the overall circumstances were concerned, east may have just been the better choice when you consider the ultimate fate of the Donner Party.

Chapter 2

The Characters in Our Story

As mentioned, our main character is a lady by the name of Wilomena Bejeesus Farnsworth-Miller, otherwise known affectionately around town as "Ma." Ma is a direct descendent of Jedediah and Rosemary, and she never lets anyone forget that she is, in fact, related to the settlers of East Puddleduck, with the "Miller" part being her married name. Also as mentioned, Ma is an in-your-face kind of lady, likes to use profanity, never lets her opinion go unnoticed and, she's always prepared to back it up. She stands about five foot nothing, is a bit plump, and almost always wears a floral pattern dress with a bell-shaped skirt down just below her knees, and typically an apron over it. She's a hard-working, boot-wearing woman. Rarely does she wear shoes when she's not working and certainly nothing that would have heels. Her long, graying hair can usually be found all put up nice in a bun, with one or two long hairpins holding it tight. Ma's face is care-worn, and at times she needs to wear reading glasses but she doesn't like them. She often squints and crinkles her nose when she looks at you, especially if she's paying any attention to what you're saying to better hear you, as if crinkling her nose improves her hearing.

Ma is a true Mainer, and more specifically, a true East Puddleduckian, to the point that she really doesn't care much for anyone not native to or residing in the town. Not even residents from the next town of Skunksquirt, which is a bit larger and only a few miles down the road. In fact, anyone not from East Puddleduck is not-so-affectionately referred to as a "foreigner," by Ma, especially anyone from out-of-state or country. Ma is the type of person that if you just met her and after listening to her speak for a few minutes, you'd most likely initially accuse her of being a bigot or maybe even a purist. After those first few minutes, you'd realize Ma is neither, she's just

"Ma." The truth is, Ma, although being quite serious about not liking anyone who's not from town and at times appears to be quite unfriendly to even the citizens of East Puddleduck, is actually very protective of the residents and loves just about every one of them. Although, she'll never let onto that fact. And, although she can seemingly be mean to just about everyone in town, it's simply her nature and they all love her and would happily stand up in her defense because she's truly protective of them. Regardless of her overall demeanor, she in fact is everyone's "Ma."

Ma owns and operates the town diner. Now, why you ask would such a small town require a diner? The truth is because nobody living in town has the ability to cook a decent meal. You see, most, if not all, of the working folks need to travel for their jobs. Many of our residents either work for one of the local logging companies or for the railroad in Fort Sampson where the product is transported by rail and road, both further north and south to existing lumber mills that are still in operation. Even the people who remain in town each day work very hard but rarely does anyone have time to make a decent meal, so literally, everyone stops at Ma's Diner to fill their bellies.

And, it is in fact, called "Ma's Diner" and it's the staple of the town. Ma's is the place to go, and everyone does just that each and every day. The other part of this is that East Puddleduck is very rural, with only a small general store for the basic necessities and quite the travel to the nearest large supermarket or department store. This adds to the challenge and why nobody can cook a proper meal other than the homemade food available at the diner. Ma runs a neat, clean diner which is located on the main road in the northern section of town on a sharp corner, just a few miles before the road dead-ends. Ma's prices are reasonable and barely charges over what it costs for her supplies and basic living and operating expenses. You also don't ever tip Ma, as she wouldn't have that. Instead of a tip, you're much better off simply paying it forward by buying someone else in the diner an extra cup of coffee before you leave. More to come later on the diner and the significance of the "sharp corner" mentioned.

Ma is married to Elmer "Junior" Miller, otherwise known around the area as "El." Now, there are those who say that after being married for so many years a couple can begin to resemble each other, and none was ever the truer about Ma and El. In fact, if it wasn't for his long red beard and that he doesn't wear floral pattern dresses, you'd swear he and Ma were the same person. All except for the other detail in that El is a bit quieter person and is certainly more polite than Ma.

Runyon Farnsworth-Miller is the thirty-ish year old son and only child of Ma and El. Runyon lives in his own tiny cabin on the Farnsworth-Miller homestead. Unlike his parents, he's a bit taller and skinnier, sports a jet-black handlebar mustache, and longer hair. He has a bit of a '60s hippie look going on. He's a nice enough fellow, quiet like his dad, and a hard worker. He primarily works for the diner and on the homestead but also performs other odd jobs around town. He's sort of like the superintendent of an apartment building, only for the entire town, being very handy and self-motivated to assist others. Runyon's unmarried right now; however, always open to the possibility, and his mother considers him quite the catch for any lucky lady. Obviously, she'd need to be a Puddleduckian to be eligible to join the family. It's rumored that Runyon has a serious girlfriend who's a native Skunksquirter, a minor detail that he certainly doesn't want his mother to know about.

The Farnsworth-Miller homestead is the largest privately owned plot of land in town, being handed down by the original settlers. Ma and El's large farmhouse sits on the homestead along with an equally large barn where they keep a bit of livestock and fenced-in areas for the animals to roam safely. The aforementioned tiny cabin that Runyon lives in is located on the property and many acres of fields and woods surround the buildings. The homestead is full and busy but also clean and neat as Ma likes it that way.

The diner itself isn't located on the homestead. As described a bit earlier, it sits right on the main road and the dining room has eight booths surrounding four tables and a counter-bar where you can also sit and eat. The motif is rustic, with the bar made from a thick piece of pine board and the walls all unfinished dovetailed pine as well. Two buck deer heads are mounted to the dining room walls along with pictures and paintings of black bears, white-tail deer, and other Maine scenes. There's a large corkboard display where townsfolk pin up pictures of themselves hunting, fishing, and whatnot plus, plenty of nostalgic photos of the diner and patrons from years past. No alcohol is served in the diner, by Ma's choice, just good home cooking and fresh coffee. The diner is open early for breakfast with plenty of time for folks to eat and get to work even if they travel, through the lunch hour and into the late supper hour for patrons to return and get a good, hot homemade meal. Ma has plenty of townsfolk willing to work for her in the diner, and I'll let you know just who they are in the pages ahead.

Next in line to introduce you to is Robert "Bob" Johnson and his wife, Mabel. Bob is the town constable for not only East Puddleduck but also the neighboring town of Skunksquirt, being that the two towns abutted each other and both are small in population. Now, Bob, who's in his late forties, goes about 360 on a good day and not a bit of it muscle. In fact, he barely fits into his bright yellow 1973 Oldsmobile Delta '88 that the two townships pitched in and purchased as his police cruiser several years back. On the sides of the car, which sports a big, blue bubblegum light on the top, reads, "East Puddleduck And Skunksquirt Police Department." The phrase is so long and the letters so big that it doesn't fit along both sides of the vehicle. The title begins on the driver's side and wraps around to the passenger side, with the word "AND" being on the rear of the vehicle under the trunk release all by itself. Bob performed the artwork himself, and it looks terrible and certainly doesn't match on both sides. Bob is the only employee of the police force, and he can usually be seen wearing his oversized and clean, white uniform complete with his shiny black duty belt, suspenders, and a six-shot .38 caliber wheel gun that he's never discharged, not even for practice. Bob is tall as well as wide, about six-two, has a receding and thinning hairline, and a small, square black toothbrush mustache just below his nose.

Mabel Johnson, his wife, is the town gossip. Ma calls her "busy-body." If you want to know something about someone that probably isn't true, ask Mabel but only if you have an hour to spare. Mable is about as attractive as Bob and is also about six feet tall and a heavy woman if that helps paint a picture of her for you. She doesn't have the thinning hair or mustache, though. That is, unless of course she wears a brunette wig and waxes and we just don't know about it. Bob and Mable make a good pair, and they're quite content with each other. Mabel occasionally works for Ma in the diner as one of her waitstaff when Ma has other things to tend to, such as picking up supplies during the week or when she's fishing or hunting on the weekends.

Wallace Marmaduke, otherwise known as "Old Marmaduke." Marmaduke has roots that can be found in Canada and speaks with a heavy French accent along with his Maine accent, which makes him a bit difficult to understand at times. Old Marmaduke is in his late 60s, if not 70s, and he's tall and skinny. He sports a full head of snowy-white hair and a matching beard nearly down to his belt line. He wears jean overalls and suspenders most, if not all, of the time, and a red flannel jacket. His is the first house you come to as you enter town, and certainly the worst property as far as overall attractiveness or neatness. His cabin is old, with graying logs, and his front porch is dilapidated. His big yard and property are littered with junk cars, and he's never mowed his lawn, not even once, even though there are several junked lawnmowers lying about. He does drive, he simply has a habit of purchasing aging vehicles that don't tend to last very long. Once they give out, they find their permanent home somewhere on his property. He likes to tell people that one day everything on the property will be considered "antiques" and he'll open a museum and charge people money to come and look at it all.

Old Marmaduke is a nice guy who worked hard all his life. He's a widower of many years. He's not a bum, he just prefers to live like one. In fact, there's a rumor that there was quite a bit of money in the Marmaduke family, if not money that he himself had earned, that just might be hidden somewhere on the property. Maybe even buried deep in the ground under one of the jalopies. When Marmaduke's not at the diner he can regularly be seen sitting on his rotting porch in his wicker rocker, always on the left side of the porch, smoking his corncob pipe and watching what's left of life go by. Even though there's another wicker rocker on the right side of the porch, he always sits on the left. Someone once asked him why he doesn't ever sit in the other chair and his response was, "It would upset the balance of nature." Marmaduke's a fairly easygoing person, as you can probably tell.

Old Marmaduke is also known as the voice of reason in town. If it doesn't make sense to him, he'll let you know it. He's worldly and possesses quite a bit of knowledge about things in general. If you ask him a question, he'll most likely look to the ground, stroking his white beard a couple of times, might even chuckle to himself, and then provide you with an answer that you should probably assume is correct.

As an example, the town church needed new shingles on the roof a few years ago and many of the townsfolk gathered together to pitch in and rebuild it. Someone decided to suggest a metal roof because the logic was that overall they're less expensive and might quite possibly last longer than asphalt shingles. On the day of the conversation, Old Marmaduke stood outside the church with the group and said in his heavily accented voice, "If you do that, it'll rattle like a tin can on rainy Sundays. You won't be able to hear the preacher preaching or the choir singing." His wisdom being based on the fact that the church roof is uninsulated and paper thin. As you can well imagine, and as sometimes occurs when a group of would-be know-it-alls are standing together arguing about how to get a job done, his wisdom was unfortunately ignored and the roof was built out of metal regardless. From that moment on, and on every rainy Sunday, the pastor is required to yell and everyone just sits there in the pews wondering what Bible verse he's quoting and responds, "Amen," quite often at the wrong times. There's always a long, uncomfortable pause after services are done because you can't tell that the pastor has completed his sermon. About this time, Ma usually stands up and yells an obscenity or two as she reminds everyone that they should have listened to Marmaduke, to which she must immediately excuse herself for cursing in church.

Speaking of the pastor, his name is Percible Winkin. Ma refers to him as "Father Bubblehead." He's sort of like one of those television evangelists, very outspoken but in a low-voice kind of way when he's engaging in casual conversation. You know, he speaks to you like you're a child but he can be quite animated and loud during his services. He'll talk along in a low, monotone voice and then suddenly wave his hands high into the air and blurt out a quote that may or may not be from the Bible, many times causing you to jump in your seat.

Ma likes to poke fun at the pastor quite often. She'll say things to him like, "Look here, preacher, if I invite the devil himself into my diner and give him a free lunch, will he be nice to me when I get to his place?" Father Winkin's usual response is to shake his head and say in his pompous voice, "Bless you, my child," and then move on.

As you can probably picture, the pastor is traditionally seen in his flowing black frock and white collar, carrying the good book in one hand and driving around in his shiny, older model Cadillac. He stands a bit tall along with a bit of weight on him, and to look at him you'd probably guess him to be in his 50s with trim-cut brown hair, and he also wears driving glasses on the bridge of his nose. When he speaks to you, he looks down on you through the glasses and has the uncanny ability to always make you feel like a five-year-old with his arrogant demeanor and tone.

Next are Wally and Joshua McIntyre. The McIntyre twins, even though they weren't born in the same year or resemble each other in any way, operate the local automotive garage, gas station, and used car lot. The boys are both in their late 20s. "Strapping young men," as Ma would say. Neither are married yet but both date local girls. Between the two of them, their IQs don't amount to double digits but there isn't anything with an engine that they can't fix and their used cars are reliable and come with limited warranties.

The boys are trustworthy and always willing to help out anyone in town regardless of the time of day. They share a house that was left to them by their parents who were both killed in a lumber mill accident a few years back. Ma looks over them both like they were her own and she warns them often of the consequences if they don't behave. For the most part, they listen to her and, along with the other townsfolk, there isn't anything they wouldn't do for Ma.

The town's mayor is Rupert Wiggleswort. He's also a descendant of the original settlers, which puts him and Ma at odds quite often. Rupert, being the elected mayor, fancies himself as the decision maker in town when in reality nobody dares to defy Ma, such as the way it was with her great-great-great-grandmother Rosemary and the Farnsworths.

Rupert has the gift of gab, gaining his experience having formerly been employed as a car salesman in the nearest larger city of Van Brethren. He's now retired from sales and is our full-time local politician. To picture Rupert, all you really need to do is visualize the mayor of Munchkin City from the *Wizard of OZ*, only make him a bit taller and his voice a bit deeper. The mayor, who can almost always be found in his office within the tiny municipal building, traditionally wears a loud, colorful suit coat, dress pants, and a poorly tucked-in dress shirt and tie that certainly doesn't match. Shaped like a pear, Rupert is in his 50s and holds his mostly hairless head high as he speaks and is the typical baby-kissing, promise-making politician type.

Rupert is married to Eleanor, a strong, outspoken women herself. Her deep voice is loud and her laugh even louder and could shake the shingles off any roof when she gets going. Eleanor's hair is gray; however, died a dark blond with split ends and no makeup to speak of. She's somewhat thin, and the two together resemble a Laurel and Hardy pair. Similar to Ma, Eleanor can usually be seen around town wearing a sundress and she wears flat shoes.

Rupert's sister, Myrtle Watson, will also be mentioned in the stories ahead.

Myrtle is an older lady, older than her brother, and in times of past, she would have most likely been best described as a spinster. She married only once at a very young age and then divorced only a week after, never having married again, and never intending to. Forever blaming her ex-husband for the failure of their brief marriage, she doesn't mind providing her opinion on other people's relationships, fancying herself some sort of expert in the matter. Myrtle is now married to her work, being the town office clerk, which also affords her the opportunity to be included in the various rumor mills offered by all that are required to visit the tiny municipal building to perform their town business. Myrtle also volunteers her time at the church as the organ player and leader of the church choir.

The other two that make up the town's select board are Paul Doody and his wife, Matilda, and Jacob Daley and his wife, Valerie, or "Val" as she prefers. To simplify things about the two select persons, they're the bookends for the mayor. They're both quite average and rather normal in their appearance with nothing fancy to set them apart from each other. The two look more like each other than the McIntyre brothers do, even though they're completely unrelated with the only significant difference being that Paul has a bit larger nose than Jacob.

Now, to put this in better perspective as it relates to these two families, the two men are simply dorks and do exactly what their wives tell them. The two families are all in their early 50s as far as age, and the wives are more professional-looking than the two men and certainly more attractive. Both Val and Matilda are pleasant-looking ladies. Val is a bit more down to earth with Matilda, or Mattie as she's known, with a bit of an air about her. You know, a bit of a know-it-all. In other words, she's stuck up, which places her and Ma at odds fairly often. Val, on the other hand, is one of Ma's managers for the diner and can usually be found in charge when Ma isn't there herself. Val is a shirt and jeans kind of woman, while Mattie is more of a fancy, wishing she was rich but only acts like it kind of lady, if you know what I mean.

The spouses of the three town leaders are certainly the decision-makers in their respective households, if not for the town itself. It's certain that when the mayor and his tiny select board are required to make a decision that involves the town during a live meeting, they usually move to table the item and postpone the vote so all three can go home to their wives and ask their opinions before making a formal decision at the next meeting. It's not exactly Robert's Rules of Order, but it makes for better decision-making for sure and certainly makes the town a better place. That is, of course, if Ma hasn't chimed in already during the decision-making process and provided her opinion, which results in the decision being made by someone other than the elected decision-makers, leaving the said elected decision-makers to look like the fools that they sometimes, if not always, are.

Smirnoff, whose first name nobody can pronounce, is the operator and co-owner of the general store in East Puddleduck. Smirnoff's father was from Russia and his mother was from Ukraine, which is where Smirnoff was born, and he speaks both languages and has a heavy Slavic accent. He's in his early 60s, a tall and well-built person, quite capable of lifting the heavy boxes when the supply truck arrives twice each month. Smirnoff is overly friendly, which makes Ma very suspicious, and although she'd protect him to the end if need be, he's one of Ma's "foreigners" and believes him to secretly be in the Russian mafia. And just to let you know, Ma absolutely hates it when he speaks publicly in his native language, which he gets a chuckle out of and does it quite often.

Smirnoff is married to a very nice lady he met in town when he moved here several years ago. Cicely, who's just a bit younger than Smirnoff in her later 50s and can be best described as a "handsome lady," African American, whose family moved to East Puddleduck in the early 1960s and started the general store. It was originally a haberdashery where they not only sold goods but it was also the only tiny hotel in town. Cicely now owns the family business along with her husband, who started out as one of her employees and the relationship grew from there. Once they were married in the town gazebo, they changed the name of the business to "Smirnoff's General Store." Cicely also works from time to time in the diner, when things are quieter, during which she leaves her husband to operate the store.

Puut (pronounced Pu-ut) Voisine. Puut is originally from Canada and has a heavy French-Canadian accent, worse than Marmaduke's. Ma calls him a "Dumb Canuk" and he often refers to her as a "Crazy Mainiac" when he's not referring to her as an "old woman." Very often, Puut will speak French in front of Ma, and obviously, she quickly reminds him that he's to speak English when he's around her. Puut adores Ma but finds it quite amusing to push Ma's buttons whenever he has the chance, which is quite often seeing that Puut and Runyon are the best of friends. If you get both Puut and Smirnoff in the same room with Ma, each speaking their native languages, it causes Ma's head to spin.

Puut is now probably in his late 50s and arrived in East Puddleduck many years back when he was a teenager. Puut is a handsome fellow, about six feet tall, and he's quite rugged. His hair is silver in color and has a full head of it, and he also has a long mustache. Puut can be best described as someone who lives off-grid, even in a rural town such as East Puddleduck. He's a wood and leather crafter, a hunter, and a fisherman, living and making a living entirely off the land. He makes his own clothes and feeds himself almost completely from what he catches or grows himself, although he is known to frequent the diner. Probably, and mostly likely, to poke fun at Ma and challenge her patience but he often takes the time to grab a fresh cup of coffee or a good hot meal while doing it.

Now, again, I feel the need to explain something. By now Ma is probably sounding pretty mean and nasty even though I've pointed out that at the core she certainly isn't. Ma is a no-nonsense, no-drama, get-to-the-point type of person. She isn't intentionally mean, it's in her nature and heritage, and no one who knows her well expects anything else. When she's poking fun at "foreigners" or the townsfolk with Canadian, or even Slavic heritage, it's not because she doesn't like them and they know it. Ma is the type of person whose favorite sayings are, "Suck it up, Buttercup," or, "You probably ought to grow thicker skin if you can't take it." She obviously doesn't mince words. Ma isn't politically correct, and no one intends or expects her to be. The unwritten rule is that you don't mess with Ma, not because she'll lay you out if you do. It's because the townsfolk *mostly* adore her in their own individual way, and would never allow anyone to be mean, or take advantage of Ma's naïve nature.

Lastly, Ruby "Red" Mayflower. Ruby is a very nice lady with just a shadow of a reputation. Ruby was at one time a dancer of the skimpy-dressed kind back some years ago. For a lady in her self-declared early 40s, but most likely later 40s, if not early 50s, she's comfortable to look at even though her age is beginning to show through the makeup and Botox injections. She's the type of person who calls everyone "honey," and she's quite popular with the menfolk. The women in town put up with her too, to tell the truth, mainly because they know that Ruby is entirely harmless and the fact that she owns the local beauty parlor.

Ruby, as you've probably guessed, has flowing red hair, dyed that way, no doubt. She's easy to spot in her usual spandex, high heels, and she's fairly well-endowed in what most would guess is a store-bought pair of boobs that she keeps inside her tight T-shirts. But don't get the wrong idea, Ruby's quick to respond to anyone who would dare try catcalling her, which no one from town would ever have the disrespect to do so. Ruby's the equivalent of a popular magazine swimsuit issue: you can look but you can't ever touch, or you might just lose your hand trying. Puut Voisine is especially interested in Ruby and has asked her out quite often. Ruby enjoys the attention. However, up to now, and as far as we know, she hasn't accepted his invitation. It might be due to his off-grid nature and the fact that Ruby is certainly a bit high maintenance, if you get my meaning.

The McIntyre boys swear that they have an old calendar pinup photo of Ruby hanging in their garage that they found somewhere. Ruby says it isn't her, though.

Ruby's salon is only open a couple of days a week and Ma has her waiting tables in the diner on weekends. Business at the diner tends to pick up on weekends.

Well, folks, that's our primary characters. There are certainly several other families that make up the town, making the total population a little less than a hundred people; however, the ones mentioned are the ones most worth mentioning. They're the residents that generally stand out and will show up most frequently in the stories ahead, while others tend to be more low-key and just go with the flow in town. Other townsfolk are, in some way, pretty much related to one another. However, the ones I've spoken of personally will be the characters that become most familiar to you.

◆ ◆ ◆

Now, just a bit more on the town other than what you already know. East Puddleduck is just north of Skunksquirt and (farther) west of Fort Kent, somewhere in between the Saint John River and Caribou but closer to the Canadian border. Quite a bit southwest of St. Agatha but east of the Allagash. I'm sure that clears it right up for you, now, doesn't it? The town is basically a cul-de-sac on its own, with one road in and coincidentally the same one road out. It's an island without water surrounding it. For this reason, and much to Ma's pleasure, they don't get many, if any, visitors. There's an engraved, "Welcome to East Puddleduck," sign over the road on a two-by-ten plank chained in between two cedar trees on either side of the road right on the town line. On the end of the sign is hand-painted, *"EXEPT FOR FORINERS,"* that Ma put there. Several times the townsfolk have attempted to remove Ma's artwork only to have Ma paint it right back on the sign. They even took the sign down for a while and Ma picked it out of the dump and made the McIntyre brothers put it right back up. Now, primarily out of frustration, they just leave it there.

The town has the diner, Smirnoff's General Store, a church, Ruby's Beauty Salon, and McIntyre's Garage. The town's municipal property consists of the town hall and meeting room, public safety office, library, volunteer fire department, and town public works plow truck all housed in one location. East Puddleduck has two cemeteries, with Farnsworths primarily in one and everyone else in the other, and the scattered residences and homesteads. Fire lanes ranging from "1" through "6" branch off the main drag, along with a few named roads. The town dump lies off Fire Road 6. Most residences have running water now and indoor plumbing, although some still have outhouses as their primary bathroom facilities, including Old Marmaduke's place and a couple of others. Ma and El just recently, within the last ten years, built an indoor bathroom and have running water on the homestead. If you require the services of a doctor, dentist, or laundromat you need to travel to the next town of Skunksquirt, and if you need a larger supermarket or department store, you need to go further south to larger towns such as Saint Advent.

Now, one of the problems with East Puddleduck is that there are few, if any, cellular telephone towers in range, no internet service, no streaming services, and cable television doesn't get out this way. The tiny local newspaper out of Skunksquirt, which is basically news taken from other circulations out of Fort Sampson, and is only published bi-weekly, prohibits reliable information from being easily accessible to the residents. Phew, that was a long sentence, wasn't it? Anyway, landline telephone services are almost non-existent with the more popular cellular phones being everywhere else. There is a party landline that Rupert's sister Myrtle controls from her home. She won't answer it after 7:00 p.m. when Wheel of Fortune is on or anytime when she's sleeping or getting her hair done, or when she's working in the town office or volunteering for the church choir. So, in short, she never answers it. Primarily speaking, only rumors and third, if not fourth or fifth-party word of mouth is how the town keeps up on the headlines, which by that point is a bit overblown and fairly unreliable.

For recreation and fun, those who live in town enjoy hunting, fishing in both summer and winter, ATV riding, and other outdoor activities. Not to mention enjoying a meal at Ma's, hanging out at Smirnoff's store, or bingo night at the church. Oh yes, and getting their hair done and the latest gossip at Ruby's.

Speaking again of the diner, and possibly to give you a bit of a better feeling about Ma, here's a tidbit of information for you: Ma doesn't put food prices on her "Specials" board. Written on the chalkboard that sits on top of the bar counter, just as you enter the establishment, it reads at the top, "SPECIALS," and just below is written, "Everyone Is Special at Ma's Diner." Most find this a bit amusing knowing Ma's demeanor, and in actuality, she does run specials from time to time.

So, there you have it. You've got a good idea of what East Puddleduck looks like and how it came to be, and you've been introduced to some of our residents. I do believe it's time to sit around that campfire and begin our stories, so grab a beer and maybe a marshmallow too if you like, and let's get going.

Chapter 3

The Local Election

We may as well begin here, as it's as good of a place as any to start. It's also time to formally introduce you to Ma. However, I should probably *ease* you into Ma, as it's better to do so rather than unleash her on you all at once. So, here's a little tale that's primarily about our mayor.

Fall is the time for local elections. Of course, we only have one elected official in East Puddleduck, the mayor, who appoints his or her own select board once taking office as it says they can in the town charter. So, fall of this particular year was no different than any other election year in the town.

It was about two weeks before election day and the current mayor, Rupert Wiggleswort, was busy preparing. He had councilpersons Daley and Doody paint, "Vote for Wiggleswort," signs and place them on just about everyone's front lawn. Most remained up by the property owners; however, a few were taken down like the one he had placed in Old Marmaduke's front yard, which required a bit longer stake to have it be visible above the high grass and weeds. Marmaduke claimed to be bipartisan, and even though nobody was running against the current mayor, Marmaduke said he didn't follow any political party, so he wouldn't allow the sign in his yard. He took the sign down but kept the wooden stake in place and put an old soup can over the top of it. He said this was just in case he needed a piece of wood later on for something, he'd know where to find one.

This election year Wiggleswort had done something new and ordered lapel pins with his name printed on them. He'd sent away to a company in Tijuana, which ended up spelling his name incorrectly and each one read,

"Vote for Wigglywart," which he didn't immediately notice until someone else pointed it out to him. He'd handed a pin to every potential voter he'd greeted during the final weeks of campaigning. As you can probably guess, most ended up in the garbage.

Rupert had even bought a new suit for campaigning from Choppies clothing resale store in Skunksquirt; it was bright purply velvet and came with purple suit pants, a violet dress shirt, and a bright red tie. He resembled Barney the dinosaur whenever he had it on. He'd spend his time campaigning primarily at both Smirnoff's store and Ma's diner, shaking hands with everyone as if they didn't already know who he was, hoping they'd all listen to his campaign promises and buy himself votes. You see, Rupert's been the mayor of our little village for over seventeen years now, seeing the town charter doesn't call for term limits, not to mention he's lived in town ever since he'd been born here. As a result, he's quite well known.

This day, Wiggleswort was at Ma's standing near the diner's entrance, greeting the hungry patrons as they entered for the lunch hour. He was making rounds to the tables and was more than willing to sit down one-on-one with anyone caring to listen to his campaign promises. However, all anyone really wanted to do was enjoy their meals in peace before going back to work. Rupert approached Constable Bob, who was seated at his usual counter bar seat, and the mayor promised him a new police cruiser. In response to which the lawman just rolled his eyes at the mayor. Bob knew how tough it'd been to squeeze the current cruiser out of the two townships, and he also knew the mayor didn't have it in him to make such a promise. Rupert moved on to the McIntyre brothers who were seated next to Bob and the mayor's promise to them was a new plow blade on the town truck to make it easier for the brothers to clean up after a storm snowfall, as the boys are the town's contracted winter plow operators. They didn't believe him any more than Bob had. Today, the mayor had even promised Ma a billboard just outside of town to advertise the diner.

"Go tell your lies to someone else!" Ma barked at him as the mayor followed her through the diner while she was attempting to wait her tables. Noontime during the week at Ma's Diner is regularly light, and for this reason, Ma traditionally covers the lunch hour and only uses waitstaff during breakfast, at supper time, and on weekends, when she brings in extra help. As mentioned before, weekends are her time for fishing and other more important things. During the weekday lunch, she cooks and waits the tables herself. Preparing the food and waiting tables alone does take a bit longer, but the townsfolk are patient and her home cooking is well worth it. Ma wears an apron most of the time, but especially when she's covering the kitchen and preparing food, which she doesn't bother to remove when she exits the kitchen to wait on patrons in the dining room. She figures that the food stains on her apron from preparing it all in the kitchen are the same food that's on their plates, so why not show it off? She also wears flat-bottom shoes instead of boots when she's working the floor to keep her feet from tiring out. Normally, Ma's quite cordial when she's working the dining room, except for when she's offering an opinion, asked a question, or any other time she speaks. But today the mayor was annoying Ma more than usual, which isn't hard to do. Not to mention, she'd already heard his promises each prior election year and had grown tired of them.

Ma was holding a hot meal in each hand that she needed to get to her hungry patrons. "And get your ass out of here unless you're eating!" Ma turned and said to the candidate, frowning at him and having to tilt her head back to avoid their noses poking each other as Rupert was following right on her heels in hopes she would listen to him. She turned back around and delivered one dish, haddock and chips, to Smirnoff who was seated at a center table, and the other, a hearty bowl of hot, homemade beef stew to the corner booth where Puut Voisine was waiting in his favorite seat.

"Might be good advertising for you, old woman," Puut looked up and said to Ma in his heavy French-American accent. The mayor, who was right behind Ma's backside, nodded and pointed at Puut in agreement.

"Oh, shut up!" Ma barked at the Frenchman as she set his stew down on the table. "You know he can't make that happen. Plus, I don't need any more out-of-towners, or worse, *foreigners* coming into my diner, let alone into town at all! It's bad enough that I have to deal with all you flatlanders! Just look around, I've got a Frenchman here and a Russian over there! Up at the counter I've got Tweedle Dee, Tweedle Dumb, and H.R. Puffinstuff! I can't handle any more!" Ma reached over to the next booth, grabbed the salt and pepper shakers for Puut, and set them down next to his stew, then pointed at the man seated in her booth with her stubby finger. "You and I both know he's full of shit! Plus, as usual, there's nobody running against him anyway, so why bother me?! You need anything else?"

"No, Ma, I'm good. Thank you," Puut said politely as he admired his beef stew. Ma turned to go back to the kitchen, only to be face to face with the mayor again, as they both stood the same height. She frowned at him and the mayor took the hint, stepping aside to let Ma pass, smiling nervously and tipping his head. As she passed by his table, Ma looked at Smirnoff and raised her eyebrows as if to ask him if he required anything else. Smirnoff just smiled and shook his head to her, letting Ma know he was content. Ma nodded with a frown on her face and she continued to the kitchen. Rupert made the smart decision not to follow her.

Of course, although it was true that even though nobody was running against Wiggleswort, he was quite worried about the write-in candidates. It wouldn't take many votes for *Mickey Mouse* to cause him to lose the election, and on a recount two years ago that very thing nearly occurred, so he continued his campaigning and proceeded to further annoy the patrons of

Ma's diner.

♦ ♦ ♦

A few days later Rupert held a "Meet the Candidates" night in the church Sunday school room. He scheduled it during bingo to make sure someone would be present to hear him speak. He stood up next to the bingo ball picker, Father Winkin, who always uses acronyms from the Bible when calling the bingo letters. The mayor was animated and loud as he attempted to strengthen his campaign. Standing tall, sort of, next to the pastor, he proceeded to speak, pretty much only succeeding in annoying everyone in the room who only wanted to hear their bingo numbers called.

"I promise prettier flowers, greener trees, good weather next summer, and a light winter this year!" Wiggleswort announced, testing to see who was listening. Nobody was.

"B, three. Bartholomew three," Father Winkin yelled over the mayor's campaigning as he pulled the tiny, numbered ping-pong balls from the hand-spun wheel and carefully looked down his nose and through his driving glasses at each one he plucked. The preacher was wearing his usual long, black frock and white collar and his Bible sat next to the bingo ball machine.

"I'll have a new bandstand built for the school band! It'll make the kids sound better!" Wiggleswort promised.

"I, twenty-eight. Incarnation twenty-eight."

"No more self-serve at McIntyre's gas station. Full service at the same price, three cents cheaper!" The wannabe mayor blurted out, looking around the room and noticing that still not many, if any, were listening to him.

"N, thirty-six. Nefarious thirty-six."

The current mayor began to perspire a bit and attempted a more attainable campaign promise in an attempt to have himself noticed. "I'll fill the two potholes in front of the church. Really, I promise this time!"

"G, fifty-five. Gospel fifty-five." Not one person was looking up from their bingo cards.

The mayor was becoming more and more anxious at the thought that no one was paying attention to him. He attempted to bolster his promises a bit. "Lower taxes!"

"O, seventy-one. Obeyeth, seventy-one."

"Bingo!" busybody Mabel Johnson gleefully cried out. She'd won again for the third time this evening.

"Increased tourism!" The mayor yelled out.

"Bingo, my ass! Increased *what!?*" It was Ma's voice that immediately cried out. Everyone else in the room went quiet, all nine of them, which included the reverend and the mayor. All eyes were wide and waiting for the inevitable verbal beatings to begin. Some contemplated hiding under their tables. Ma stood up and pointed at the mayor with her stubby finger and yelled, "What in Hell's Kitchen did you just say, Wigglewort?! *Tourism*?! We don't need no *goddam* foreigners in East Puddleduck!"

"No swearing, please," the pastor said in a calm, monotone voice.

"Shut up, Bubblehead! I want an answer from that chunky monkey standing next to you!"

A look of fear crossed the mayor's face and he began to sweat quite uncontrollably. Ma had been listening, either that or she was just programmed to hear certain unpopular phrases and the mayor just committed a fatal election snafu, and Wigglewort knew it right away. He'd just lost the Farnsworth-Miller family vote, and possibly most of the rest of the townsfolk along with it if he didn't have Ma's political backing. Mickey Mouse was looking like a sure thing if he didn't think of something quickly. He might actually be defeated at the polls by a cartoon character, but what was he to do? All eyes were on the mayor for a response as the sweat began to trickle down his brow.

Wigglewort smiled nervously and looked straight at Ma, who was sending a gaze toward Rupert that terrified the man. With a troubled look on his face, he cleared his throat. "Well, what I meant, Ma, was…" The mayor blanked and Ma raised one frowning eyebrow. *Think of something, you fool,* the mayor thought to himself. Rupert's eyebrows raised high and he opened his mouth to speak, only to have his statement come out as a question. "More Skunksquirters spending their hard-earned money in your diner if I'm elected?" *Oh, goodness, that was terrible,* the mayor thought again to himself.

"Skunksquirters ain't necessarily foreigners!" Ma came back, still pointing her finger at the mayor. "They're just nosy neighbors! You know *damn* well that you meant Massholes, Canuks, and outta-staters!"

"Oh, come on, Ma," Wigglewort's tone turned to whining, "I'm just trying to get some votes here. It's not like this stuff really happens anyway. You need to give me a break." The mayor was sweating terribly under his velvety suit jacket, whispering loudly directly at Ma as if no one else was in the room other than the two of them, "I'm not really going to bring in tourists. I can't even lower taxes or make the gas cheaper. I can't make the flowers prettier or the summers warmer like I said I would! Truth be told, I can't even fill a pothole."

"Bah!" Ma waved both her arms towards Wigglewort in an *I don't care* fashion and sat back down, still upset that Mabel had apparently won that round again, collecting her fifty percent of the winnings. Which, at twenty-five cents per bingo card put her take at around $8.75, with the other half always going to the church collection fund. Ma looked back up at the mayor as she sat down as if it was his fault that she hadn't won the round, then looked over to Mabel who was grinning back at Ma in a way that annoyed her greatly. Ma wiped her ten bingo cards clean and whispered to herself,

"Sonovabitch."

The mayor turned to the reverend, smiled nervously, and proceeded to leave the room. The reverend gave him a pompous smile back and nodded as he prepared for the next round by tossing the balls back into the clear plastic contraption that resembled an oversized guinea pigs exercise machine.

◆ ◆ ◆

Voting day. The only voting station, located at the town hall, would be opening at 8:00 a.m. Wiggleswort was standing at the door ready to shake hands and give out more lapel pins. He was uneasy and trembling a bit, rocking up and down on his heels and checking his watch often; it was 7:55 a.m. He'd arrived at the town hall at 4:30 this morning.

Eight o'clock arrived, and Rupert opened the doors to the voters. There weren't any right now but it was still early. Wiggleswort went back inside to check the blank ballots and make certain his name had been spelled correctly in large, bold lettering. The ballots looked okay. It wasn't as if he hadn't checked them already this morning; he had, 28 times. He'd also made certain the space for the write-in candidate was very small on the town-made copies of the local ballots that his sister, Myrtle, had printed for the election. He checked the old wooden ballot box; no absentee votes had magically appeared since he'd checked it last, ten minutes ago. He checked the single, portable voting booth that was set up inside the tiny meeting chambers. It had a nice, sharp pencil for casting the vote and a chair for the older folks to sit and make their decision on the single-question ballot. The town charter says a person can't vote for themselves, so Rupert had decided early on not to vote at all rather than write in a cartoon character's name that may, in fact, beat him by one vote.

10:00 a.m. The current mayor had gone through his thermos of hot coffee and he needed to pee badly; however, now he was being careful to stand at least fifteen feet away from the front entrance of the town hall and wouldn't go inside to use the restroom. He knew if he was spotted standing any closer he could be accused of campaigning too close to a polling place, which could cost him the election. He also didn't want to miss the opportunity to greet any incoming voters, so he chose to resist the urge for the time being.

By noon no voters had shown. Wiggleswort was still sweating, checking his watch often and continuing to wear out his soles by rocking on his heels. Partially from nerves but mostly because he still really had to go. At 12:15 he couldn't take it anymore, his bladder was floating. He darted into the building to relieve himself and quickly ran back out, checking his fly twice before getting out of the building and once more in the parking lot. He glanced over at the twelve, "Vote for Wiggleswort," signs he had put out on the town hall lawn early this morning. Eleven were still up, with one blowing over in the breeze as he watched. Rupert quickly waddled out and put it back up.

Two o'clock. No voters. Wiggleswort ate the sandwich he'd brought with him and had a glass of lemonade. The sandwich was warm and soggy, his ice had melted in the zip lock baggie he'd put in his brown lunch bag to help keep it cold. Not to mention it had been in the bag since he'd gotten up at 3:30 a.m., and at that early hour he'd known better than to wake Eleanor and ask her to put up a lunch for him in the wee hours of the morning, so he'd done that himself.

Three o'clock. Wiggleswort was pacing in the parking area. He heard a car coming down the main road and he sprinted curbside, stood up straight, checked his plaid necktie that matched his suspenders, and smiled. The car blew past doing about forty, tooting the horn as it went by. The dirt dust on the country road being kicked up by the speeding vehicle's tires made Rupert winch and cough as he brushed the dust off his velvety suitcoat. He was fairly certain he'd recognized the car as his sister who'd driven right by and hadn't bothered to stop and vote.

Four o'clock. Wiggleswort had sweat so terribly that he now had his coat off and was pulling at his plaid necktie to get it to loosen a little. Luckily, he'd worn a dark-colored dress shirt, so it managed to hide the sweat stains fairly well. He sniffed his underarms and now wished he'd brought some deodorant. He recalled that he had a can in his desk drawer; however, hadn't thought to grab it earlier when he went inside to pee and it was too late now.

Five o'clock. His necktie was now gone. Still no voters. The polls were due to close soon.

Six o'clock *post merīdiem*. Wiggleswort shut the town hall doors and turned the rusty old deadbolt, locking them behind him. Absolutely no one at all had bothered to vote this day, not even the mayor's own wife or sister, nor his two appointed board members. The volunteer ballot clerk hadn't even bothered to show up to tally any votes. Wiggleswort slumped down in a chair beside the empty ballot box. He rested his arm on the box and looked over again at the stack of blank ballots with his name correctly spelled on each one, and the spot for the write-in candidates made really small. A smile crossed Rupert's lips and he chuckled to himself, lifting his head proudly and cocking one eyebrow.

Rupert Wiggleswort had won the mayor's race by default again this year.

Chapter 4

Dirty Chickens

Early fall in northern Maine. This is the real fall that takes place beginning anywhere from the first of September all the way into December, depending on when the first snowflake drops. Maine truly has only two seasons, fall and winter. I suppose you could count preparing for winter as a third season if you really wanted to. At the onset of fall the leaves on the trees are a combination of green, yellow, orange, and red. The view from just about any mountaintop is a kaleidoscope of colors, and the leaf-peepers traditionally come out in droves, going wherever the local weatherperson tells them is the best spot in Maine to see the colors before they all fall to the ground in the first good autumn windstorm. The temperature is about forty-five above the donut on any given day early in the season with the nights getting nippy, and smoke from wood-fired stoves can begin to be seen floating from the chimneys of every residence.

Hunters are gearing up for the preferred game. Fisherman are thinking of fixing up their ice shanties, as this is their downtime with open water coming to a close and they're all waiting for ice-in, which on most bodies of water isn't until January 1st.

And the fair has come to town. Well, close to town anyway, with the annual event being held at the local fairgrounds in Skunksquirt. The fair is an annual tradition in Maine with many communities having its own, whether it be a cultural event with primarily crafts, show animals, and horse pulling. Or possibly an all-out, something-for-everyone extravaganza with carnival games, rides, and a variety of high-cholesterol foods. Our local fair is a bit of both.

◆ ◆ ◆

The cavalcade of tractor trailers had rolled into the fairgrounds a few days earlier, bringing all the carnival rides to be assembled by the carnies, which are made up both of local folks looking for a little extra part-time work and the paroled convicts from all around the eastern seaboard. The logo on all the rides is the same, "Smittie's Fun Follies," a company based out of Florida and now on their usual annual tour of the northern New England state and local fairs.

One of the interesting aspects of a fair is the haggling with the carnies if you're into that sort of thing, and seeking to play a game in which you win some cheap toy that would cost you much less if you simply went to the local dollar-store and purchased it. The carnies that traveled with the fair can be especially annoying in their attempts to draw you into their cubbyholes. You simply can't walk down a midway without the carnies taunting you to spend your money and come play their game. If they're a good carnie, they'll practically reach out and grab you, and they're willing to dicker with you over the price of the game or the prize if you win. If the game is two balls for a buck, you can usually talk them into three. It doesn't matter to them, they know that chances are you won't win the game anyway, or you will stay on to spend many more of your hard-earned dollars playing the foolish thing until you win several times and continually work your way up to that normally two-dollar stuffed animal that ultimately costs you about twenty. You may walk away with empty pockets but with a feeling of accomplishment for a few moments.

The other incentive to visit the fair is the food. You can get burgers for several times the amount it costs to prepare them. Footlong hot dogs, sausages, or cheesesteaks full of green peppers, onions, and mushrooms that have been sautéing for hours, if not days, are so tasty. The cheesesteaks are the ones that soak the buns so terribly that all of the fixings squirt out long before you're done eating, and it takes a roll of paper towels to begin to wipe the grease off your hands.

Ma has a dough-boy shack at the fair each year, one of her favorite side goodies to make. This year they stuck her between the dunk tank with the clown that yells out obscenities and the game where if you pop a balloon with a dart you win a framed girly photograph. Ruby had shown up early while they were setting up the games to inspect the merchandise, fearing there may be an old photo of her among the prizes and she wasn't about to allow that.

Ma did it up right in her shack, she'd plop a dollop of dough in the grease pit, and it would come out the size of a flat basketball. She generously covers the treat in powdered sugar and cinnamon for you, and she adds a soda pop for the same price. For the short period of time it takes you to eat the tasty treat, you're in cholesterol hell and loving every minute of it. Ma's shack has flashing neon lights all around it and a big neon sign on the top that reads,

"Ma's Other Diner." Very often she'll have Val, Cicely, or even El working the shack either along with, or for her, and Runyon helps keep it clean and well-stocked for the long weekend the fair is in town.

Now for some, especially the teenagers, their goal in visiting the fair is to see how much food they can pound down and then hop on all the rides on the midway. It seems as if their purpose is to determine how much greasy food and watered-down soda it takes to cause them to hurl on the spinning and twirling rides. When you see the carnies throwing down cat litter near the tilt-a-whirl, you know someone's achieved their goal.

There are, of course, other aspects of our local fair. Each year they have ox, horse, and tractor pulls; 4H animals; a hayride; the demolition derby on the horse track; and the freak shows. This year they featured a fake, stuffed, two-headed cow that they won't allow you to get too close to so you can't see the fake fur and poor stitching.

The ox-pulling in particular always seems to be a favorite among the older folks. Local ox owners chain their animals to big cement blocks at one end of the grandstand arena and drive the animals to the other end to determine whose oxen are the fastest and strongest. They grunt, snort, and dangle wooly-boogers from their snouts the entire way. Some of the oxen do the same, but mostly it's the boisterous, drunken farmers while the bystanders cheer them on as the large beasts tug and pull on the cement load. All so their owners can receive a tiny ribbon if theirs is the winner.

For the most part, the annual fair is a good time had by all.

"My hog will win this year!" exclaimed Ma, speaking of her self-proclaimed prized pig. Ma named the beauty "Buster Hog." Buster weighed in close to 400 pounds and was lounging in one of the long barn stalls used throughout the rest of the year by equestrians of the horse racing season. Each stall measured ten feet by fifteen feet and was separated by cedar log fencing. Buster was wallowing in the muck as Ma squirted more water into his pen from a long garden hose attached to a spigot that feeds water to many of the stalls. Ma herself was wearing her usual older, floral-patterned sundress that she didn't mind getting dirty, and her muddy swamper boots on her feet. This was her usual annual stall, and Ma was looking over the gate fencing hoping she'd finally have the ability to hang a first-place ribbon on it for the remainder of the fair for everyone to see and something for her to gloat about to all that passed by.

Animal shows are not only fun for people to wander through and admire, they're also a source of fierce competition among the locals for the prize of their animal being judged number one. More importantly, the bragging rights that come with the honor. You see, older folks around here don't have the luxury of having been a basketball, baseball, or football star, or have ever experienced the feeling of being on the winning team. They only have the annual, "Best in Show," if their extended family member wins at the annual fair, and the right to brag about it for an entire year as a result. There are also no "categories" to win at our local fair, there simply isn't enough folks with the time or energy to bring their animals to the fair, nor are there enough animals to begin with to hold individual competitions. There's simply one category, one winner, and the competition is tangible for the contestants.

And Ma wanted it.

"I don't know, Ma, Mattie's chickens are looking pretty good this year," Runyon remarked, glancing at the snowy white hens two stalls down. Each of the nearly dozen chickens having a tiny red bow scotch- taped to its neck feathers.

"Whaddaya mean!?" Ma spouted as she looked down towards Mattie Doody's stall, "Buster has it all over those skinny chickens and their hen-pecked owner!" Ma studied the clean little chickens, then looked back at Buster who was rolling in the mud, then back to the chickens again.

"I dunno, Ma. Those chickens are pretty spiffy, and Buster's looking pretty muddy. And he doesn't have a red bow, neither. I think the chickens have a good chance over the hog to win."

Ma contemplated the situation and began thinking that Runyon might be correct in his judgment, and just maybe the clean and bow-tied hens did look a bit better than Buster who was currently all covered in slop and not smelling very fresh. Ma stood there and thought, her garden hose now limp and just trickling water on her own boots.

"Judges will be coming soon," Runyon said, pointing. "They're just down a bit looking over Ruby's cats."

Ma knew Ruby's furball-ridden house felines didn't stand a chance, but she was now a little worried about the chickens. Ma spotted that Mattie was leaning into her stall, her bit-larger-than-normal butt up in the air and she was adjusting the little red bows just so, while the chickens pecked at her hands, hoping they were full of seed for them. Ma's eyes squinted and her nose crinkled. "Them chickens seem to need a little dirtying up," whispering beneath her breath, one eyebrow cocked up.

Runyon had overheard her as he peered at the chickens and knew Ma was plotting something. And knowing Ma quite well, whatever it was that she was contemplating wasn't going to be good. "Don't do anything stupid, Ma," he said looking back at her. "You'll get yourself disqualified if you get caught, just like you did last year when you tried to tie the floppy ears on Paul Doody's rabbits together."

"Shut up, boy, judges are getting close," Ma grumbled as she looked down the line just in time to see one of Ruby's cats take a swing at judge number three as he held the feline up in the air to look it over. She watched as the angry kitty hissed at the judge, taking the opportunity to pee on his leg as it did so.

Runyon could tell by his mother's demeanor that he was better off being somewhere else, or he just might be deemed an accomplice when the ca-ca-poo hit the fan from whatever Ma seemed to be plotting. Runyon snuck out of the barn onto the midway while El remained oblivious to everything that was going on around him, fast asleep in the old rocking chair he'd brought along and had set just outside of the pig stall. El was fast asleep, slumped down in the chair, and rocking instinctively.

Ma saw that the judges were now working their way up to the Wigglewort's goat stall. She watched as once they arrived the mayor began to brag to the judges on how wonderful his goats were. He had three of them all on dog leashes as he opened the stall door and let them out for the judges. Rupert had his hands full as the honoree goats proceeded to head-butt the judge's knees and screeched loudly. The goats screeched, not the judges. Well, one of them did. Ma knew she had bought herself some time now that the mayor's gums were flapping above the gleating of his goats. She looked over at El and frowned, realizing he was going to be of no assistance in the matter, as he was snoring under his straw hat that was down covering his eyes.

Ma dropped the trickling hose and shuffled over to Mattie's stall. Mattie was dressed in a nice, clean white dress with a red bow in her hair, disturbingly resembling the chickens themselves. "Chickens are looking a little tired, Mattie," Ma claimed. "They'd make a good stew, though, except they're a bit peaked and wouldn't feed too many. You look like you're enjoying the fair grub, though."

"My chickens are just fine, Wilomena," Mattie said arrogantly, knowing well that Ma disliked being referred to by her formal name. "A lot better looking than your dirty pig." Mattie motioned towards Buster, whom she noticed was just getting done eating a big gob of muck, most of it drooling down his snout. Mattie took a second puzzled glance, having never seen a pig smile; however, Buster seemed to be at the moment.

"We'll see. Well, good luck, Ma-til-da," Ma said sarcastically, a fake smile crossing her lips as she turned to walk back to Buster. When she turned away, the smile turned to a frown as she returned back to her stall. "I'll take care of your chickens, you hen-pecked witch," Ma whispered to herself, along with an evil little laugh under her breath as her frown turned to an equally evil smile.

Ma looked back and saw that the judges were doing their best to break away from the mayor's jaw-jacking, their knees now aching as another goat rammed its head and tiny horns into one of them. One judge had managed to step into goat poop and was shaking his boot as he turned to walk away. And yet another lady judge was headbutted to the back of her thigh by one of the tiny, stubborn creatures. Ma knew time was running out. She looked down at Buster. "You're a good-looking pig, Buster, but not good enough. We've got to do something. You need to win, and I want that award!" Buster just snorted happily and rolled on his back in the mud, pretending to know what Ma had said to him.

The judges were on their way, now going past Myrtle Watson's guinea pig, and Mattie's chickens were next. It was go-time and Ma had no intention of losing. *But what to do*, she thought. She looked around for something, anything. Finally, in a desperate effort, Ma grunted and reached down into the pig pen, scooping up a big handful of pig slop, mud, and straw. She made certain no one was looking and took careful aim, and slung it at Mattie's chickens, hoping to dirty up the little buggers just before the judges looked at them. Ma's aim was spot on and she had a good arm, sending the muck the two stalls over. Unfortunately, though, it was at this particular moment that Mattie had bent down over again into the stall to give a good-luck kiss to one of the chickens. Instead of hitting the chicken, the muck hit Mattie right upside of her head, the surprise knocking her balance off and she fell over the gate and onto the floor of the chicken pen, forcing the door of the stall wide open. Mattie's spooked chickens took advantage of the opportunity to leave the pen and spread out among the other animals in the barn but not before the surprise of Mattie falling into the pen caused them all to cluck loudly, fly up, flap their wings violently, and send feathers and little red bows everywhere. When Mattie raised back up onto her knees from the faceplant she'd incurred, she had feathers and a tiny red bow stuck to her slop-covered face, and her pretty white dress was now quite soiled.

Mattie began to get up as she watched her chickens fly from their respective coop and she turned towards Ma. "Miller! You old cow!" There was vengeance in her eyes, as pig slop dripped from her temple. "I'm going to fry you like a side of bacon!"

Ma's eyes widened. She had never seen Matilda quite so angry, but Ma wasn't one to back down from a fight. "Come get it, you wimp!" Ma quickly scooped up another handful of slop, ready to go on the defensive.

By this time El had awoken, mostly due to one of Mattie's chickens landing in his lap. Everyone else in the barn, including the judges, quickly made their way to the door openings at either end of the long building, whichever they were closest to, knowing that this was going to get even uglier than it already had. Mattie raised both arms preparing to block the oncoming slop, made a fist in each hand, and slowly crept towards Ma.

"Keep your distance, Doody!" Ma exclaimed as she raised up the slop, ready to let it fly. Mattie didn't stop, and when she got to be within just about an arm's length from Ma, she sprung with her arms outstretched and screamed like a banshee. Just as Mattie became airborne, Ma let a yell out of her own as well and let go with the slop. The handful of muck hit Mattie in the bosom, further staining her once-clean white dress. When Mattie came down, she grabbed Ma around the waist and the force landed them both in Buster's pen with a "*Splash!*" into the muck. Buster let out a loud squeal as he attempted to wiggle out of the way of the two fighting women. Mud and pig goo flew everywhere, including all over El and the chicken that was in his lap, which Ma caught a glimpse of as she landed backward in the mud with Mattie's arms tightly around her. "Ha! Got one of 'em anyway!" she screamed into Mattie's face. El decided he didn't want any of this and headed towards the exits with the others, carrying the muddy little chicken in his arms.

The two women tangled, tumbled, and squirmed in the muck. Buster did his best to stay out of their way. Pig slop and chicken feathers filled their section of the barn. People watching from outside both ends of the building were all in shock. A couple of the older women screamed, and one passed out, having to be fanned back to consciousness by the judges using their notebooks. One judge was fanning his own pants leg where the cat had peed on him.

"Somebody needs to do something!" a random voice cried out.

Runyon made a pass through the small midway, listening to all the carnies attempting to convince him the play their game. On the second pass, he heard his calling. "Shoot until you win!" a voice cried out. This drew Runyon's interest.

The game looked simple enough with four rows of wooden sticks, evenly alternating and spaced apart, each with a different prize rubber-banded to a stick of wood. The prizes ranged from a plastic bug to what appeared to be an actual twenty-dollar bill. "All you need to do is knock the stick completely over," the carnie said from under his hat which looked like something Dr. Suess should be wearing. The man was tall and skinny with greasy hair, and he had on dirty clothes to match his filthy hands, your typical fair carnie. His petty criminal record was most likely as tall as he was.

The pop gun was a rifle that ejected a tiny little cork from the end of the barrel. "You stick the cork in the end of the barrel, cock the gun once, aim, and shoot," said the carnie. "Shoot until you win, two bucks my friend!" Runyon almost thought of attempting to talk him down to a dollar, but he figured he was going to win something anyway so he might as well spend the money. He put his two bucks on the counter and the carnie quickly snatched it up in his dirty hands and put it into the equally grimy pouch that he had tied around his waist.

The carnie placed a plastic cup full of corks on the counter in front of Runyon and told him to pick any gun on the counter, telling him they were all the same. Runyon chose a weapon, cocked the gun, stuck his cork in the barrel's end, leaned on the counter, and took aim at a twenty-dollar bill with a rubber band holding it tight to a stick.

"*Pop!*"

Runyon missed. The cork seemed to fly to the left of the stick he'd aimed at and flew between two other prizes. Runyon frowned and looked strangely at the sights on the toy rifle. He cocked the rifle again, putting a cork in the end, leaned on the counter, and took his time taking a more careful aim. Behind him, Runyon hadn't noticed Constable Bob, who'd been patrolling the fairgrounds nibbling on a doughboy, was now running through the midway in a general direction towards the animal barn. His big belly and the gun belt around his waist were battling each other with neither seeming to win, nor backing down.

"*Pop!*"

Runyon missed again. His cork took the same path, just to the left of his intended target. On the third try, Runyon aimed at the empty space just to the right of the twenty-dollar bill, believing that if his instincts were correct, this time he'd hit it.

"*Pop!*"

This time Runyon struck the twenty-dollar bill dead center; however, the stick didn't move. He stood up annoyed, "Hey! I hit it and it didn't go down."

The carnie was busy at the opposite end of the counter trying to con another person into playing the game and almost hadn't heard Runyon's plea. "No, you didn't," the carnie said, not even bothering to turn to look at Runyon.

"Yes, I did!"

This time the carnie turned and looked Runyon straight in the face. "No, you didn't, pal. Keep trying."

Screw this, Runyon thought to himself, frowning and turning back towards his target. He put another cork in the barrel and cocked the gun twice and took aim as before, just to the right of the cash.

"*Pop!*"

He struck the twenty-dollar bill again, only this time the stick seemed to turn just a hair to the right on impact but still didn't fall down. "You've got the damn sticks nailed down!" Runyon pointed at it and yelled to anyone who happened to be listening while looking over at the carnie.

"No, it ain't. And no cursing!" the carnie replied, looking straight back at Runyon, speaking, and then quickly looking away at a couple of cute girls walking up the midway, catcalling his sales pitch to them as they went by.

"*Sonofabitch,*" Runyon whispered to himself. This time Runyon cocked the gun several times, put his cork in, took aim, and fired.

"*POP!*"

The cork exited the barrel, spun out of control, and knocked over a stick one row up and four over that had a plastic bug attached to it.

"We have a winner!" The carnie shouted for others to hear as he walked over and handed Runyon a plastic bug from hundreds of others he kept in a cardboard box beneath the counter. "Want to play again, my friend? Two bucks."

"Oh yes," Runyon growled in a low voice and a smirk on his face as he put down two more dollars with one hand, throwing the plastic bug over his shoulder onto the midway behind him with the other. It landed among many other, multicolored plastic bugs.

"Good luck, my friend!" the carnie said with a big, shit-eating grin that displayed some of his teeth that weren't missing as he scooped up the two dollars, leaving another cup of corks and heading towards another potential sucker at the other end of the counter.

Runyon again pumped up the rifle more than a dozen times and put his cork in. Again, the carnie was haggling with passersby at the other end of the counter, attempting to get people to play his game and fill his filthy cash bag. Runyon took careful aim as before, just to the right of his intended target, taking his time to make certain he was going to hit exactly what he was shooting at.

"*POP!*"

"*Yeeooww!*" The carnie screamed, his body stiffening straight up and then bending backward, and finally, he fell down, grabbing his backside as he went. Runyon had waited for the carnie to turn around and then shot him in the ass, having aimed just a bit to the right of his target.

♦ ♦ ♦

"What the hell is going on in here?!" Constable Bob shouted from the open barn doors, his belly still jiggling from stopping too soon. "Ma! Mattie! Get out of that pig pen!" he yelled, oddly enough with authority. Just then, through the screaming of the two women and screeching from the animals, a big gob of pig mush came flying out and hit Bob on the oversized sterling silver-plated badge he had pinned to his chest. Bob was visibly annoyed that his normally clean, white uniform had fallen victim to violation from a pig pen. Bob stretched his arms apart, "Stand back, folks," he said as if he was stopping anyone who was going to assist him, which nobody was intending to. "I'm going in."

"Be careful," a voice from behind. "They're both nuts!"

Bob yanked up on his gun belt and proceeded into the barn. The deafening sounds of animals clucking, mooing, barking, and squealing filled his ears. Not to mention the cursing coming from both women.

Bob carefully made his way the short distance through the flying mud and feathers to Buster's pen, squatting and ducking as he crept towards it. When he arrived, he found the two women covered in mud. Ma was eating one of

Mattie's red bows off her muddy dress, and Mattie was trying to poke Ma in the side with her own hair needle. The constable stood up outside the pen and mounted his hands to his sides. "Get up, both of you, and quit this foolishness!" Bob attempted to reach down and grab onto one of the women; however, he was unsuccessful as it was just like trying to grab a greased pig, so to speak.

"This is between Mattie and me!" Ma grunted as the two women continued to wrestle in the mud. "Get your fat ass outta here before you get dirty too!" Buster was squealing and trying his best to squeeze out of the pen between two logs. As it turned out he was too big to accomplish the task and was stuck in the pen with the two battling women with nowhere to go.

"That's it! Ma, you're headed to the pokey for causing a public disturbance!" Bob knew what he had to do. He had a duty to cease this ruckus and he intended to perform his job to the best of his abilities. Unfortunately, his *abilities* are where he was lacking expertise. He took one step into the pen and immediately his right leg slid out from underneath him, and flailing his arms in a desperate attempt to take flight and remain on his feet, he landed on his tuckus in the mud. Religion overtook Bob as he yelled "*Jeesus!*" as he went down. "*Splash!*" The constable wobbled like a weeble trying to get back up, covering his uniform in pig goo and crying out, "That's it, you're both underrest!"

Bob managed to get back onto his knees, grabbing onto the logs on the side of the pen. He then lunged both hands towards the two women, grabbing Ma by the hair and Mattie by her arm, and managed to pull the two apart, wheezing like he was having a heart attack while doing so. Mud was dripping from his brow. "Stop it!" Bob yelled, and the women ceased momentarily. "Just look at you two, you should both be ashamed of yourselves! You're scaring the pig!" Bob motioned his head towards Buster and mud flew from his brow.

The two mud-covered women looked over at the oversized and terrified hog. Finally, after a few tense moments which seemed more like minutes, the two women who were obviously pooped both nodded reluctantly at Bob. He let each go and they both fell back, sitting up in the muck and breathing heavily. Mattie's white dress and Ma's standard floral-pattern dress were both now entirely stained grayish-brown by the mud. Both women looked as if they'd participated in a Pay-Per-View mud-wrestling competition that neither had won, nor that anyone would want to pay to watch. A brief ovation came from the onlookers in response to Bob's ability to finally calm the situation.

El walked back into the barn and looked down at Ma, shaking his head in disgust as she glanced up at him. "*Awe*, shut up!" Ma yelled and took the opportunity to clean her muddy hands by flicking them one last time at Mattie, striking her in the face with muck.

Mattie flinched and closed her eyes. "You ruined my dress!" she whined as she wiped the mud just above her brow and began to stand back up.

"Oh, for *Chrissake*, make yourself another one! You got more curtains in your house!" Ma replied. "It ain't like you've never been dirty before!"

The rest of the onlookers re-entered the barn to calm their animals and resume their caretaking and spectating. The judges also began resuming their duties.

"Bob, there's a disturbance on the midway. A shooting!" The constable's two-way police radio squawked as he struggled back to his feet in the pig stall.

"What now?" Bob sarcastically said to himself as he grabbed his radio, which had a big wad of muck on it. He pulled it from its dirty cradle and keyed the mike, replying, "Ten-fowa." Bob moaned and groaned as he got back up and took off waddling towards the midway, perspiration, and pig slop dripping from his face.

Ma stood up and paused for a second or two as she wiped the mud from her dress, and then it dawned on her. "Holy shit! Runyon!" She too waddled quickly toward the midway.

◆ ◆ ◆

Runyon and the carnie were at a standoff, both with their pop guns cocked several times and corks ready to shoot at each other. The carnie was ducking behind his counter with just the uppermost part of his body exposed. Runyon, showing no fear was out in the open on the midway about fifteen feet from his prey pointing his gun straight at him, or so, a bit to the right.

The midway, too, had come to a standstill. Rides ceased, and food stands stopped selling. People had taken shelter behind whatever they could find, food stands, rides, games, behind larger people. All peeking out, gawking, and waiting to see who would shoot first.

Constable Bob, still dripping with pig muck, arrived and came to a halt just a few feet from the two with Ma right behind him, nearly bouncing off his backside when he stopped. "Put those guns down!" Bob shouted at the two.

"Runyon! Put that damn pop gun down!" Ma bellowed, seemingly hiding behind Constable Bob.

"The game's rigged, Ma. They nailed the sticks down!" Runyon said, not taking his eyes off the sights or his target. "This guy's stealing money from people!"

"The game's not rigged!" the carnie exclaimed from behind the counter, never taking his eyes off Runyon. "This asshole just can't shoot straight!"

"I'll show you how straight I can shoot!" Runyon yelled down the barrel of his pop gun and straight at the space just to the right of the carnie's head.

"Don't shoot, Runyon," Constable Bob said in his best, and certainly inexperienced, negotiator voice. "We can work it out." Bob's arms outstretched and his hands motioning in front of him as if he was trying to telepathically get Runyon's gun to lower. "Nothing's worth shooting someone over." Attempting to calm his voice even more and convince Runyon to put the pop gun down, "We just need to talk the situation out." He was nearly to a whisper now.

"Put the *goddam* gun down, boy!" Ma bellowed at the top of her lungs from behind Bob.

Bob's eyes rolled in disbelief. "Shush, Ma, I got it under control."

"Sure looks like it, fat boy! They're both ready to off one another!" Ma said as she walked out from behind Bob, now facing and talking to him as if nothing else was happening at the moment.

"Gimme back my pop gun or I'm gonna shoot you!" The carnie yelled at Runyon, "I've had enough of this crap! I put up with bullshit all day long from people like you! I can't take it anymore! I'll shoot you, I swear it!" The carnie's voice now crackling and his hands shaking.

"No one is going to shoot anyone!" Bob yelled as he pushed Ma aside, realizing that raising his voice again was only going to agitate the situation. Bob was seemingly stumped. He had two fools ready to shoot each other with pop guns and a growing crowd of fairgoers in the crossfire. Too many thoughts were running through the constable's head. This wasn't in his training manual. *I'm not a negotiator*, he thought to himself. Bob's evenings were spent watching old episodes of *COPS* on their DVD player and it hadn't prepared him for this type of tense situation. *Should I call for backup? No, that's embarrassing, they're using pop guns. Maybe I should just shoot them both? No, that would look terrible in the local papers. "Police officer guns down two people pointing pop-guns at each other." Is there even an arrestable charge for pointing pop guns at each other? Dammit, I'm hungry and those doughboys really smell delicious. Crap! Stay focused!*

Not entirely knowing what to do, Bob did the next thing he thought to himself and he reached over and grabbed a third pop gun off the counter nearest himself, put a cork in it, and cocked it a few times. This didn't seem to faze either suspect, whose eyes were currently locked on each other. Bob waved his new toy weapon back and forth between the two. "If either one of you shoots, they get it right back at them!" The constable was sweating bullets, so to speak, never to have been in this type of situation before. The perspiration was keeping the mud on his uniform moist.

"Oh, this is classic! Why haven't you called for backup yet? Where's the tactical team? Why don't you radio for one of them hostage negotiators, Johnson? Embarrass yourself even more!" Ma stated, scolding the constable as if he were a child.

"Shut up, Ma," was Bob's reply, not letting his eyes leave the two armed suspects, and still waving his pop gun back and forth between them.

It was quite a sight, three men, three pop guns, ready to shoot like an old western standoff. Along with the bystanders on the ground, in the melee of the midway ceasing completely, people were stuck on rides that had stopped. Many were looking down from the Ferris wheel and teacup rides from above. It invoked fear in some of the spectators and simply made others chuckle. It caused quite a bit of amusement to Ma. "If you do have to shoot him, son, make it right between the eyes so he don't come back!" she yelled to Runyon.

"Shut up, Ma!" Bob cried out. "You're not helping the situation!"

Just about this time, Old Marmaduke came strolling by, having visited the fair for a bite of his favorite carnival treat, a deep-fried sour pickle which he was taking his time munching on, savoring each and every bite. As Marmaduke walked straight into the middle of the mess like some brave warrior, he stopped and looked over the situation carefully. He took notice of the three men armed with pop guns, and the two completely covered in mud. He shook his head as if any of this didn't surprise him and casually said, "It figures," and took another crunchy bite of his pickle, strolling up beside Ma to watch and be amused as to how this situation would ultimately end.

Several tense moments went by in silence as Bob continued to wave his pop gun between the two, just waiting for one of them to act. It was finally the carnie's shaking trigger finger that got itchy first, either by choice or by nervous accident, and he shot.

"POP!"

The cork flew from the barrel and hit Runyon square on the chin, snapping his head back for a moment. There was a half-surprised look on the carnie's face when it happened, and his eyes widened. *"Oh, shit,"* he whispered.

"You sonofabitch!" Ma exclaimed and pointed at him. "You shot my boy!"

Bob's eyes widened as well. He knew what was coming next. He looked at Runyon who was regaining his composure and began to re-establish his aim. "Don't do it, Runyon!" Bob shouted, and with one-time courage from out of nowhere, the constable hurled himself between Runyon and the carnie just as Runyon pulled the trigger.

"POP!"

The cork struck the officer in the forehead right between his eyes. Bob went down and as he hit the ground his pop gun went off.

"POP!"

The cork flew, ricocheted off the tilt-of-the-whirl, and came back to hit Old Marmaduke in the shin. Marmaduke went down, his half-eaten pickle striking Ma in the bosom as he threw it away to grab his aching shin as he tumbled to the ground.

Three shots, three immediate casualties.

♦ ♦ ♦

As dumb luck would have it, the county ambulance had been set up on the fairgrounds along with the volunteer fire department, each collecting donations. The EMS attendants all had a good laugh as they treated the cork bruises on the four victims. Constable Bob had a big red welt between his eyes, which were now both blackening. Runyon had one big welt on his chin. The carnie, refusing to drop his pants for the attendants, had unknown injuries but sported an obvious limp. And Marmaduke swore to anyone who cared to listen that his leg had been broken, even though it wasn't, and he was out half-a-pickle. All four refused transport to the county hospital.

Bob made the carnie give Runyon back the four dollars that he'd spent on the game. He then made Runyon give the money to Marmaduke to buy another fried pickle. He also made Marmaduke promise not to sue him for inadvertently shooting him in the shin. Ma and Mattie sort of apologized to each other, and they both, along with Constable Bob, all went back to the horse barn to be hosed off.

Ruby Red's cat was announced the first-place winner, with Myrtle Watson's guinea pig taking a close second. Wigglewort's goats received an honorable mention ribbon.

The fair ended without further excitement four days later; however, games with pop guns were prohibited from any future events and it was declared that judging for animal contests would all be performed by secret ballot in the future.

♦ ♦ ♦

The next week Ma ran a special in the diner. Chicken fried ham. And no, Ma didn't cook up Buster but Mattie's chickens were never seen or heard from again.

Chapter 5

A Fishing Trip

As mentioned, weekend days in any season are Ma's time for recreational activities and she has other people that she trusts tending to the diner. Today, Val Daley was managing the establishment while Ma had other things on her mind this fine late spring Saturday.

◆ ◆ ◆

"Get your lazy ass up!" Ma yelled to El, who was busy sitting in his favorite easy chair and watching the morning news. The fabric on the chair was cat-clawed on all sides from Ma's big tabby. Ma's cat was quite overweight from eating anything it felt resembled food. It was simply a huge ball of white-ish hair that she'd affectionately named "Fluffbutt."

"All the fish will be gone for the day before we get out on the pond!" Ma was all dressed and ready to go fishing. On her feet, she had her olive-green swamper boots that came up to her knees. Not because she planned to wade in the water to fish but due to the fact that the boat had so many leaks she couldn't keep up with the bail bucket without getting her feet wet. She had her bright yellow fishing hat on over her hair bun. She wore a faded yellow and stained rain jacket, and, of course, she had on her old fish-stained floral pattern dress that she kept just for such occasions. Finally, a fish gut-stained apron for cleaning the day's catch and wiping her hands on. She had her favorite fishing pole, a six-foot long Shakespeare with a Zebco Spincast reel, ready with a silver spinner, bobber, weights, and hook all prepared and ready to have fresh live angle worms in place of the crusted dead ones that were still stuck to it from the last outing. Ma wanted to get an early start, knowing that the misty morning hours were the best fishing.

El stretched and yawned an old man groan out of him as he pretended to have a hard time lifting his butt out of the chair. El was never happy when

41

Ma would bother him before he got to see his favorite weather lady on the morning news show. Of course, television reception this far north wasn't so great, so the weather girl usually looked a bit fuzzy anyway, but El could dream of what she might actually look like.

Ma was getting more and more agitated and restless as El took his time putting on his old, tan shit-kickers with the leather on the toes nearly worn down to the steel and his equally old, gray fishing hat, which sported all his retired fishing lures stuck into it. All except for the one hook that was placed there from his own wrongdoing. That one was from a bad cast and the hat had kept the top of his noggin from having the hook driven into it. He decided to leave it stuck there with the broken line still attached as he felt it was good luck.

Ma kicked open the porch screen door and yelled out, "Runyon, do you want to go fishing?!"

"Are you going fly fishing?" a muffled voice emerged from inside the barn where Runyon was tinkering on his pickup truck engine. He'd gotten up early that day to get a head start and change the oil out, which was several thousand miles overdue.

"Nope! Trolling and bobbing!" Ma yelled back. "Nope."

"Fine, be that way!" Ma echoed back and started back into the house. She stopped herself and yelled back out, "When you're done with that foolishness, get over to the diner and replace that leaky toilet faucet, and make sure them one's I got working today aren't messing around! I'll be in for the dinner hours!" She heard Runyon's "*Okay, Ma*" echo back as she let the screen door slam behind her.

Ma already had the ten-foot and badly dented steel johnboat bungee strapped to the bed of the pickup truck. The boat was powered by an old '67 Evinrude fifteen-horse outboard. Ma threw in a couple of wooden paddles and a round rock about the size of a football with a rope tied to it, which made a fine anchor in case they happened to troll over a hot spot and decided to stop and plug fish. She'd also tossed in a couple of buckets and two life-preservers.

"Where are we going today, Ma?" El asked as he readied himself, and as if he didn't know. Pug Hole Pond was always the spring destination unless they were headed to camp. Today would be no different. Many fishing days were spent with the conversation being about trying different lakes and streams, especially if the fish weren't biting but it was always Pug Hole Pond that they returned to.

"Pug Hole! Where else?!" Ma barked and El cracked a smile.

They both climbed into the old '78 Chevy, which at one time was bright, fire-engine red in color. Now, many years later, it was a combination of faded red, rust, bondo, and a bit of duct tape. Ma was in the driver's side as she climbed in and plopped her butt on the sofa pillow she used to keep the exposed springs on the bench seat from poking her in the tush. El had an old toilet seat on his passenger side for the same reasons. Ma shifted the long standard gear rod into neutral and let out the brake, and the truck began to roll backward a bit as she clutched hard and turned the key. The truck gave a resounding groan, coughed a couple of times, and thick, black smoke shot from the straight pipe with a loud backfire that rattled the license plate that was held on by zip ties through two rusty holes in the rear bumper. Ma looked at El and sighed, "Huh." El looked back at her and just shrugged his shoulders. On the second turn of the key, the old truck roared to life, and they were on their way. After fifteen minutes of El's back-seat driving and Ma telling him repeatedly to, "shut up," they arrived at the pond.

Pug Hole is not a large pond, about one-quarter mile wide and little more than a stone's throw across. The deepest it gets is about twelve to fifteen feet. It has an inlet on the north side where the brook trout spawn each September. The inlet is fed from a stream that leads to the larger Bottleneck Lake. It's not uncommon to see a moose wading on either end of the pond, and if you're lucky, you might just see one swimming straight through from one side to the other.

Oh, and just as a side note, Ma really has no use for moose.

◆ ◆ ◆

As the flashback goes, it was 1975, and one winter's night Ma felt the urge to visit the outhouse about one o'clock in the morning. At that time the small two-seater toity was thirty feet from the front door. Due to a recent and windy nor'easter, the aging crapper was missing part of the roof and one window facing the rear had broken out. Ma had only brought a small flashlight with her but it was a moonlit night with plenty of stars to see through the tall pines and fir trees. Ma had been in a hurry, so all she had on was a pair of drawers under her robe and her work boots slid onto her feet. Ma was squatting on the frigid potty, gazing up at the stars through the holes in the roof, whispering to herself, "Lazy bastard." Referring to El and how he hadn't repaired the tiny building yet as she began to shiver.

Ma was looking for the Big Dipper and waiting for her business when all of a sudden she felt a warm breeze through the cold that hit her on the back of her neck. Frowning, Ma turned to see where the strange wind was coming from. She turned her head and squinted her eyes to see through the broken window and out into the darkness. What Ma saw in the moonlight was two large nostrils at the end of a snout that was a quarter-way through the window and staring her straight in the face. Attached to the snout was a rather large bull moose with a huge rack of horns that was preventing him from poking his entire head through the broken window.

Ma's eyes grew wide just as the moose nonchalantly let out a snort directly in Ma's face, leaving a dripping trail of snot and misting mucus. Ma proceeded to instinctively let a yell out of her louder than any loon, and with similar vocals. The startled moose let out a loud, deafening bellow, whose force took Ma's hair out of its bun and shot her hair needle into the door of the outhouse like an arrow into a bullseye.

Ma, with one hand on either side of her underpants; however, not taking any time to pull her skivvies back up, bolted out of the outhouse towards the house. She tripped on her britches and took a header off the top step and into a snowbank with her ass straight up in the air just as the frightened moose bolted in the opposite direction back into the woods.

Ma managed to get herself up out of the snowbank. And, with a bit of swearing to assist in the effort, pulled up her skivvies and went back inside the house to the bedroom where El was snoring loudly and deep in dreamland. Ma walked to his side of the bed and smacked him as hard as she could upside his sleeping head which startled him awake. She then told him in no uncertain terms that he'd better get on it and perform the necessary repairs to the outhouse before any more moose had the chance to stick their snouts through the open holes and disrupt her business.

Ever since that fateful night when Ma felt the urgency, she'd take a 30/06 rifle with her to the potty. She also made certain El fixed the outhouse and replaced the broken window with a piece of plywood.

It wasn't too long after that they had indoor plumbing installed.

◆ ◆ ◆

Ma backed the pickup down the landing and they slid the boat into the pond. As soon as the boat hit the pond, it began to take on water through the several tiny holes in the steel construction. They both climbed into it, Ma taking the back seat next to the motor and El up front. Their "life preservers" were a couple of old boat seat cushions that supposedly doubled as a floatation device that, in reality, probably wouldn't keep a chipmunk afloat if need be.

The old Evinrude had seen better days too. The cover had been lost years ago; however, it had pushed many-a-boat during its time and still ran decently most days. Ma pumped up the portable gas tank that fed the motor with the fifty-to-one mixture of gas and oil, pulled the choke on the Evinrude, and began cranking on the motor. After five or so pulls and some encouragement with the ball primer, it made a hesitant sputter. The engine shook, smoked, and dumped gas and oil into the pond but still wouldn't start. After ten pulls, Ma was sweating and swearing. She stood up in the boat now, rocking it back and forth. Fifteen pulls, nada. El reached for the paddle. "Put that damn thing down!" Ma blurted. "She'll start! Give her time!" Twenty pulls, nothing. Ma's hair had now fallen from her bun underneath her hat. "Give me the damn

WD-40!"

El handed Ma the can that was kept under his seat. Ma removed the spark plug with a plug wrench she kept in the outboard's engine compartment. She hosed the end of the plug, squirted some straight into the carburetor and put the plug back in. Twenty-one, twenty-two, twenty-three… *"Sputter…sputter… sputter, sputter, sputter…varoom!"* The old engine came to life, and Ma turned down the throttle to a low idle that kept the engine from shaking too much. Ma sat back down, sweat making her graying and stringy hair stick to the front of her face. "I told you it would start!" El just shook his head and faced the front.

They tried trolling for a while, doing circles near the outlet in hopes of catching a nice brookie. The pond is known for trout, white perch, and bass. After an hour of trying, they hadn't even had a nibble between them. "Enough of this! I'm parking it in the middle!" Ma barked. El didn't particularly care, he had his pole in the lazy fisherman mounted to the gunnels, had his hat halfway down over his brow, and was spread out in the front of the boat, dozing to the rocking of the waves. Ma found her spot somewhere near the middle of the pond, shut down the Evinrude, and tossed the rock overboard. Once the rope went limp as the rock found the bottom, she gave the makeshift anchor a few feet of slack and tied it off. They both put bobbers on their lines and casted out. El went back to dozing, while Ma sat patiently and watched for her bobber to dance on the water.

The pond was as clear as glass that day, with no wind and a clear sky. Ma could see her reflection in the pond and took the opportunity to use it to help return her hair to its normal bun and make certain she looked good. She winked at herself in the pond-mirror just as a moose walked out of the woods on the south side of the pond near the big casting rock and waded into the water up to its underbelly, dipping its snout occasionally into the water, its tail swatting flies on its back. Ma looked up and spotted the oversized critter. "Should've brought the moose gun," Ma whispered to herself. El cracked a smile, overhearing Ma's comment; however, not bothering to open his eyes or adjust his hat, he knew what she must've been referring to. "Keep your distance, Bullwinkle!" she called out as the moose's head came back up out of the water with a nice trout between its jaws and showed the prize to Ma. "Damn it! We're fishing the wrong deep hole!" Ma cried out.

"You parked the boat," El replied nonchalantly, not moving from his comfortable spot.

"You're no help at all," Ma said. "And you're some fisherman too, ain't ya?! The damn moose got one before you did!"

"He's been fishing for more years and he's better at it than me," El groaned. "Plus, they got that little twingy-thingy on their tongues that attract the fishies when they dunk their heads and open their snouts."

Ma gave El that "look" that tells him he was full of shit. "Twingy-thingy on their tongues," she quipped sarcastically. "I'll give you a twingy-thingy…"

El looked up from under his hat and smiled. "Oh baby, you haven't given me the twingy-thingy with your tongue in years!"

"Dirty bastard!" Ma's was a look of disgust as she focused back on her bobber. Then it dawned on her. "Wait a minute! Moose don't even eat fish! What's that damn moose doing with my fish?!"

"Must be protecting it from you," El said as he closed his eyes again under his hat, giving a little giggle at the thought of Ma losing her prize catch to a moose that didn't even like fish.

It was around this time that a big moose fly made its way out to the boat and began to "bug" Ma. And for those interested and not knowing, a moose fly is one step above a horse fly, which are slightly larger than a house fly. "*Goddam* fly," Ma said as she started swinging her yellow seaman's rain hat above her head trying to shoo it away.

"Let him bite you and then he'll go away," was El's poorly timed suggestion.

"Are you stupid? Their bite's worse than getting poked with a needle!" Ma continued swatting at the elusive little creature, her hair beginning to come out of its bun again.

"You're rocking the damn boat, Ma. Cut it out!" El now being forced to give up his comfy position and grab the gunnels of the boat in an effort to remain on his seat.

"Shut your trap!" Ma managed to hit the moose fly once or twice, but it didn't seem to faze it as anyone who has battled a moose fly knows, they're tough little buggers. The fly just kept buzzing around Ma's head. "That's it, I've had enough!" Ma bellowed as she grabbed one of the paddles and stood up in the boat, giving it a big rock and this time El slid off his seat into the puddle of water in the bottom of the boat, grabbing onto his hat before it fell into the pond.

El cried out, "What the hell are you doing, Ma?! *Jeesus*, that water's cold! You got me all wet! Just sit your ass down!"

Ma didn't respond to his request. Instead, she kept her stance with her feet spread apart to each side of the boat as it rocked gently and watched the air around her. In her hands was the paddle, prepared for battle, and she looked around in an effort to locate the fly, which for the moment had disappeared. Not seconds later Ma spotted the moose fly coming at her from the front of the boat straight over El's head. Ma reared back and swung the paddle as hard as she could and whacked the fly, and El, right on the side of his noggin. "*Thwack!*" El's hat flew off his head as he tumbled over and back onto the wet floor of the boat again, his head landing in a bucket they very often used for live bait smelts when trolling for salmon. The fly went splat onto the surface of the pond. Ma had hit a grand slam home run.

Ma pointed to the dead fly floating on the water, "See, I got him!" She looked down at El. "What the hell are you doing with your head in the fish bait bucket?!"

"It's tastier than the worm bait bucket," El gurgled. "You hit me, that's what!"

"If you weren't in my way you wouldn't have gotten hit!"

"I ought to throw you over the side!" El grunted as he struggled to pick himself back up, kneeling on his knees, dripping from the bath he'd taken in the bottom of the boat.

Ma swung the paddle again and hit El on his right butt cheek as he attempted to get back on his seat. "*Whack!*" "I'd like to see you try it!" El slipped and went right back on the floor of the boat.

"You old witch! You wait until I get myself up!"

"Try it and you'll land in the pond on the next one!" Ma raised the paddle back up to swing again. Just then out of the corner of her eye, she spotted El's pole bend over the side of the boat, the tip jigging just above the water. "You got a fish!" Ma shouted.

El raised himself up, the bait bucket still on his head. He cocked the bucket up to one side so he could get one eye out from under it and saw the tip of his fishing pole dancing up and down. Sure enough, there was a fish on. The tip of the pole was bent right close to the surface of the water and El saw that the bobber had disappeared below the boat. *This is a good one*, he thought to himself. El reached over and grabbed his fishing pole, got himself back up, and sat back down on his seat to begin reeling.

"Play him out, you don't want to lose him!" Ma belched, still standing up in the boat and holding the paddle.

"I know what I'm doing!" El replied as he slowed down his reeling and tilted his head back to get both eyes out from the bucket and on his line. The line was dancing in circles near the boat, making round ripples on the water.

"He's a good one," said Ma in a calmer voice, her anger seemingly now turned to joy in the fact that one of them had a fish on.

"He's a fighter all right," El said, doing his best to play the fish out. The bait bucket fell back to his nose, blinding him again.

The bobber on El's line appeared, jumping out of the water. "He's close now!" Ma blurted.

"Get the net!" El pushed the bucket back up over one eye.

Ah yes, the net. Ma looked around the boat and suddenly remembered she had forgotten the net. It wasn't surprising, she always forgot the net. "Don't got a net, El. Just reel him into the boat. Not too fast or you'll lose him."

El reeled in the fish right up close to the boat, just below the water. The fish jumped out of the water; it was a rainbow trout, over a foot long from El's best guess. The fish jumped out of the water again and El adjusted the bait bucket with one hand once more so he could see with both eyes.

"He is a good one!" El shouted with joy as the fish fought against him. The reel screeched from El reeling and the fish pulling against the effort. El wasn't even noticing now how bad his head and ass hurt from the paddle-whacking. "I'm bringing him in!" El yelled as the line went to the front of the boat and El caught sight of the whopper once more as it swam sideways near the surface. "He's a biggun!"

El gave a last hard tug just as the fish again jumped out of the water. The huge trout came soaring into the boat past him. Ma, who was still standing right behind El, caught the trout in the kisser, knocking her off balance as the boat rocked hard to the left. Ma let go of the paddle, swung her arms up over her head, and lifted her right leg in an ill-fated attempt to keep herself, and the boat, upright. She lost all balance and tried to catch herself on the gunnel as she went overboard on the port side.

"*Shiiiit!*"

"*KER-SPASH!*"

El, being seated and facing forward, was able to stay on his seat when the boat rocked and didn't immediately notice that Ma had gone for a swim. Tunnel vision and deep concentration had kept him from hearing Ma's profanity and the splash when she fell into the pond. El pushed the bucket up again out of his eyes. The trout had swung back in front of him and was dangling from the pole that he was now holding up. El sat and admired the catch, it was about a three-pound rainbow. "See, Ma, I told you it was a good one," El remarked excitedly, turning around to get Ma's approval. She wasn't there. "Ma? Where'd you go?" El finally removed the bucket from his head with one hand and looked around the boat, as if Ma was hiding somewhere in the small vessel. With the other hand, he kept a tight grip on his loaded fishing rod.

"You asshole!" a voice echoed next to the boat as two hands reached over the gunnels. Ma's head popped up, her stringy, gray wet hair back covering her face again, causing her to resemble Cousin It from the Addam's Family.

"What are you doing in the pond, Ma?" As he was tilting to look down at Ma and grab his fishing hat out of the water, El didn't realize he was holding his pole so that his catch was dangling out over the water rather than in the boat. He put his drenched hat back on his head and water fell over his brow.

"I thought I'd try fishing like the moose was, you idiot!" Ma was about to start the process of climbing back into the boat when she noticed El's pole. "Don't hold him over the pond, you fool!" When she pointed to the fish with one hand, her other hand slipped off the gunnel and she went for a second dip below the surface of the water.

El glanced back at the fish. The fish looked back at El. Their eyes met, Junior Miller and Mr. Rainbow Trout. El's eyebrows turned up as the fish's eyes seemed to say to him, "*Forget it, buddy, you blew it.*" The fish even seemed to smile. El knew then that he had committed a fatal-fishing snafu and a frown crossed his lips as his eyebrows sank. The trout swung its tail, flipped in the air, and spit the hook out straight into El's hat, adding another ornament to its brim. "*Splash!*" The trout returned to the pond. The fish was free.

Ma bobbed back up, rested her head on the gunnel of the boat and groaned. Her fish-stained floral dress and apron ballooned up around her body in the cold pond, and her water-filled swampers weighed her down. She glanced up at the empty fishing pole in El's hands and the hook snagged in his hat with a thin line connecting the two, and no fish.

"You dumb sonofabitch."

This was a typical day of fishing for the two lovebirds.

Chapter 6
A Story for the Birds

Just about every city, town, and neighborhood in New England has its issues with pigeons. The pigeon population in East Puddleduck has always been plentiful but certainly not as bad as it was this particular year. In fact, the town became semi-famous for pigeons that summer.

♦ ♦ ♦

It seemed as if every rooftop, powerline, and whatever else that didn't move in the wind had a pigeon or two, or more, perched on them. Ma remarked that it looked like winter in July with all the bird crap covering everything. The birds were just simply everywhere.

The townsfolk were forced to all wear hats when they went outdoors just for the reason mentioned. You couldn't walk down the main road without getting showered with pigeon poop. The cooing of the birds drowned out any conversation you attempted to have in public areas. People were practically tripping over the fat, feathered creatures each time they walked outside. Of course, at the diner, it was twice as bad with the smell of food drawing the birds in. The funny thing was, though, the pigeons only came out during the daytime. Every evening they flew away to the west and returned at daylight. The pigeon problem became so bad that the townsfolk had to call a special town meeting in an attempt to figure out what to do about the issue.

Constable Bob made up the posters and put them around town:

Mayor Wiggleswort and his board of two sat at the select board's folding tables in the town hall's small council chambers. Many of the townsfolk were seated in front of them in the audience, all three rows of them, and many others standing. The tiny chambers had never experienced so many people in it at once except for during the Christmas get-togethers and the annual craft fair.

The town hall itself was a fairly old structure built around 1910 with one main floor and an attic area for storage. The basement was of no use anymore with its damp dirt floor and crumbling stone foundation. The building houses the tiny municipal office where as mentioned before Myrtle Watson works as the town clerk in a cramped office, an adjacent office in which her brother the mayor occupies, and a third tiny office near his for the public safety department, namely Constable Bob. A tiny bathroom is located next to Myrtle's cubbyhole. Beyond the offices at the end of the hallway are the old wooden double doors to the public meeting chambers. In the same parking lot, separate from the town office, is a large, old garage with several bays that house the town road equipment and fire truck.

Many had shown up to complain about the pigeon problem. The coat rack was full of rain gear covered in bird doo-doo and a variety of baseball caps, fishing hats, and ladies wide-brimmed summer hats all similarly speckled in bird poop. The complaining was so loud in the chambers that the mayor needed to use a gavel to get the attention of the crowd.

"Order! Come to order!" Wiggleswort yelled as he banged the gavel. The crowd focused their attention on the mayor for a moment. He was seated in the center as usual with select persons Jacob Daley and Paul Doody to either side of himself, and Constable Bob in a metal chair off to the side of Daley. "We're here to discuss our pigeon problem and what to do about it," the mayor announced.

"They're all over the place!" Mattie shouted from the audience.

Wally McIntyre pointed out, "The pigeon crap is eating the paint of all our used cars in the lot!" His brother, Joshua, sitting beside him nodding in agreement.

"I got bird poop everywhere!" Marmaduke yelled. "I can't sit outside and enjoy the scenery anymore 'cause I just get crapped on! It's Pearl Harbor, every day!"

Cicely joined in, "No one can visit us! When they all walk out of the store, their groceries get pooped on!" Her husband Smirnoff nodded, agreeing with her.

"I'm about ready to run a special at the diner and call it mystery chicken!" Ma yelled out. Most in the room acknowledged her comments with an "*ewww*" expression on their faces and wondered just what was in the soup special earlier in the day.

Wiggleswort acknowledged everyone by nodding to people's complaints. "What can we do?" he asked the crowd.

"We could catch them all in a big net," Puut Voisine suggested.

"You're a dumb Canuk!" Ma blurted out, glancing back at him and then swinging back around. "Make them the special of the year at the diner, my freezer would be stocked for months!" She suggested again while everyone in the room looked at each other and made another "*ewww*" expression on their faces, none knowing whether to take Ma seriously or not.

"I had to use an ice scraper to get the dried poop off the cruiser windshield after I stopped to have my lunch," Bob Johnson chimed in, leaning forward and speaking directly to the mayor.

Ruby interrupted Bob's disgusting comments, "No one is coming to the salon! Well, why would they knowing that when they walk out looking fabulous they'll immediately get shit on!?"

It was El's turn. "Them *goddam* birds parked themselves on our boat at the pond! They loaded it with bird crap like it was their own personal toilet! I can't go fishing without a bunch of birds tagging along with me, sitting in the boat, and staring me in the face! We need to figure a way to do away with them!"

"El's on the right track, we gotta kill them," Wally McIntyre said, pointing in no particular direction as he made his statement.

Wiggleswort could see no other choice other than to agree but also had to reason with the crowd. "How are we going to do it? We can't go out and shoot a thousand birds in broad daylight! We can't catch them in anything. We can't leave truck-loads of rat poison lying about town, and we can't sneak up on them."

"You should follow them at night and see where they're going." A monotone voice in a heavy French accent had come from the back of the room. Everyone turned to see it was the usual voice of reason, Marmaduke, who had the idea. "Birds are all going somewhere after dusk, find out where they're nesting first and then figure it out. It'll probably be easier to deal with them all in one place." Everyone in the room began nodding and silently agreeing with Marmaduke's wisdom, primarily due to the fact that no one else could come up with any better ideas.

"Marmaduke's right!" Doody exclaimed, breaking the low-volume talk in the room. "We need to follow those birds and hit them where they live when they're asleep!" The crowd in the room nodded to each other at Paul's suggestion.

"Okay, it's agreed then! Let's get a few of us in a posse to meet back here at dusk with your vehicles ready to go!" The mayor declared as several hands went into the air to volunteer for the mission, including Ma's. "Leave your shotgun home, Ma!" Wiggleswort motioned towards her, giving her a stern look and pointing his gavel.

"*Bahhh!*" was her usual response as she waved her hands in discontent toward the mayor.

◆ ◆ ◆

The scene resembled an all-terrain street race about to begin, with everyone waiting for the waving of the starting flag. Several four-wheel-drive pickups, ATVs, and other modified all-terrain vehicles were lined up in the town hall parking lot, all with their engines on and lights off, ready for sunset when the pigeons would take flight. Everyone was dressed in rain gear and slickers, and plenty of head protection. Some even wore helmets just to keep the bird poo off their noggins. It was a bright, clear evening and the group felt they could stealthily follow the birds by moonlight. They hadn't taken into consideration that even though all headlights and spotlights were off, the sounds from the factory and modified engines were loud enough to scare the birds away on their own. The last vehicle in line was Runyon's bright green '74 Ford Pinto station wagon. All modified with oversized, off-road tires, a lift kit, and a supercharged 5.0 V-8 diesel Hemi that sat mostly above the engine compartment with exhaust pipes that went high above the hood and shot fire when charged with ethel. The engine put out about twenty-five hundred horsepower. Runyon had hand-painted orange flames on the hood and front fenders of the vintage auto, and overall, the car was fairly butt-ugly. Runyon traditionally only used the monster of a vehicle for the tractor pulls at the local annual fairs throughout the county, but he figured they may be going off-road this evening and he'd need the extra power and ground clearance. Not to mention that Ma was in the old Chevy pickup already on a tangent and ragging on El, so Runyon had decided early on to go it alone in this modified beast of a vehicle.

All eyes were on the roof of the town hall, which was covered with the pesky birds, waiting for them to fly towards the west as they did each evening. The sound of the cooing nearly drowned out the sound of the loud, revving engines, but not quite.

Just as the last of the sun went below the horizon and as if someone had rung a starting bell, all of the pigeons took flight from all over town. The evening sky went black with them. All of the waiting vehicles were immediately pigeon-bombed with poop, with those in open all-terrain vehicles taking the worst of the fallout. However, they had thought ahead and planned a bit in advance. Puut was assigned the job of using the town office's outside spigot and spraying off windshields and those in the exposed ATVs as they went by him when the chase began. The birds, and the soiled wagon train below them, were all off and heading west, with Puut hosing everyone down as they left. Of course, this hadn't been the best of ideas and mostly the addition of the water just made the situation worse and created an even filthier substance for everyone to deal with. Windshields, goggles, and helmet visors were covered in slimy goo, and windshield wipers only made the situation worse by smearing it across the glass rather than wiping it away.

It was easygoing at first as the birds could be seen from the Main Road. About a mile into the chase, the birds turned slightly in the direction of Deerlick Drive, and the posse followed on the roadway. The pigeons were dense and didn't fly very fast, so the group below had the ability to keep up fairly well. A few times someone would stray off the road into the puckerbrush, due to the fact that everyone was looking up towards the sky rather than on the road, and windshields were crusting over, causing drivers to poke their heads out the side windows and get bombed from above. A lot of near collisions were taking place.

Three miles up Deerlick Drive the direction turned just slightly onto Porcupine Way. Another quarter mile and the pigeons turned more to the south. The posse was forced to stop, there was no road to follow here, only woods. Everyone came to a quick halt and a panic ensued. To keep up with the birds, they needed to find a way to follow before they all flew out of sight. With everyone's engines still humming, the townsfolk got out of their vehicles and stood at the edge of the road, contemplating their next move and watching the flying carpet of pigeons quickly going by.

"We can't let the birds get out of sight!" Wally McIntire screamed, with everyone trying frantically to think of a way to follow them.

"We'll never keep up with them on foot through the woods!" Ma exclaimed. "And it's going to get darker than the inside of a cow if we lose the moonlight! They'll blend into the night sky and we won't be able to see them!"

The birds were disappearing into the tree line above. "What are we going to do?!" Wiggleswort yelled out. "They're getting away!"

Runyon, who was still sitting in his Pinto, studied the area. He looked up at the direction the pigeons were flying, then looked at the dank woods. He studied for a moment and then recalled hunting in this area a few years back. He'd never gotten a deer out of it but he did remember one important detail about this particular patch of woods. The roar of Runyon's engine shifting back into gear rang out and everyone looked to the back of the cavalcade to see what he was up to.

"What's Runyon doing, Ma?!" Wiggleswort yelled out

"I don't know what's in his head," Ma yelled back. The two were standing literally beside each other; however, the noise of the modified engines was drowning out their words, requiring each to yell out loud to be heard.

Runyon leaned out of the front of the car where the windshield should have been but had been long since removed, and he reached out and sprayed nitrous oxide straight onto the exposed carbs. Fire shot from the pipes high into the air and the Pinto took off. Runyon pointed her towards the woods between two tall trees. He nearly launched the car into the air off the small ditch on the side of the road and sailed through a small patch of woods. Everyone looked at him like he was insane as the Pinto nearly disappeared into the trees, throwing mud and dirt high into the air when his wheels came back down and he dug into the earth as he continued. About 50 feet from the road the group watched as Runyon turned the Pinto sideways into woods and his headlights illuminated an old tote road that looked as if it hadn't been used in years. The birds were headed in same the direction the old road was pointed.

"That's my boy!" Ma said as everyone locked their hubs into four-wheel drive, got back into their vehicles, and shoved them all into their lowest gears. The posse was off again, spinning their wheels down through the woods with dirt, mud, and ground moss flying everywhere. Vehicles were bouncing up and down on the rough terrain like ships on the ocean. Headlights were required to make it through the woods, and lights flashed up and down, reflecting off the trees like strobe lights in a dance hall.

Runyon was leading the group and didn't see the peat bog that had formed over the years quite soon enough. His tires spun around and around as thick mud flew everywhere. Runyon tried as best he could to get through the bog but to no use; his rugged wheels became stuck and the other vehicles behind him were all forced to stop. All engines ceased and headlights dimmed. Everyone grabbed flashlights, jumped out of their vehicles, and prepared for a foot race.

"Quick," Ma said. "After the birds!"

The group took off on foot and most made the mistake of trying to run straight through the bog to get back to a dry road. Sucking sounds and swearing could be heard as many lost their boots to the ankle-deep quicksand-like mud that ate their footwear up. They were tripping over one another, and the majority were getting quite wet and messy as they slowly trudged through the bog; however, they did all help each other, pulling and tugging on one another in the mud, and they finally found dry ground again and kept on going.

After what seemed like hours but in reality, were only minutes, the road took a sharp bend just ahead of them. The birds flew around the bend and disappeared. Sweaty, wet, grunting and groaning townsfolk made it to the turn, Ma now leading them, surprisingly enough, swearing with each and every step her bare feet were taking. Ma rounded the bend, stopped quickly, and put both arms out to stop the others behind her and whispered a loud *"Shush!"* to silence the posse. Everyone stopped quickly right behind her, although they all began groaning and panting. Not one of them were in any shape for this night's workout. They all crouched in the overgrown undergrowth.

"Jeesus, I'm going to have a heart attack," the mayor panted.

"Shut your trap!" Ma blurted in a loud whisper, panting just as hard as the mayor.

Just up ahead and barely in view was an old, three-story farmhouse quite dilapidated with grayed, rotting lumber, boarded-over windows, and much of the roof missing from age and weather. Attached to the farmhouse was a large barn, much larger than the house, leaning considerably and just as run down as the main structure. The hayloft doors were mostly off their rusted hinges and swinging in the breeze. The moonlight was shining through holes in the barn roof. Inside the barn were the pigeons, hundreds, if not thousands of them all perched on the old rafters over the decaying hayloft. The cooing from the barn was deafening.

"That's old Skeeter Dyer's farm," Joshua McIntire whispered as the group all crouched down around each other. "He was our great uncle on my dad's side. He passed on years back. He and Dad would go trapping together near Brownbrook Stream on the other side of Skunk Mountain. I can remember some good times when I was young and we visited this place. We had some good meals in that house, and Skeet would let me drive his old tractor in his corn and potato fields."

"I heard tell in later years he became a hermit," Doody chimed in.

"It's true," Ma whispered back. "Skeeter turned hermit in his old age, never left the place, and finally died right there in that barn. They found him three weeks after he croaked, stiff as a board and still sitting in his old rocking chair he'd put up in the hayloft."

"I heard the place is haunted," Daley offered. "I heard that Skeeter's ghost can be seen in that hayloft every night."

"That's a bunch of horse manure!" Ma came back. "Ain't no such thing! He was just an old hermit and he died! That's it! Ain't no ghosts! Now, shush up!" Ma had always been a bit superstitious.

The bird hunters were crouched in the brush, not wanting to alert the pigeons of their presence. There were a few minutes of silence and staring, each person waiting for the other to come up with an idea, any idea. The group looked at one another in the moonlight, hoping someone would say something. Shoulders were shrugged and heads shook slowly.

There was sobbing coming from Joshua.

"Oh, *Jeesus*! Joshua's blubbering about his childhood," Ma whispered.

"I'm sorry, Ma…" *Sob…sob…sniffle…* "I just remember old Skeet letting me milk the goats in that barn…" *Sniffle, sniffle…* "and then he'd let me jump off into the big bales of hay. Those were such good times…”

“Oh, for the love of Pete! Get a hold of yourself, boy!” Wiggleswort whispered loudly.

“Where the hell was I?” Wally inquired, a bit of annoyance and jealousy in his voice.

“You hadn’t even been born yet…” *Sniffle, sniffle, snort…* Tears were beginning to flow down Joshua’s cheeks now. “I got my first kiss from Mary Ellen Dyer right there in that barn hiding behind a bale of hay when we were both twelve. She was such a sweet girl. There was no need for her to fall off that tractor the way she did… Skeet knew better than to have her on the hay baler at that young age. If only he hadn’t drank so much apple cider that morning, he might have seen the cows in time to stop.” Joshua’s eyes swelled shut with tears.

“Oh, for *Chrissake*, the boy’s going to go into the fetal position if we don’t do something,” El remarked.

“She never did get used to that eyepatch, and her pegleg was always an inch shorter than her right leg from after the accident…If only he’d taken her to a real doctor…!” Joshua’s voice squeaked and he was seemingly sobbing uncontrollably.

“Hey, *asshole!* I’m still seeing her!” Wally offered angrily in a loud whisper.

“She still sees you too, with her good eye anyway.” Runyon leaned over to Joshua and pointed towards the barn. “I bet you were conceived right there in that barn, Joshua. Your mom and dad right there in the hay.” He chuckled. “Or maybe your mom and old Skeeter!”

“Bwwwahh, haw, haw!” Joshua was down on his knees fully in tears.

“Can we go down memory lane some other time, please?!” Ma was quite annoyed with where the conversation was heading.

A few more moments of silence followed. Well, silence except for Joshua’s constant sobbing and the sounds coming from the pigeons. The uneasy lull was finally broken again by Ma. “What the hell do we do now?!” Speaking directly to the mayor; however, startling everyone when she spoke out, “This was Marmaduke’s dumb idea, and he ain’t here to guide us, so what do we do?”

Wiggleswort thought for a moment, not really certain what to do. He glanced up at the sky, at the barn, and down to the ground. He finally whispered again, “We’ll retreat and hold another town meeting tomorrow. We need to think on this a bit and come up with a solution. We’ve got time to plan it out now that we know where they’re going at night.”

“Yeah, and we know where they’re *going* during the day! All over everything!” Ma whispered back loudly.

The posse retreated and walked back to town and the following day would be primarily spent watching the McIntyre brothers towing their vehicles out of the peat bog and Ma having to convince Joshua that old Skeeter wasn’t his real father.

That next evening the townsfolk gathered again in the select board chambers to discuss the birds for a second night in a row. The pigeon problem was just as bad this day as it had been any previous day. East Puddleduck was starting to look like they'd purchased stock in a tarpaulin factory. Everything was covered with blue tarps, and the tarps were covered with pigeon poop. The only folks making out like bandits was the hardware store in Skunksquirt, which carried and quickly sold out of tarps and canvases of all sizes.

Wiggleswort banged his gavel on the folding table. "Order, order, please! We are here to discuss what the next step is in dealing with the pigeons! We know they're roosting at the old Skeeter Dyer farm; now how do we rid ourselves of them?!"

"We need to get rid of all this pigeon poop, too," Constable Bob stated. "It's everywhere, and really starting to stink!"

"Yes, yes, yes. The poop too. First the birds, then the poop." The mayor continued, "We know where they're sleeping at night, now what?"

Ma stood up and yelled out, "Burn the building while they're sleeping!"

The townsfolk in the room started talking to one another about the idea. Whispers of, "Yes, burn the building," and, "That's a good idea," could be overheard. Finally, Mattie voiced the opinion out loud, "Ma's got a good idea! We should burn the old Dyer farm tonight!"

Joshua McIntyre teared up and began to sob again.

"It's the only way to get rid of all of them at once," Puut replied. "The old farm's in the middle of the peat bog anyway. No chance of a forest fire. We should burn the barn with the birds in it!"

Runyon spoke up, "It's good training for the fire department, too! We can set up the portable tank on the road and run lines to the barn. Get some of that rusty old water out of the tanker and flowing through those hoses. It'll be a good test of the pumps!"

"I'll bring the hot dogs and beer!" Smirnoff's voice came from the crowd.

"And marshmallows!" Cicely chimed in gleefully.

Mabel Johnson cried out, "I have plenty of lawn chairs!"

Ma stood up and turned to the crowd. "A nice, big bonfire! She'll smell like a chicken barbeque! Once we're done, we'll use the fire pumper to go around town and hose all the bird shit down and be done with it!" She turned back to the mayor for confirmation.

"Well, I guess you're all right," Wiggleswort said, looking to either side of himself for his board's approval. Both Doody and Daley nodded their heads to the mayor in stereo. "Everyone seems in agreement. We'll burn the barn tonight." The mayor's gavel rose and prepared to come down.

"No, you won't!" a voice came from the back of the room. All heads turned to see a tall, well-built gentleman, wearing a dark gray suit, black tie over a very clean white shirt, very shiny black shoes, and mirrored sunglasses. He was standing in the back and apparently had quietly entered through the chamber's double doors in time to hear the planning. "You cannot burn the pigeons, nor will you harm them in any way," Mr. Sunglasses remarked sternly.

"And may I ask who you are, sir?" Mayor Wiggleswort inquired sarcastically, "And just what interest do you have in our pigeons and how we get rid of them?"

"They're not *your* pigeons," exclaimed Mr. Sunglasses. He then peered around the room and spoke to everyone sternly, "My name is D.W. Washburn, Department of Environmental and Wildlife Protection! And the species *Columbidae* belong to the *people*, not you, and they cannot be harmed!"

"The Columbian what?" Runyon leaned forward and asked El who was seated in front of him. El just turned his head and shrugged his shoulders.

"Then tell *the people* to take care of the damn pigeons so they won't crap on *us people*!" Ma shouted at Mr. Sunglasses.

"Who called you?" Mayor Wiggleswort asked defensively, pointing his gavel at the tall man.

"That question has no bearing on the situation at hand," Mr. Washburn replied as he started marching towards the board table, displaying paperwork in his left hand. "And furthermore, you cannot dispose of the waste in any transfer station or other locations without proper permits."

"We need a permit to clean up pigeon shit?!" Ma barked as Mr. Washburn walked by her.

The tall man paused and he turned to Ma, gazing down at her through his sunglasses. "Yes, you need a permit to clean up *pigeon shit*. There are toxins and chemicals in the waste that require special treatment before they can be properly disposed of. Their fecal matter contains Salmonellosis and it's highly probable that dust from their feces has already made its way into your air supply. Without proper treatment and disposal, it can result in contamination to your groundwater supply."

Constable Bob looked terrified at the mayor. "What did he just say?!" The mayor returned the look with an equally puzzled expression on his face.

Ma shook her head in disbelief, and chatter amongst the audience began, most wondering what the man had just attempted to explain to them. Ma looked at the floor and whispered, "Special treatment for pigeon shit. Just unbelievable."

Mr. Washburn stood in front of the mayor like a statute and slapped the paperwork down on the table. "Here is the injunction prohibiting you from touching the pigeons. Do you wish to put in for your form MW-50 to permit you to dispose of the waste properly?"

Wiggleswort looked down at the paperwork, entirely befuddled, then back up at the tall man. The mayor never had to deal with a situation such as this.

His political expertise consisted of judging the best-looking baby contests at the annual fair and sampling pastries at the diner. This was out of his league. The mayor stood up, leaned to Mr. Washburn, and looked up, coming only to about the tall man's chest even when standing and whispered, "Look, Mister, ah, sunglasses…we're just a small town with a pigeon problem. We just want to get rid of the birds so they won't crap on us anymore. We don't want any trouble."

Mr. Washburn bent down a bit and placed his large hands on the table, still towering above the mayor, and whispered back, "You have an obligation to protect the wildlife of Maine, no matter what form they are. I sympathize with your problem but I cannot let you harm the birds, nor can I allow you to dispose of their waste without proper permits. You simply can't burn a barn full of live birds."

Runyon happened to glance out the window around this time. Outside he noticed several vans had arrived and were parked all up and down the main road. Each one seemed to have a small satellite dish extending from their van tops way up high into the air and wires were strewn everywhere on the ground. Men with cameras and bright lights were taking pictures of the pigeons and the poop. Tall, fancy-dressed men and women were speaking into microphones in front of some of the cameras. Many were smartly carrying umbrellas. It appeared that somehow the media had caught wind of the situation and the circus had arrived.

Runyon slapped El on the shoulder and motioned to the windows. More people in the room were now taking notice of the commotion going on outside. Mayor Wiggleswort and Mr. Washburn had also noticed the media running around outside the windows and knew they were going to enter the building soon.

Still whispering to Wiggleswort, the tall man said, "Now, Mayor, do you really want those people out there taking pictures of you striking the match that lights the fire that burns a barn full of defenseless pigeons and showing it live on all of the social media platforms?"

"Shows it on what?" the mayor whispered back, a terrified look now on his face as he stared out the windows.

"The boob-tube, Mister Mayor. The idiot box. Television. Do you want them to see you torturing and killing those birds on live television?"

Wiggleswort, eyes widening and still glancing at the reporters outside the windows, unconsciously shook his head. He thought for a moment. He thought hard. He then looked around the tall man and at the townsfolk who were all frozen in place and staring at him for a response. "Folks," the mayor said softly, "We have a problem…"

♦ ♦ ♦

The doors of the town hall flew open. Wiggleswort was leading the way with Daley to one side and Doody on the other, and Mr. Sunglasses right behind them as they stepped out onto the front stairs. The rest of the townsfolk crammed into the tiny hallway behind them, all looking outside at the reporters and cameras. The mayor held his head high and he adjusted the suspenders under his velvety suit jacket, preparing himself for the media. Bright lights pointed in his direction and reporters began reaching out with their microphones.

"Is it true, Mister Mayor, that you're thinking of killing the pigeons?" one reporter yelled out as cameras started flashing photos, causing Daley and Doody to squint and duck each time they flashed. Mr. Washburn was standing tall and not twitching at all as flashbulbs reflected off his sunglasses.

"Don't you feel that pigeons are part of Maine's wildlife too?" Another reporter shouted, "Is the town willing to harm Maine's wildlife?"

And yet another, "Mayor Wiggleswort, are you willing to take responsibility for the deaths of thousands of pigeons? Not to mention the tens of thousands in fines from the Department of Environmental Protection?"

The mayor stood tall, or at least as tall as he could, and he put his hands on the lapels of his suit coat and took a deep breath. He smiled at the media circus before him, confidence was written on his face. "Ladies and gentlemen, I would just like to say that we love our feathered friends, the pigeons!" He pointed to the crowd. "And we won't cower to any rumors that we intend them harm in any way! We intend on doing nothing less than working with the Department of Wildlife Protection in order to provide them with a natural habitat here in East Puddleduck!"

A distant voice from inside the town hall that sounded similar to Ma's voice cried out, "Pussy!" The mayor's eyes rolled just momentarily; however, he kept his confident posture.

"Now," he continued, rocking a bit on his heels, "I'd be happy to entertain any questions…"

◆ ◆ ◆

For the remainder of the summer, the town was forced to put up with piles of pigeon poop and the odd bird watchers that arrived in small numbers from around the state and country. All seeking to get a glimpse of the pigeons and keep close tabs on how the town was treating the birds like they were some sort of endangered species. Ma wasn't happy with the influx of *foreigners* at all. They all wanted vegan meals served to them at the diner and were generally poor tippers.

Cicely and Smirnoff didn't mind, though. For the remainder of the summer, they were able to re-open the second floor of the general store and restore Cicely's family haberdashery, earning a bit of extra money on the side renting rooms to the curious ornithologists.

Ma did manage to keep the pigeon population under control at the diner without anyone from away taking notice. She'd taken an old electric bug zapper and removed the protective outer shield and mounted it up underneath an awning she'd set up behind the diner near the dumpster. She put the bug zapper in the center of a two-foot-by-two-foot piece of plywood with a lip on the outside edges to create a large bird feeding station and ran the power extension cord back to the building. She hung it all up under the peak of the awning so you couldn't see it from the outside from a distance. She then roped off the awning on all sides with bright yellow police caution tape she'd gotten from Constable Bob so that no one could get within ten feet of the awning, and she put up a sign that read, "STAY OUT, PIGEON QUIET AREA." She loaded the electrified feeding station with bird seed and diner scraps and also scattered the ground with chicken feed. When the birds came in to snack, they quickly figured out that more food was above them on the feeding station and they'd fly up to eat off the perch. Periodically you could hear, *"Bzzzzzzz…POP!"* and see a bright blue flash from under the top of the awning, and singed pigeon feathers would drift to the ground below. Ma had the contraption on a timer to start at dawn and stop at dusk, which is when she'd go out and toss the carcasses that piled up on the feeding station in the dumpster after closing the diner each evening.

As usual, every resident knew what Ma was up to but none dared tell her not to do it. And as long as Mr. Washburn didn't return, none was worse for the wear, except for the pigeons.

For the remainder of the summer, Joshua McIntyre went back and visited the old Skeeter Dyer farmhouse and wept on the broken-down porch steps every Wednesday evening, reminiscing about his childhood and wondering who his real father was. He wore a full rain suit and held an umbrella over his head during every visit.

Chapter 7

Foreigners Buried Here

Days come and days go. For the most part, in other areas of the state, they come and go pretty much as the one before. Here, in East Puddleduck, it's sometimes a little different. You might recall that I mentioned early on that Ma's Diner sits on the main road on a particularly sharp corner, and that detail would become important later in the story. No, really, I mentioned it at the beginning of the book, go back and look.

It was early afternoon on that sunny summer's day; the lunch crowd was a bit heavier on this day than normal. Ma was out running errands with Runyon and she'd left a couple of local kids that she had hired for the summer to work in the diner, one in the kitchen and one on tables. She trusted the youngsters and was generally impressed that any youth would have the drive to provide an honest day's work, so she gave them opportunities. They didn't manage the diner, though. These responsibilities, when Ma was away, were given to more mature employees. This day it was Val Daley in charge. Elmer was also in the diner, eating lunch and waiting on Ma and Runyon to return. Several other locals were enjoying their noontime meals as well.

Ma and Runyon were just pulling into the dry, dirt parking area. The old Chevy pickup bounced in the driveway, leaving a trail of dirt dust and creaking on its rusty springs. Vegetables, paper goods and other supplies loaded into the bed of the pickup were bouncing up and down as they came to a stop in front of the diner. Ma had her own parking spot, being the owner and all. It wasn't marked or anything, it was just commonly known that this was Ma's space and everyone else better stay out of it.

Ma slid off the toilet seat and exited the passenger side. She bent down to dust her dress and apron off. "Wish it had rained this morning; wouldn't be so dry."

Runyon just smiled and said, "Ayah," as he climbed out of the truck.

As the dust rose from Ma beating on her dress, her expression suddenly changed. She stood back up slowly, although not all the way up straight; her head turned just as slowly and she glanced back up the road, eyes squinting, nose crinkling, eyebrows frowned, then one eyebrow cocked upwards. She even seemed to give out a low growl.

Runyon started to grab the load out of the back of the truck when he saw Ma peering down the road. His expression turned to one of nervousness. He knew that Ma could tell, even though he couldn't. He stretched his neck and looked up the road but didn't see it yet even though he knew it was coming just from the posture of his mother. He'd seen Ma looking and acting this way once before.

El, who was glancing out of the diner's front window caught a glimpse of Ma and he put his spoon back down into his fish chowder before it reached his mouth, which was still open as if to receive it. He too recognized her demeanor, and he also knew immediately. He'd only seen this particular look on Ma's face and this posture once before, just about two years back in exactly the same spot she was standing now, and he'd hoped he'd never see it again. He looked up the road and even though he didn't see it yet, he knew it was coming.

"What's up, Ma?" Runyon inquired as if he didn't know, however, still inquired cautiously in a low voice as he saw Ma frozen in her stance. She was slightly bent forward and staring straight up the roadway. Runyon looked over towards his father in the diner window. His father looked back at him; both had terrified looks in their eyes as they met.

Like a cat's sense of danger and a bat's keen sense of hearing, Ma could tell it was coming. She could tell every time. "I hear me a foreigner coming this way," Ma growled in a low, deep, almost demonic tone.

◆ ◆ ◆

The muscle car had Massachusetts license plates that read "EATMY-DST." The car itself was a bright green, a fully restored '69 Pontiac GTO with a four-barrel 389 V-8 engine. Its owner and operator appeared to be a thirty-ish gentleman from Boston who was on his way to a classic auto show in New Brunswick and hadn't been paying attention, nor did he feel he had the time to waste. He was driving his supercharged hotrod far too fast and had missed a crucial turn further south and was now definitely on the wrong road. The classic car didn't have a GPS, and this road he was now speeding down didn't lead to the border as anticipated; it led straight to Ma.

The driver looked like Elvis with his jet-black hair all slicked back. He was traveling at seventy-four miles per hour, a huge cloud of dirt dust behind him from the dry roadway. He was only maybe seven or so miles from the diner and had already passed underneath Ma's town sign that he hadn't paid any attention to, nor could even have noticed at the speed he was traveling. He believed the Canadian border was ahead of him. Little did he know how wrong he was. It was too bad that he missed the sign at the town line; that was his first, last, and only warning.

♦ ♦ ♦

Ma finally broke her frozen posture when she reached back into the truck, slammed the bench seat forward, and reached behind the seat, never once taking her eyes off the road. She pulled out a twelve-gauge, double-barrel shotgun that she kept there for moose, fully loaded with two, double-aught buck loads. Escribed on the stock were these exact words;

"USE FOR MOOSE and FORINERS."

By now El had removed his napkin from where it had been tucked into his collar; he threw it into his chowder bowl and was on his way out the of diner towards Ma. "Put that thing away, Ma!" he pleaded at the doorway. "There's too many people in the diner this time! Remember, Constable Bob warned you about shooting at any more outta-staters!" El was referring to the incident two years ago that was still fresh in his mind and was the basis of his warning to Ma.

"Shut your trap, I gotta job to do," Ma growled again as she took a shooting stance, standing straight up with the gun raised and her eyes traveling down the barrel. She cocked both barrels, *"click, click."*

Mayor Wiggleswort and his wife Eleanor, who were sitting at their regular center table, glanced outside simultaneously at Ma when they heard El's warning. Their eyes widened. "Ma's got a gun!" the mayor yelled out. They both dropped out of their chairs and attempted to take cover under their table.

Puut, who was in a corner window booth, had also taken notice. He picked his bowl of beef stew up off the table in an effort to keep eating, as he had to strain to see out the window from his vantage point and he didn't want to miss anything. "Crazy woman's going to hurt someone if she ain't careful," he whispered to himself.

"Must be another out-of-stater coming up the road again," Joshua McIntire said quite nonchalantly to his brother, who were both seated at the counter bar. It was their lunch time too and they both had ordered the chipped beef on toast, which they were both enjoying. Neither immediately turned around to look out the window; however, eventually curiosity took over. After they gave a cautious gaze to each other, they both got up from the barstools and went around to the employees' side to get a better look and use the bar as a bit of cover, and continue with their lunch. Behind the counter, they found the young waitress ducked down and hiding.

Cicely and Smirnoff had closed the store for the noon hour and decided to have lunch together here in the diner, something they normally didn't do but business had been light today. Cicely approached the front windows carefully to get a better look and Smirnoff remained seated at their table to continue his lunch. "In Russia, they'd put the old woman in front of a public firing squad after she did this the first time and taken care of the problem," Smirnoff said to his grilled ham and cheese just before taking another bite.

It was the cook, Reverend Percible's nephew Stanley, who made the call to the county dispatch center from his safe area in the kitchen.

◆ ◆ ◆

Bob was in Skunksquirt, stuck in his cruiser as usual with his belly crammed up against the steering wheel. He was at the local burger joint inhaling a double quarter-pound beef burger with extra cheese, mayo, and bacon. The special sauce was dripping on his uniform shirt. Normally he didn't miss a meal at Ma's Diner. But today he'd been called to a cat stuck in a tree in the neighboring township during the lunch hour and was forced to eat the fast food, not wanting to go hungry and all. He figured he'd just grab a late afternoon, pre-supper snack at Ma's later.

"*Dispatch to Puddleducksquirt-One, we got trouble on the east side,*" the radio squawked. "*Large woman with a shotgun in the parking lot of the diner. Reported to be the owner.*"

Bob grabbed the mike. "Ten-fowa," he replied, smearing the special sauce all over the key. "Dammit, Ma!" he said to himself out loud as he slammed the Bonneville into drive, turned on his big blue bubblegum light that was mounted to the roof of his cruiser, activated the whaling siren, and pulled onto the main route towards East Puddleduck. His "Super Big" soda that was sitting on his dashboard at the time slid straight off and into his lap.

"*Oooohhh!* That's cold!"

◆ ◆ ◆

The speeding driver had one hand on the steering wheel and his other arm resting on his open window. The engine roared as Queen's "Fat Bottom Girls" blared from the modified sound system which was particularly heavy on the bass speakers that were mounted in the trunk. Elvis's head was bopping as he sang the lyrics out loud.

♫ *"Hey, I was just a skinny lad!" "Never knew no good from bad..!"*
"Heap big woman you've made a bad boy out of me!" ♫

◆ ◆ ◆

"Ma! Please don't!" Runyon pleaded with his mother. "You're going to get into big trouble this time!" He was on the opposite side of the truck from Ma, ready to take cover behind the truck bed if need be.

"Down, boy," Ma grumbled as if talking to her dog. "You're gonna make me screw up my aim." She was solid as a rock with the barrel of the shotgun pointed down the roadway.

Runyon ducked lower behind the bed of the pickup truck. "I'm warning you, Ma, don't do it!"

El was standing back a bit closer to the diner's door. "You should listen to the boy, Ma. They'll put you in the pokey this time!"

Ma didn't answer. She just stood like a statue, waiting.

◆ ◆ ◆

The speeding vehicle was only one mile away. The driver was still completely oblivious to the fact he was most certainly on the wrong road, in more ways than just one. He increased his speed to seventy-eight miles per hour and turned the music up louder.

♫ *"Oh, but I still get my pleasure..." "Still got my greatest treasure..."*
"Heap big woman you done made a big man of me!" ♫

◆ ◆ ◆

"Report: the woman is pointing her gun down the roadway and not responding to requests to cease," Bob's radio spoke out. Bob was already pushing the cruiser to its limits, the tires nearly leaving the roadway on the humps and screeching into the turns. He too recalled the incident two years prior. *"Jeesus, Ma, don't do it,"* the officer said to himself out loud as he tried to control his speeding cruiser and keep it on the roadway. His crotch cold from the ice that was melting through his uniform.

◆ ◆ ◆

♫ *"Oh, you gonna let it all hang out!"*
"Fat bottomed girls you make the rocking world go round…" "Fat bottom girls you
make the rocking world go around!" ♫

The foreigner came around the last corner before the stretch that led straight to the diner, about a quarter mile away. He wasn't paying attention to anything other than the song. Not the speed he was traveling, not the fuel gauge that you could almost watch drop from the fuel consumption on the big V-8. Not the engine temperature which was running a bit high…

…And not the short, stalky, floral-pattern dressed woman in tan shit-kicker boots holding the twelve-gauge double-barrel shotgun just ahead to his right in the parking area of the local diner, just before the sharp L-curve in the road ahead.

Elvis finally took notice of the curve coming up very fast with little warning. Ma had consistently removed the "'Sharp Curve Ahead" sign, just for this reason. She knew someday another *foreigner* would come speeding past. As Elvis was about to slam onto his brakes to make the forty-five-degree turn to the right, he caught a fleeting glimpse of Ma and his smile turned to an open-mouth gasp and his eyes bulged in fear when he saw the two shotgun barrels pointed in his direction. He immediately changed plans, cranking his steering wheel hard to the left to instinctively avoid the danger, and he pushed the brake pedal to the floor; however, it was too late. The car began to swerve sideways as it went straight into the hairpin turn.

Just as it went past the diner Ma, like a sharpshooter pointing at a skeet that had just been launched, swung the barrel along with the movement of the vehicle and let go with both barrels as the car went by the diner.

"BLAM, BLAM!"

Everyone watching from the diner instinctively flinched when the gun went off. The force of the shots pushed Ma back into the passenger door of her pickup, the gun barrel flashing and smoking as it unloaded both barrels. Her target was the car's grill and right front tire. As the tire blew out, the car went off the corner of the road where a berm of dirt had formed over the years from the snowplows pushing sand into the turn. There was an opening in the trees right on the corner seemingly just large enough for a car to go through, and that's just where Elvis's vehicle flew, sideways, and launched off the berm into a field on the other side of the trees that sat lower than the road. As the vehicle left the roadway, it went airborne and began turning over mid-air but not before the terrified driver, who was clutching the wheel tightly, noticed a hand-painted sign just beyond the trees in the mouth of the field that read, *"FORINERS BURIED HERE!"* with an arrow pointing out into the field.

The car flipped over in the air once, making a complete revolution before landing hard on its axles in the field. The impact blew out two more tires.

Upon impact it bounced back up and forward, making another complete revolution from front to back and down on its wheels again. On this landing it lurched to the right and began tumbling over and over on its sides until it was several hundred yards out into the field, finally coming to a rest on its roof.

It took a moment for the dirt and dust to settle. Elvis was frozen upside down in his seat, hands still clinging to the steering wheel. He looked to his left, then to his right, then straight ahead at the pile of dirt his front end was buried in, the same dumbfounded look of disbelief still remaining on his bruised face.

It was then that Elvis realized that he had a tremendous headache.

Ma was looking over the smoking barrels of her shotgun. "Ain't never missed a Masshole yet, two for two," she said to herself, turning towards the onlookers. She flipped open the break and the two spent shells ejected into the air. Like magic, she took two fresh shells from her dress pocket and reloaded the weapon, using only one hand to flip the barrel shut again like a professional gunslinger. "Heh, heh," she chuckled and threw a nod and a wink to everyone.

Runyon stood back up, as did the people cowering in the diner as they approached the windows and door, all looking towards the field. El sat down on the diner's front step, shaking his head. "You can't be doing those sort of things, Ma."

"Bah!" was her response. The faint sound of a siren could be heard in the distance.

It was a minute or so before Elvis's head appeared at the embankment as he struggled to crawl out of the field and back up onto the road. He was bruised from head to toe, and dust was coming off his tattered clothing, looking as if he'd been on fire and someone had put him out. He stopped on top of the berm when he saw Ma and her gun.

"Didn't you see that sign at the edge of town, boy?!" Ma yelled to him.

"Sign? No, ma'am, just the one in the field," Elvis said gingerly; he was trembling as he raised his hands in front of him. "Please don't shoot again."

"I'm not going to shoot you! I'm just sending you along with a warning!" Ma replied. Everyone's attention quickly focused on the speeding cruiser that was approaching.

Bob's cruiser came to a sliding halt sideways at the edge of the parking lot. A dirt dust cloud rose up and engulfed the cruiser, seeming to hide it for a few moments. Bob swung open the door and got one fat leg out before the door swung back at him and struck him in his shin. *"Goddammit!"* His belly was still caught on the steering wheel and he needed to slide his big gut under the wheel to get out as the dust settled. "Ma! I told you once before, no more shooting the outer-staters!" he grunted as he finally made it out of the cruiser, the empty cup from his soda falling beside him to the ground as the dusk settled along with it.

"You piss yourself, fat boy?" Ma inquired.

"No, you old crow! You made me spill my soda with this foolishness!" Bob said as he fanned his crotch with one hand in an effort to dry the wet spot as he walked up to Ma.

"She's nuts!" Elvis yelled out, pointing at Ma and ducking at the same time in anticipation of some retribution for the comment to come.

Ma warned, not bothering to look in his direction as she said it, "That isn't anything that a *Masshole* wants to say to an old woman that still has a loaded gun in her hands!"

Bob walked up to Ma and took the gun out of her hands. Elvis looked surprised at seeing how easy it was to disarm the crazy lady. Bob opened the break, emptied the two fresh shells onto the ground, and handed the shotgun back to Ma. "Put this thing away."

Elvis pointed and began to open his mouth in protest to the crazy woman getting her gun back, then stopped himself, thinking twice about speaking quite yet. He quickly realized that she might just be able to produce more live shells from her dress pockets.

Bob towered over Ma, pointed at her, and scolded, "You know, you're really in trouble this time, don't you? I told you two years ago what would happen if you did this again! I ain't got no choice, I gotta take you in!" The constable's demeanor changed and what he said next was with a bit of sadness in his voice, "I can't keep letting you get away with this stuff, Ma; twice is one time too many. People are starting to talk and wonder why you get away with such things. I really have to take you in this time."

The foreigner's eyes widened more as he wondered what happened to the "other one" that Bob had referred to. He glanced back into the field for the possibility of a grave marker.

Now, Constable Bob had threatened to arrest Ma on many occasions for this, that, and the other but this was the first time that it seemed he was going to have to do it for real. "Are you gonna come easy, Ma?" he whispered and whined. He really didn't want to arrest Ma.

The rest of the onlookers had equally sad looks on their faces. For as crazy as Ma was, this was "Ma," and she wasn't made for an orange jumpsuit and to be behind bars. As insane as she sometimes makes herself out to be, right or wrong, Ma was the glue that held the town together. Ma was simply, Ma.

Wilomena Farnsworth-Miller turned to look at the sea of sad faces in the diner's windows and doorway, and then looked back up into the constable's eyes and could see he was nearly tearing up. She bowed her head and nodded. She knew the officer was fighting his emotions at the thought of arresting his favorite person, which she believed herself to be. She truly felt bad for making him do it. Plus, she didn't want to embarrass the officer in the performance of his duties by putting up a fight that she felt she'd most likely win. Bob took Ma by the arm and started leading her to the cruiser and she went reluctantly but willingly.

Now, while all this had been going on, Runyon had wandered over to the side of the road to glance at the foreigner's upturned and shot-up sports car. With its three blown tires pointing straight up and puffs of smoke coming from the engine compartment, he wondered how the McIntyres were going to get it out of the field. He also didn't seem to be too worried that his mother was in the process of being arrested, for real this time. Runyon had a contingency plan. He gazed at the wreck for a moment or two, giving it a good looking over, finally cocking his head sideways as he looked at the vanity license plate, and a smirk crossed his lips.

Runyon wandered back over to the constable just as he was opening the cruiser door to put Ma inside and he tapped the police officer on his shoulder. Bob leaned to Runyon to hear what he had to tell him. Runyon whispered into his ear, motioning towards the embankment where the car rested below. Bob's eyebrows raised as he listened to Runyon's secret news. When he was done, Bob looked at Runyon, then let go of Ma and walked over to the embankment. Both Ma and Elvis looked puzzled. Ma looked up at Runyon, who simply smiled and winked at her.

Bob stood at the edge of the field and looked down at the wreckage. He cocked his head sideways as he looked the vehicle over and finally stopped at the license plate. He formed a little grin on his face. The constable turned back and took Elvis, who was still standing on the berm, by the arm and escorted the confused and tattered visitor back to his cruiser. The limping Elvis was about ready to begin screaming at Bob as the constable put his hand up to motion the man to hush.

"Your license plates expired two months ago, sir," Bob said to the man. "And did you know that it's illegal to operate a motor vehicle unregistered in this part of the state?"

"No, I didn't know that," the man said in a sarcastic tone. "What does that have to do with anything?"

Nothing really, but I'll come up with something, Bob thought to himself. "Unregistered motor vehicles carry a big penalty in this county," Bob said to the man, using a bit of authority in his voice. "At least six months minimum and…*errr*…five thousand in fines," looking confident as he recited the trumped-up charge.

"Six months?!" A look of disbelief on the man's face as he yelled out. Everyone in the diner looked as bewildered as the man, as they hadn't caught on quite yet.

"Maybe longer. Depends on the judge and how sober he is. Looks like your tailpipe's a bit modified too." The two glanced over into the field to look at the upturned auto, its now-bent straight pipe revealing itself. "Modified ve-hi-cles carry a hefty penalty to add to it. I'm sure that's not the only modifications that you've made to that car, now, is it? Probably quite a few more violations, each with hefty penalties around these parts." Bob's imagination was on a roll. "Fines don't necessarily matter to the judge. We call him the Sledgehammer. He likes to see people in the pokey instead. You'll like it, though, Ma here serves up the meals to the inmates from the diner scraps she throws away. They're kind of cold and mushy, coming a day late and from the garbage can. I'd be a bit careful eating your portion, though, with you pissing her off and all today. Ma tends to carry a grudge."

Ma's eyebrows raised but she kept her mouth shut, she knew what Bob was up to.

"And don't forget he was speeding, too!" a voice came from the diner door. It was Val Daley, pointing and nodding her head in confidence as she spoke out. "He was going like a bat out of hell! Could've killed someone if he'd hit them!" The other onlookers nodded in agreement to her words.

"And he was operating on the wrong side of the road when he took the turn," El chimed in from the front steps.

Ma looked at the onlookers, an endearing smile that she couldn't control appearing on her face.

"And he'd certainly have killed himself when he hit the dead end up ahead! Driving like he did was dangerous to others! Ma probably saved his life!" Mayor Wiggleswort cried out, his wife Eleanor standing right beside him nodding in agreement with a stern expression on her face.

"Quite a number of charges," Bob continued on. "I tell you what," the constable started, as he made the effort to stand up straight in confidence and put his arm around the Elvis look-alike. He began to turn him away from Ma, although it was difficult to display any authority with his crotch still wet from the soda. "You forget about the situation here with Ma and the gun, and I'll look the other way on your vehicle defects and driving issues. Otherwise, I'll just have to arrest you along with her. And out of the two of you, you just might end up with the more time in the pokey. You got a lawyer? If not, I'm sure we can call one to get up here by next Tuesday, or maybe the one after, I can't recall what rotation they're on this month. You'll be fine, though; the jail's got a lovely view of the town dump and sewer treatment plant right outside. Smell's a bit funky, but not too bad. It's up to you. If I do take you in, I'm hoping the jail's not too full or they'll have to put you in with Farmer Hugo, the town drunk. He's a regular and he's been away from his sheep a couple weeks now in the tank drying out. He gets a bit lonely when he's in jail and we're careful about doubling up in his cell unless we're overcrowded, which is pretty often with the types of folks we got living around here." The constable looked down at Elvis and motioned his head toward the diner crowd. "It might not be the most pleasant of visits for you; you might want to be careful about falling asleep. Just some sound advice."

Elvis's eyes couldn't have been open any wider at that moment, even with his bruised face attempting to swell them shut. The man thought for a moment, not really knowing how to respond to the wealth of information and bullshit the constable was shoveling towards him. He was well into the woods of northern Maine and out of his element. He looked over at the diner crowd and thought they all could double for the cast of *Deliverance*, and banjos just might start playing at any moment. He looked back up at the constable. "What about my car?" he whined. "It's wrecked!" He looked toward the field with puppy dog eyes.

"Joshua!" Bob shouted towards the diner. "Get your wrecker out here!"

◆ ◆ ◆

The wrecker was parked on the corner and a winch cable had been stretched out to the severely damaged and upturned sports car. Wally ran the cable from the truck as Joshua gave him commands with his hands from the berm as the winch motor whined and the chains turned the heap back over, the final tire blowing out as it bounced back onto its axles. It creaked loudly as it hit the ground and blew up a cloud of dirt-dust smoke. The boys continued to winch the dented and mangled sports car out of the field and back up onto the shoulder of the road.

Bob walked around the car with his arm still on the man's shoulders and finally guided him back to the driver's side door. "There she is, my friend. Practically as good as new. And don't forget to register her when you get home." Bob released his arm from the man and tugged at the driver's door to open it, and for obvious reasons, it wouldn't budge. Bob grabbed the handle with both hands, put one foot on the rear quarter panel, and yanked until the front door came off its damaged hinges and dropped to the ground, the handle disconnecting from the door and still in Bob's hands as the door fell. "Sorry." Bob handed the foreigner his door handle and picked up the door to put in the trunk, now that the trunk lid was permanently open and damaged to the point it would never shut again. "Don't worry, it'll make a good insurance claim for you. You'll probably end up with more than what you had into her. I'll do up a nice accident report for your insurance company, you'll see," Bob said with confidence as he assisted the man into his vehicle.

Elvis slumped down into his car and tried turning the key. He received a rather large argument from the engine. Joshua tugged on the snagged hood, literally pulling only half of it up as the other half remained pinched into the engine compartment. Elvis sighed loudly as Joshua looked at Bob with an "oops" look on his face and shrugged his shoulders. Joshua leaned in and adjusted a few things under the hood as if the car only needed a minor tune-up. "Try it now!" Joshua called out. Another turn of the key and more groaning and the engine eventually, quite reluctantly, turned over. Just as it started, the radio blared loudly as if it hadn't been damaged at all, startling everyone;

♫ "Fat bottom girls you make the rocking world go around!!!" ♫

"Sorry," Elvis smiled nervously up at the constable as he quickly turned off the radio.

Wally had been busy putting four bald and not-the-same-size tires on the car in record time as if he'd performed a pit stop. The tires wobbled a bit as Elvis slowly pulled onto the road and back in the direction he'd come from. Smoke poured out of the mangled tailpipe, and the front of the car tilted downward due to its broken axle.

"Why don't you cite him for a noise complaint too?" Ma kidded with Bob as she walked up to him.

"Shut up, Ma." Bob said under his breath as they all watched the foreigner slowly drive away and leave their town. Elvis even managed to pick up a little speed before disappearing around the turn and out of sight.

"Heh, heh. Can't teach anyone nothing, can you?" Ma slapped Bob gently on the back. "Come in the diner, Johnson. I'll heat up some nice fish chowder and we got some fresh pecan pie. On the house."

The thought of one of Ma's pies made Bob feel better and he smiled down at her. *Oh well, at least I kept the peace in the town today after all,* he thought to himself. They turned to walk to the diner together. "You've really got to stop shooting at foreigners, Ma."

Ma reached up and put her arm around Bob as they walked together. "Constable, someday when I'm dead and buried, you won't have to worry about it."

Chapter 8

A New Rule

It's late October again. The leaves on the trees have all turned a variety of colors and many have already fallen to the ground in the fall wind and rains. The town is all decorated up for Halloween and the general store has stocked up on candy.

And the annual deer hunting season has arrived.

Runyon was up before daybreak in his tiny cabin. He'd put on his faded red wool jacket, rabbit skin trapper's hat with the fluffy ear flaps dangling down, orange wool gloves, red flannel pants, orange vest, and tan leather boots, in which he'd put several coats of silicone on to make them as waterproof as he possibly could. He also had on long johns and a red scarf. Attached to his belt he had a hunting knife, a short piece of rope, extra 30/06 bullets for his bolt-action rifle, and on the back side he had a hunter's "hot seat" clipped to his belt that bounced against his tush when he walked. This was obviously to keep his butt warm in the event that he wanted to sit in the woods and wait for a deer to come to him. Runyon enjoyed walking through the woods, and rather than have a deer stand set up in a particular area, he enjoyed spreading out and trying different locations to find his prey.

Runyon's rifle, a Winchester 30/06, was given to him by Elmer when he was just old enough to go out hunting. The barrel of the gun is a bit rusty, and the stock has a few scratches from years of use; however, it's a good and accurate deer hunting rifle.

Today, Runyon was going hunting with Puut Voisine. *This should be interesting*, Runyon thought to himself as he prepared. Runyon hadn't been out with Puut in the past and he wasn't even sure if Puut knew how to hunt deer. He assumed he did, as Puut primarily lives off the land, but Runyon wasn't certain just how legal his methods might be or how much Puut knew about Maine hunting laws.

However, Runyon wasn't worried about Puut. He was far more concerned about other hunters. Hunting is a tradition amongst Mainers, and for the most part, everyone uses proper precautions in the woods. Lately, though, it seemed that more and more out-of-staters were in the woods, and even crazier, younger Mainers that weren't as careful as the more mature and experienced ones. In recent years it seemed to Runyon that anyone with a gun was out there trying to shoot at something. It was usually fairly safe this far north, not too many horror stories of hunters getting a bullet in the tush from other gun crazy wannabes, but Runyon knew that you could never be too certain. Runyon knew the spots to hunt too, as he'd hunted this area for many years with his father. Hopefully today he and Puut would be alone on their expedition with no one else around.

As Runyon exited his tiny house on the Farnsworth-Miller homestead, he caught a glimpse of his mother climbing into the Chevy. She was getting ready to head to the diner for the breakfast hunting crowd. She always makes it a point to open early during the hunting season.

"Seeya, Ma. Going hunting with Puut," Runyon called to his mother as he climbed into his own pickup truck.

"Not doing breakfast first?" she yelled back.

"Nope, headed straight out into the woods. Had a cold Pop-Tart a few minutes ago."

"Suit yourself. That ain't a good breakfast, though. And don't let the dumb Canuk shoot you!"

◆ ◆ ◆

Puut had a long, wooded driveway. As Runyon turned down the winding drive, he viewed all of Puut's signs that he'd read many times in the past. As he drove through the iron gate that Puut never bothered to close, he spied the first one; Puut had carved a piece of wood into the shape of a rifle and tacked it to a tree. Across the sign it read, "*We Don't Call 911.*" There was a frog-shaped carving tacked to another tree that read "*Frog Ally.*" One that always made Runyon chuckle was the piece of wood that Puut painted, "*Crazy Canadian Ahead,*" that he'd suspended from a pine branch over the driveway. Amongst the many other signs and just before the house, Puut had a short log with four sticks holding it up at the base. Nailed to the log was a piece of wood carved in the shape of a head with two eyes painted on it. Next to the log was a sign that read "*Beware of the Dog,*" and it pointed to the log-dog.

Puut's a bit weird, Runyon again thought to himself, *or would eccentric be the better term?*

Runyon pulled up next to the house and admired the unique structure as he always did when he visited. Puut had built his entire house himself out of firewood-size logs. There wasn't a log in the two-story construction more than eighteen inches long. It's quite bizarre in its jigsaw puzzle design. A large, detached garage near the house has also been built in the same manner.

Puut also never had inside running water. Instead, he has a pond out back and a hose that he runs from the pond to an old shower stall on the back lawn. Near the top of the stall is a hand pump to operate the shower, and on the very top is mounted a metal garbage can that he pumps the water from. The metal can heats up in the daylight sun to create a warm shower. The door to the shower only covers chest-to-knees, and it's a bit breezy in between. It doesn't hide naked body parts very well. Too many times, Runyon thought to himself, he's arrived to find Puut out back singing in the shower and showing way too much of himself to the wildlife.

To the side of the shower stall is a cast-iron kitchen sink. Puut has a second spigot from the trash can that points into the sink for cleaning dirty dishware and whatnot. Puut's outhouse is just four feet from the shower stall so he doesn't have to travel too far to wash up after doing his business.

"Hey, Puut!" Runyon yelled as he climbed out of the truck. He reached back in and blew the horn of the old Ford. It sounded like a moose in some sort of distress.

Puut appeared from around the side of the house. He was dressed all in khaki from his hat down to his boots. He had even painted khaki stripes on his face. He looked like a member of the Marine's Special Forces.

Runyon's eyebrows raised when he saw what Puut was wearing. "What the hell are you dressed like that for?"

"I don't want the deer to see me," Puut replied in his heavy French accent.

"The only thing that will see you is another hunter thinking you're some sort of game. You're liable to get a bullet in your ass dressed up like that."

"I thought the point was to not be seen by the deer?" Puut remarked.

"You need to put some orange on. It's the law; plus, you may just survive the day. You got any red or orange?"

"Yeah, I got some red, wait a minute." Puut strolled back into the house and returned a few moments later looking exactly the same except for a pair of new red wool gloves that he'd put on, the price tag still on one of the gloves. "There, are you satisfied now?"

"I guess that'll have to do. Where's your gun?"

"Ahh, hold on." Puut reached into his old, olive green 1944 Jeep Willey that still had the original rusted shovels and jerry cans mounted to its sides and rear, and in the back Puut pulled out a large plastic case. He opened the case and removed a very mean looking, military-style semi-automatic rifle.

"What the hell is that?!" Runyon asked with a very confused look on his face.

"It's an AR-15, .223 caliber semi-auto with an infrared laser sight and retractable stock. I just bought it in Alberta a couple weeks ago. Got a good price on it. Had a bit of trouble at the border with them boys; they're a bit picky with things like this but we got through it. Why?" he asked, a bit surprised that Runyon had even inquired to begin with. Runyon just rolled his eyes as they climbed into his pickup. "Where are we going?" asked Puut.

"Near Skunk Mountain, about four miles north of the pond," Runyon replied, still glancing in disbelief at the rapid-fire cannon Puut had purchased to use for hunting. "*Jeesus*, Puut, there's gonna be nothing left of any deer you shoot with that thing."

"No, but listen," Puut went on, "I shoost a bear with it a week after I bought it. Near the house."

"You *shoost* a bear with it? You *shot* a bear out of season?" Runyon shouldn't have been surprised, but he sounded it.

"Yah, the bear kept waking me up in the middle of the night. He'd come into the yard looking for food and was scratching at my front door, every night for a week. I got tired of that quickly. I called the warden and told him I'm going to shoost the bear. He told me don't shoost the bear. I shoost him anyway out my window one night. I heard him scratching at the door, I waited for him to come around the corner of the house, I open my bedroom window, and I shoost him. That bear come around the side of the house and...bang! Good-tasting bear! I give you some meat when we get back. Plenty in the root cellar."

Runyon just shook his head at the man's description of his bear encounter. "You are a crazy Canuk."

"Yah, maybe, but better than being a dumb Mainiac."

♦ ♦ ♦

On a four-by-four post were engraved the words "Skunk Mountain Road." Once making the turn, Runyon found a spot to pull off the road and park. The sun was just peeking over the mountain to the east. It was going to be a nice day; probably later on it would get up to thirty-five or forty degrees at best. Right then it was a chilly thirty-two. The two hunters got out of the truck, and both could see their breath in the air. The aroma of fresh pine gave them a good feeling and they both took in a deep breath of it.

"You want to hunt together, or do you want me to go up on the ridge and see if I can scare something down to you?" Runyon asked of his hunting partner.

"Don't matter to me, whatever you think is best, you know the area."

"You got a compass?" Runyon inquired of his khaki-clad friend, as he checked the brass one he had pinned to his own vest.

"Got one here." Puut pulled one out of his pocket. It looked like something he'd gotten out of a snack box at the five and dime.

Runyon noticed. "Wait a minute, you look like an airborne ranger that just dropped out of the sky, carrying a gun that would make Rambo jealous, and you have a compass that looks like it came from a Cracker-Jack box?"

"It wasn't Cracker-Jacks. It was Fruity Pebbles."

Runyon just sighed and pointed. "Head southeast for a bit, I'll take to the ridge up above and see if I can scare anything down your way. There's a goat path bout half mile in, take it when you find it and head south and I'll meet you somewhere along the way. If you get something, sound off again with two quick shots."

"Sounds good." Puut took a compass reading and started walking into the woods. As he disappeared in the trees and underbrush, Runyon heard him say, "Gonna get that thirty-point buck today." Runyon just smiled to himself and shook his head again.

Runyon wandered down the road to a spot near the base of the ridge and then he walked into the woods. He took a compass reading and walked southeast, up to and along the ridge from the lower ground where he'd told Puut to walk. It was a gradual slope, and he could see the base of the mountain through the trees every so often, hoping to see some wildlife to send Puut's way, or maybe see a deer along the ridge to take a shot at himself. Walking was fairly easy on the higher ground; the trees were spread out enough to get through without too much trouble and the slope wasn't steep. Runyon went along just fine, being careful with his steps to keep the noise down. He checked the wind direction regularly by licking his pointer finger and holding it up. The morning breeze was coming out of the northwest, just where he wanted it. Runyon was enjoying the sights and smells of the countryside as he went. For him, it was just as enjoyable to be walking through the woods as it would be to get a buck, if they were lucky enough.

Runyon walked for the better part of an hour before seeing any fresh signs of deer. He came to a spot where it appeared the deer had been munching on the brush earlier. He knelt down and looked closely and saw fresh tracks and soon found fresh droppings. *Deer have been here this morning*, Runyon thought to himself, and the signs showed that they were headed down towards Puut. Runyon kept on, being as quiet as he could and keeping his eyes open. He was beginning to sweat as the temperature began to creep up above freezing in the morning sunlight, and the morning frost had now disappeared.

More signs and tracks continued ahead of Runyon as he gradually made his way off the ridge nearest the spot where he figured he'd pick up the old path he'd mentioned to Puut. He hoped that if he was driving a deer in Puut's direction, that Puut wasn't too far ahead or behind him. Just as Runyon reached the old path, he heard the gunshots.

Bang!….Bang! Bang, Bang, Bang, Bang!…Bang, Bang, Bang!

"*Jeesus*," Runyon said very quietly to himself. "How many shots do you need?"

Runyon picked up the pace to find the location the shots had come from. When he reached the base of the ridge, through the trees he spotted Puut pointing across to the woods to the other side of the old tote road, his gun barrel had smoke pouring out it.

"Big buck!" Puut whispered loudly, huffing and puffing. "He just jumped the road over there." Puut sprinted to the spot where he said the deer had jumped back into the woods and he leaned against a tree to catch his breath and looked back at Runyon. "I took a couple of shots at him!"

"A couple? You don't really know how to count, do you?"

"I think I got him," Puut panted. "Look here, down here." Puut pointed to the ground and a few droplets of red were sprinkled onto the dry leaves. "I got him, there's a bit of blood here."

"I can't see how you could've missed him. Well, let's get after it," Runyon looked down at the blood as they both started into the woods. "Watch for more blood and tracks." Runyon hadn't taken notice that there was another spot of red on the tree just above the blood on the ground, about shoulder high.

Puut went out a bit ahead, and Runyon didn't try to catch him. He knew Puut would need rest breaks if he went along too fast and became winded. He also knew that if the deer was hit, they'd both be on his trail. And, if the shot, or shots were good, the deer would be lying dead up ahead. "Buck's wounded, Puut. You don't need to run," Runyon called out. He could already see through the forest that Puut was leaning against another tree to rest.

"Don't see it yet," Puut said as Runyon caught up to him. Puut was huffing and sweating. "But I got tracks going this way." Puut started off again at a quick pace.

Runyon spotted the next red stain on a tree the same height as the one he'd missed, just about five feet high, and it was fresh. Runyon took a compass reading and looked ahead; the deer was still heading southeast along the base of the ridge and along the old trail. He thought to himself that it can't be too much longer before they find it. He looked up, Puut was now out of sight as he continued on. Again, several hundred yards from the last one, and along the deer's tracks, Runyon spotted a stain about the same height on another tree trunk.

"Keep up, he's going this way!" Runyon heard Puut call out as he spotted him through the overground vegetation on the trail up ahead, once again Puut was resting.

"That buck's sure going along strong for being shot!" Runyon yelled and then spotted another stain, a larger one than before trailing down a trunk about five-feet high. "You shoot him in the head or is he just a really tall deer?" Runyon cried out, puzzling a bit as to how this deer was still going along if he's been wounded as badly as it seemed to be.

Runyon caught up with Puut about five minutes later, and after having passed by two more spots with stains similar to the others; however, the deer seemed to be bleeding worse each time that Runyon located another spot on a tree. Puut was resting again, sweating and breathing heavily. Runyon too had worked up a sweat during the chase, his wool jacket now unbuttoned, and he'd taken the scarf off and tied it to his belt. The heavy wool clothing in the morning heat was making him perspire something awful.

"More stains here," Puut said pointing to a red stain on the tree he was leaning against. "Tracks keep straight through those trees." Puut pointed ahead.

"Something ain't right, Puut. He should be slowing up or lying dead around here somewhere. There's too much blood and he can't be getting any better."

Puut disregarded the comments and continued on as before getting out ahead. Runyon picked up the pace a little as well. His hot seat was spanking his buttocks as he went along. A few minutes later Runyon finally felt the need to stop to rest. He took off his hat and wiped his brow, looking up at the sun. *Something just isn't right*, Runyon thought. *When is this damn deer going to slow down?*

Runyon came to the next stain. It was a bit higher up on the tree than the previous ones, almost to Runyon's height. "What the hell?" Runyon asked aloud. He looked up ahead. "Puut! Where'd ya go?! I think that damn deer's trying to climb a tree!"

"I'm still chasing him!" a voice echoed from far up ahead in the woods.

Runyon now slowed down considerably, too hot and sweaty from the chase to care anymore. He also couldn't figure out why that deer was, for some reason, seemingly still going strong. He continued to follow the deer tracks and the trail of blood stains. Puut was way out ahead somewhere. Another few minutes later Runyon stopped completely on the trail. He knelt down and looked at the tracks in front of him and saw that they were turning towards the ridge. As he stood back up, he glanced to his right and saw a blood stain on a tree, the same height as before. He looked again to the tracks to his left, and then back to the blood stain to his right. "What's going on here?"

Runyon knew that Skunk Mountain Road was still to his right, the same direction the blood seemed to lead. So, rather than chase the tracks up the ridge, he decided to go to the road. If he didn't find the deer before he got to it, he'd head back towards the truck, call it a day, and wait for Puut. Runyon continued on, and by the time he reached the mountain road, he'd passed by three more trees with stains on them. Runyon exited the woods and found Puut sitting on a large rock near the roadway. Puut had shed his heavy jacket, hat, and gloves, and was still sweating and breathing heavily. He looked spent.

As Runyon got closer to him, Puut looked up and started chuckling. Runyon squinted his eyes and looked at the ground beneath the rock that Puut was sitting on. Beneath Puut there was a spot where there appeared to be a blood stain, and more stains on the rock. Runyon's eyes widened. "You find that deer, Puut?" Runyon looked around and didn't see it lying anywhere. "Where is it?"

"No deer, didn't find it."

"*Jeesus!* You didn't end up shooting yourself, did you?!"

"No, I'm not that stupid," Puut said. He then picked up his new red wool gloves from the rock, held them out in front of him, and wrung the sweat out of them. The bright red liquid dripped to the ground, adding to the stain that he'd created the first time he'd wrung the gloves out when he stopped and rested on the rock.

Runyon now realized that what the two had been chasing the entire time were the spots where Puut kept resting, leaning up against a tree and leaving sweaty, red stains from the dye in Puut's new pair of gloves. The more he'd chased the deer in the rising morning sun, the more he'd sweat, and the stains would get larger, making it appear as if they'd been chasing a badly wounded buck. Puut probably had seen a deer; however, he'd never hit him with one single bullet.

"I sweat a lot for an old man, eh?" Puut remarked, still laughing. "Yeah, and you're a terrible shot, you son of a bitch." Runyon too leaned against the rock, exhausted.

Puut, still chuckling, ultimately was able to have Runyon laugh with him. What else could they do but laugh? The two sat on the rock, sweaty and tired, their laughter echoing off Skunk Mountain.

A hunting rule was made from that day forward by Runyon. Anyone hunting with him, including himself, was never allowed to wear red wool gloves, especially not new ones.

Runyon got his buck three days later although it was only an eight-pointer. Puut shot another bear the next day.

Chapter 9

The Big Show

"Ma, we got news!" Mayor Wiggleswort came running into the diner all out of breath during the supper hour. Ma was standing at the end of the counter bar, wiping her hands on her apron and talking with Constable Bob, who was having his usual big bowl of beef stew. The diner was full of patrons, being after work and all, and it was a busy Friday evening.

"What's so exciting that you feel the need to run in here huffing and puffing?" Ma asked, "You want your usual liver and onions?"

The mayor almost hesitated, wanting to get out his news, then stopped himself. "Yes, please and thank you…But, Ma! I got news! I just got off the phone with a big-time promoter out of Boston! It's exciting, Ma! Your all-time favorite county music star is coming to town! Zac Brown is going to be right here in East Puddleduck!"

Ma's face turned angry and she pointed her stubby finger at the mayor. "Don't mess with me, Rupert! That ain't funny to run in here and tell stories like that! You know I love that band! I'll probably never get to see them in my lifetime, so quit your funny business!"

"No, it's true, Ma! Zac Brown's promoter contacted me at the town hall and said he's touring the east coast and has two shows scheduled further south in Bangir and Portland. Says he's headed into Canada soon after. Said he's got a day in between and wants to come here up north to see some of his fans that he doesn't get to see, or that can't get to the big cities. He's really coming to us!"

The mayor, who was practically yelling the news and didn't realize it, now had the diner's attention. Ma's face turned from anger to a wide-eyed stare straight at the mayor, who actually leaned back a bit and raised his hands in defense, not knowing what was coming next towards him if she didn't believe him. Ma was still pointing at Wiggleswort, with her finger nearly touching his nose when her eyes suddenly rolled back in her head; she let out a loud sigh and fainted forward down to the floor. *"Thump!"*

Nobody immediately paid attention to the fact that their matriarch was unconscious on the floor, due to the excitement that had taken over the room.

"Is Zac Brown really coming here?!" Joshua McIntyre blurted out.

"Yes, it's true," said the mayor, stepping around Ma to get closer to Joshua. "I spoke to his promoter myself!"

"I don't believe it! He's a big-time star!" Wally blurted out.

Bob glanced down at the floor, pondering whether or not he should provide assistance to Ma.

Ruby Red stood up from her table and spoke to everyone in the diner. "Oh my, he's dreamy and can really sing. He's got that really popular song that I love that he does. What's it called? 'Dixie Chicken Lickers'? I sing along to it every time it plays in the salon!"

"No, no, 'Dirty Chicken Tenders' is the name of the song!" Val spoke out from where she was standing near the opposite end behind the counter bar.

"No, no, no," Cicely Smirnoff exclaimed as she sprang from one of the booths. "That isn't it, I believe it's called 'Nickel Chicken Dinner'!"

Puut chimed in from his corner booth, "You're all wrong. I've heard it on the radio, it's called 'Fried Chicken Gizzards.'"

The mayor, with a wide, elated smile on his face as he listened to everyone, glanced over at Bob. The constable's eyes motioned between the floor and the mayor as if to telepathically let him know that someone was still passed out below. The mayor didn't pay attention.

Runyon exited the kitchen and corrected everyone, "No, it ain't neither! It's called 'Little Chicken Peckers.' Ma plays it all the time on the record player at the house. She's nearly worn it out."

"You're all stupid," Mabel Johnson spoke up from where she had been seated beside Bob. "It ain't called none of that, it's called 'Fried Chicken Feathers'!"

"It's called 'Chicken Fried,' you assholes!" a voice echoed from the floor below as everyone stopped and looked down. "And somebody better be helping me get up off this floor!"

Everyone looked back up at each other and nodded in agreement that Ma was correct in the name of the song. Meanwhile, the mayor and Bob both leaned over and assisted Ma up off the floor. "Are you sure he's coming?!" Ma barked at the mayor again as she stood up and dusted off.

"Yes, Ma! The promoter said Zac Brown. Said he'll be here in three weeks, Saturday night," the mayor exclaimed as he brushed Ma off and reached for

Bob's glass of water to hand to her.

Constable Bob asked the mayor, "Where are we going to put him? We don't have a big stage anywhere and he'll draw in a few hundred, if not more."

The mayor thought. "That's true, he's going to draw in a bunch of people. The stage at the fairgrounds is barely big enough for Zippo the Clown's balloon animal show. We can't put him there. We need him in town, it's good for business and our economy." The mayor nervously turned to Ma and handed her the water. "Gonna bring in a lot of people, Ma. Lots of foreigners." The mayor prepared to duck.

Every patron quieted and was staring at Ma for a response. For just a moment or two, Ma herself went completely silent, squinted her eyes, and her left eyebrow twitched. Like magic, she came out of it. "It's only for one day, and it's for Zac Brown; let's do it!" There were smiles and an ovation from everyone in the diner.

The mayor spoke back up, "We still need a location. I say the best spot is the field right here across the road here. Plenty of space, and we can build a stage right in the middle!"

"We can get the dozer out there and plow it over. We'll make a nice, level parking area," Wally McIntyre offered. "We'll put in a gravel drive through Ma's opening on the corner." Wally got up from his meal and approached the diner's owner, "We might need to take your sign about foreigners down temporarily, Ma. It's not very friendly or inviting."

Ma's left eye began to twitch again.

"We'll build a nice, big stage," the mayor continued. "Smirnoff, you and Cicely must have a contact for lumber and such things through your suppliers. Or maybe try the mill in Fort Blasphemy." Smirnoff winked and nodded to the mayor. The mayor then turned to Constable Bob. "You'll need plenty of extra help during the event, too."

"I'll get in touch with the county sheriff and see what he offers."

The mayor continued, "We'll need volunteers too, although I'd expect the band will come with plenty of their own staff."

"Oh, this is so exciting!" Ruby Red couldn't contain herself as she bounced up and down. The menfolk in the diner took notice as their eyes widened and their heads bobbed as if they were watching a puppy jumping up and down. Her tight, plastic cleavage bounced like two bobbers on a lake, each with a fish on. The women in the diner watching wide-eyed as well, mostly in amazement.

"That reminds me," the mayor spoke, his eyes still on the bouncing redhead, "we should get some big balloons and have banners made up welcoming Mr. Brown to our town and advertising ourselves." He finally had to force himself to look away. "Smirnoff, can you get some advertisements made up? A big banner for over the town sign and plenty of balloons and other memorabilia to sell?"

"Yessir, I can look straight into it," Smirnoff replied. "Banners, balloons, T-shirts, and hats that all say East Puddleduck. Cicely and I will get right on it."

"We'll make sure the banner for over the town sign says, 'Welcome, Zac Brown Band!'" Cicely yelled out.

"We'll do just that," Smirnoff said. "This is going to be spectacular! Very exciting! Very, very zakhvatyvayushchiy!"

"English, you asshole! Speak English!" Ma barked. Smirnoff just winked at Ma and blew her an air kiss.

A childlike grin was on the mayor's chubby cheeks and he clasped his hands together. "It is exciting, isn't it? Oh, this will be a whole to-do! People will know all about me…I mean, East Puddleduck, before they leave! We'll promote the town right." The mayor then looked back over his shoulder and saw Ma right behind him, her face turning back to a bit of concern.

"Just one day, Wiggleswort! One day of foreigners, that's it! I mean it!" The mayor simply nodded to her in return.

"I bet those are going to be some pricey tickets," Runyon said to no one in particular.

"No, no, that's the other thing," the mayor replied to him. "They said the tickets are nice and cheap, and half of every ticket goes to a charity of our choosing. All the tickets are only twenty dollars."

Marmaduke spoke up from his corner booth, "That's going to bring in a lot of money, Mister Mayor. Which charity do we give it to?"

The mayor turned to the old man. "Anyone we want, I suppose. We get to pick one."

"We don't have any local charities, you dunce!" Ma barked as the mayor turned back to her. Ma was doing her usual pointing and frowning. "Everyone around here works for a living, Rupert! We don't have charity cases, and we ain't sending the money out of town neither! Who are we supposed to give it to?"

"We'll have to come up with something," the mayor replied. "We need to give it to some type of charity, especially if they're good enough to let us have it. And Marmaduke's right, it will probably be a good pot of money. We're going to have to think on that, but we'll come up with something." The mayor began addressing the entire diner again, "The promoter also said to let him take care of all the ticket sales and advertising the event. All we have to worry about is selling any extra tickets at the door and he'd bring us the tickets on the day of the concert."

"I can't wait to hear the 'Chicken Finger Licker' song!" Constable Bob blurted out with glee.

"It's 'Chicken Fried,' you asshole!"

◆ ◆ ◆

Construction began shortly thereafter. Cicely and Smirnoff had gotten right on the supplies and several volunteers began building a ten-foot-by-twenty-foot stage in the center of the field across from Ma's diner. Over the stage, they built a nice, big awning in case of foul weather, and under it, they'd placed a large generator that's usually kept in the town garage in case power goes out during the winter storms. Joshua and Wally brought in the heavy equipment, including a bulldozer and several loads of dirt from the town gravel pit, and began leveling the field, creating a large parking area and a driveway into the field from the road. They even knocked down the sand berm that had been created by the snowplows and made a separate exit by taking down a few of the trees further up the road, creating an "in" and "out" for traffic.

Cicely had two large, "Welcome Zac Brown Band," banners made and they'd hung one up below the welcome sign at the town line. Ma even let them cover over her artwork with cardboard temporarily so it wouldn't appear as if they were being unwelcoming to what would most certainly be a diverse influx of both local fans and other groupies from out of the area. At the mouth of the field Ma's other sign, "FORINERS BURIED HERE," was temporarily replaced with a sign that simply said, "CONCERT PARKING." Ma held on tight to her sign, though, for after the concert.

Cicely and Ruby used some creativity and designed T-shirts and baseball hats that advertised East Puddleduck. On the front of each shirt was a picture of what they thought puddles the duck might have looked like, and on the back they added all the local businesses as each had donated a bit to the cost as sponsorship. Of course, "Ma's Diner," was the first name on the shirt. Below that was, "Smirnoff's General Store," "Ruby Red's Hair Salon," and, "McIntyre's Garage & Used Car Emporium." The price for each shirt was set at five dollars each. Unfortunately, Cicely had allowed her hubby Smirnoff to place the order and he'd mistakenly ordered five thousand of them. In his excitement, he'd actually made the error of basing the shirts on the cost in Russian rubles instead of American dollars. He also ordered three thousand hats, and he'd done the same when he ordered the balloons that each said, "East Puddleduck, Maine," with the picture of a duck on each one. The town ended up with twenty thousand multi-colored balloons.

"Oh, this is going to be dandy!" the mayor exclaimed, as he watched the McIntyre brothers hang the banner over the stage.

Councilperson Doody, standing right beside the mayor and holding a clipboard and pencil, was checking off his "to-do" list. "Rental chairs should be here tomorrow with the helium tanks for the balloons. The portable toilets on Thursday. This is getting a bit costly, Mister Mayor."

Annoyed, the mayor replied, "It doesn't matter, we'll make it up on the other end with the memorabilia and concession sales!" Pointing, the mayor continued, "We're going to have two tables right over there with the T-shirts and baseball caps, and Ma will be set up over there with the popcorn, hot dogs, and vinegar fries. Over there will be the vending machines with water and soda pop." He turned to Doody. "Did we give Schmoozes Bar in Skunksquirt that liquor permit to set up a beer tent or not? I can't recall and I'm a bit worried about selling booze."

"No, we didn't yet. You said you were going to think about it and didn't get back to him. You said you had to look up in the town charter and see if we could do that or not."

"Ah, well, probably should," the mayor said nervously. "Can't really hold a proper country music concert without serving beer."

"Ma's going to be angry."

"Tell me something new," the mayor answered back over his shoulder to Doody.

"If you let people get drunk right across from her diner, not to mention letting another vendor from out of town set up here, it's going to piss her off something awful," Doody pointed out.

"Oh, well, she's going to have to get used to it for one night. Did Smirnoff order that novelty toilet paper with the town's name on it for the portable toilets?" The mayor glanced down at Doody's clipboard.

"I don't know."

Constable Bob arrived and drove onto the field, kicking up a cloud of dirt dust with his cruiser as he came to a stop near the mayor and Doody, causing each the need to dust off their clothes as the officer exited his cruiser. He slid his big belly out from underneath the steering wheel, which was adjusted to its highest setting. Bob was sweating more heavily than usual, even though it was a comfortable day.

"Mayor, the sheriff's department said they won't send any extra deputies for the concert!"

"Well, why not?" The mayor was obviously annoyed, still puffing dust off his light blue velvety leisure suit coat that had little duck figures all over it. He'd had to special order the coat. Doody tried to help the mayor dust it off when he was done with himself, only to have the mayor slap his hands away.

"They said they're too short-staffed and they don't believe he's coming anyways."

"Well, of course the band's coming! I spoke to the promoter myself, twice now! They're just jealous that the band ain't coming to any of their hometowns! We'll have to make do!"

"But that's a lot of traffic to control!"

"We'll get Joshua and Wally to help you out. We'll put some orange vests on them and give them flashlights. We'll deputize them for the evening. It won't be an issue unless you make one of it!"

Bob looked up at the stage and seemed to forget what he had previously been complaining about. A big grin crossed his face and he squeezed his hands together. "Oh boy, I can't wait. Zac Brown right here in East Puddleduck! I'm going to be right close by when he sings 'Deep Fried Chicken Fingers'!"

"It's 'Chicken Fried,' you asshole!" Ma barked as they all turned to look and spotted her tromping towards them from across the field in her sundress and swampers. "Wiggleswort! Don't get your hopes up that this will be a permanent concert venue! I want this all down next Sunday morning after the concert!"

"It'll be down, Ma. I Promise."

"And what's this about Schmooze's serving beer here?! It's bad enough we're going to have foreigners, now we have to have drunk foreigners?! And why didn't you ask me to do that?!"

"We need to have a beer tent, Ma. All music concerts have one. People won't come if you don't serve alcohol; it goes with country music. And Schmoozes is used to doing it, you're not. You won't even serve alcohol in your diner!"

"And another thing!" Ma pointed at the mayor as she marched straight up into his personal space, the soles of her swampers making her nearly one inch taller than the mayor who was wearing flat soles. "Them portable crappers! I don't want to see too many balloons tied to them! We don't need one of them floating away with no one in it. And I know for a fact that dumb Russian ordered way too many balloons! It'd be just my luck that a good wind would carry a rented toilet over my diner and something nasty would happen!"

As Ma spoke a long, brown '78 Cadillac Eldorado drove down onto the field and pulled up next to Bob's cruiser. Dirt dust kicked up onto the group and once again they were required to dust themselves off and everyone coughed a bit. Once again, the mayor had to swat Doody's hands off his suit coat. The Reverend Percible Winkin emerged from the driver's seat of the Caddy.

"What do you want, Bubblehead?" Ma greeted him.

The reverend ignored her and spoke to the mayor with his head tilted back in his usual arrogance, and his driving glasses sitting on the bridge of his nose. "Mayor, I'm concerned. This is just too much. Too many people in one place. The noise, and so many from away. I've heard about these rock band groupies. I watched the movie Spinal Tap last evening and I was appalled! And what about the alcohol and the possibility of illegal drugs?"

Ma interjected, "We got the alcohol covered, preacher. If you want to sell the drugs, we can set you up a spot over beside the beer tent."

"That's not funny, Wilomena," the reverend said, not bothering to look at Ma when he replied to her.

"Which kinds do you want to sell? I heard the mary-jo-wanna goes pretty good with these things!"

"Bless you, my child." This time the reverend turned his head and looked directly down at Ma.

"How's this look?!" came a yell from one side of the stage where the McIntyre's were up on ladders, each on opposite sides of the stage mounting the banner.

"It's crooked!" Ma barked, "Wally's side is lower than yours!" Ma noticed that Joshua's side was all the way up and mounted just below the awning, and Wally's side was about halfway between the stage floor and the awning.

"Wally's scared of heights and won't go any higher!" Joshua yelled out.

"Oh, for Chrissake! We can't have a crooked sign; we'll look foolish to the band! Lower your side then if he's too scared to go up!" Ma commanded and then turned her attention back to Reverend Winkin. "Let me know if you're planning on selling the pot so I can load up on extra munchies in my booth, and we'll make sure the ambulance is parked nearby too just in case," she said sarcastically to a less-than-impressed preacher. Ma looked up again at the crooked sign and shook her head. She turned back to the mayor, "And don't forget, no floating crappers! And make sure all this is gone by Sunday morning!" Ma began to stomp back towards the diner. As she walked past the temporary ticket booth that had been borrowed from the fairgrounds and set up near the entrance, she admired the sign tacked to it that read:

TONIGHT ONLY – ZAC BROWN BAND
$20 PER TICKET
HALF OF THE PROCEEDS TO BENEFIT THE FUTURE
"ANIMALS THAT GET HIT BY CARS"
CAMPAIGN TO PURCHASE SAFETY EQUIPMENT FOR THREE-
LEGGED DOGS

The reverend too shook his head at the whole situation and began to leave just as the mayor turned back to Doody and remarked again, "Don't forget to check on that toilet paper."

◆ ◆ ◆

It was the day of the concert, about one o'clock in the afternoon. The weather a clear and bright seventy degrees with no rain predicted. The stage was ready, having been painted and other finishing touches the day before. The rented folding metal chairs had arrived and they'd set up for five hundred concertgoers. Any more and it would be lawn seating with people having to bring their own butt comfort or stand up through the show. Ma's concession trailer was parked off to the side where she had Runyon and El working. They were preparing boxes of popcorn in advance, extra heavy on the butter and salt, and had fixings for the hot dogs sizzling on the griddle. Schmoozes had a red-and-white beer tent set up, all roped off so as to only allow those over twenty-one inside and they also offered to sell cold water and soda. The Smirnoffs had memorabilia tables set up for themselves and the band's crew, who were sure to be selling the band's T-shirts and whatnot.

Joshua and Wally McIntyre had set up orange traffic cones they'd found in the town garage. They had two lanes coned off leading up to the field entrance and they were both in their orange reflective traffic vests that they'd written, "EVENT STAFF," on the back with black permanent markers. Both had flashlights on their belts, and they were out in the roadway preparing for early comers, not to mention the band itself that was certain to arrive soon in several large tour busses.

Ma, the mayor, Doody and Daley, Constable Bob, Ruby Red, and a small group of other locals were standing ready at the ticket gate just outside of the field looking at the row of traffic cones and staring down the road. Each one had on a new, different-colored town shirt with the logo and sponsorships printed on them, and baseball caps to match. Ruby's shirt was far too tight, and it was apparent she wasn't wearing a bra. They were all watching for the band to arrive, when they weren't glancing at something else, or should we say, a pair of somethings.

"Should be here soon. I'm sure they need time to set up and all," the mayor stated, checking his watch again. "I can't imagine it'll be much longer."

"That promoter better remember the extra tickets, unless they've considered it a sell-out already," Daley noted.

"It better not be! We don't have our tickets yet!" Ma barked, her T-shirt a bit tight too; however, this was due to the fact that she was only wearing an extra-large and she required at least a 2X. Unfortunately, Smirnoff hadn't ordered anything larger. Luckily, Ma was wearing a bra, not to mention her normal sundress underneath.

"We shouldn't need tickets, Ma, we're sponsoring the event. They'll probably hold us some seats right down front," the mayor said with confidence, stretching his neck out as if that would allow him to see further down the road and spot a tour bus approaching.

Constable Bob whined, "Where's the early-comers? I heard tell that them groupies can come as much as a day early and camp out on site. There ain't no one here yet."

"They probably went to the *Bangir* or Portland shows. They probably won't come here," Doody responded.

"I can't wait! I'm going to sit right up front and throw my bra at Zac Brown!" Ruby bounced up and down and blurted out through a wide smile that sported far too much red lipstick.

"You'd need to be wearing a bra before you can take it off and toss it!" Ma shouted at her, "And keep those big fake things inside your shirt during the concert! And don't forget, you're taking a shift in the hotdog stand tonight! And keep your tits inside your shirt while you're in there too! I don't need El having a heart stroke or Runyon getting jump-started into pooberty!"

Ruby stopped bouncing, although her body stopped before her breasts did, and she made a poo-poo pouty-face at Ma.

Bob and Doody just looked at each other behind Ma's back, puzzled, each amazed in that other than the fact that Ma mispronounced the word, the fact that Runyon was over thirty years old now.

The mayor inquired of their matriarch, "I'm getting worried, Ma. Where is everyone?"

"You did get the day and year right, didn't you?!"

"Of course I did, Ma!"

Just as the mayor said this an older model blue Dodge van coming up the road towards them was spotted. Ma saw it first. "Must be a groupie in that old shag-wagon. Here we go, probably all liquored up and smoking them funny cigarettes before they even got here. Goddam foreigners!"

The van slowed as Joshua took the opportunity to practice his direction-giving and waved the van in between the cones. The vehicle came to a stop on the corner near the "entrance gate." Exiting the passenger side of the van, which appeared to be full of people, was a short, older man with long, graying hair under a red, white, and black checkered Balmoral hat. He had a long, gray mustache, had on a white shirt, knee-high white socks, black bog shoes, and to finish it off a red-and-white checkered kilt.

"See, I told ya. He's higher than a kite. Goddamn fool has a dress on," Ma leaned into the mayor and said.

"Howdya do?" The man approached in a friendly manner.

"Fine, buddy. It's twenty-bucks per person and stay away from the beer tent. You're gonna be searched under that dress, too. No drugs allowed." Ma motioned to Constable Bob, who looked a bit dubious at the mere thought of having to perform a search on a man who was wearing a skirt.

"No, no, my fine lass. We're here to play. I'm Zacharia Hercules Brownstone," the man replied in a heavy Scottish accent, extending his hand to the mayor. "We're the band ready to set up in your fine little town. You must be the welcoming committee. Honored, for sure. So, what kind of music do you fancy us playing? We specialize in the finest of the Scottish polkas. We can also do some clog dancing fer-ya too."

The small group just stood there, all with their mouths open and each had the deer-in-the-headlights look on their faces. Uncomfortable silence took over for a moment or two as the mayor cautiously extended his hand. "Ah, excuse me? Who did you say you were again?"

"We're the Zacharia Brownstone Band. Straight from the Iverlocky Castle in the beautiful Whales, Scotland. Ready to play fer you all. Do you have enough microphone jacks set up for the bagpipes and squeeze boxes, lad?"

"Bagpipes?!" Did you say, bagpipes?" the mayor asked and then looked to others standing beside him. "Did he say bagpipes?"

"Well, certainly, lad. Ya can't really have a proper polka without lots of bagpipes. Are you all ready to dance?"

Still stunned, the group stared at the funny little man before them. Joshua and Wally wandered up to everyone, with Wally finally breaking the silence. "Scotland, huh? Is that Loch Ness Monster thing for real?" As he questioned their strange-looking visitor, Joshua backhanded his brother in the gut and frowned at him in response.

"Shut up, McIntyre!" Ma finally barked, turning to the mayor, "What did you do, you idiot?! This isn't Zac Brown! Where's the big tour busses?! Where's the roadies and groupies?! Where's the steel guitars?!" Motioning both of her hands toward their visitor while screeching at the mayor, "Who the hell is this little man in a dress?!"

The mayor, perspiring and realizing something certainly wasn't right, asked their visitor, "You're not Zac Brown, the country legend, are you?"

"Oh, that. Yes, we get confused for them quite a bit. Quite a band, aren't they? We like their song they do, 'Sticky Chicken Fingers.'"

"It's 'Chicken Fried,' you asshole!" Ma reared back and wholloped the mayor in the back of his head, knocking his East Puddleduck baseball cap off, flying forward, and hitting their visitor in the chest. "You moron! You booked the wrong band! This isn't Zac Brown! This is Charlie Brown and his Irish bag-piping hurdy-gurdy band!"

"We're Scottish, not Irish."

"Shut up!" Ma was fit to be tied. Constable Bob had to grab onto her arms from behind to keep her from ripping the mayor limb from limb. "We're not going to sell one ticket to anyone to listen to Scottish polkas! I'm not going to sell one hotdog! We're not selling one single T-shirt! Let me go! I'm going to kill this shithead until he's dead and then I'm going to kill him some more! We've got twenty thousand balloons and two banners welcoming the wrong band! No one is going to show up to this, and I'm not going to get to hear 'Chicken Fried'!" Ma's voice raised up several octaves as she screamed directly at the mayor and struggled to get out of Bob's grip.

The mayor, looking like a terrified child, holding a hand to his aching head and winching at the tongue lashing he was taking from Ma, responded, "Well, that's not entirely true, Ma. We did advertise this all over town and in Skunksquirt too. We'll probably get at least a hundred or so…"

"…Yeah, all thinking they're here to see the Zac Brown Band, you dunce!" Ma was still tugging hard against Bob who had a good grip on her, her hair bun coming loose from under her baseball cap as she struggled. "How are you going to explain this to all of them?! Are you going to blast Zac Brown through those speakers and expect this dress-wearing leprechaun and his merry band of elves to karaoke it?! No one's going to buy it, you dipshit!"

"That's true, Mayor," Bob said, planting a foot hard to help keep Ma back from him. "They're all going to expect a famous county music band on that stage. What are you going to tell them all?"

All eyes were on the mayor for an answer. The mayor, who's a politician who's supposedly trained to think on his feet and make sound decisions, pondered for a moment or two and then turned back to the kilt-wearing musician, "You wouldn't happen to know the song 'Chicken Fried,' would you?"

"I'm sure we can put it to a polka."

◆ ◆ ◆

The mayor had been correct, that evening around a hundred or so locals from East Puddleduck and the neighboring townships attended the Zacharia Hercules Brownstone and Friends concert. Wally and Joshua had tacked cardboard over the two banners so they simply read, "Welcome, Brown Band." And oddly enough, it was the largest crowd that the band had played for all season long. All of the initial confusion and disappointment washed away for the most part when the spectators were each provided a free T-shirt, a baseball cap, several balloons, and a box of popcorn. The beer tent was pretty popular as well, and it was soon discovered that if you mix good food and alcohol with a catchy polka and throw in some free swag, it makes for a fairly fun evening. And the concert itself was something out of the ordinary for the normally mundane residents to enjoy.

Even Ma, after getting over her initial anger and frustration, caught herself bopping her head as she dished out vinegar fries during the group's bagpipe and accordion rendition of 'Chicken Fried.'

And their new charity raised over one thousand dollars.

The diner did quite well that evening too, prior to the start of the concert during the dinner hour, and it remained open late after the show was over. Ma even donated part of the proceeds back to help pay for some of the costs related to the event. The Smirnoffs began selling T-shirts and hats in their store, and the McIntyres bought up the remainder of the balloons for their used car lot, tying them to the vehicles for sale to bring attention to their stock.

Chapter 10

Lost in the Woods

"C'mon you old fart! Do I need to find a wheelchair and push your lazy backside through the woods?" Ma was standing over El, who was doing his best impersonation of a dead body lying on the couch. Fluffbutt the cat was lying on his chest with her tail flapping back and forth across his face.

"All right, I'm up," was El's response, without even opening an eye. He'd gotten dressed in his hunting attire early on and then he'd sat back down on the couch while Ma had been busy getting the hunting rifles, ammunition, and other gear loaded into the truck, which she had warming up outside. It was just about six thirty in the morning and there'd been a light snowfall during the overnight, just enough to see the tracks of their prey in the fresh powder. "Why do we have to go deer hunting anyway, Ma? I'd rather just lay here and do nothing, probably be just as successful as hunting with you."

"We ain't hunting for deer!" Ma barked. "We're going after a moose!"

"A moose?!" Elmer said, now opening his eyes and leaning up, much to Fluffbutt's agitation, and she jumped down to the floor. "For Chrissake, Ma, they don't do nothing but stand there in the woods and stare at ya."

"Fine with me. I don't want to have to chase one! Only good moose is one with his head stuffed and mounted on my diner wall and the rest of him on the special's menu."

"How'd we get a moose permit, anyway, Ma?"

"I put in the for the lottery, got one for me. If you shoot one first, I'll tag it. The game wardens will never know anyway."

"Where we going, Ma? I don't want to have to walk too far," El whined as he hoisted himself off the couch, just before Fluffbutt was preparing to jump back up onto him.

"The other side of the pond down on Muskrat Point," Ma answered as she headed for the door. "C'mon, let's go!"

El reluctantly followed. "Pretty thick woods through there, and it's not Muskrat Point, it's called Muskrat Bog, and for a reason! You know, Ma, we ain't gone through that part of the woods before. If we do get a moose in there, how we gonna get him out?"

"Whaddaya think you're coming along for, your good looks?" Ma climbed into the Chevy on the driver's side. "That's your job, to get him out!"

"I was afraid you were going to say that," Elmer said beneath his breath as he climbed into his side of the truck. The brisk morning air was cold, El's toilet seat was even colder. "I thought you warmed this thing up?"

"I tried. Heater don't work anymore, looks like it blew out the coil. I'll get the McIntyre boys to take a look at it later."

♦ ♦ ♦

The long-since honeymooners parked near Pug Hole Pond and began their day in the woods on the west side where the elevation was lower, and El was certain to be correct, there'd be a bog in those woods somewhere. They both jumped out of the cold truck, loaded their rifles, and walked to the west side inlet where there was an old, rotting wooden bridge over the inlet stream, obviously built some years ago. Just across the bridge, the landscape took a downward slope into the damp woods.

"We're going to have an awful time trying to get a moose across this if we get one," El's whining continued as they crossed the bridge together.

"Quit your complaining! I don't want to listen to it all day, and neither does the moose!" Ma barked back.

Ma was leading, wearing her aging, faded, red flannel hunting jacket. She didn't wear a hat but had a special "hunting" hairpin in her bun that was red. Ma had also borrowed Runyon's hot seat and had it pinned to her tush over her green wool pants. Hunting was one of the few times she didn't wear a floral-pattern sundress; she didn't want the thorny bushes scratching her legs. She was wearing her usual swampers on her feet and heavy wool socks. Elmer had on basically the same type jacket, red wool pants, and an old red flannel hat that had a few holes in it. On his feet were his worn, tan shit-kickers.

Neither had worn red gloves. They'd heard told a bad story about them.

As they headed into the dense woods, "You bring a compass, Ma?" Elmer whispered.

"Don't need no compass! I know these here woods like my backyard!" Ma whispered back loudly as she looked down at the brass compass she had pinned to her jacket. "Shut up and keep your eyes open for moose droppings!"

"You must get awful lost in our backyard," Elmer mumbled to himself.

"What'd you say?"

"Nuthin'."

The two walked for several minutes until they came to what appeared to be either an animal trail or a very old tote road that crossed their path going in both directions. Ma knelt down and studied it closely while El took the opportunity to rest on a tree stump. "Moose's been through here this morning. Some deer too," Ma said as she kept looking both ways, choosing a direction. "It looks like the animals have been up and down the trail. Got some fresh moose poop over here."

El was already dozing on the stump. "Why don't you keep the droppings for a souvenir in case you don't get the moose, Ma? At least the day won't be a total loss."

"Why don't you bite my hot seat! Now, get your lazy ass up! We'll take both directions. You go left and I'll go this way. Maybe the trail will go around the bog and meet up again on the other side."

"What if it don't, Ma? We may be wandering a good while if it doesn't."

"If it don't, I'll give a two shotgun blasts about noon and we'll get out of here," Ma whispered.

"Ayah. I don't have a watch, but I'll keep my eyes to the sky and listen."

Ma warned, "And don't you stop and fall asleep neither! And no shooting a deer! I want a moose's head on my diner wall! I've already got two deer heads now and a freezer full!"

Ma crept off the trail to the right. Elmer stood up and waited for Ma to disappear into the woods. When he couldn't see her anymore, he sat back down to rest for a minute. "I said get up and get your ass moving!" came a whispered yell through the woods.

Elmer got up and started off to the left, shaking his head. "How in hell does she always know?"

Ma crept low, watching her footsteps and following what were most likely fresh moose tracks on the trail in the night's snow dusting. The snow was just beginning to melt off in the morning sunlight; however, the moose tracks remained visible on the trail in the soft earth. Ma knew that by now that El was probably dozing again somewhere, so it was most likely up to her to find her moose.

About twenty minutes went by and Ma, who was so bent on spotting her prey, hadn't noticed that the tracks seemed to turn off the beaten trail and the ground beneath her had now turned to mud and saturated moss, which was creeping up around her swampers. Her boots began making a slight sucking noise with each step. After several more minutes and Ma didn't realize until it was too late that she was walking right smack into the middle of the bog that El had warned about. Finally, when the tracks seemed to disappear altogether in the saturated, soft earth, Ma stopped and looked around; her ability to maneuver through the bog was quickly nearing impossible. Ma's boots sunk further, and she looked around mostly to see nothing other than old, dead-standing trees and thick growth all around her.

"Awe, crap! He was right for once." She looked around again, "Well, I ain't going back, so might as well go forward," she whispered to herself.

Ma's stubbornness put her deep into the bog. She had to crawl over, under, and then through thick trees and branches, both alive and dead, and the wet moss was consuming her boots with each step. Ma was sweating and quietly swearing. She also discovered that one of her boots had a hole in it just above the ankle. "Goddam bog!" she said to herself as she hoisted her leg up to get over another fallen tree and stuck her foot into another deep hole of soft, wet ground. When she attempted to swing her other leg over, she caught it on the log and went down. She had all she could do to not cry out loud as she went face-first into the wet moss. She fumbled back to her feet and looked around again, seeing no signs of an end to the bog that she was now lost inside of.

"Sonofabitch."

◆ ◆ ◆

El was continuing to wander along the trail, taking in the sights and smells of the morning forest. So far he'd managed to say "howdy" to three small chipmunks, one big gray squirrel, and a red fox. Along the way, he'd seen signs of moose, deer, and even a bear, but he really wasn't paying much attention to any of them. Each time he came upon a big rock or stump that looked halfway comfortable, he'd sit and rest a while. "There ain't no way I'm dragging a moose out of here," he'd mumble to himself every time he rested.

It was during one of his rest stops that El heard something walking through the crisp, dry fallen leaves up ahead, coming towards him on the trail, and it sounded fairly large. El got up and quietly stepped off the trail and waited. "Just my luck," he whispered to himself, "I'm going to end up being the only one that finds Ma's moose."

Squinting, El spied an orange coat through the trees. He breathed a sigh of relief and stepped back onto the trail as Joshua McIntyre walked up to him.

"Hey. El, howya doing?" Joshua asked.

"Not bad for an old man. You out for a deer?"

"Yessah. Ain't seen one yet. How about you?"

"Seen signs but haven't spotted one yet. Ma's out for moose anyway. I'm out for a walk."

"Yeah, Wally's wandering around here somewhere. I figure between the two of us we'll come up with something. Have you ever hunted these woods, El? I haven't been down here before. I heard there's a bog that you don't want to get into." Joshua looked around as if the bog were nearby.

El replied back, "Nope, never been down in here. I know there's a bog in here, though, just haven't come upon it yet. But if you're headed where I just came from, lookout for Ma. She's back there a ways somewhere and on a rant as usual."

"Thanks, I'll do that. Good luck," and with that Josh was back on his way.

"Don't need luck. I ain't shooting nothing anyway," El remarked as he looked ahead for his next resting spot.

♦ ♦ ♦

By the time Ma had turned herself around in circles several times and finally managed to make her way out of the bog, she was quite wound up and in a bad mood, worse than usual. "I better find me a friggin' moose! I got a real need to shoot something!" she said out loud, not even attempting to be quiet anymore. Ma had dried leaves in her hair and her feet were soaking wet, having discovered holes in both boots now. She'd also lost her hot seat and the compass she'd pinned to her coat, both having been snagged on dry branches in the bog and torn from her clothing. The branch that caught her hot seat had bent right over after catching it, and when it finally let go, it shot the hot seat way off into the air. The compass had been caught on another log that Ma was forced to crawl over and had fallen to the ground, only to sink in the moss and be lost forever.

Ma continued through the woods in no general direction, as the trail she'd been on before she'd strayed into the bog was now long gone. However, it didn't take long before she came upon more moose tracks. She stopped and studied them; they looked fairly fresh. Ma looked around to try to get a bearing; she looked left, right, and up. Frowning, she asked herself, "I wonder where the hell I am?"

Ma's head snapped forward when she thought she heard an animal attempting to walk quietly through the woods up ahead. Even though animals in the wild are excellent at hiding themselves, Ma had a good sense of telling when one was near. Unfortunately, though, she had a horrible sense of direction in the dense woods. The animal she was apparently listening to was behind her, not in front. It probably wouldn't have mattered anyway, what she was hearing behind her was a huge twenty-eight-point, dark-haired swamp buck and not a moose.

103

♦ ♦ ♦

El's trail stopped at a clearing where it appeared to have been logged a few years back. He noticed some old skidder tracks and dried, graying slash piles to each side. He walked out into the clearing and looked up to admire the sky; the sun was getting high. He figured that he'd been walking for a good amount of time now, a couple of hours at least. He located a fallen tree at the edge of the clearing that had a bend in it about knee high and decided this was as good of a place as any to sit and rest until he heard Ma's noontime gunshots. Elmer got comfortable and rummaged through his coat pockets to see what he may have left inside them from past hunting trips. He found a stick of wrapped beef jerky that was homemade at Herb Shorey's Maple Barn in Skunksquirt. El recalled buying the jerky last year just before the season and shoving a few in his pockets. "This stuff don't ever go bad," El mumbled and unwrapped the tasty treat. He relaxed and chewed on the hard beef stick.

♦ ♦ ♦

There's something up ahead of me, Ma thought to herself as she tried to find either tracks or droppings. She couldn't locate any. "Might be my moose, and might not be." Ma gave a puzzled look as she spoke. "I need to stop talking to myself out loud, it's the first sign of going crazy." Ma crept on forward, still thinking that the animal she was hearing was up ahead of her. What she didn't realize was that, once again, the animal was behind her. This time instead of a deer, or even a moose, it was a rather large black bear. The bear had found the old, complaining woman in his woods and he was curious and had begun to follow her, and only about ten feet to her rear, literally. Its big, black nose was twitching and sniffing, it smelled of mothballs, and possibly some beef jerky.

♦ ♦ ♦

El was still resting and chewing when he spotted the majestic creature. It wandered out into the old log yard across from him, not realizing that he was there with the breeze being to El's advantage. It was a little less than a hundred yards away from where El was lounging and it was the largest bull moose that El had ever seen. The creature wandered out into the clearing with its huge rack held high and simply stood there for a few minutes. El just sat and admired it, remarking quietly to himself. "You don't need to worry about me, Mr. Moose. I'm not going to shoot you. And Ma doesn't really need your snout sticking out of her diner wall, neither." El took another bite of his hard jerky.

The moose, detecting El's presence, wandered off back into the woods a couple of minutes later. After the moose disappeared, El stood up. "Enough of this. Time to get my butt out of these woods and back on my couch." El looked around. "Well, I know where I came from and I don't know where this trail comes out, so which way?" Elmer took a compass reading. "Road should be off to the east and not too far. I suppose that's better than going all the way back the way I came." El chose a spot to enter the wood line and started back on his journey. As he did so, he shook his head and said to himself, "I really need to stop talking out loud to myself, it's a sure first sign of going crazy."

◆ ◆ ◆

I can't find one single sign that there's anything up there, but I can hear the damn thing, Ma thought to herself. She crinkled her nose and squinted to try to see through the trees and underbrush and catch a glimpse of her elusive animal that she was certain was ahead of her. She crept on forward, the black bear still right on her tail, only about six feet away, stopping every time Ma stopped and then continuing on with her as if they were in a conga line. His big, hairy backside swung side to side as he walked, very similar to Ma's backside when she walked along too.

Ma finally discovered what was going on behind her when she popped her head through some thick branches and stopped quickly at the edge of a stream that was about a foot below the edge of the bank, about eight feet across and maybe a foot deep with clear, slow running water. The bear hadn't been so quick to notice and went snout first into Ma's tush before realizing she'd come to a stop. The bear's twitching nose bumped Ma's butt and sent her tumbling ass-over-teakettle into the brook.

"Holy shiiiiit!"

"SPLASH!"

"Goddammit!" Ma managed to turn herself turned around so that she was sitting upright, the water up to her midsection as she sat on the edge of the brook's cold bottom. She looked up to see what, or who had pushed her into the stream. Just then the bear poked its huge head through the brush and Ma gazed at the bear. The bear leaned over the brook and was twitching its nose into Ma's hair bun, poking its nose on the long, red hairpin and grunting. Ma's eyes almost popped entirely out of her head and her mouth was open wide enough to catch a fish if one decided to jump from the brook at that moment. And for once, she had absolutely nothing to say. Nothing out loud anyway.

It was about this time when Runyon's orange hot seat floated past her downstream. Both Ma and the bear turned their heads to watch it float by.

◆ ◆ ◆

Elmer came upon an old set of railroad tracks. "Huh, never knew these were here," he said to himself, stroking his long, red beard. "Haven't been used for quite some time by the looks of them." As he said this, El looked up and spied some type of vehicle coming in the distance towards him on the tracks. He looked puzzled. "Now I know that ain't no steam engine coming." He chuckled as what he saw was Puut Voisine coming down the tracks on an older model three-wheel ATV that looked as if it had been hand-painted olive green. Puut had his semi-auto bungee strapped to a gun rack mounted to the front handlebars. And, as usual, Puut was dressed in khaki from head to foot. He even had on a khaki Yukon hat with green wool ear flaps. "My goodness, there's more traffic in these here woods than on Main Street in town," El said out loud, noticing that once again he was talking to himself.

Puut putted along and stopped beside Elmer. "Afternoon, Mister El. You out for a walk in the woods?"

"Ayah, and Ma's hunting for a moose. She's somewhere, I don't know where. What are you out for, Puut?"

"I'm going to shoost me a bear!" Puut smiled and said jovially. "Have you seen any?"

"Nope, not today. Saw me a moose, didn't shoot it, though. Hey, Puut, where do these railroad tracks lead to?"

Puut pointed behind himself and replied in his heavily accented voice, "All the way to the north border at Saint Decayeth, then on into New Brunswick to an old lumber yard in Edmonton. Rails haven't been used in many years." He then pointed forward. "This way goes towards Skunksquirt for a bit, I think. If you head the way about another quarter mile, it will come out right beside the road. Probably be easier walking back to your truck on the road than in here if that's what you're looking to do." Puut looked around. "Where's Ma at? She ain't got a gun, does she?"

"Sure does. Watch yourself, Puut. She'll shoot you if she thinks you're a moose coming down the rails."

Puut nodded and began to roll forward. "Okay then, see you around." Puut was off again driving slowly on the tracks. El heard him say as he drove away, "Gonna shoost me a big bear!" El just smiled and shook his head as he started walking again.

◆ ◆ ◆

What the hell do I do now? Ma thought to herself. I've got a big bear sniffing my head, and my ass is really cold. Plus, I'm all wet. The frigid water was running over Ma's legs and around her waist. Ma's hands were starting to go numb from where she was leaning back on them in the stream, looking up at the bear. Ma glanced down without moving her head, she could see that her rifle was under the water about three feet to her left, just out of her reach. She knew there was no way to get to it without moving, and for the moment she didn't feel like moving.

The bear sniffed its way down to Ma's cheek and then it pressed its nose against her and licked her face with its long, rough tongue. Awe shit! Now I got bear snot and drool on me! The bear licked her again. Ma, without really thinking first, spoke out loud, "Quit licking me, you dumb animal!" Ma paused. Uh-oh, did I say that out loud?

The bear pulled its head back a bit, pointed his snout upward and gave out a little grunt. Ma, in her usual fashion, began to get cocky without thinking first. "Look here, you hairy beast! Don't grunt at me! You're the one that knocked me in this damn stream, and now my ass is freezing! Go sniff someone else!" pointing straight at the bear's snout with her shivering, wrinkled, frostbitten finger, flicking cold water onto the bear's snout.

The big black bear, wide-eyed from his scolding, leaped up onto his two hind legs and let out the biggest bear roar Ma had ever heard.

"Awww, crap!"

◆ ◆ ◆

"It's got to be past noontime," Elmer said as he looked at how high the sun was in the sky. "In fact, it looks as if it's around one or maybe two now. Haven't heard me no gunshots from Ma neither." El was continuing along the railroad tracks until he came to a spot where the tracks crossed a small stream. There was an old, partially rotted wooden bridge where the rails crossed. Elmer stopped to study it. "They used some good timber here," he said to himself, admiring the aging craftsmanship. He walked out onto the bridge. "Still strong too. Could probably still put a steam engine over it." El was about halfway across when he spotted something round and orange floating down the brook coming towards him. El squinted and spied an orange hot seat floating on the water. He leaned down, listening to his bones creak on the way, and waited for the object to float to him. El scooped it up. "Now, how did you get in there? I wonder who it belongs to?"

"It's Runyon's, you old fart!"

El looked up to see Ma walking towards him on the tracks. He also saw a big black bear waddling behind her, right on her heels, carrying a long red hairpin in its mouth. El's eyes went wide and he scrambled to get his gun up. "Holy shoot, Ma! Watch out for that big bear behind you!"

107

"Pipe down! He ain't going to hurt you!" Ma barked. "He's harmless. Not sure what his problem is, just lonely I guess. He's beginning to be a nuisance! I can't get him off my backside. I ain't never gonna get a moose with Smokey here on my heels!" Ma turned to her new friend and pointed. "I'm not friggin' Grizzly Adams, you know!" The bear seemed to nod and grunted.

El was stunned and put a hand on his shaking head, watching as the two neared and realizing that Ma was correct, the big bear was happily following her. El was cautiously backing up off the bridge as the two got closer, keeping his distance from the bear. The bear happily followed Ma across the bridge, grunting and swinging its huge head back and forth, seeming to be enjoying playing with Ma's hairpin. When Ma stopped on the other side of the bridge, her new friend also stopped and sat back on its huge, hairy hind end, seemingly waiting for Ma to move along again so he could follow.

"Ma, it's just amazing what kind of crowd you attract."

Ma and El, along with their furry friend, started walking in the direction that Puut had recommended. It was quite a site to see El and Ma walking through the woods with their newfound friend, a big black bear, following right behind. All three hoped that Puut wasn't nearby.

"Hey, Ma," El noticed, "why are you all wet?"

"Just shut up and keep walking!"

Chapter 11

The Duck Shoot

Runyon realized that he should have learned a lesson from his previous hunting trip with Puut. However, he enjoyed Puut's mannerisms and the eccentricities that made him unique. Runyon knew well and good that Puut did things a little differently sometimes, but then we all have our oddities, he'd thought to himself. He'd agreed to go duck hunting with the Frenchman.

◆ ◆ ◆

It was late November and Puut was dressed in camouflage again, from the chest up, and from there down he had green chest waders. He'd painted green stripes on his face. However, none of this is what caught Runyon's attention. It was what was on the top of his head that did.

"What the hell is that on top of your noggin, Puut?" It appeared that Puut had taken a wooden duck decoy and hollowed it out, tacked a baseball cap and visor to it, added some freshly broken pine branches, and created a hat out of it, complete with a strap around his chin to keep it on his head.

"This is my homemade decoy. It will help bring the ducks to us," Puut said proudly.

"The only thing that will do is make you look like an idiot. Just how deep do you plan to wade into the pond, there, Puut?"

"Deep enough so from above they think I'm a swimming duck," Puut replied, again quite proudly, standing straight and smiling.

Runyon just shook his head. "We're hunting out of the boat, and you better not jump out of it when you see ducks flying," pointing at the strange

109

man.

"Not me. I'm wading into the pond. Got me a duck call too." Puut held up a tree branch he'd hollowed out to about one inch in diameter and five inches long. Runyon noticed that he'd whittled himself two reeds and stuck them in one end. In the other he'd shoved in two flat cattail leaves he'd cut short, hoping they'd make the correct noise when he blew into the call and they vibrated together.

Runyon just stared blankly at the spectacle in front of him, a funny Frenchman with a duck on his head holding a stick of wood.

◆ ◆ ◆

Runyon attempted to convince Puut to take the hat off during the ride to Pug Hole Pond. He didn't want any townsfolk to see Puut with a duck decoy on his head. He was unsuccessful; Puut wore it the entire ride. Runyon had also hoped none of the local game wardens were around today. Runyon figured that they would think Puut to be pretty drunk and hold them up just long enough to figure out that Puut was just nuts and probably they'd take both of their guns away and the hunt would be over.

The two arrived at the pond around 7:30 in the morning. A cool early winter breeze was in the air and it was a bit overcast. Runyon removed his green, overturned johnboat from the truck bed. Under the boat was Boris, Ma's bloodhound, asleep as usual. Boris was about eight years old and quite overweight from a combination of Alpo and scraps from the diner. Runyon had brought the big, old mutt along to retrieve any ducks that would drop into the pond when shot. Runyon's plan was to put the boat in and just paddle and drift mostly, with his eyes in the sky looking for ducks to fly in. He began to wonder if he did shoot a duck in the pond, who would get to it first, Boris or Puut?

Puut and Runyon flopped the boat into the water and Boris jumped into it and immediately found a comfortable spot on one of the dented metal seats, and he went fast to sleep. Boris was a smart dog; he wasn't about to flop down on the bottom of the boat, he knew most of the Farnsworth-Miller watercraft leaked. Runyon threw in his twelve- gauge and a handful of shells, two paddles, and pushed himself away from shore.

Puut took his own shotgun, which he had all wrapped in camouflage tape, and began to wade in the water. His duck-mounted head held high and looked up in the sky for his prey.

"Hey, Puut…"

"Don't bother me, I'm looking for ducks." Puut kept wading in further and looking around in the sky. He gave a blow on his homemade duck call. It didn't exactly sound like a duck; it sounded more like a constipated bear fart after being fed stale beef jerky. It was the saddest sounding thing Runyon had ever heard. It even caused Boris to open one sleepy eye to see who, other than himself, had let one go.

"Puut, you're forgetting something," Runyon tried to tell him.

"Hush up. You're just jealous that you didn't think of this first." Puut kept wading in deeper and blowing the sickly duck call. "Blaaaat! Blaaaat!"

"Fine, you dumb Canuk, keep walking," Runyon replied with a hint of sarcasm.

"Better to be a dumb Canuk than a stupid Maniac," Puut said just loud enough for Runyon to hear. Runyon's smile grew as Puut kept wading out and looking up. When the water was about chest high, about twenty-five feet from shore, he took one more step and disappeared beneath the surface with only the duck decoy above the rippling water. A second later his head bobbed back up above the surface. "Ho-shit! That's cold!" The chilly pond water having filled Puut's waders. He took one step back towards shore to get his head and chest above the water line. Runyon drifted up beside him as Puut looked up, "Okay, smarty pants, is that what you wanted to tell me?" The Frenchman inquired, shivering violently.

"Yup. Hope your damn duck hat keeps you afloat when you forget about that drop-off again. It's always been there, you know."

Puut waded back to shore and took off his hip waders to pour out the water. Runyon wasn't surprised to discover that his friend didn't have on any wool pants inside the waders, just a pair of tight white underpants with little red hearts on them. "There's something I didn't need to see today," Runyon said to Boris, who had his paw covering his eyes to block out the morning sun. "You got the right idea, there, dog. Don't look, it'll just upset you."

Puut drained his waders, put them back on, and waddled back out, being a bit more careful this time to avoid the drop-off. As he waded back into the pond, he attempted his duck call again, only to have water and the soggy cattail leaves squirt out the end and now it made more of a sad bubble-blowing sound. *"Plhhhhht."* Puut gave it a dirty look and tossed it into the pond. Runyon couldn't help but chuckle.

It was two hours later when Puut came wading by the boat for the umpteenth time after making circles around the pond's edge. Runyon noticed his friend still shivering, "Why don't we call it a morning before you catch a flu bug, there, Puut? Clouds are thickening up, probably going to rain soon."

Puut just kept wading past with his eyes to the sky. "Few more minutes, they'll come in soon." And for once, Puut was right. Just a few minutes later, off in the distance the two began to hear the faint sounds of quacking, which was soon followed by the "V" in the sky that the incoming ducks formed. Puut was near the inlet where the weeds were thicker above the water line and he crouched down in the pond to the top of his waders and pointed his shotgun skyward.

"Wait till they get close, Puut. I'll tell you when," Runyon whispered while drifting right up beside Puut, and he too raised up his twelve gauge. "Get ready, dog!" Runyon said to Boris while looking up through his sights and down the barrel. Boris was snoring and didn't hear a word that was said to him. There was a long string of drool coming from his jowls to the soggy bottom of the boat. The ducks were nearing. "Which one are you intending to aim at?" Runyon inquired.

"The first one. The leader. I got my sights on him," Puut whispered.

Runyon set his sights on the front of the pack as well. "Almost, Puut. Wait a second longer. Okay, ready? One…two…"

"KABOOM!!!"

Puut's gun went off like a cannon that had been packed far too tight with gunpowder, the shockwave creating ripples on the pond. Not to mention the force of the blast sent Puut backward into the water again with another big. *"SPLASH!"*

"Jeesus-kee-riste!" Runyon cried out as his eyes bulged open wide and he clearly saw the lead duck, and two more behind that one, explode in a frenzy of feathers. Boris nearly crapped himself as he leaped up off the boat seat and began howling with his front paws on the gunnels. The boat rocked, and the remainder of the ducks flew off in random directions, squawking loudly.

Runyon lowered his gun as Puut came bobbing back up, dripping wet and yelled, "Got 'em!"

"Got them?! There's nothing left of them! What in hell are you shooting with?!" Runyon asked as feathers floated down around the boat and it began to resemble a big pillow fight. Boris sneezed as a feather landed on his howling snout.

"Ten gauge with triple packed buckshot. I loaded the shells myself. Why?"

"Oh, no reason. You just blew up three birds, that's all! Guaranteed no more are coming back today! Maybe never!" Runyon shouted. "That thing could kill a moose!"

"Already has. Didn't I ever tell you the story…"

"Shut up," Runyon said sarcastically and looked around in the feather-filled boat; the dog was now missing. "Boris, where are you boy? See? You scared him right out of the boat into the pond! He's probably halfway to town by now." The two began looking around for the dog through the floating feathers. Raindrops were beginning to fall from the sky as well.

Puut spotted Boris first. He was doing the doggie-paddle towards the boat with only his head above water, and he had two ducks, mostly featherless, in his snout. Puut pointed, "See, I only blew up the first one. The other two are fine. Two for the price of three! Now, we can go home and eat."

Runyon just shook his head as Boris swam up to the boat. "I don't believe it." They both helped Boris back in the boat and Runyon held up the naked ducks, both featherless but intact for the most part. "Okay, let's go home. And take that dumb duck hat off."

"It's the hat that did it, you know," Puut said as he undid his chin strap and pulled on the hat. "Oh, shoot!"

"What's the matter?"

"Pine sap from the branches I used. The ugly thing is sticking to my head!"

The three duck hunters, Puut, Runyon, and Boris, went back to Puut's cabin. Puut put on pants and other dry clothes, fired up the wood stove, and Boris fell asleep in front of the heat. Runyon cooked up a nice, afternoon duck dinner, while Puut used goo-gone to remove the duck hat and pine sap. All three enjoyed the roast duck brunch.

Chapter 12

Who Can Snort the Loudest?

Ma was under the hair dryer at the salon, flipping through one of the Maine magazines Ruby had lying about for patrons to read while they waited for various hair-related matters. Mabel Johnson was in the dryer next to Ma and Eleanor Wiggleswort was in Ruby's chair having her hair dyed blond from her natural silver color, or so she expected.

The magazine was one of those publications that highlighted other Maine businesses and their achievements. The particular article that Ma was squinting at had to do with ideas on how to boost the Maine restaurant business, increase revenue, and basically advertise the food service industry in a particular way in an effort to have it be noticed.

Now, Ma didn't need to boost business, nor did she necessarily want to. Advertising caused too much chance of bringing in more foreigners and Ma wasn't hurting for profits. However, she was a bit jealous of the other food establishments that were being highlighted and thought how it might be nice to read about her diner in a local paper once in a while. Through her reading glasses she took particular notice of the innovative ideas that others had used to get their establishments noticed. Some had special dishes they cooked up, some had cute names for the entrees like Roadkill This or Maine Something-Or-Rather That. Many of them she was reading about specialized in lobsters and were coastal-based establishments. "Hmph, that don't seem right," Ma said to herself.

The more of the article that Ma read while waiting for her hair to dry and

Eleanor's color to set, the more Ma thought she might want to try one of these gimmicks in an effort to get her name in the papers.

"Whatcha reading, Ma?!" Mabel yelled over the sounds of the dryers.

"Just some nonsense about other eatin' places in Maine."

"Wouldn't it be interesting to see your diner in one of them," Mabel mentioned, which didn't help Ma's current train of thought on the subject.

"Yeah, maybe," Ma said under her voice and flipped to another page.

When the tin foil and goop was removed, Eleanor's hair was a not-so-lovely shade of reddish-brownish-yellow, and her natural silver. Ruby stood back and looked proud of her accomplishment. Ma and Mable just stared in awe at the spectacle that Ruby had created on Eleanor's head.

Now, sometimes Ma has good ideas. Sometimes they're bad. And then there was this idea…

◆ ◆ ◆

"I'm going to hold a bucksnort contest!" Ma said to El as he was sweeping up after closing time in the diner that June evening.

"I don't think that's a good idea, Ma."

"Of course it is! It's got to be something no one else has thought of. I read about that, it's got to be unique or it won't make the papers."

"Oh, it's all that, and then some. I still don't think you ought to do that. Doesn't seem quite right for an eating establishment."

Ma, who was sitting in one of the booths wrapping clean silverware into the napkins, looked up at El. "It's perfect for an eating establishment! What do you think causes a person to fart?! Good food, that's what!"

Runyon emerged from the kitchen, wearing an apron and carrying a rack of clean drinking glasses. "I have to agree with Pa, that isn't a good idea. It could hurt business, Ma."

"Ain't neither! Where else are people in this town going to eat? Right here as always, that's where. I'm doing it! Loudest and longest toot wins! I'll have the local paper in Saint Sagacious send a reporter over and see where it goes from there. I bet it makes it all the way to the Bangir Daily News or maybe even channel two!"

"How are you planning on arranging this here contest, Ma?" El asked. "How are you figuring on people all having the urge at the same time?"

Ma looked up, squinted, and pointed. "Do you remember the night when that idiot constable thought he'd be funny and sprayed a dab of his police-type pepper spray in my bean chili? Do you remember when he ran for the toilet not two spoonfuls in? He told me afterwards that fire nearly shot from his ass and he had the gas something bad for nearly three hours. I looked that stuff up, it's nearly ten percent pure pepper!" Ma went back to rolling silverware. "Now, I read that there's a hot pepper out there called the Alabama Reaper that's nearly twenty-five percent pepper! I'm going to order me a tub of that stuff and mix them in with my bean chili and add a nice, big side of coleslaw, heavy on the cabbage. I'll have them wash it all down with carbonated soda-pop. Won't take but a minute and they'll all be ready to explode!"

Both Runyon and El looked at each other and had the "ewwww" look on their faces as Ma described her diabolical plan.

Ma stroked her chin and glanced up to the ceiling. She was thinking hard. "We'll have them sit pretty far apart so's not to influence each other, and we'll need to time them on a stopwatch."

"Not leaving any details out, are you, Ma?" El remarked.

Ma looked back at him. "Do you think the McIntyre's got one of those decibel meter thingies? You know, them things that measure the temperature of the loud noises?" Ma's excitement and enthusiasm was becoming creepy to the two others.

"Doubt it."

"Ah, well, just have to rely on audience participation and the judges then."

"Who are you going to get to participate in this?" Runyon asked while putting the clean glasses away under the counter bar.

"Well, it can't be family as a contestant or a judge. I don't want the papers accusing me of nepotism. But I'm certain they'll be plenty of people wanting to get in on this."

"I ain't so sure about that." El continued on with his sweeping.

Ma was partially correct, most of the people were present simply out of morbid curiosity. The diner was fairly full that fine afternoon and the newspaper did send a pleasant-looking lady reporter to see if it was for real and what it was all about. Ma had advertised it as, "Ma's Diner's First Annual Bucksnorting Contest," promising free chili for life to the winner, one bowl per day limit.

Three contestants had signed up, the first being Smirnoff, who really enjoyed chili. Second, of course, was Constable Bob Johnson, who never turned down a free meal. Lastly, and oddly enough, was the mayor himself, Rupert Wiggleswort, whom Ma would have guessed may have wanted to be a judge in the contest; however, he'd signed up as a participant. And oddly enough, he'd treated it similarly to the mayoral race. He'd been Ma's best advertisement, having spoken about it for days in advance of the contest that he'd ultimately be crowned the winner. The truth was, he too probably just wanted the free chili, and the attention.

The judges consisted of Ruby Red Mayflower, who really hadn't wanted to participate but Ma told her she had to, being she was an employee and all. Second was Matilda Daley, mostly due to the fact that Ma had made a bet with her that she wouldn't do it. Lastly, and oddly enough again, was Old Marmaduke. Ma wanted the town's voice of wisdom on her jury, plus she felt that he'd done a good amount of farting during his time and would make a sound choice if the other two judges got sick and had to leave during the competition.

Ma spent the previous twenty-four hours prior to the contest simmering her special dish. She'd strayed off the traditional recipe a bit and began to wonder just how hot she'd made the kettle full of chili. One thing she did know was the ten-pound box of Alabama Reapers was empty by the time she'd started the concoction to simmering. She had a heaping of boiled cabbage in the coleslaw too.

On the day of the competition, Ma had the contestants seated apart with Bob at the counter bar, Rupert at his usual center table and Smirnoff at a corner table. Other spectators were seated about, none too close to the contestants, and plenty of folks standing around. The judges were set up at a table with a good view of the three contestants. The reporter had been interviewing Ma in the kitchen, turning down an opportunity to sample the hot chili. At noon the two emerged into the dining room.

"Okay, folks, here we go!" Ma yelled out, getting the crowd to quiet down. "Here's the rules…"

Just then Bob farted.

"What the hell are you doing? We ain't started yet?!" Ma barked. "Sorry, Ma, just warming up and clearing out space."

Ma turned to the judges, "Don't count that! It wasn't an official entry!" The judges, and everyone else, winced. The air wasn't circulating very well in the diner, even though all the windows and doors were open, and all the overhead fans were forcing unpleasant smells downward. Bob's test run wafted for a moment or two in the air.

Ma continued on, crinkling her nose a couple of times. "Like I was saying, when I say go, the three contestants will start eating, as much as they want. When the first one feels the urge, they'll let it out and the others have to wait, and so on until all three have submitted their snorts. If anyone farts while another one is being judged, they get disqualified. Only one chance per contestant! Once all three have gone, the judges will make a decision on a winner. Loudest and longest toot wins! Smell ain't a factor!" Many faces in the diner went from excited smiles to the "ewwww" look as Ma described the afternoon's anticipated festivities; however, no one decided to leave. It was similar to watching a bad car accident as you pass one on the highway; everyone still had the urge to see just what kind of a train wreck Ma's idea would turn out to be.

As Ma was explaining the rules, Runyon went around the room providing a clothespin to anyone who wanted the primitive, smell-blocking device. In addition to the judges and spectators, Ma had also arranged for the local volunteer ambulance service from Skunksquirt to be on-site just in case either the contestants, the judges, or others in the room required their services. The ambulance personnel had brought plenty of barf bags, just in case they were needed.

Ma was pleased that such a large crowd had shown up, and that her diner was going to be famous for such an innovative idea. Maybe even be mentioned on television. Ma hadn't even planned on the side bets that a few in the room had arranged, although, truth be told, Fat Bob was the favorite with the odds being two-to-one. Ma had dressed for the event in a new, floral-patterned dress, her hair all done up nice in a bun, and even had on flat-bottom shoes instead of her usual boots. She had on a new apron and was all smiles today, proud of her apparent, disgusting accomplishment. The apron, along with three bibs for the contestants, all had been printed up with a "Ma's Diner" logo, and underneath it read, "First Annual Bucksnorting Contest," with the cartoon picture of a smiling buck deer just to be cute.

Ma motioned to El and he exited the kitchen pushing a handcart and wearing a clothespin on his nose. He went around to each contestant, plopping a hot, steaming bowl of chili in front of each, along with a big side dish of coleslaw, and a large carbonated soda.

"If you need refills before you feel the urge, just speak up!" Ma yelled to the three.

The reporter was taking notes and occasionally snapping some photos, seeming to take an actual interest in the putrid event.

Ma looked to the judges, who all had on nose clips now. "You all ready?"

Ruby, whose expression was one of disgust as was Mattie's, spoke first. "Ma, this is really revolting," she said in a nasally voice.

"Shut up and judge!" Ma barked as she put her own clothespin on.

"Something to be proud of, Ma," Marmaduke said, and Ma smiled and gave him a little wink. Marmaduke chose not to pin his nose.

"Repulsive," was Mattie's word for it, clothespin in place. Ma didn't pay any attention to her.

"Okay, everyone ready?" The three contestants all held their spoons up in the air. "Go!" Ma yelled.

All three began eating, one cautious spoonful each. As soon as Bob and the mayor each had their spoonful in their mouths and attempted to swallow, each squinted and began to perspire uncontrollably.

"Jeesus, Ma! This is hot!" Rupert managed to spit out.

Ma giggled. "Yeah, I know."

Bob looked like he'd just sucked on a lemon. "Tastes like chili covered in pepper spray, Ma!"

"Heh, heh, heh…" Ma was in heaven, joyfully chuckling at the sight unfolding before her.

Smirnoff wasn't even breaking a sweat, shoveling two…three…four spoonfuls in. "This all you got, old woman? This chili is a bit chilly! I thought you said it would be hot?!" Everyone in the diner, including Ma, looked at Smirnoff in amazement.

The mayor managed his second spoonful, sweat dripping down his brow, and he was moaning as he struggled to swallow.

Constable Bob made it to his third, ate a bit of coleslaw, and took a big gulp of soda. His eyes were tearing, and he was wheezing as if close to a heart attack.

The reporter pulled out a mini tape recorder and visited the three contestants, beginning with the mayor. "How do you feel, Mayor?"

"Like I'm going to die." The mayor groaned and began to whimper, chili dripping down his chin.

She next turned to Bob. "And you, sir?"

Bob's eyes were nearly closed and chili was also dripping down his chin and onto the nice new bib, mostly simply because Bob was a messy eater. He managed to speak, "It's rough going, but we're trained for these types of situations…" He cut himself off by shoving another spoonful into his chubby face.

The reporter then walked over to Smirnoff and asked the same question. He responded, "Pretty soon I'm going to put my winter parka on, it's getting cold in here. Ma! Heat up the next pot, would you?!" His bowl was nearly empty.

Ma leaned over to Runyon and whispered, "What's that man's stomach made of anyway?"

Runyon just shook his head slowly in disbelief and whispered back, "I dunno. I'd guess coming from another country he eats some pretty strange stuff, Ma."

"He ain't right," Ma said back. She then looked over to the mayor who was nearly crying like a baby now. She leaned back to Runyon. "You better have the ambulance people get ready, Rupert looks like he's going down." Runyon nodded, and just as Ma said this, the mayor dropped his spoon in his bowl, causing chili to splash on the table and onto his nice new bib and bright red velvety suit coat, and he put his hand up in the air. Ma nearly climbed over the spectators as she ran to his table and held her hand over his head. "Contestant number one is ready! Here we go!" She looked around at Bob and Smirnoff. "Everyone else hold your farts!" She put her hands back down on Rupert's shoulders, "Go ahead, Mayor, give us a good one!" Ma then took three steps back and held her arms out to her sides. "Watch out, everyone, he may just explode!"

The mayor lifted his head, his face was chili and tear-stained. He took a deep breath, closed his eyes, and gritted his teeth.

Ma cried out, "This is going to be a good one!" She turned to one of the EMS attendants and pointed, "You might want to be ready with some oxygen, just in case he passes out!"

Everyone in the room winced, ducked, and prepared for the worst. Rupert put both hands on the table and his body stiffened. He then let out a yell, "Ungggghhh!!!"

"Pooffft."

A slight noise came from the mayor's tailpipe, and he collapsed in his chair and fell forward, placing his head on the table between the chili bowl and coleslaw.

"What the hell was that?! Ma yelled at him, walking around to the front of the table. "My cat farts louder than that!"

Huffing and puffing, the mayor looked up at her and responded, "Sorry, Ma. It's all I got. I just need to rest now."

"All that moaning and groaning and all we get is barely a burp?"

Constable Bob turned to the two. "The silent ones are the deadly ones, Ma," sounding a bit nasal with his nose clip in place.

"Shut up! We ain't judging on smell, we're judging on loudness and longevity! Now eat your slaw!"

Marmaduke held up a large card that had the number "3" on it. The other two judges each held up cards that had a "1" on them. Ma walked over and barked at Marmaduke, "That wasn't even worth scoring, and you gave it a three?!"

"It's the effort that counts, Ma."

Ma noticed El pointing to Smirnoff, who had his hand up. Ma ran over to him and put her hand above his head. "Contestant number two is now ready!" she yelled. "Go ahead, sir!"

Smirnoff, who wasn't sweating or breathing heavily. In fact, he didn't look phased at all and his meal was entirely gone, sat up straight and gave a cheesy grin as he let out a rather normal, common everyday fart.

"Phhhhfffft."

Ma's arm lowered and she gave the big Slavic man a, "Really?" look, quite disappointed. "What the hell's going on here?"

"Maybe your chili doesn't pack the punch you thought it would," Runyon observed.

"The hell it doesn't! The whole meal is chock-full of fart-makers!"

The judges all held up the same number across the board, "6." Ma shook just her head. There was a faint, pathetic applause from the audience in response to the scoring.

"Ma, can I get another soda?" Bob called over to her, now turned around in his seat to plea for liquids, or possibly a fire extinguisher.

"El, give him some more to drink; he's our last hope," Ma said, looking over to the reporter, who seemed quite disinterested at this point. Ma's expression turned to desperation and disappointment.

When Bob turned back around to his nearly empty bowl, the motion must have churned something up in his gut. The lawman froze, face forward, and a loud gurgling sound came from his stomach that everyone in the diner overheard and took notice of. A moment later he slowly raised his hand above his head. Ma sprinted to the counter bar. "Contestant number three is up!" she called out.

Bob grabbed the counter bar with both hands and tilted his body sideways as the gurgling in his stomach grew louder. He took in a deep breath as Ma arrived just opposite on the other side of the counter, staring Bob straight in the face with anticipation in her eyes. Bob looked straight back at her. Their eyes locked. All of a sudden Bob sighed heavily and tilted back straight up in his chair. Ma's expression turned to fear. "No, boy!" she whispered loudly. Bob lifted his right hand and put up his pointer finger to her in a "hold on" fashion, tilted his head slightly, and smiled. Ma's eyes grew wider. Bob then took a second deep breath and tilted his body again so his left butt cheek was off the stool. Ma slowly cracked a smile and winked at him.

What came from Constable Bob's backside next was monumental, to say the least. It began as a low growl that gradually grew louder, then it revved like an engine three times before letting out a loud "Boom!" like a cannon going off, only to be followed by the loudest and longest fart that anyone in the room had ever heard. Some compared it to a growling lion, others to a loud, groaning bear. Bob stood up, squatting with his arms tucked to his sides tight and his eyes closed as he continued to give birth to his fart. After what seemed like minutes, the loud, extended bottom- burp sent a shockwave that began to cause the big man's butt cheeks to shimmy together, and his farting clapper appeared to give itself a standing ovation as his butt cheeks spanked together. People in the room stared in amazement. Finally, the flatulence began to dull down slowly, and as it completely left the man's colon, it ended rising up in tone to a high squeak and one last "Pop!"

Bob slumped back down onto his stool as the spectators broke out in clapping and cheering. Ma threw her arms up and cheered along with them. The three judges all held up cards with the number "10" on each as a smiling Ma yelled out over the crowd, "Did anyone get a time on that?!"

"Twenty-five seconds!" the reporter yelled back.

Ma threw her arms over her head. "We have a new record!" Ma cheered. "And a winner!"

As the cheering continued, Ma patted Bob on the shoulder and looked to see if the other two contestants were being good sports about it. She looked over at Smirnoff, who was sitting straight and had a blank look on his face. She then glanced over to the mayor, who had sat up as well and had the same look on his face; he was staring straight at nothing and his eyes were glazed over. She then looked back at Bob, and as he looked back up at her, she could see in his face as well the signs of what was soon to come.

"Everyone, make way!" Ma yelled out as the three contestants all fumbled to stand up, each holding their stomachs. "Make sure no one's in the crapper!" Ma screamed just as each of the contestants bolted towards the restroom. Ma yelled over to the EMS attendants, "Make sure the ambulance is standing by!"

Bob, Rupert, and Smirnoff nearly tripped over each other rushing to the head as the crowd all backed up and made room for them. Luckily, Ma had thought it out in advance and had three buckets in front of the three stalls just in case it was either end that the chili was coming back out of. And it was certainly lucky that the diner had the three stalls, except for the fact that one was a urinal, so it wasn't going to work out so well for the mayor…or the urinal. Sounds of more flatulence, barfing, loud groaning, crying, stalls shaking, and noises of other bodily functions could be heard coming from the diner's toity for the next several minutes.

As the fallout was occurring in the potty room, Ma was still smiling and shaking hands with the judges and others in jubilee of a successful contest. That is until Ma along with the others in the diner removed their nose clips pretty much at the same time, thinking it was safe with the three wise men all currently suffering in the crapper. The foul air affected everyone all at once.

"Jeesus! It smells like something died in here, Ma!" El groaned as almost everyone, including the reporter and the EMS attendants, began to retch to the terrible smells wafting through the establishment.

"Good lord! This will melt the paint off the walls!" Ma coughed, bent over, and wretched.

Puut cried out through his hacking, "Kee-riste! This is worse than a barn full of skunks all munching on raw eggs on a hot August day!"

"This will never come out of my clothes!" Cicely yelled out as everyone started towards the diner doors to get outside and into the fresh air. Cicely, Eleanor, and Mable were fleeing along with everyone else even though their husbands were all suffering in the restroom. There were a few brief moments when the diner doors were blocked with bodies, all attempting to free themselves from the horrible stench. Everyone had their hands over their mouths and noses, trying hard not to puke on the person in front of them.

"We're trapped!" someone yelled out.

"My God! We're not going to survive!" another voice cried.

Finally, everyone made their way through the doors and out into the fresh air. Marmaduke was the last one out, casually strolling out without having ever used one of the clothespins. He stood in the doorway with his hands in his pockets, watching all of the spectators, including the reporter and the EMS volunteers, all retching and heaving in the parking lot. Everyone had involuntarily picked a spot to hurl. He watched as Eleanor Wiggleswort literally passed out onto the ground. Marmaduke smiled and shook his head. "Heh, heh, toughen up, buttercups." He chuckled to himself.

Three people ended up being transported to the local hospital for de-lousing and oxygen. The mayor was one of them, along with his wife, Eleanor, and one of the ambulance attendants.

♦ ♦ ♦

The diner opened again two days later after a good airing out. The restroom re-opened five days after that, all except for the stall with the urinal; it required replacing completely.

Constable Bob came back on the first day the diner was open again for his first of many free daily bowls of chili.

The reporter had made the difficult decision to not run any sort of story on the event. She simply didn't have words to describe what she'd witnessed and been a part of. Instead, she ran a story highlighting the town's newest charity organization benefitting three-legged dogs.

Ma was so overjoyed with the results, and even though she was disappointed that it didn't make the papers, she's scheduled another identical event for next year. She figures it will catch on and ultimately someone will write a decent story about it.

Chapter 13

Another Fish Story

The 1st of January, New Year's Day. The temperature this time of year can average anywhere from ten above to twenty below, depending on the wind. Now, generally speaking, you might think that everyone would want to stay nice and toasty warm in their homes, all cozied up to their wood stoves and fireplaces.

Not Ma, she never misses the first day of ice fishing season.

Ma was up good and early before dawn. She wanted to be on the ice at daybreak. She yelled out the front door, "Runyon! Get out here and give me a hand hooking up the shack!"

Runyon appeared at his tiny cabin front door in his red, long john one-piece and wool socks. "Ayah, Ma," he yawned and stretched. He slid on his snow pants and heavy wool jacket, put on his rabbit-skinned trapper's hat with the big wing flaps flopping down over his ears, and slid his bean boots over the wool stockings.

Ma was dressed similarly to keep warm. Today she had wool pants on under her floral dress, which looked a bit funny to see the lower part of her dress hanging out over the pants and her wool coat on over it. She had two pairs of wool socks on under her swamper boots.

The ice shack was built out of the old outhouse after they'd put in the indoor plumbing and after the "moose" incident. It had sat a couple of seasons and been aired out pretty well before converting it into an ice shanty. It had the half-moon cut out on the door and it had been a two-seater in its day, just in case you wanted to bring a friend. In the two potty holes is where Ma had cleverly wound fish line onto the old toilet paper rollers and created a system on the rollers to trigger a flag to let you know a fish was on the line. For the flags, Ma used thin gauge metal survey stakes with orange plastic flags. Although, once you heard the old toilet paper roll squeaking and going like crazy, it was a good sign a fish was on before you ever noticed that the flag had sprung up. El had put an old gas heater in the shack and mounted a five-pound propane bottle to the outside. Ma would usually only fish from one hole and kept warm sitting on the other toilet seat that she'd normally toss a hot seat onto because cold air and all still made its way through the hole if she didn't. El had jacked up the "half-moon" shanty and mounted metal skids underneath it for towing across the ice. It's unique in its own way, as is everybody's ice shanty.

It was a cold morning, closer to zero to begin with. Ma was outside putting the tow chains on the ice shack which was already up on the old eight-foot flatbed trailer, along with their '74 John Deer 400 snowmobile in the bed of the truck. The reliable old machine has a 340cc engine and a reverse gear in it, and always starts on the first pull. As one of their backups, they have a 1970 Arlberg 340 that's just as reliable. That one doesn't have a reverse gear and usually requires a little ether in the carb to get the Sach's 336cc engine to turn over. As a rule, it blows fire at you once or twice from the carb horn that points straight at your midsection before starting. Ma was bringing the John Deere just in case they needed it; however, the plan was to drive the truck straight out onto the ice.

Ma had her creepers tied to her boots to keep from slipping on the frozen pond. Once she managed to get the shack chained up, she commenced to putting their gear inside the shanty. She had the gas-powered auger, plus an old hand auger. A one-gallon can of pre-mixed 50/1 gas for the power auger. A five-foot ice chisel and two ice-hole scoops, a Coleman single-burner propane stove, and a teapot. She didn't take fresh water; pond water was good enough for her. She had an old plastic pink sled with a wicker basket tied to it to drag the ice traps around the pond. Lastly, the ice-fishing traps. Ma's preference is the underwater traps to keep the lines from freezing in if it's particularly cold. El still uses his own homemade tip-ups. He uses an old fisherman's trick of tying pine boughs to the line to give it a little "jig" and to keep his lines moving in the breeze to prevent them from freezing into the holes on really cold days.

With everything in place and the ice shack full, Ma and El were ready to hit Pug Hole Pond. Of course, El was finally ready after everything was loaded up and chained down, and he eventually emerged from the house.

"You could help once in a while, you know," Ma said to him.

"Looks like you're both doing fine," was the reply as El climbed into his side of the pickup.

Ma ignored him and started to get in the driver's side. "You coming today, Runyon?"

"Nope, got other things to do." "Suit yourself."

The old Chevy smoked from the tailpipe and argued a bit as it usually does; however, it started up. Joshua McIntyre had fixed the heater, so after about time they arrived at Smirnoff's store to pick up a dozen or so shiners, the truck was good and warm.

"Raised your bait prices again this year, didn't you!" Ma grumbled to the Ukrainian-born store owner. "They're looking kind of tired, too!" Ma quipped as she netted the best ones herself from the tanks that the Smirnoffs had. Smirnoff just smiled, winked, and blew Ma an air kiss. He knew to take Ma's comments with a grain of salt, she was just being "Ma" as usual.

The Smirnoff's opened early as the ice fishing season is prosperous as far as bait and grocery sales, as ice fishing is a popular winter sport and pastime. Many a Puddleduckian spends their winter weekend days on the ice. Some folks have shanties so fancy that they're all set up to spend all night in them. During the season, Smirnoff has two bait tanks, which are housed in one of the back storage rooms running with air twenty-four seven and keeps them full of all sizes of shiners in one tank and smelts in the second one. The Smirnoffs pay the local youth fairly well to go out and catch bait and to keep their tanks stocked throughout the winter months, and still keep the bait prices reasonable. Not to mention theirs is the only bait shop in the area.

In the summer on special occasions, and when they can get them, the Smirnoffs use the tanks to hold live lobsters for Ma to serve in the diner. Of course, Smirnoff cleans the tanks between seasons, mostly because one species requires salt water and the other fresh water.

Ma filled their bait bucket with cold water from the tanks and scooped up two dozen nice shiners. She preferred shiners over smelts, due to the fact they were cheaper and they remained alive longer in the cold water.

♦ ♦ ♦

Ma stopped the truck at the edge of the pond at the boat landing. It was barely daylight. The pond was well frozen over with just a few inches of snow on top of it, the freshest from the dusting the night before. They both studied the frozen pond.

"Where we gonna put the shack this year, Ma?"

Ma looked around through the semi-frozen windshield. Through the dawn of morning, she spied Joshua and Wally McIntyre's bright blue tarp-covered shack that was already at the mouth of the brook, and Puut's fancy mini log cabin shack, complete with a tiny pot-bellied wood stove was dead center on the pond. "Dammit, I knew we should have gotten here sooner! All the good spots are taken!" Ma barked, and then she pointed, "There's a deep hole to the north side close to the edge, and a sand bar running across it. Let's pin her down over there."

"Sounds good enough."

They both got out of the truck, Ma locking the hubs to the front tire on her side and El doing his side. They climbed back in and Ma shifted the old bomber into four-wheel drive. "Hold on!"

El grabbed onto his hat as Ma gunned the truck and drove out onto the ice, spinning all four tires. She barreled through the wind-drifted snow at the shoreline and began fishtailing down the ice, the truck going in one direction and the trailer and shack in the other. She came to a sliding halt sideways over the spot where she determined the deep hole to be. The force from the trailer caused both truck and trailer to spin around once completely before coming to a stop.

El gave Ma one of those looks. "Kinda rough on the equipment, weren't you, Ma?"

"I don't like driving over water, even if it is frozen!" she answered back.

Ma and El dismounted and El loosened the chain and removed the bolt on the tilting bed of the trailer, and the shack slid down onto the ice. They hammered four ground stakes into the ice and tied the shanty down for the season, first mounting it up on wooden blocks knowing that in the hot sun come late February and March the shanty would sink a bit into the soft ice.

Ma climbed into the shanty to get the equipment and start the heater, and El grabbed the power auger. "I'll cut some holes, Ma," he said as he primed gas into the machine, choked the engine, and tugged on the pull cord several times until it started. El had to brace himself as the old auger was built with only one handle. If you didn't hold onto it tight on takeoff, you were likely to get the handle spinning around and catching you in a spot you really would rather not be struck in.

Ma fired up the heater and it began to reflect warmth against the tin foil she'd tacked to the wall behind it. Ma cracked the window in the rear of the shack to let gas fumes pass out into the fresh air. She grabbed the long chisel, opened up one of the two toilet seats, and began to chisel the indoor hole. *"Thunk, thunk, thunk!"* The sound echoed as little ice chips flew back up out of the hole. Once she had a good base started, she used the hand auger to finish the job. The ice was thick, at least fifteen inches, and cutting the hole was tiring. Finally, like a toilet flushing, so to speak, the water rushed up through the hole and onto the top of the ice under the shanty.

Ma reached in and cleaned the hole out with her scoop. She then dipped her tea kettle in, filled it with pond water, and set it on the propane stove. By the time Ma was done setting up her toilet trap, baited with a nice three-inch shiner, she looked out to see that El had cut several holes and had scooped them out, and was pounding the frozen ice off the end of the auger.

Ma came outside and yelled to him, "How many times you fallen on the ice so far?"

"About a dozen."

"Well, that's what you get for not wearing your creepers." Ma chuckled, grabbed the pink sled, and started setting ice traps in the outside holes he'd cut. She built a snow wall into the breeze at each hole to prevent wind flags. She hooked each shiner in the back, just below the dorsal fin. She lowered the lines, placing some of the bait just below the ice line and the rest just off the bottom of the pond. Once they had their first fish on, she'd set them all to the depth they'd be biting this day. El went around and tied pine boughs to his sets. They both hoped they'd see a flag go up early on, a sign of good fishing to come throughout the day.

When they were done setting traps, and as El was walking back to the shack for some heat, he slipped again on the ice. Both feet went up and his tuckus hit the ice. Ma giggled to herself when she saw him go down and she started back to the shack herself. When she got about halfway between the furthest trap and the shanty, she was looking around for flags when she stepped straight into an ice hole that had been cut but hadn't been used and it wasn't scooped out. *"Splash!"* Her calf was wet with freezing water almost up to her knee.

"Sonofabitch! Elmer, get me out of this friggin' hole! And quit cutting holes that we don't use!"

"Don't step in them and you won't have to worry about it." El chuckled under his breath, which could be seen in the brisk morning air.

El slid back over to Ma, grabbed her under her shoulders, and tugged. She was stuck in the hole. "Why in hell didn't you set a trap in this damn hole?!" Ma shouted and grunted each time El tried pulling her up.

"You were setting the traps, I only cut the holes. Besides, we always do extras and move them around. Now, quit complaining and push!" El tugged again and had Ma up just a little, then lost his footing. He slipped on the ice, one leg on either side of Ma, and went down on his rump again. Ma splashed back into the hole. Water sloshed out of the hole like a toilet being plunged, splashing Ma between the legs and cold water ran under El's tush.

"Goddam, that's cold! Why in hell didn't you wear creepers?!" Ma barked.

"Don't need 'em!" El barked back as he wiggled and struggled to get back to his feet.

"Bullshit!" Ma yelled as El got back up and started tugging again. Up, *"slosh!"* Down, *"splash!"* Up, *"slosh!"* Down, *"splash!"* Ma's foot was caught just beneath the ice line.

"Might have to cut another hole, Ma. Either that or cut your leg off," El suggested, still tugging on the old woman. Ma wasn't a bit amused by his comments.

Just then Ma saw it out of the corner of her eye. A bright orange flag sprang up on one of her traps about thirty feet away, the flag waving back and forth in the cold air. Ma pointed at it. "Flag!"

El looked up to see it. "You gotta fish, Ma."

Ma replied in a sarcastic tone, "Goddam, you're smart! Nothing gets by you, does it?! Go get it!"

"What about your leg, Ma?"

"Don't worry about it, go get the fish before it takes out a half-mile of line. Go!"

El let go of Ma and she splashed into the hole again, washing water up her leg, out of the hole, and under her frozen tush. "Dammit!"

El started chugging towards the waving flag, doing his best to remain upright. "Don't forget the bait bucket and scoop to skim the hole!" Ma shouted, bracing herself on the ice and pushing to get her tush up off the frozen water and keep an eye on what El was doing. El grabbed up one of the ice scoops along the way that one of them had left on the ice and kept heading towards the flag. When he arrived, he looked down into the water and could see the reel, still full of line and standing still under the ice.

"It's a wind flag, Ma!" he yelled back to her.

"Shit! Well then, get back over here! My legs freezing up!"

Just then another flag went up on a second trap another thirty feet away. "Flag!" Ma shouted and pointed.

El took off for the second one, only a bit slower this time. As he neared the hole, he could hear the whining of the reel under the ice. When he arrived, he knelt down and pulled Ma's trap out of the water, the reel spinning round and round, and the line cocked off to one side of the hole. "No wind flag this time, Ma. You got a fish on!"

"Well, don't just stand there gawking at the reel, get that walleyed bastard!" Ma shouted, twisting her foot to see if that would help release her boot from below the ice line.

Walleyed bastard, El thought to himself and chuckled. Ma's word for a pickerel, a common winter catch here on the pond. Another word she used for them was "alligators" for their green color, long snout, and sharp teeth. El set the trap down on the ice and began pulling on the line. "It's a fighter, Ma!"

"Whachya doing sitting on the ice, Ma?!" a voice echoed from behind her. "You got a fish, there, El?!"

Ma turned herself to see Joshua McKintyre calling to her, standing next to his shack. His old, yellow-and-orange single-cylinder '73 Ski-Doo Bombardier Olympic with the duct-taped seat parked next to the shanty. He'd just arrived for his day of fishing on the pond.

"Sonofabitch." Ma said to herself, "Just what I need, people seeing me with my leg in a water hole." Ma shouted back in Joshua's direction, "Keep to your shack, McIntyre! Don't be nosy!"

Joshua wandered a bit closer, stretching his neck out to see. "You got your leg stuck in the ice, Ma?"

"I'm just resting! Get back to your shack!"

Joshua started to laugh and continued walking towards her. "You have got your leg stuck, don't you, Ma?!"

"Shut up, McIntyre, I don't need your crap! And as long as you know anyway, get over here and get me out of this goddam hole!"

El was still pulling in the line, the fish fighting back against his efforts. "Almost got him, Ma! Took out a bit of line, though!"

"Be careful, don't lose him!"

Joshua strolled across the ice over to Ma and took over where El had left off, planting his creepers, grabbing her under her armpits, and tugging at her while she pushed against the ice. "Jeesus, Ma, you need to quit eating your diner leftovers. You're getting a bit weighty."

"Shut up, asshole! I'm just as trim as I was thirty years ago! Now pull!"

You must've been pretty fat thirty years ago, Joshua thought to himself; however, he was just smart enough not to say it out loud as he tugged on the woman.

El could see the fish near the top of the ice hole. He was careful not to tug too hard and lose it. It appeared to be a nice-sized pickerel. He could see the shiny greenish coloring and spots as it swam by the top of the hole in an effort to get free. "Here it comes, Ma!"

Ma pointed her boot downward as much as she could under the ice and Joshua gave a good yank. Ma's leg slid up out of the hole, her swamper making a loud sucking noise, and more water ran out of the hole onto the ice. Joshua, being what you'd call a fit young man, pulled her straight up to her feet. Ma emptied her boot, took her socks off, and shook her frozen leg to get some feeling back in it.

"Thanks, Josh, you're a good boy," as she slid her cold boot back onto her bare foot.

"Anytime, Ma." Joshua was steadying her on the ice. "You need to get yourself into the shack, Ma, and get warmed up."

Ma looked over and saw that El had both hands on the line and was kneeling over the ice hole, ready to pull the fish out. She watched El stand up, back to her and positioned his feet on either side of the hole.

"Don't stand up!" Ma yelled out, just as El slipped and both feet went out from under him again. He unintentionally yanked on the fish line and a twenty-three-inch pickerel came shooting out of the hole into the air, over his head and flew behind him. The leader line snapped in the cold air and the pickerel was immediately airborne, flipping and flying over and across the pond.

Ma and Joshua saw the fishy torpedo headed their way and both pointed at it. "Fish!" Joshua yelled out.

There was no time to duck. "Sonofabitch," Ma said under her breath as the fish flew over and whacked her straight in the face, the force knocking her backward into Joshua, and both went down. Joshua landed tush first back into the hole that Ma had just come out of. *"Splash!"* The wet ice around the hole was just enough to fit all of Joshua's butt inside of it, and Ma fell straight backward onto Joshua's lap, making sure his ass was good and stuck in the hole.

"Get off me, Ma! My butt's freezing!" Joshua yelled as he tried to pry himself out of the hole.

"You got waders on, dontcha?! Quit your bitching!" Ma crawled off Joshua and stood back up. "El! Get over here and help get McIntyre get his ass out of the hole, I'll get the fish!" Ma waddled over and scooped up the pickerel, which was flopping on the ice nearby. She had the fish in one hand and her wet, freezing socks in the other.

El got back up and started sliding toward Joshua. He glanced at the other traps on the ice, no more flags yet. El was moving much slower than before with a little limp, his rump was definitely beginning to ache from all the tumbles he'd taken on the ice so far this morning.

Ma was admiring the catch when suddenly she dropped the pickerel and her socks and looked around. She could hear a "whirring" noise. She looked around and didn't see any more flags up on the ice. She turned back and glanced at the half-moon shack and realized the sound was coming from inside. "My line's spinning out on the toilet roll, we got a fish in the shack!" she cried out as she sprinted to the shanty with an obvious limp as well. Her creepers dug into the ice as she went. *"Clip clap, clip clap!"*

El made his way to Joshua and started tugging on him, falling down often as he made the effort. "Owe! Watch your footing, El, this ice hurts! Feels like my butt's in a frozen meat grinder!"

Ma climbed into the shack and noticed it was nice and warm inside. She saw that the line was reeling quickly off the toilet roll with a good amount already gone. "Crap! Damn fish has a mile of line out already!" Ma grabbed the line and started to pull it back in. She pulled and pulled, and pulled, letting the line hit the floor of the shack rather than put it back on the toilet roll just yet. Finally, the line got to a point where it wouldn't pull anymore. "Dammit!

The fish went to bottom and wrapped himself around a log!" She gave a couple of tugs to try and free the line, and not lose the fish in the process. The line wouldn't budge.

♦ ♦ ♦

"Owe! I'm telling you, El, something is pulling me back into this hole! I swear it!"

"Don't be dumb, it's just your butt numbing up from the cold water and the suction your hip waders are causing! If your ass wasn't so skinny, you wouldn't be stuck!" El tugged hard again, holding Joshua down around the waist now, with his head resting on Joshua's shoulders. "Now push!"

"I feel like a mother giving birth!" Joshua said sarcastically as he pushed against the ice again. "Owe!"

♦ ♦ ♦

Ma tugged the line a little harder, it still didn't budge. This wasn't anything new; there had been many times when Ma hadn't paid attention to her traps and a fish had taken enough line to swim around a log or large branch sitting on the bottom of the pond. It happens every year. Usually, after a while of gentle tugging it will come free and you save the fish. Sometimes you lose it all, the fish and the rigging. This one was caught good, though, Ma thought as she tugged again. "Come on, you walleyed bastard! Let go of the log!"

♦ ♦ ♦

"Jeesus, this really hurts! Hurry up and get me out of this hole, El!" Just as Joshua said this, El slipped down onto one knee again.

"I can't get a good footing!" El braced himself using the knee that was on the ice. "Get ready, Joshua, when I say go, push real hard! One, two, three…go!"

Joshua pushed hard and El pulled. Joshua's butt came out of the hole, the suction pulling water and ice chunks up with it. El fell backward onto the ice once again. Joshua caught his balance and was squatting over the ice hole, water dripping from the seat of his pants back into the pond. Just then, a puzzled look came over Joshua's face as he realized that something was spanking him on the ass.

"Joshua!" El cried out and pointed. "Your butt!"

Joshua, still squatting, leaned forward and looked under his crotch between his legs. While upside down he saw the tail of a pickerel slapping back and forth against his backside. The fish was biting him in the tush, feeling as if its sharp teeth were going through all of his layers of clothing and seemingly straight into flesh.

El exclaimed, "You've got a pickerel on your ass!"

However, Joshua knew this already. He also spied a red, braided thirty-pound test fishing line extending from his butt back down into the ice hole. "There was no trap in this hole," Joshua said to his crotch, feeling a bit confused.

♦ ♦ ♦

The red, braided thirty-pound fishing line yanked out of Ma's hands. "What the hell is going on here?!" Ma asked out loud. She grabbed the line back up and pulled again slowly, it was still caught on whatever it was caught on. Ma was a bit puzzled and decided to give a little harder yank.

♦ ♦ ♦

"Whoa!" Joshua yelled and stood back straight, flailing his arms as he almost lost his balance backward towards the hole.

"Fish has got a line in its mouth!" El said, just a bit bewildered.

"No kidding! And I don't care if it's smoking a cigar, I need it to stop biting my butt!" Joshua yelled, trying to reach around to get a hold of the slippery, slapping fish.

El got back to his feet again and tried to grab the flailing pickerel by the tail. His hands slipped off the fish several times. "Hold still, Joshua!"

"I am holding still, it's the fish that's moving around!"

♦ ♦ ♦

"Enough of this!" Ma said to herself as she wound the fish line around her gloves a few times. "Either she comes or she breaks!" Ma gave the line a hard yank.

♦ ♦ ♦

The fish slipped out of El's hands as it headed straight back for the ice hole, still biting into Joshua's butt, which also was headed for the ice hole once again along with it.

"Splash!…Rip! Tear! Rip!"

Joshua's backside lodged into the hole again, cold water and ice splashing out of the hole and up over him. El seemed surprised to see Joshua sitting in the ice hole for a second time.

"Christ! My balls are going to freeze together!"

♦ ♦ ♦

Ma pulled on the line. "Heh, heh. Let go of the log, didn't you, you little devil?!" Still annoyed that the fish had taken so much line, Ma noticed there was no further resistance. "Tired yourself out, too. Serves you right!" She hoisted the pickerel out from the ice hole and began to pull it through the toilet seat when she noticed a large piece of material in the fish's jaws. "What the hell is this?" she said to herself. Ma pulled the fish up through the crapper hole and dangled it in front of her. In the fish's mouth was a large, tattered piece of thin rubber-like material, attached to what appeared to be a piece of wet flannel material, attached to what appeared to be a full pair of men's tightie-whitie under drawers. Ma's face displayed a confused expression as the oddity in front of her spun slowly around and around on the line. "What the hell?"

♦ ♦ ♦

El managed to get Joshua out of the hole for a second time, and as Joshua stood up, water poured out from a rather large tear in the rear end of his chest waders. El looked at Joshua's backside and said quite casually, "Josh, you lost the seat of your pants."

Joshua turned his torso to look at the missing pieces. What he discovered was that he was missing a piece of his waders, a piece of his flannel pants, and all of his underwear, which the fish had ripped clean off him. The crack of his ass was starting to freeze in the frigid air and water. "Goddam, that's cold!"

They both heard laughing and turned to see Ma at the doorway of the ice shack. She was dangling the pickerel in front of her with one hand, holding her belly like Santa with the other hand. In the fish's mouth was the seat of Joshua's pants, both layers, and his underwear. Through her laughter, Ma blurted out, "Fish was hungry today! I guess your butt was the main course to the shiner he'd started with as an appetizer! You should've stayed at your shack, McIntyre!"

Chapter 14

Number Three Pond

It was early spring and Ma had heard that there was a pond just the other side of the Hyattsville Woods that had the best white perch fishing in the north. The only name she heard tell of it being called was "Number Three Pond."

Old Marmaduke had bragged on the spot several times when telling stories to Ma over a meal at the diner. He'd also sworn it was the best fishing north of the Allagash and south of the Canadian border. He'd told her that he'd fished it many times and always caught well beyond his limit. His directions, which Ma had taken the time to write down on a napkin, were fairly understandable:

Take the Main Road towards Skunksquirt.

Take a right onto Cornfield Road.

Go all the way into Fort Cornerstone and hop onto Route 63.
Just before Saint Behemoth hang another right on Moosetail Lane just before the cemetery that you can see ahead of it.

Drive 2 miles to the corner store that ain't there no more.

Hang a left at the corner store and find the second dirt road well into the Hyattsville Woods. End of the dirt road is Number 3 Pond boat landing. Can't see the pond from the road.

With her limited knowledge of the area southeast of Fort Cornerstone near Saint Behemoth, Ma had convinced Puut to go along with her and Runyon, thinking between the three of them they should have the ability to locate the popular fishing hole fairly easily and with the use of Marmaduke's directions.

It was early, about 4:00 a.m. Ma yelled out to Runyon to make certain that he was up and dressed, because of the long drive to the location and she didn't know exactly where they were going. She figured the trip would take about two hours to get to the pond.

The boat was ready to go on the trailer, bungee corded well so as not to bounce too much on any rough roads. She had two cords on the outboard motor. This one wasn't Ma's usual johnboat; this one was a little larger ten-foot Boston Whaler that Ma had picked up from the McIntyre's when they had taken it in trade for a used car the summer before. The boat is a bit more comfortable when you have more than two people on the adventure, and has a bit larger outboard engine of twenty horsepower. The trailer, all registered, has its beaten license plate zip-tied to it. Sometimes the directional and brake lights worked on the trailer, but not today when Ma checked them.

Ma and Runyon started out, stopping briefly to gas up the truck at McIntyre's station. The station wasn't really open this time of day but Joshua always trusted Ma and other townsfolk to pump their own gas and leave the money in the mail slot in the door. Runyon fueled up the boat tank too, poured about three ounces of two-stroke outboard oil into the can, and shook it to make certain it had mixed to a near 50/1 ratio. They continued on and proceeded to pick up Puut, and were on their way to Number Three.

Ma had Runyon drive and Puut rode in the center. There was no extra cushioning for him on the bench seat, so he got poked by the springs a bit more than the other two. Traveling was okay, not too many potholes on the northern Maine roads, and Runyon was usually pretty good at avoiding them anyway. The good thing about Maine roads up north is that they're marked fairly well. If not by the state or the townships, then by someone else who's tacked up a handmade sign to refer to, warning you of any obstacles.

Of course, traveling through the Hyattsville Woods can seem to go on forever, it being miles and miles of nothing but road. Not to mention too that Ma, being superstitious and all, believed the tales of ghosts and such things that roam the woods and the road that traveled through them. Plus, the fact that these dense woods have a lot of wildlife, it's not uncommon to have a deer, bear, or moose dart out in front of you and cause some nasty damage, especially near dusk or at night. Ma's old truck was a magnet for animals, more to come later on that tidbit of information. Ma didn't want a moose ending up where Puut was sitting between the two in the front seat. That would certainly ruin the fishing for the day.

It took just about what Marmaduke had said it would, about two hours, to get to the landmark on Moosetail Lane where they spied the cemetery. They turned and continued until they found the closed corner store, where they turned left again and began seeking the second dirt road.

"Can't be far now, Ma," Runyon observed.

"Well, just take it easy. And keep your eyes open for the second road."

Puut smiled, thinking to himself, What a dumb saying, keep your eyes open. How would we find it with our eyes closed?

They traveled a few miles down the road they were on. A bit of a problem was that there were many potential turnoffs that looked like private drives, not to mention places where it appeared that old logging and tote roads once were but nothing yet resembled any stand-alone or well-driven roads spurring off from the one they were traveling.

"Old Marmaduke didn't say if the road in here had a name, did he?" Runyon inquired.

"Nope, just said second dirt road." Ma checked her napkin again just in case. "As a matter of fact, he didn't even mention left or right."

Runyon took a sharp corner and there just on the other side was a road to the left. "Whoa," he called out as he hit the brakes, stopping just a bit beyond the road. There were no markings, but also no camp signs. That's another thing about Maine: if someone has a camp along a dirt road, they usually feel the need to advertise themselves by tacking a sign to any tree near the end of the road to let the world know that's where they are. There were no signs here.

"Do you think this it, Ma?" Puut asked, stretching his neck out to peer out Runyon's window.

"I don't know. Is this the first or second road we've seen?"

"First, I think," Runyon answered, looking back out the window and around. "Could be a boat landing road, I suppose. There's no other signs here."

Ma barked, "You'd think if it was a boat landing road they'd put up a sign! Well, if it's the first road we better keep looking for another one. But then again, if this is our road, we don't want to miss it."

Runyon backed up the truck and trailer and turned down the mystery road. They did; however, notice that the road had recently been dragged, taking that as a good sign that it might be the correct one. Runyon barreled right along, and the old pickup and trailer bounced along, kicking up rocks and creating dirt dust. Every once in a while Ma would give Runyon a nasty look for hitting a hole a little harder than he should. Each time they came to the top of a hill, they could see water off to the right through the trees in the distance.

"Must be Number Three," Ma said, pointing to the water. "We can't be too far from the landing, keep your eyes peeled in case it comes up quick. You can't be too sure. And slow down!"

After cresting another knoll, the pond disappeared. Runyon kept on as before; however, he kept looking to the right to catch another glimpse of the body of water that they believed to be Number Three.

Ma checked the time on the digital watch that she'd bought and used Velcro to attach it to the dashboard of the truck. It read 7:45 a.m. "Not too bad for time, looks like we're still going to hit it early enough."

They passed a spot where a logging crew was hard at work. There was a skidder and a loader where the road opened to a clearing, and two large flatbeds waiting to be loaded parked off to the side. Logs and slash were scattered around. The three smiled and waved to the loggers as they went by. "Goddam stump jumpers," Ma grumbled to herself as Puut and Runyon chuckled at her comment. As much as Ma respected the logging industry, she hated seeing clear-cutting.

Runyon figured they had traveled four miles down this road as they sat at a fork, and another dirt road bearing to the right, the Chevy's engine idling loudly and as the tailpipe shimmered and shook while they looked over the situation. The road looked a bit rough ahead in both directions. Off to the right, the trees appeared to be grown up around the road, and the middle of the road had a rise in it with grass all grown up quite high.

"Could this be it, Ma? It seems to turn in the general direction of the pond we spotted."

Ma looked it over, then looked at her napkin notes again. "That old idiot didn't say nothing about another road off this one. It don't appear to be too well traveled, neither."

"I think maybe this was the first road, not the second one," Puut chimed in. "Marmaduke is a smart fellow, I'd follow his directions."

Runyon shoved the gears back into second, with first gear not being worth much of anything, and proceeded to turn the truck and trailer around. They drove back by the loggers, waving and smiling again, although their smiles were a bit less broad than before, and made it back to the main road. They turned left and began seeking another dirt road. It wasn't long before they located one, same as before, it was on the left and had no markings.

"Whaddya think, Ma?"

"It's got to be the one. Take it!"

The truck bounced and the trailer rocked down the roadway. This road wasn't as level as the one before and was even more rough going. As they traveled down the road it became narrower, the dense trees and bushes scraping the sides of the truck and boat. Long branches slapped Ma and Runyon on the arms they both had resting on the open truck windows. Actually, Ma was more so hanging onto the door as Runyon's driving was causing the truck to bounce up and down. On the up-hills, there were ruts where the rainwater had run over the road and caused damage. One the downhill, the same. There were bends and curves and deep puddles on the lower portions of the road. Large rocks caused the bed of the pickup to bottom out on the springs several times.

Ma's hair bun was coming loose as it hit the roof of the pickup on one of the bounces. "Goddammit! There better be one hell of a perch pond here or Marmaduke's in for a world of hurt!"

"I'm still seeing that pond off to the right on each hill," Puut observed. "It can't be too far away."

The truck hit a particularly large rock. *"Bang!"* Ma leaned forward and gave Runyon a dirty look. "Don't worry, Ma, the truck can take it," Runyon calmly replied, looking straight ahead and avoiding his mother's expression towards him.

A quarter of a mile later, and after cresting a hill that Ma swore the old truck and trailer wouldn't make it over, the road widened out to a woodlot and piles of tree slash. There was an old skidder ahead with a big hole in the plow where it looked as if a cannonball had blown through it. Just beyond that the road ended.

"This ain't the goddam road to the pond!" Ma yelled. "It's a friggin' old logging road!"

Runyon leaned over the steering wheel and pointed. "Looks like the skidder's seen better days there."

"I don't give a crap about that skidder!" Ma barked. "That dumb asshole gave us the wrong directions!"

They all exited the pickup and Puut climbed to the top of a pile of branches and trees the loggers had left some years ago. He pointed to a body of water he could see looking over the tops of the trees to the east. "Pond's over there! Only about a stone's throw away!"

"Well, that doesn't help us here, does it?!" Ma barked back as she glanced at the clock. "Get back in the truck, we need to find that pond! The fish will all be done with their lunch and napping by the time we get to them!"

The three climbed back into the truck and turned around again. Runyon had to go back and forth a few times to get the boat trailer to come around, and they headed back towards the main road. Traveling was just as bad going back out as it was on the trip in.

When they reached the end of the wrong road, Runyon asked Ma, "Which way, right or left, Ma?"

"Let's keep going left and see if we find another road; the water we've been seeing is still off to our east side. Maybe we shouldn't have counted this road."

Puut chimed in, "It's not that hard to count to two."

"Shut up, Frenchman! No one asked you."

Puut, smirking, couldn't help poking the grumpy bear a little more. "One, two…Uno, dos…Un, deux."

Ma turned to Puut and nearly stuck her stubby pointer finger up his nose.

"You'll speak English when you're riding in my truck! You hear me?!"

Puut's smile got bigger. "Ah deen, dvah."

Ma leaned forward still with her finger in Puut's face and looked over at Runyon. "What the hell was that?!"

"It was Russian, Ma."

She sat back, "Goddam it!"

Runyon continued down the road they'd traveled in on. Every few turns and bends they all thought they could see what they believed to be Number Three through the woods. They came to yet another road to the left. The truck's brakes squeaked loudly. This road looked worse than the two before.

"Think this is it, Ma?"

Ma gazed at the road, tree branches enveloping it and ground vegetation fairly high. "How the hell should I know? I'd like to strangle that old fart right about now! We might as well try it, that pond isn't getting any closer with us sitting here."

Again, the truck bounced up and down the narrow, rut-filled road. Ma nearly gave up putting her hair needle back in place on each bump that loosened her bun. The bench seat in the truck sounded like an old bed spring and Puut's bum was hurting pretty badly but he wasn't one to complain. After a few more minutes, and several more hills later, the truck came to a stop where a white birch tree had fallen into the road. Just beyond the tree, the road itself looked like a tunnel with branches hanging down over it from both sides.

Runyon threw open his door and jumped down out of the truck. "I'll be right back," and he crawled over the downed tree and began to walk through the tunnel.

Ma herself just sat in the truck fixing her hair in the passenger rearview and looking fairly disgusted with the entire situation. Puut took the opportunity to crawl out the driver's side and stretch his back, rubbing his tired bum as his feet hit the ground.

Not a minute later Ma heard Runyon yelling, "Ma, come over here, I see the pond!"

Ma climbed out of the pickup mumbling to herself, "So have I, it's only a stone's throw away. Bullshit!"

Ma crawled over the tree, Puut chuckling as she got her fishing dress caught on a branch on the way over, and she wandered through the tunnel of trees. Just around a bend, there was a field that appeared to have been fairly recently mowed. The road stopped at the edge of the field, and two large boulders had been placed at the end of the road to keep vehicles from driving into the field. On the other side of the field, only a couple hundred feet away, was the edge of a pond.

"Sonofabitch," Ma whispered.

Runyon gazed at the pond. "Can't get the truck through here, Ma. Too far to carry that big old boat and this must be someone's private property."

Ma just stared across the field at the water. Every few seconds she could see ripples where the perch were jumping at the flies that were landing on top of the water. "It's a sign from above, boy. We weren't meant to fish that pond."

The two returned and they all climbed back into the truck. Ma looked at the clock, 10:17 a.m. The morning was fading fast. Runyon performed some fancy backing up until he found a spot where he could turn the trailer around, and they drove back to the main road.

"Where to now, Ma?"

"Let's go back to the general store. Maybe someone there knows the way. We ain't getting anywhere fast."

"That store's closed," Puut reminded her.

Ma put her head in her hands and whined in a muffled voice, "Then find them loggers again, maybe they know something."

They drove back up the road in the direction they'd come from. Just before the turn that would take them to the woods crew, they spotted an old man with a walking stick coming towards them. He looked to be in his seventies, wearing tattered coveralls with suspenders and a dirty white T-shirt. His hair was long and gray, and he had a full beard. Alongside the man was a big, hairy dog that looked about as old as his owner was, and just as gray.

Runyon slowed the truck and pulled up to him. "Excuse me, sir, could you tell me if we're on the right road to the boat landing into Number Three Pond?"

"No sir-ree." Using his walking cane as a guide, he pointed, "You go back to the tar road up here that you're following to the stop sign and turn left. Take another left and the second dirt road to the right that you come to just round a corner will take you to the boat landing."

Ma's eyes rolled and she whispered loudly to herself, "The second road past the store. Marmaduke, you're a moron!"

"Thank you, sir," Runyon replied as the man's companion jumped up on the truck to get some attention. "Best of the day to you. Fine looking dog," as Runyon scratched the hound's long hair.

"Ayah, thank you. C'mon, boy." The two continued on their morning walk, the happy dog's tail wagging in the air as they left.

Runyon drove the three back to the closed-down store. He turned left, and within a quarter mile came to the turn they should have taken initially. Within a mile of that, they were sitting idle at the second dirt road to the right, all looking up at an aging sign tacked on a tree at the mouth of the road that read, "Number Three Pond Boat Landing."

"Why didn't that dumb sonofabitch just say to look for the sign?!" Ma yelled out, pointing at the sign. "It ain't like they just put it here just for us!"

"This isn't the pond we were looking at back a ways, Ma. It can't be, we were looking off to the left, and this here pond is to the right. We must've been looking at another pond over there."

Ma just sat leaning forward and gave Runyon a dirty look. "You ain't as dumb as you were born to be," she remarked quite sarcastically.

Runyon shifted the truck back into gear and started down the road. And sure enough, a short way in they came to the landing at the edge of the pond. Another sign carved into a piece of old, graying wood that was tacked to a post mounted on the water's edge read, "Number Three Pond," with an arrow pointing down into the water. Runyon backed the boat into the pond and the three unloaded it from the trailer.

Puut picked all of the branches out of the boat that was left from the journey to get there, "I hope they're still biting, it's pretty late morning."

They all settled into the boat and Ma primed the fuel tank as Runyon cranked on the throttle a couple of times and turned the key to the electric start. The twenty-horse came to life. All three baited up their fishing poles and they began trolling for perch.

◆ ◆ ◆

Five hours later the three were drifting in the middle of the pond, engine off and plug fishing over the sides of the boat. The bait can was still full of live worms, the fish bucket still empty. They'd also all gone through every lure they'd had between them. None had so much as a nibble all day long.

"Guess they were biting early on, Ma," Runyon observed, swatting at a mosquito on the back of his neck.

Ma just sat hunched over in the boat, looking disgusted, watching her bobber still floating on the water. "Bullshit! There ain't no fish anywhere in this pond! Never was! Just a pond full of weeds, that's all it is!" She growled.

Another hour went by and then they finally gave up. None of the three had caught a fish, any fish. Late afternoon had rolled around, and they knew it was going to be a long ride home. It was nearly 6:00 p.m. when they finished loading the boat back onto the trailer, bungeed it down, and started the journey back home. No one said a word on the ride back, and they didn't get lost going home.

◆ ◆ ◆

Ma stormed into the diner around 8:30 p.m., one-half hour before closing. Old Marmaduke was sitting at the counter bar sipping a cup of coffee, using both hands to hold the cup. In front of him was his dinner plate, all eaten

144

down to the last few French fries. Ma wandered behind the counter in front of him as Marmaduke glanced above his cup and smiled through his beard.

"How was the fishing on Number Three, Ma? Were the perch biting today? I bet you got more than your limit."

Ma put both hands on the counter and forced a smile on her face. "How's the coffee? Nice and hot? Hmmm?"

"Not quite, been working it for half hour now."

"Good, good." Ma reached over and took his cup away from him, it was still half full. She reached up over his head and dumped the remainder of the coffee down onto his noggin. The liquid poured over his snowy white hair and down his face, coming out the bottom of his beard and dripping onto his plate. Marmaduke's smile disappeared as Ma then took a glass of ice water that Constable Bob, who was sitting in the next chair and was reaching for at the time, away from him and dumped that over Marmaduke's head. Next, she took the waterspout from the bar sink, pointed it at the old man, and squirted the water, causing Marmaduke to flinch as it splashed in his face. It all created a puddle in Marmaduke's plate which caused his last few French fries to float as a wide-eyed and bewildered Bob sat and stared at Ma's actions towards the old man.

"Do you see any fish in that puddle in front of you, old man?!" Pointing to his plate, Ma inquired in a quite annoyed tone.

Marmaduke glanced down at his plate. "No," he said softly.

"None in that Goddam pond neither, you old sonofabitch! But at least you can find that dinner plate easy enough, can't you?!" Ma stormed away to the kitchen. As she went by her evening waitress and manager Cicely Smirnoff, she yelled out, "Charge him double for the mess!"

Marmaduke just sat, stunned, never having known why Ma was so angry that evening. He turned his head to Constable Bob, who simply shrugged his shoulders at the old man, and then asked Cicely for another glass of water.

Chapter 15

Full Throttle Troubles

Ma and El own a camp a bit further northwest of town. Now, camps in Maine are a popular getaway if you're lucky enough to have one. They're also a lot of work, whether it be a hunting camp, fishing camp, or a combination of the two. Very few are simply relaxation spots or weekend getaway camps. The truth is, no matter how often you have the ability to escape to camp, there's always work to be done. Whether it be picking up the mess that winter leaves behind, making general age-related repairs, or cleaning up after some dirtbag has broken into your camp, there's continually something that needs attention that takes up your time once you arrive. The Farnsworth-Miller Camp is no different.

Ma and El's camp is located in T-7, R-28 on the edge of Unknown Lake. No, really, it's called Unknown Lake. It's about a forty-five-minute drive away from their homestead and about ten miles from the nearest populated town. The three miles of road into the camp off the main drag are maintained by the logging company that owns the area. They keep the roads up for the camp owners and traditionally will grade the roads in the late spring when the mud season's over and the roads have hardened up a bit in preparation for their logging season.

Traditionally, the roads are impassable in the winter by vehicle, as they aren't plowed by anyone during the snowy months and the logging company shuts down for the season. Traveling by snowmobile is the only way to get in once the season has arrived and the white stuff falls from the sky. It was, at one time, that camp owners couldn't get to their cottages between late

March and early June due to the muddy and soft road conditions. When ice-out finally arrived, you might get there by boat, and once ATVs finally came around, the camps on the lake became accessible year-round, if you owned one of the new-fangled and fancy three-wheeled machines.

There are many camps around Unknown Lake, many of which are owned by Puddleduckians, and it's a popular getaway spot, especially for some good lake-fishing, both in the summer and winter. El and Ma have the best spot on the lake in their own little cove with no other camps until you round the bend on either side. Ma feels fairly comfortable swimming in the mostly shallow water, wearing her polka-dotted one-piece and bathing cap, floating around on her back without fear of being seen by anyone. The lake itself is about three miles long and a good half-mile across, and fairly shallow as far as lakes go with its deepest part being no more than thirty feet.

Ma and El's camp road is easy to locate. Other than the sign sporting their name at the end of the road, there's also one other marker, a five-foot-tall wooden, hand-carved statue of a black bear. It's been standing at the end of their road for many years, and no one knows where it came from or who put it there. One day Ma and El made a trip to camp and there it was. It's now a landmark, and it's not uncommon to find, when they arrive on a camping trip, that someone has put a hat, a scarf, or even a shawl on the bear, and he's usually holding a beer can or liquor bottle as well. It seems that everyone on the lake has taken a liking to the symbol that lets you know that the Farnsworth-Miller camp is just down the road.

The camp itself had once been a hotdog stand that Ma operated long before the diner. In fact, you can say it was the original "Ma's Diner" way back when. When the diner was built properly, they towed the old stand into the woods and El built a loft over it, a kitchen on one side, and a living/dining room on the other, keeping the stand itself as a first-floor sleeping and washing-up area. Once he finished construction, the original food shack remained standing in the middle of the structure and sticks out on both ends, resembling something of a hotdog itself in the center of a big bun. The nickname "hotdog camp" remains to this day. They have a water pump in the washing-up area with a hose extending to the lake, about a hundred yards or so from the front door, and an outhouse within a short walk from the back door. Kerosine lanterns light up the evenings, and the big old grill that the hotdog stand once had was replaced with a smaller gas stove and oven. There's a gas-operated refrigerator that takes hours to cool off once you light the pilot, and in the small living room area is a wood heating stove for the chilly fall and winter nights. The living room itself has three screened windows that face the lake that El staples clear plastic over in the wintertime to keep some of the heat in and cold out. The camp sits close enough to the lake that most of the time no ice shanty is really necessary. Ma and El just stay warm in the camp and watch through the windows with a set of binoculars for the flags to go up.

The aforementioned outhouse is a bit unique, as it doubles as a tool-storage and a tiny workshop area. It has a small workbench and tool rack on one end and a single-seater on the other. In the center is a small pot-belly wood stove that they keep lit late into the evenings on cold nights so when it's time to do your business it isn't quite so uncomfortable. However, the chilly winter wind can still come up through the toilet hole and gives you a good zap! There are no magazines to read while you sit patiently on the seat and wait, just a bit of scribbling on a piece of wood that El tacked near the toilet roll that reads:

> This little potty is all we got,
> We strive to keep it neat.
> So please be kind to those behinds,
> And try not to shit on the seat.

Ma gets a chuckle reading this every time she visits to tinkle or do a number two.

♦ ♦ ♦

Ma and El parked the old Chevy at what they called the junction, the last spot on the main road near the east end of the lake that's still plowed open before starting down the snow-covered camp roads that surround the lake. A fairly large parking area that the plow drivers use as a turn-around is cleared out for the camp owners. There are about twenty-five or so surnames, each hand-painted on little pieces of wood and tacked up all around to let you know just whose camps are ahead on the lake, and a row of mailboxes for the seasonal camp owners that stay all summer long.

When Ma and El arrived, they found that quite a few vehicles were already parked at the junction and Ma found a spot to squeeze in the truck and trailer. They had their weekend supplies all loaded onto a dunnage sled in the bed of the truck and on the trailer were the John Deere and another snowmobile that they own, a 1967 Snow Jet, bright blue in color. Ma likes this sled because of its lightweight and one person can pick it up pretty easily if it gets stuck in the snow. This year they'd taken the Arlberg to camp early in the season and left it behind the outhouse as an emergency sled in the event one of the others broke down during the winter. They'd planned quite a few ice-fishing trips on the calendar this year and wanted to remain prepared for anything.

They unloaded the two machines from the trailer, the John Deere coming off easier than the Snow Jet due to it having the reverse gear. They slid the heavy dunnage sled off the tailgate of the truck onto the empty trailer, then onto the snow-covered ground, and latched it onto the John Deere. Their dunnage sled has a heavy steel frame, welded together by the McIntyre boys, complete with a rear step and handrails on the sled so if need be one person could ride on the rear of the sled with the dunnage packed on the three-foot-by-four-foot wooden bed. The big, green bomber was better at towing a dunnage sled as it has the larger, twin-carb engine, and the Snow Jet, like the Arlberg, only has a single-cylinder Sachs engine. The Snow Jet's lightweight did make it good for breaking a fresh trail if need be.

Ma was dressed in a warm, two-piece snowsuit and insulated mukluk boots. She had on a wool cap and her jacket had a furry-edged hood that she pulled up over her head and tied tight. On her hands were snowmobile mitten-gloves, and in both her gloves and boots she'd put hand warmers that she'd recently picked up at Smirnoff's. El had on flannel pants over his long john one-piece with a green heavy flannel coat up top. He had heavy insulated leather gloves and his tan shitkickers with two pairs of wool socks on his feet.

The weekend supplies consisted of a cooler full of hamburger, hotdogs, buns, chips, bacon and eggs, sausages, and condiments. Ma had also put in two nice steaks for dinner and a handful of potatoes, because you can't always count on catching fish to fry up. They also had milk, orange juice, a case of beer, a half-bottle of scotch whiskey for El, and a bit of the Blackberry brandy and Tab for Ma for the evenings to sip on while playing cards and cribbage. In a suitcase they had extra clothes, although most hand-me-down and hole-ridden clothes ended up at camp anyway instead of tossing them out, so there were plenty of extra britches and warm undergarments at the camp already. They also had a pack basket with ice-fishing traps and gear, a bucket of live shiners and lastly an extra can of fresh 50/1 mix gas for the snow machines. Any other gear they required was already at the camp.

El had no issues starting his machine, the twin-carb turned over easily. Ma jumped on the Snow Jet and straddled the seat. She flipped the choke lever up and squeezed the ball primer a few times to send gas into the carburetor. She gave it a few pulls, to no avail. She then reached into the storage box under the seatback cushion and squirted ether into the carburetor horn, giving her a couple of good squirts. On the next pull the engine backfired and Ma thought the fire shooting from the horn might just light her snowsuit aflame. With the carb good and clean, and with the encouragement from the ether, the little blue snowmobile started on the next pull.

Traveling the last three miles to camp was a bit rough. Whoever had cut the trail through the snow hadn't done a good job, and it was apparent they'd either stopped or had gotten stuck often as the trail had ups and downs like riding a boat on a wavy ocean. It was too late now, as the January snowpack was deep and the trail was frozen in. They needed to snowmobile down the East Shore Road to the turn onto their own camp road that leads into their cove. They'd need to cut their own trail on their camp road; as mentioned before, there were no other camps in their cove, and with this being the first trip of the season, they'd need to start a new trail. Ma took the lead on the Snow Jet and El was right behind her with the John Deere and all their gear.

When they arrived at their camp road, and after several stops to re-adjust the bungee cords on the load and pick up a couple of items that fell off on the rough trails, they stopped and shut the machines down for a moment. Ma glanced at the bear and chuckled as on this trip he was wearing an old trapper's hat that'd seen better days and had an empty Schlitz malt liquor can in its hand. Ma stepped off the Snow Jet to check the depth of the snow that she'd need to plow through on the last quarter mile to the camp. She immediately sunk into the soft snow up to her waist and discovered there were easily three feet already on the ground.

"Get me up out of here!" she called back to El. He dismounted his machine onto the hard-packed trail and waddled to the Snow Jet, sitting on the seat and leaning over to grab Ma's arms and help pull her back to the hard pack.

"It's going be tough breaking a trail in this, Ma."

"I'll just go real fast. You wait for me here. I'll go in, make a circle around the camp, and come back. I'll widen her out on the way back before you try it with the dunnage sled."

"Ayah. Good idea."

Ma hopped back around on her little snow machine as El trudged back to wait on the Deere. Ma took off down the camp road and was quickly out of sight. She stayed on top of the snow fairly well until the first hard turn several hundred yards in. She leaned into the turn; however, the machine kept on mostly straight and Ma drove off the road into the puckerbrush, and the machine became stuck in a deep snow drift. "Dammit!" she yelled out loud, which nearly caused snow to drop off nearby branches as her voice echoed off the trees.

Ma stepped off behind her machine onto the trail she'd just created. The soft-packed trail held her for about two seconds, and then she sunk to her knees again. She attempted to pull the machine backward, and even though it was light enough, she didn't have leverage with her body knee-deep in the snowpack. Huffing and puffing from several attempts, she gave up and began the trek back out to the end of the camp road.

El spotted Ma trudging back up the road; she was sinking to her knees on every step on her new trail and was swearing loudly. When she was in earshot, El yelled out, "Did ya get stuck, Ma?"

"Stupid question!" she barked back. "Unhook that damn dunnage sled! I'm taking the Deere to camp!"

El did what he was told and Ma jumped on the John Deere and started back in, leaving El and the gear behind. The heavier machine took the turns better and Ma kept her at a good speed to keep the machine moving high on the snow. She made two trips in and back out and packed down a good trail. She and El then took the gear into camp, with El driving the machine and Ma riding, standing on the back of the dunnage sled. As soon as they arrived, El unlatched the sled and made a dozen or so circles around the camp and down to the lake's edge to create a nice, hard trail to walk on while Ma shoveled off the front steps and a path to the outhouse, using a hand snow shovel that was kept inside. They both unloaded the gear and Ma got the pilots lit on the cook stove and fridge after El turned on the propane gas at the tank outside the camp. Later, they'd retrieve the Snow Jet after getting the fire good and warm in the wood stove and after putting the food and gear away, and after allowing their new trails to harden up a bit in the cold winter air.

That evening the two enjoyed a nice dinner and played cards. They stayed nice and toasty between the wood stove and sipping on their toddies. They retired for bed around 9:00 p.m. and after El had made certain there was a nice bed of coals and fresh wood on the fire before he closed the vents up tight in an effort to keep it going through the night, knowing good and well that both he and Ma would have the urge to tinkle at least once during the night. And, the camp rule is, if you get up to go pee, you put fresh wood on the fires regardless. He also checked the pot belly stove in the outhouse and made certain that too was good and warm before going to bed.

And just so you know, there's another and even more strict, second rule at the Farnsworth-Miller camp. If you get up during the night to go pee, no slacking. You're required to go all the way to the outhouse. No leaving yellow stains in the snow just outside of the camp!

Ma and El both felt the urge to pee twice during the night, at different times, of course, and checked the fires each time.

The following morning it was nice and clear out, and the temperature was just about eighteen degrees. Ma had gotten up good and early and had cut ten holes in the ice before El was even dressed. She'd cut two rows of five straight out from the shoreline, each about fifteen feet apart from one another. They each cleaned the holes and set their traps. Ma put down her five underwater traps and El put out his five tip-ups, complete with the pine boughs on each line. Once completed, they returned to camp to wait for the first flag.

Ma cooked up a nice breakfast on the gas stove and made percolated coffee on the wood stove. They were enjoying the warmth inside the camp in front of the plastic, picture windows when Ma, using the binoculars, spotted the first flag. "You got one, El. Looks like the fourth one straight out."

"Ayah. Why don't you go check it?" El never looked up from his breakfast plate as he spoke.

Ma, lowering the glasses and staring at El remarked sarcastically, "Why don't you take your lazy ass out there and check it yourself?"

"Because you know good and well that you want to. First fish and all."

Ma opened her mouth to argue with El, then realized he was right and she really did want to check it herself. She grunted as she got up from the table, hoisted the top half of her snowsuit back up and over her shoulders, and zipped up the front. She stepped outside and decided that she'd better take the John Deere. Not that the walk was far but it did have the sled still attached with the auger, bait, and other gear on it just in case she needed any of it. She stood to the side of the Deere where the starter cord was, turned the key, and choked the carbs. She held the throttle with one hand and gave the starter cord a good hard tug with the other. The machine started immediately, and as some older model snowmobiles sometimes do, the throttle stuck wide open and the machine bolted forward without Ma on it, straight towards the lake where it had been pointed.

"Elmer! Get out here! The snow machine has escaped!" Ma yelled out and watched as the machine picked up speed as it neared the edge of the frozen lake.

El flew open the camp door as he wiggled into his coat. He looked out just in time to see the machine take off onto the ice. "Ma! Your machine's driving itself!"

Ma yelled back as she began to waddle quickly towards the lake in her snowsuit. "It took off without me!" Ma saw the direction the speeding machine was taking. "No, not the traps!" Just as she cried out, the big machine ran over the first ice trap in her line and then turned just a bit to the right. For a moment Ma thought the rest of her traps would be saved until the machine's front skis struck an ice chunk which turned the skis back to the left again, throwing the bait, the auger, and other equipment off the sled and onto the ice. The snowmobile then plowed over the remaining four traps in her line. "Awwwe, shit!" The snowmobile made a line straight out into the middle of the frozen lake, picking up speed on the snow-covered ice the farther out it traveled. Ma's snow pants sounded like fabric tearing as the legs rubbed against each other with every quick waddling step she took chasing after her John Deere.

El hopped onto the Snow Jet and took off after Ma. When he got to the lake's edge, he stopped and saw Ma chugging out after the green machine, which now was quite far out ahead of her and starting to bear left. He watched as the snow machine, just before reaching the outer edge of the cove, made a forty-five-degree turn and drove itself up into the woods. "Thank goodness," El said out loud and he continued onto the ice. By the time he got to Ma, she was halfway out of the cove, huffing and puffing, and barely at a crawl on the frozen lake.

"I'm going to have a heart attack chasing after that damn machine," she said as she collapsed on the back of the Snow Jet.

"Good thing the Deere took a turn. If not, she'd have gotten out of the cove and would've gone for three miles or better. What happened, Ma?"

"Goddam throttle stuck open," Ma puffed. Her hood was down, as well as her hair, and her hairpin was somewhere behind her stuck in the ice.

The two rode the Snow Jet out to where the John Deere had stopped just into the woods off the edge of the lake, just before the outer edge of the cove. It had struck a pine tree and the engine was revving high in an attempt to keep going. The front end was damaged fairly badly and the cowling cracked into two separate pieces. Ma jumped off the Snow Jet and waddled over to the broken equipment, pushing the kill switch to stop the whining engine.

She looked the machine over, still breathing heavily from the unintended workout she'd just endured, "Throttle cable's melted, she's done. Sled looks all right, though, except for the front end. Dunnage sled's fine far as I can tell, tow bar's a bit bent."

The two spent the morning towing the wreckage back to the camp and picking up the mess it had left behind when it wiped out Ma's traps and threw the gear off the dunnage sled. Ma chipped dead shiners out of the ice and found several still alive in the bucket. She salvaged what she could of her traps. The only saving grace for the morning came when Ma did find a fish on the line of El's trap where the original flag had gone up earlier before the snowmobile incident. It was a nice, fat white perch.

El spent some time in the outhouse work shed where they kept extra traps and set Ma up with five more while Ma brushed the snow off the old Arlberg and removed the tarps that were covering it. She siphoned out the old gas, using a long, thin plastic tube they kept in the shed. She put one end into the machine's gas tank and sucked inward on the other to start the flow. The taste of old gas and oil didn't bother Ma as she got some in her mouth and spit it back out before the flow was steady in the tube and emptying out onto the snow. She replaced the old gas with the new mixture they'd brought with them and eventually revved up the old black-and-red machine with some assistance from the can of either and a fresh spark plug. The aging Sach's engine sounded like a low-flying aircraft coming out from around the crapper. The vintage machine didn't have any speed and not much power to her but she was reliable.

By the time all this was said and done, they were both spent and decided to call it a day and start fresh in the morning. They retired to the camp and had another nice, hot dinner and laughed a bit over the day's events as they ate. They laughed a little more after the evening toddies while playing a few games of cribbage.

◆ ◆ ◆

The next morning brought overcast skies, a light snowfall, and a bit lower temperature than the day before. Once again Ma was up early, eager for another try. She'd put the dunnage sled on the Arlberg and was on the ice just before dawn re-cutting the holes that had crusted over during the night. Ma noticed that her bones were a bit achy this morning, especially in her legs.

El wandered out and helped set the traps with the few live shiners they'd managed to salvage the day before, and the remainder with dead ones. Once again, they returned to the camp for a hearty breakfast after all ten traps were in.

After breakfast, Ma decided to walk down to the lake to check the lines, and El told her he'd be along shortly. When she got to the lake's edge, she didn't immediately see any flags, so Ma found a spot to sit. Just off to the side of the cove and under a big pine tree there's a large rock with a flat spot on it that's perfectly shaped for Ma's butt, and she uses it for this purpose quite often. Ma sat down on the cold rock and looked out over the frozen lake, enjoying the brisk morning air. She spotted someone fishing on the point off the end of the cove that she thought might be the McIntyre boys, as they had a favorite spot they often visited to do some day fishing. There's a sandbar off the south point that extends to a small island, ironically named Big Island, right in front of Ma's cove where the salmon like to hang out. She squinted and looked through the light falling snow and spotted two snow machines just off the point that she recognized with one being the yellow-and-orange '73 Ski Doo Bombardier, which confirmed for her that Joshua and Wally were out there for the day.

It wasn't long before Ma heard the loud banging of the camp screen door slamming shut and knew El was on his way out onto the ice to join her. She listened as she heard the familiar sound of the Snow Jet cord being tugged on as El attempted to get it started. Ma heard the engine roar, loudly, and then went silent. "Flooded her out, didn't you?" she said to herself. Ma listened for a few more moments and didn't hear the machine start again. It was about five minutes of more silence when Ma figured she needed to walk back up and start the snowmobile for him.

Grumpy, she walked out from her cozy spot on the rock and looked up at the camp. Neither El nor the snowmobile was in sight. "Where the hell did you go?" Ma said under her visible breath as she trudged back up towards the camp. As she walked to the spot where the Snow Jet had been parked, she saw new machine tracks leading behind the camp. She rounded the corner behind the camp and found El sitting on the back end of the snowmobile. The front end of the machine was off the ground and up the trunk of a white birch tree. As she got closer, she saw El's face and noticed that his nose wasn't where it had been the last time she'd seen him; it was now quite crooked and mostly under his left eye. El looked up at Ma and cracked a painful smile. He was also missing his two front teeth.

"What happened?!" Ma blurted out. "You look terrible!"

"Feel that way too, Ma. Damndest thing, I started the machine and the throttle on this one stuck open too. I tried to ride her out and stop it. Didn't go so well, we both ended up this here tree and whacked my face on those steel handlebars pretty hard."

"El, you've broken your nose bad! It ain't where it's supposed to be! We need to get you to a hospital so they can put it back where it belongs!"

"Ayah. Probably a good idea." El sounded quite nasal as he spoke.

"We must be cursed!" Ma's superstitious side kicked in. "Two throttles sticking in two days!" Ma looked at El's nose; it appeared to resemble a 'Z' in shape. "Jeesus, El, we need to go now."

"Okay, need to get the gear out of the ice first. Don't want the game warden coming by and get us for unattended traps." El began to stand up.

Ma knew El was being serious; he wasn't about to leave the camp with traps in the ice. As she helped him to his feet, she noticed he was quite wobbly. "I'll get the traps, you go inside and clean yourself up. That nose is going to start gushing when your blood starts flowing again out of this cold air."

El was a tough old bird and Ma knew he wasn't about to complain about the tremendous pain he had to be in. She helped him to the door of the camp and sent him inside to wrap a towel around his face while she ran down and quickly scooped the ten traps out of the water. One had a nice perch on it. "Freebie!" she yelled out as she tossed it out onto the ice for the eagles to snatch up.

When Ma got back to the cabin, she found El in the washroom area. He'd cleaned himself up a bit, his eyes now both turning black. His nose had bled, and by the looks pretty badly with stains on his green, wool jacket. She also discovered that he'd wrapped a towel around his chin and tied it to the top of his head. The tied ends of the towel resembling to long, floppy rabbit ears.

"You idiot! You put the towel around your head the wrong way! How's that supposed to keep your nose from squirting everywhere?"

"I had to, it hurt when I tied it the other way around it."

Ma took a closer look at El's face, getting in close and squinting to see the damage. El's nose was cocked off sideways and appeared to be broken in at least two places, along with his missing front teeth, and now his black eyes that were swelling shut.

"Did a number on yourself, didn't you? Looks like you went twelve rounds with George Foreman."

"Did I win?" El attempted humor with his now toothless smile.

"No, you didn't. Did you do anything else while I was taking care of the traps?"

"I cleaned up the mess I made in the sink the best I could. Then I stoked the fire, put in some wood, closed the vents, pulled the curtains over the windows, and checked the back door to make sure she was locked."

Ma stared at him blankly. "Well, shit, why didn't you fix the leak in the roof while you were at it?" Speaking sarcastically, "I meant did you do something for your nose, you fool! Did you take anything for the pain?"

"A few shots of my whiskey."

"Okay, that should do you." Ma knew that El wasn't much of a whiskey drinker, normally sipping on just one throughout the evening, so she figured a few shots would probably knock him out before they reached the truck. "We need to get going and have the doctor put your nose back where it belongs. Traps are all out of the ice, let's go."

"Okay, Ma. You hop on one sled and I'll take the other," El said with all seriousness.

Ma replied back, again a bit sarcastically, "Well, there's two problems with that idea, Einstein. First, you drove your snow machine up a tree and that's where it still sits. Two, you can't see out your swollen eyes past your broken nose! How do you think you're going to drive a snow machine?! I'm going to put you in the dunnage sled and tow you to the truck. We'll need to go across the lake; I don't think you could take the three miles on the up and down trail. You just hold onto the sled with one hand and to your nose with the other."

"Ayah, okay, Ma."

Ma knew the ride to the truck wasn't going to be comfortable for El, so she took a few of the camp's couch cushions and put them in the sled for El to park his butt on for the hard ride across the lake in the steel and wooden sled. She figured his face was hurting bad enough, his rear end didn't need to ache as well. She also gave him the remainder of the whiskey bottle to sip on in case he needed a little more pain medication. They both bundled up in extra warm clothing, and Ma handed El an extra towel for his face. El sat in the dunnage sled and they took off slowly across the lake towards the truck.

♦ ♦ ♦

157

Wally and Joshua were busy tending their traps, having just pulled a nice, fourteen-inch salmon out of the ice. Wally was re-baiting his hook with a smelt and Joshua was holding up their catch and admiring it. They both looked up when they heard the loud snowmobile in the distance. It was snowing a bit harder now and they strained to see the snowmobile and sled coming towards them out of the cove.

"Sounds like the old Arlberg. Looks like Ma and El are heading this way to see how the fishing is," Joshua said, squinting his eyes a bit more. "Looks like someone might be getting a ride in the dunnage sled."

Wally finished baiting the hook and was resetting the trap. "Ma's probably driving around her traps to scare up some fish. You know how superstitious she is about things. She still thinks the sound of a snow machine on the ice will bring the fish around."

"No, she's definitely heading this way," Joshua remarked, holding his gloved hand over his eyes as if to block the sunlight that wasn't there.

As the Arlberg drove closer, it became clear to the boys that Ma was driving and El was riding in the sled. The boys started walking to their shanty to meet the two where they figured Ma would pull up, and where they had some hot coffee percolating on the propane stove. When the snowmobile was close enough to make out the details, the boys spotted El, sitting in the dunnage sled with his head wrapped in a towel the wrong way and the damage to his face. When Ma slowed the snow machine down as she neared, El opened his blackened eyes, waved one hand to the boys, and took a sip of whiskey from the bottle in his other hand.

"Jeesus kee-rist!" Wally said to his brother while pointing at El and grabbing Joshua's shoulder. "Look at that! Look at his face! Ma's finally whooped the tar out of old El!" Joshua's eyes grew wide as Wally continued, "And she's toting him around on the ice to show off what she's done! Lord, have mercy! He's got blood all over his jacket. She's beaten the piss out of him and she's proud of it!" Wally took a step behind his brother as if attempting to hide. "What are we going to do, Joshua? What if she decides she don't want no witnesses?!" Joshua gave his brother a dirty look in response. He knew better.

As Ma pulled up beside the boys on the ice and turned the engine off, El smiled a toothless grin to the boys and yelled out, "Happy New Year!" waving the nearly empty bottle high up in the air.

Ma turned to El and gave him dirty look, then she turned back to the boys. "Whiskey's kicking in!"

"Did whiskey do that to El's face?!" Wally blurted out.

"No, you idiot! Driving a snowmobile up a tree did that to his face!" Ma barked.

"Why'd he go and do that, Ma?" Joshua inquired. "You didn't let him get all drunk and drive a snow sled around, did you?"

"No, you moron! He just started drinking a few minutes ago. He drove the machine up the tree earlier because he thought he saw a flying fish! Don't be as dumb as your brother! His damn throttle stuck open when he started the Snow Jet this morning! We've lost two machines so far this weekend!" Ma said in a disgusted voice, then remembered why, in fact, she'd driven out here. "You got your truck out here on the ice? I need to get El to the doctor to fix his nose! It'll take me all day to get him back across the lake to our truck on this sled."

"Yeah, Ma, it's parked right around the corner on the lake's edge. We can get him to the hospital in Saint Sanctuary in no time." The brothers jumped onto the back of the dunnage sled and Ma drove the three to Joshua's pickup truck. Joshua and Wally helped El up off the sled and into the front seat, and Joshua started the truck to get the heater warming up.

Ma turned to Wally, and before she could say anything, he put his hand up and spoke, "Yeah, Ma. I know. You want me to get the snowmobile out of the tree."

"If you would. And there's probably a mess in the camp, too."

"Go ahead, hop in and see that El gets to the hospital. I'll take care of it."

Ma gave Wally a big hug, probably the only one he'd ever get from her, and then she piled into the truck. She knew Wally would take care of the camp for her. She also knew when this was all said and done, she'd owe the boys a hot meal at the diner, or possibly two.

The three headed out across the frozen lake. Joshua didn't stop at the junction; he drove them both straight through to the hospital. El, in his whiskey-driven state, kept yelling out "Happy New Year" to everyone they passed along the way and sang, "Auld Lang Syne," the entire hour's drive to the emergency room, sounding quite nasally and inadvertently whistling from time to time through his missing teeth.

Once they arrived at the hospital the doctor put El's nose back in place and also had to use three screws to re-align his cheekbone that he'd busted up. Joshua didn't leave the emergency room until he knew El was going to be okay and that Ma was going to be with him in his room. Ma gave Joshua a big hug too before he left the hospital to drive back to the lake well into the night to pick up his brother.

When Joshua arrived back at the camp, he'd found that his brother had taken care of the busted snow machine and cleaned up the place all nice. They remained the night as the snow that had begun earlier was now an all-out storm. The following morning, the two brothers made certain the camp and outhouse were secure and even loaded the two broken snow machines into the back of the truck before heading out to get home and check on El.

El ended up staying in the hospital the remainder of the weekend and, to this day, El can't walk through an airport metal detector without setting it off. That is if he ever had a reason to go through an airport metal detector. Which he hasn't.

◆ ◆ ◆

Wally and Josh ended up repairing the snow machines, using parts from others they had lying around or scrounged up. They also received a few free meals at the diner for their troubles.

And you can be certain that nothing from that weekend's events ever deterred Ma and El from future ice-fishing trips at the camp. It was just another chapter in their book to reminisce about over a sip of whiskey and a brandy and cola on cold winter nights at the lake.

The actual "Hotdog Stand" camp.

The trailer can be seen, which ran the length of the interior of the camp and stuck out on both ends. The front, pictured above, shows the three windows that faced the lake, and the loft over the top and the kitchen (below far right) were on the back side.

The '74 John Deere and Steel Dunnage Sled. Behind it,
the work shed outhouse.

The 1970 Arlberg

The '67 Snow Jet and the Arlberg.

The Bear that Stood at the End of the Road.

Chapter 16

Town Meeting

In July of every year, East Puddleduck holds its annual town meeting. The purpose of any town meeting is to allow public input on municipal-related matters such as the budget and taxes. It's a forum for public discussion, or more so complaining, about things in town that need attention and where the money will generally come from.

And then there's East Puddleduck's annual meeting.

Mayor Wiggleswort gaveled down the crowd. As usual, on the town council board seated at the folding tables were himself, Selectperson Daley to his left, Doody to his right, and Constable Bob Johnson seated in a metal chair on the end next to Daley. In the audience were the McIntyre brothers, Puut Voisine, Smirnoff, Mattie Doody, Old Marmaduke, the mayor's wife Eleanor, and Reverend Winkin. And Ma and El, of course.

After the bean-hole-bean supper that Ma had made for everyone, set up buffet style off to the side of the meeting room with fresh hot rolls and a strawberry shortcake for dessert, and around seven in the evening, Wiggleswort called the meeting officially in session.

"I'd like to thank everyone for coming." The mayor glanced around the room. "Seems like more people this year than last. First order of business," he said as he put on his spectacles and glanced at his hand-written agenda, "is how much are we're going to pay the McIntyres to plow and sand the roads this coming winter. Last year it was twenty-five a storm, thirty for a nor'easter."

Joshua spoke up from the audience, "We need some new tires on the one-ton this year, and the front-end loader is up to the gravel pit with a dead battery. Can we go thirty and thirty-five?"

Ma glanced over at Joshua and scowled. "Are you trying to cause my taxes to go up?!"

Joshua pleaded with her, "No, Ma. It's just that every year things get more expensive."

A recommendation came from Councilperson Daley to the mayor, "I move that we give them twenty-seven a storm and thirty-three for a nor'easter."

"Any discussion? Any opposition?" The mayor purposely looked toward Ma. "Hearing none, all in favor?" All hands in the room went up. Ma's too, a bit reluctantly. "It's decided," the mayor declared as he struck the gavel to the little piece of wood he'd cut for just this purpose, as striking a folding table really didn't have the same effect and made the tabletop vibrate.

Joshua stood up, took his baseball cap off, and thanked everyone while Wally tried to do the math in his head, looking a bit puzzled.

The mayor checked his notes and continued, "Next is a suggestion to put a new sign at the edge of town. The old one's been there for quite a few years and faded a bit, and the posts are starting to show signs of age." Again, he glanced toward Ma, knowing there would be discussion on this item, primarily from her.

"Ma will just scribble on the new one if we do! The old crow will just put her little welcome to out-of-staters on it before the paint dries," Mattie declared. Ma cracked a grin and chuckled to herself.

"It's true," the reverend spoke up. "What happens when she ruins a new sign this time, Mister Mayor?"

Everyone looked at the board of selectpersons. This was one of those many occasions that the board had the deer in the headlights look on all their faces, it occurred every time they were required to make a decision. Daley finally broke their uncomfortable silence and moved to table this item for another year. The vote was reluctantly unanimous.

"Let's pick it up, Wiggleswort! The meeting's already gone on two minutes longer than last year!" Ma pointed out, as she was the official minute taker and secretary to the annual meeting. Her job was to take notes on what everyone was saying and keep track of the time. Smirnoff, who was seated directly behind her, leaned forward and glanced at her notes. There were no words on the paper but there was a nice little drawing of a moose with an arrow through its head. Smirnoff cracked a smile and leaned back.

"We're getting a lot of complaints about that pothole on the main road right near the town line, Mayor," Bob Johnson had spoken up. "Same complaints as last year."

The mayor turned to Bob and asked quite sarcastically, "And might I dare to guess? Are you the one doing the complaining, there, Constable?"

"Yessir." Bob looked like a puppy dog, bowing his head. "I keep hitting the hole with the cruiser. It's ruined nearly half a dozen hubs over the past year."

"That hole isn't even in the travel lane. In fact, you have to try hard to hit it! Not only that, it's on the other side of the town line. We called the mayor of Skunksmell last year and they promised to fill it back then." Wiggleswort shook his head, "I guess we need to call him again."

"You mean to tell me we can't just go out and put a handful of dirt in that hole ourselves?!" Ma yelled out, "Why have we got to pay for a phone call that won't amount to getting anything done?"

"It's not our responsibility, Ma. That section of road isn't in our town. Let them pay to fix it," the mayor whined. "I'll give Mayor LaFluer, LaFlower…whatever his name is a call and let him know that we got our second complaint in two years and they need to do something about it." The mayor gaveled and continued, "Next is the appointment of officers. Daley and Doody have served on the board of this here council for going on fourteen years and I recommend that they be appointed again for the upcoming year. Any discussion?" Again, the mayor looking out at Ma specifically.

The reverend spoke up over his driving glasses, "Maybe someone else ought to try it for a year. No offense intended, boys." Daley and Doody appeared confused, not entirely understanding what the definition of "offense" was.

Ma's sarcastic voice chimed in, looking over at the preacher while waving an arm towards the three seated at the head table, "What difference does it make, Bubblehead? Outside of special meetings and the once-a-month that nobody shows up to, we only all get together on this night once every year, and the decisions are mostly made by their better halves anyway for Chrissake!"

"No cursing during town meeting, please," Marmaduke spoke up from the back row.

Ma wiggled around in her seat to glare at Marmaduke. "Shut up and pipe down, you old fart! That wasn't swearing. Real swearing is them other two words!" Ma pointed at him and shook her chubby finger, causing Smirnoff to lean back in his seat to avoid Ma poking him. "And don't aggravate me anymore and make me say them!"

Marmaduke just smiled, tipped his head to her, and blew her an air kiss. Disgusted, Ma turned back around and faced front to find that the mayor was grinning. This was the first time since he could remember that there was ever a debate on any agenda item at a town meeting. This was exciting to him.

"Who else would want to do it anyway?" El asked the crowd in general.

Ma turned to him and spoke up, looking confidently at Elmer. "Maybe I'll give it a try."

Mattie broke out in arrogant laughter, "Hah! Just because your dumb drunk grandaddy, who couldn't tell a duck from a loon, founded this town doesn't begin to mean that you have what it takes to try and help run it."

"She runs it anyway now," Wally leaned to his brother and said under his breath. Joshua cracked a big smile and nodded.

The reverend, with his head still tilted back, again looked down through his driving glasses on the bridge of his nose and up at the mayor and responded arrogantly, "I think this calls for a decision from the person in charge. Mayor? Penny for your thoughts on the matter?"

The mayor snapped back from whatever he was busy daydreaming about. "Who? Me?"

"Oh, yeah, good idea, Bubblehead. Do you really think Wiggleswort can make a decision about something like this? He can't even put a necktie on straight," Ma pointed out.

The mayor frowned as he glanced down at his necktie and then looked out at his wife, Eleanor, who had actually tied it for him earlier in preparation for the meeting.

"I move to nominate Jacob Daley as a board member to the mayor," Jacob Daley himself proudly announced.

"You can't nominate yourself, moron!" Ma barked. "Someone else has to do it."

"Do I hear any nominations for Jacob Daley?" The mayor asked the tiny crowd. All was silent except for Ma grunting in a sarcastic fashion. "Well, I suppose I can nominate him again and put the vote to the room and see how this goes a second time," the mayor stated nervously and looked straight at Ma again. He then changed his tone, "I shouldn't have to do this! Charter says I can appoint my own board!"

"There's fourteen people in the room, Wiggleswort! And that includes you, plus Dumb and Dumber to either side of you and Tiny Tim on the end! If the board can't vote, that leaves eleven! Eleven residents that can make a decision! Which, by the way, is eleven more people than what showed up for your election!" Ma replied, "So, screw the goddam Charter!"

"Watch the cursing," Marmaduke spoke out, again in his monotone voice.

Ma stood up, turned around, and pointed toward him. "You say that one more time, you old fart, and I'll come back there and sit on you!"

Old Marmaduke gave Ma another wink and blew her another air kiss.

The mayor interjected, "Well then, all in favor of keeping Daley and Doody on as board members, please raise up your hands."

All hands in the room went up, even Ma's as she sat back down and turned back to the council. She saw Daley and Doody's hands in the air.

"You can't vote for yourselves, you idiots!" Ma's voice rang out. Both men, with confused looks on their faces, lowered their hands back down slowly.

"Motion passes!" The mayor banged the gavel. "Any other business?"

"I move that Ma start serving alcohol in the diner." It was Smirnoff's voice.

Ma immediately pointed a finger at the mayor, who looked surprised seeing that he hadn't even made the motion. "I don't serve alcohol! Never have, never will! People in this town are stupid enough without me adding to it all with booze!" She wiggled her bottom around to face Smirnoff. "You just want to up your business by selling me liquor! Probably want me to buy some homemade Russian vodka that you fermented in your own basement, don't you?! Well, forget it!" Ma swung back around with remarkable agility and pointed back at the mayor. "And don't think you can force me into it, neither!"

The mayor, with a bit of fear on his face, spoke up, "It wasn't my idea, Ma. Just calm down."

Wally McIntyre spoke, "What do you have against a cocktail with dinner, Ma? Or a beer?"

Ma frowned and looked over at the brothers. "Nothing!" Her expression softened a bit and she spoke more quietly, "I'm all for a nightcap. My personal preference is the berry brandy and a Tab cola. Or a bit of the whiskey if I feel a cold coming on or to warm me up on a frigid winter's night." Her expression turned to a frown again and her voice raised back up, "But not in my diner! It ain't no sports bar where everyone thinks they can drink themselves silly! Next thing you know you'll all want Ruby dancing on the bar and flashing her big plastic knockers when she's working Saturday nights!"

There were smirks and giggling from the men in the room when Ma painted the vision for them. Even the reverend had a quick thought that would cause him the need to go to confession.

The mayor shook his head like a cat to bring his thoughts back to reality. "All right, enough of that. Is there any more other business to attend to?"

"I'd like to personally thank Ma for the supper tonight." Bob nodded his head at Ma. "Best beans ever, as usual."

Everyone in the room nodded in agreement and Ma cracked a little smile. "You'd eat the back end out of a cow if it was cooked right and not complain, Johnson."

Bob smiled back, he knew this was Ma's "thank you" to him. The constable then leaned a little to the left, winced, and let one go, "Oh boy, they've got a good after effect too."

"Jeesus, Constable! Couldn't you hold it for a few more minutes?!" The mayor held his hand to his nose and gave the lawman a foul look.

"Well, that was unnecessary," Mattie commented, crinkling her nose and holding a handkerchief up to it. The aftershock of the constable's wind-breaking was now wafting throughout the hall. Everyone was wincing and fanning the air with their hands.

The mayor, now cupping his hands over his nose and mouth, said, "I need a motion to adjourn so we can all get out of here and into fresh air!"

"So moved!" Yelled El, "Someone open the doors and windows!"

Everyone was already up out of their seats by the time Wiggleswort was done bringing the gavel down for the final time at this year's annual meeting. Marmaduke was the last to stroll out of the hall and stopped at the doors with his hands in his coverall pockets. "Ayah," Marmaduke mumbled to himself, "same way last year's meeting ended."

Chapter 17

Ma Breaks a Record

The townsfolk believed it was Runyon who made the long-distance telephone call. It was right after Ma had pulled back into the diner that fine day in late August. It was about midday and Ma was returning from picking up supplies at Smirnoff's. She wheeled into the diner just as Runyon was coming out of the kitchen door for a bit of air. He'd been puttering with the plumbing on the dishwasher, having been a bit clogged and in need of attention. Runyon glanced at the old Chevy as Ma pulled into the yard and dismounted.

"That a new dent, Ma?" Runyon pointed at the driver's side, his attention to detail was spot on.

"Yup, another deer on the main road. Someday I'm going to start serving up roadkill."

"First you'd have to hit one hard enough to kill it," Runyon stated.

The truth to the story was that the old Chevy was riddled with dents and dings caused by animals in the roadway. The odd thing was, none of the animals had ever been seriously hurt or died from Ma bumping into them. And there were many; the old truck seemed to be a target for critters, and not a spot on it other than the roof had managed to avoid them.

"How many does that make, Ma?"

"Too many to count without taking my shoes off," she grumbled as she tugged on the tailgate to get it to drop down so she could unload her bounty of supplies. It too had its number of dents and dings. Finally, Runyon had to wander over and help her tug on the tailgate to get it to release.

"Goddam animals need to stay out of my way! They're going to ruin the truck!"

Runyon glanced at the many dents and scratches on the old pickup. So many, he thought, that you couldn't recognize what model Chevy it was anymore between the animal damage and rust. "I think they already have, Ma," he remarked casually.

◆ ◆ ◆

It was about three weeks later that Ma arrived at the diner, again mid-day. She and El wheeled in fairly fast, and Ma abruptly hit the brakes just before hitting the side of the diner, stirring up a cloud of dirt dust in the dry air. The two bounced in the cab as she brought the pickup to an abrupt halt in her parking space.

Ma jumped out and dusted herself off. El slid out of his side as Ma rounded the front and stopped to bend over and pick feathers out of the front driver's side fender and grill. "Friggin' turkeys! Why'd that big, stupid gobbler feel the need to cross the road just then?!"

"Don't know, Ma," El said as he bent down to look at the damage as well. "Maybe you should've asked him as he was flying away."

"Excuse me, ma'am." A voice from behind Ma startled her.

"Jeesus!" Ma exclaimed as she sprang back up and swung around. She found herself face to face with a gentleman about her height that appeared to be in his early fifties wearing a clean, blue suit and tie and shiny, clean shoes. He had slightly graying hair, receding but neatly trimmed. He was obviously a foreigner, having arrived in what appeared to be a rented sedan with Texas license plates. Ma gave him a quick once over before speaking, squinting, and crinkling her nose as she looked him up and down. "Not from around here, are you? Didn't you see the sign at the edge of town?!"

"Yes, I did." The man spoke with a friendly but slightly pompous air about him. His accent was not quite American and sounded as if he had a bit of English in him. "I was quite amused by it." He continued, "Allow me to introduce myself, my good lady. My name is Frederick Palin. I'm with Guinness…"

Ma cut him off, "Oh, salesman, huh? Well, you're wasting your time here, we don't serve alcohol in the diner. You can be on your way."

"No, my dear. You don't understand…"

Ma stuck her chunky finger in the man's face. "No, you don't understand. Let me speak slower. We…don't…serve…alcohol!"

"Let me start over." A pompous smile crossed the gentleman's lips. "I'm with the Guinness Book of World Records."

"Worldly records? You got some Charlie Daniels in your car?" El turned to Ma. "He's selling records, Ma, maybe he has some Zac Brown."

Ma perked up and she excitedly asked the worldly foreigner, "Does Zac Brown have a new album out?"

"No, no, no. World records. You must have heard of us, world records. World's tallest man. World's shortest woman. World's largest..."

"Largest what?!" Ma barked and cut his sentence short. "You be careful what you say next! If someone called you claiming that I'm the world's largest woman, you're in for trouble!" Ma turned to El. "I bet it was that busy-body, Matilda Doody! Her and I are going to have words later!"

The gentleman placed his hands on Ma's shoulder. Ma's eyes grew wide. "No, my dear lady, it has nothing to do with how overweight you are. I was called because of your pickup truck."

"My what? My pickup truck?"

"It's not for sale, mister," El responded.

"No, no. I don't wish to purchase it. We heard that your pickup truck, along with the unfortunate fact that it has been struck by so many animals, just might qualify you for a place in our annual publication!" the man said gleefully.

Ma's expression turned to disbelief. "You mean to tell me that just because a bunch of dumb animals decided to bounce off my bumper, you're going to put me in your book? That's worth mentioning in your publication? That's a category?" Ma broke out in jolly laughter. El was smiling as well, something he rarely did.

Mr. Palin interrupted, "Well, not currently. However, we're always seeking new ideas. We've also been told that none of the animals have suffered serious injury or died as a result."

Ma was still laughing and caught her breath. "Well, that's true. They've all gotten back up and gone about their business afterward and we just drive away."

"Just how many times have the creatures struck your truck?" Mr. Palin inquired as he removed his hand from Ma's shoulder and looked over the truck.

"Well, let's see," Ma began to walk around the truck and count the number of dents. Mr. Palin and El followed right behind with Mr. Palin looking hard at each dent through the reading glasses he was holding onto and adjusting as Ma pointed them all out, one by one. When she rounded the fourth side of the truck, "...Thirty-eight, thirty-nine..." Ma looked it over hard and found one more dent. "Forty!"

"Extraordinary!" Mr. Palin exclaimed, jumping Ma and El a bit. "And these are all caused by animals jumping out at your vehicle? How is that possible?"

"I dunno, never asked them. They all get up and scatter after doing it. The truck's just a shit magnet, I guess."

Mr. Palin walked around the truck again, closely examining each dent and ding for a second time. Ma gave a dubious look to El, both being a bit confused and wondering if the funny little man was for real. El just shrugged his shoulders. Mr. Palin walked around opposite the two and bent down to examine a few lower dents with Ma and El stretching their necks out to try to see what he was doing. All of a sudden, he popped back up, holding his spectacles to his eyes, surprising both Ma and El, who jumped back. "Can you prove this is all true?!"

Ma frowned. "You want proof? What do you want me to do, drive down the road and smack a deer? I can't predict when it will happen!"

"Ma, do the thing," Elmer replied. Mr. Palin's expression seemed very curious upon hearing El's statement.

"That don't always work!" Ma barked back.

"Try, Ma. You never know."

"Oh, all right!" Ma went into the diner and came back out moments later holding some dry oatmeal in her hand. "This worked once when I was unloading groceries and dropped a bag off the tailgate," she said as she walked back up to the two. "Stand back." El and Mr. Palin took two steps back from the truck. "You better back up a bit more, just in case this works," Ma said to them both, and they did as they were told.

Ma stood a few feet from the truck as well and looked into the woods surrounding the diner. "Probably come from there," she whispered to herself and then tossed the oatmeal at her truck, which bounced off the driver's side rear quarter panel and to the ground. Moments later an eight-point buck came leaping from the woods where Ma had figured it would and charged for the truck. The deer dropped its snout to nearly the ground as it arrived at the truck, seeking the oats; however, it disregarded the truck entirely. It struck its head and horns hard against the side, causing a brand-new dent and a few more scratches, and then fell unconscious to the ground into the oats from the impact.

"That's amazing!" Mr. Palin blurted out. All three approached the truck cautiously and the funny man looked through his glasses at the new damage. He then looked down at the deer. "But the deer appears to be dead."

Ma put her arm out and began to push Mr. Palin back gently, "You may want to back up a bit, it won't be long." As the three stepped back again, the deer began to shake its head and then sprang back to its feet, wobbling, with all four legs out to steady itself. The deer snorted, shook its head again, and bolted back for the woods, leaving the oatmeal on the ground. The little Englishman was watching, quite astonished, while Ma and El just acting as if it's happened before.

Mr. Palin, still stunned, turned back to Ma. "Does that happen every time?! Are deer the only species that it works with?!"

"I don't know about that, mister," Ma said. "But it ain't just deer. Every animal around here has hit the truck one time or another. Deer, turkey, fox, groundhog. Everything. All except a moose, they don't dare, they know I'll hit the gas if they jump in front of me! I even had a bear sitting on my tailgate a while back, but I didn't hit him, he followed me out of the woods. I had a hard time convincing him to get off my tailgate and go home too."

El just nodded in agreement, "Maybe the animals are just drawn to old, rusty Chevy pickup trucks."

Mr. Palin, with the same enthusiasm and now back to examining the truck continued on, "Of course, to be eligible for the award there are certain criteria that we'll need to meet."

Ma and El followed him around the truck once again. "What criteria?" Ma inquired. "It's just a bunch of dumb animals drawn to denting my truck!"

"Well, first, we'll have to examine any historical records to determine if this has been achieved before."

"Before? Before what?" Ma pointed her finger at Mr. Palin from behind, "Do you honestly think in the history books somewhere it says that Marc Anthony's chariot suffered from random deer damage?!"

Mr. Palin stopped and turned around to Ma, nearly poking his own eye out on her stubby finger. He adjusted his glasses. "And we'd need to be certain this won't cause an international competition."

"Do you mean Ma may just have created a new sport with this?" El turned to Ma, "Think about it, Ma. You may have created the new NASCAR!"

"Bah!" Ma threw up her hands in disgust and turned to walk away, the little man right behind her.

"You also can't use your record for advertising purposes."

Ma swung back around. "You mean I can't advertise my diner?!" The man closed his eyes and shook his head. "Good! No need to bring in any more foreigners to town that hear about this! In fact, I don't want anything to do with this!"

"Might be good for the town, Ma" El chimed in.

"My good woman," Mr. Palin continued, "if certified, you'll simply be mentioned in our annual publication. No one will necessarily know, there's no media involved in a record such as this unless you want there to be."

Ma stopped and thought for a moment. My name in a book? Now that thought appealed to her. She turned back to the funny little man. "Do you mean that no one will hear about this? No advertising? Just my name in a book somewhere?"

"Exactly, my fine, portly friend." Ma scowled as he said this. "You'll simply have the gratification of reading your name in our publication each year that it's published until someone else breaks your record." The man turned to the truck and adjusted his glasses. "And it's doubtful that will ever occur." He turned back to Ma. "All we need to do is make the anomaly occur one more time while I officially record the results. We can arrange for that within a matter of days."

Ma thought for a few more moments. "Okay, let's do it." She pointed her finger at Mr. Palin again. "But I'm warning you, no muss or fuss!"

◆ ◆ ◆

It was one week later, mid-afternoon on a nice, warm, sunny early fall day. Ma, Elmer, and the funny Englishman were standing on the stage the town had built for Zac Brown in the middle of Ma's field. Mr. Palin had official paperwork in his hand in which to record the pending results and certify Ma's truck as a Guinness world record holder. Ma's dented truck was parked directly in front of the stage.

Behind that was the entire population of East Puddleduck and most of Skunksquirt too.

Ma, with her arms folded and looking fairly disgusted, looked over the crowd. El leaned into her, "Who'da known that the mayor was listening out the diner window when we was talking about this last week, Ma? Nothing we could have done about it."

Ma grumbled back, "And that idiot took the opportunity to turn this into a circus!"

Just then the mayor stepped up onto the stage and walked up to a podium he'd had Daley and Doody bring from the town office, and they'd also set up a microphone and speakers. After the 'big concert' fiasco, they'd removed the generator from under the stage, so a multitude of multi-colored extension cords were running the length of the field, over the road, and to Ma's diner to power the microphone. The mayor was all dressed up in a nice, turquoise suit coat and pants, and a purple dress shirt. His tie had ducks on it. He even had on a shiny, black top hat.

"Quiet down, quiet down, everyone." The mayor's voice loudly squeaked over the speakers. He turned to Ma, "We're awful proud of you, Ma." He turned back to the crowd and said a bit softer, "Even though we know you're pretty pissed about it."

Ma started to reach out and El stopped her, shaking his head at her.

"Ma's about to set a world record right here in our little town!" The mayor continued, "The good people at Guinness have taken notice of her accomplishment, her truck having been struck forty-one times by various animals that have never been hurt or died as a result!" While the crowd cheered, he said the next bit under his breath, "And somehow that's a noticeable accomplishment," shrugging his shoulders. He then blurted out, "Today, she'll go for an official forty-two, setting herself, and our little town in the record books forever and for everyone to take notice!" The crowd broke out in applause and cheered again. Ma's frown deepened and her crossed arms stiffened.

Within the cheering could be heard such phrases as, "Way to go, Ma!" and, "We love you, Ma!" from various townsfolk, causing Ma's demeanor to soften just a bit and she unfolded her arms. Ma looked quite nervously out of place up on the stage, wearing her usual faded, floral-patterned sundress, apron, and shitkicker boots. Ma had refused to dress up for the occasion; however, now she was beginning to enjoy the attention. She finally smiled and waved at the crowd as El, and even the mayor, put their arms around her and she didn't attempt to push them away or lay them out. The mayor then motioned to Mr. Palin to come forward.

Mr. Palin approached the podium. "My good friends, today your fine matriarch will attempt to make history and set a new world record. In a few moments, she will make the attempt and I'll record the official results and, if successful, declare her to be a Guinness record holder!" More cheers from the crowd as he continued, "The key to the success will be that an animal does in fact make impact with the vehicle and that it doesn't get hurt in the process and, the truck is still in operating condition when it's completed. I'd like to ask that the crowd remain quiet during the attempt for the highest level of success, please."

Ma's nerves began to get to her. The pressure was starting to build. She leaned to El again. "There ain't no guarantees this will work, you know."

"Just give it your best, Ma," El responded and smiled at her.

Mr. Palin turned to Ma, "Are you ready, my lady?"

"I suppose now's a good of a time as any," she responded over the loud applause and cheers. Just then a fairly large, pink brazier flew up on the stage and landed, hanging off the corner of the podium. Ma frowned and looked down, locating Ruby in the crowd, her tight T-shirt and body bouncing up and down as she cheered, indicating she obviously wasn't wearing a bra anymore. Ma shook her finger and yelled, amplified tremendously by the podium's microphone and speakers, "This ain't no country music concert, you twit! Keep your boobs in your shirt!" Ruby stopped bouncing and Ma read her lips when she said, "Sorry." All the menfolk momentarily strained to see Ruby's frontside before refocusing their attention.

Ma walked down the stage stairs and around to the front of her pickup truck. The area had been cordoned off with bright orange contractor's paint that Constable Bob had sprayed on the ground to keep the crowd at least twenty feet back from the truck to give any animal in the area plenty of room to charge at the vehicle. Ma began to perspire in her dress, worried that this would be the one day her trick wouldn't work. She gave the crowd a nervous smile as she walked around to the front of the stage, the applause and cheering remaining loud. When she reached the truck, Runyon walked up to her and handed her a small bag of oatmeal, then took several steps back into the crowd. Mr. Palin motioned for the crowd to hush, and the cheering diminished. Everyone went quiet and stared in anticipation.

Ma looked around at the wood line at the edge of the field in each direction. She wet her pointer finger with her lips and held it up. "Hope this works," she said under her breath. Ma chose a direction, stood back, reached into the bag, and tossed a handful of oats against the truck.

Everyone looked around in all directions to see where the animal, any animal, might emerge from. On the stage El, Mr. Palin, and the mayor were doing the same. Nothing immediately happened. Five seconds went by. Ten seconds. Fifteen. Ma was fully perspiring now. She was also looking around for any animal to show itself. Doubts came from the audience. Doubts came from the stage. Ma was nearly dripping sweat now as she reached into the bag for another handful; however, with her palms sweating, the oats just stuck to her hand. She realized she wouldn't have the ability to throw them. All hope was beginning to be lost.

And then, it happened. At first, the faint *"Clomp, ca-clomp, ca- clomp..."* could be heard from somewhere in the woods. Ma looked over to the north side of the field just as everyone else looked to the south side. Ma was always poor with the direction of animal sounds in the wild. Emerging from the south side, the crowd watched as a huge bull moose was on a dead run toward the truck. Ma's head snapped back around just in time to see the beast barreling toward her.

"Holy shiiiiit!!!" Ma screamed just as the moose knocked her with its massive shoulder, taking her off her feet and sending her backward into the crowd. The moose dropped its snout, missed the oats, and ran its head and massive horns straight into the passenger side of the truck, buckling the door and quarter panels inward nearly halfway into the cab and engine compartment, as the passenger side, front, and rear windows shattered into pieces. The impact lifted the truck, and the passenger side wheels came up off the ground about one foot before dropping back down. The moose immediately fell sideways from the impact and landed on the ground unconscious. Dust rose from both the impact of the truck and the moose falling to the earth.

Everyone remained silent and still as they all watched the moose. Ma, who'd been caught and kept on her feet by Puut and Marmaduke crept back towards the animal; however, keeping her guard up. Ma was able to get within a couple of feet of the animal when it suddenly awoke and wobbled to its feet, its legs spread wide to stabilize itself. The moose looked straight at Ma, whose eyes popped open wide as the moose snorted, shook its head, reached over, grabbed Ma's hairpin, and sprinted back towards the woods, disappearing into the wood line to the south side of the field.

The crowd broke out in applause and cheering again. El and the mayor joined in, nodding to each other with huge smiles.

"Had to be a goddam moose, didn't it?" Ma said to herself as her hair fell over her face and the cheering continued.

"Quiet, please! Quiet, please!" Mr. Palin said into the microphone. His expression was one of seriousness as the crowd began to quiet down.

The mayor interrupted him, "Well, that's certainly one for the record books, isn't it!" The cheering began again.

Again, Mr. Palin called for the audience to quiet down. "I'm sorry, I'm sorry. I can't certify this record." The cheering diminished as he looked down at Ma. "I'm going to have to disqualify the attempt, my fine lady. Again, I'm sorry."

The mayor interrupted, quite angrily. "What do you mean?! Ma did what you asked for!"

"I'm sorry, the good lady violated the rules by using profanity during the attempt. We have strict rules against the use of profane or offensive language during the attempt of any record-breaking."

Ma yelled back up, "What profanity?!"

Someone in the crowd echoed Ma, "Yeah, what profanity?!" Several more echoes of the question followed, everyone obviously annoyed.

Mr. Palin spoke down to Ma from the podium, "Well, to be specific, you cried out 'holy shit' as the animal approached."

Ma barked back up, pointing and shaking her chubby finger at Mr. Palin, "Well, of course, I yelled out holy shit! You're lucky I only yelled it and didn't do it! Did you not see the big-ass moose coming at me?! You would have yelled it too!"

The crowd backed Ma up with many echoing her words, "Yeah, you would have too!"

"I'm sorry, that violates our long-standing rules!" The speakers squelched. "Not to mention, your vehicle obviously doesn't operate anymore." Mr. Palin shook his head as he gazed at the heavily damaged vehicle.

Ma, and everyone, looked at the disabled truck. The moose had caused extensive damage to the passenger side. The T-boning of his head and horns had left the truck crinkled nearly in half, and the passenger door was in a twisted heap in the center of the cab.

Ma turned back to look up at Mr. Palin. "Do you mean to tell me if that truck starts and moves on its own, we still get the award?! And you'll overlook the whole cursing thing?!"

"My good woman…"

"Stop calling me that and answer the question!" Ma pointed behind her, still looking up at the stage, "Do you see all these people here behind me?

Do you?! They're hard-working people! They don't have much to call their own but they were good enough to come out here today and show some excitement for this stupid contest and to cheer an old woman on! Are you going to let all these people down because of my foul mouth?! Have you ever had a moose come at you like I just did?! I still feel like I'm going to shit in my pants right now!"

The crowd joined in again and things such as, "Yeah!" and, "You tell him, Ma!" could be heard from many of the onlookers.

"But, my dear…ah, I mean, Mrs. Farnsworth, how do you expect that vehicle to still be operable? It's in ruins."

"Just answer the question!" Ma barked.

"Well…yes." Mr. Palin smiled. "Yes. If that vehicle starts and operates without someone having to push it or tow it off the field, then I'll certify the record!"

Ma yelled out a big "Yes!" and the crowd cheered and applauded again.

Mr. Palin used the microphone again to speak over the crowd, "But I really don't see how this is possible." Once again, the crowd went silent. "Your truck has been destroyed."

"Runyon!" Ma yelled and he emerged from the crowd and walked up to his mother. "Get in." Ma motioned to the truck.

"No problem, Ma." Runyon went around to the driver's side and the crowd began to whisper, many questioning whether the truck would run again. Runyon opened the driver's side door and swept broken glass off the bench seat with his hands. He crawled up in; it was tight but he squeezed in, not having a lot of room between the driver's side and where the crinkled passenger door now was located nearer the center of the cab. The shifting stick was bent towards him a bit. Runyon used both hands to straighten it and put the truck in neutral. He reached up to adjust the rearview mirror; however, the windshield wasn't there anymore, so neither was the rearview mirror. He held the steering wheel, pushed down on the clutch and gas, and turned the key. Without hesitation, and for the first time ever, the truck turned over on the first turn of the key.

The crown erupted in glee. Runyon looked over to his mother and gave her a cheesy grin and winked.

Mr. Palin, although pleased, was still skeptical. He turned to the mayor. "But will it still move?"

The mayor, with a similar grin on his face, said to the man, "Just wait."

Ma walked around to the driver's side and stepped up on the running board, grabbing the open window to pull herself up, and she said casually to Runyon, "Take it over to McIntyre's, they'll need to straighten her out a bit and put a new door on the other side." She looked the truck over. "Probably need a new hood too, and it may be time for the oil change. Can't tell, the sticker was on the windshield. I don't care what color the parts are. Tell them I want it back by next weekend," and Ma hopped back down.

"No problem, Ma." Runyon clutched and the old truck groaned hard as he shoved it into second gear. It was a bit difficult with the bench seat pushed up a bit from the impact, somewhat blocking the attempt, but he found it. With the crowd having gone silent again with anticipation, he gave the truck a little gas and let off the clutch. Smoke billowed from underneath where the tailpipe was now bent and broken, and ever so slowly the truck began to lurch forward. Runyon sat up straight and stretched his neck upward to see over the badly mangled hood as he drove the truck off the field as cheering and applause erupted once again.

As it pulled away, Ma gave the truck a slap on the tailgate and chuckled to herself. She watched as her truck bounced up and down in the rough field, creaking on its damaged springs and a few more parts falling off before it left slowly down the roadway. She looked back up on the stage and winked.

Mr. Palin, who had a grin on his face, looked down through his reading glasses at Ma, winked back, and motioned with his head for her to come back up on the stage.

As the crowd closed in, patting Ma on the back and telling her what a good job she'd done, she made her way back up the stage stairs. El gave her a smile and a wink and the mayor patted her on the back as she approached the podium. Mr. Palin handed her a framed certificate that she held high above her head to the continuing cheers of the crowd. Nobody had ever seen a smile on Ma's face as big as the one she had right at that moment. She then turned back to her new foreigner friend, "Thank you, Mister Palin. There's a seat in my diner anytime for you."

Mr. Palin gave the endearing woman a big smile and said to her, "Holy shit, my dear lady, I didn't think you'd pull that one off."

Ma proudly hung the certificate on the diner wall for everyone to see, and it's still there to this day. Most likely the record still stands too, in case you want to pick up the next issue of the record book and look it up.

Chapter 18

The Three Wheeler

"It's a good little machine. I bought it new in '82. I've done a lot of hunting with it," Puut was explaining to Runyon.

"Why are you selling her now?"

"Bought me a new one." Puut opened the door to his garage, the very one built out of fireplace logs.

Puut's garage is fairly large and has two stories. It measures about twenty feet square with a large single bay door on the front and he'd built it on a nice granite slab. The upper portion, which you can only get to from a set of stairs in the back, is where his workshop is located. On the lower portion are his "toys" and where he keeps his Jeep Willey parked.

The two were looking at Puut's old three-wheel all-terrain vehicle that he was now willing to part with. And "part" was the keyword here.

"What model is she, Puut? I can't tell by looking at it."

The ATV appeared to be quite well used and also looked as if Puut had pieced it together from several models, not to mention he'd painted the gas tank and sides an olive-green color and there were no rear fenders. Sticking out of the back were two rugged tires, quite a bit smaller in size than the knobby front tire. The rear tires had a deep tread and appeared to have been mounted to a modified rear drive shaft that was wider than the original, making the rear tires look more like training wheels than drive wheels. Behind the duct-taped camo seat was a three-foot square welded steel rack that resembled an oversized barbeque grill, painted black although rusting a bit. This is where Puut told Runyon he'd mount whatever he'd been hunting and drive it out of the woods. On the front, over the olive-green fender, and on the handlebars was mounted a gun rack that could hold at least two rifles.

"I'm not certain. Could be mostly a Honda, maybe some Suzuki, certainly a bit of Kawasaki." Puut responded as he looked around his garage. Inside the large but messy bay, along with Puut's old Willey, there was a newer four-wheeler and many, many disassembled three-wheeled machines and parts strewn about.

"Did quite a bit of tinkering to her, didn't you, Puut?" Runyon asked as he admired the tools and miscellaneous parts inside the garage.

"Yessir, she's been well used and repaired a few times. I used what I could find to keep her going. But she runs good now. She's got four forward gears plus reverse and starts most every time. I lost the keys years ago, so all you need to do is tie these two wires together and pull the choke here before cranking on her." Puut was pointing at the many wires the machine seemed to have hanging off the engine compartment. "Kill switch don't work; touch this red wire here to the frame and short her out when you're ready to shut it down. She's got an automatic clutch and one good brake on your right foot. Shift down into gear with your left foot and hold this button here and shift up into reverse. Neutral's in the middle."

"Good looking rig," Runyon said as he looked at the machine, giving it the once-over. It was missing the headlight, had a trailer hitch welded to the rear, and the tailpipe had a piece of straight pipe welded to it. The pipe extended about a foot behind the machine and appeared to have ladies' pantyhose and steel wool stuffed inside the end of the pipe where the spark arrester should have been located. "Whatcha looking to get out of her?" Runyon inquired.

"How about seventy-five, that sound fair?" Puut asked.

"Give you sixty."

"Deal." The two shook hands and Runyon paid the man.

◆ ◆ ◆

"What the hell is that ugly thing?" Ma said as she was looking over the 'new,' olive-green lawn ornament. "Nice training wheels, where's the pedals?"

"Got it from Puut," Runyon replied.

"That explains it. Does this thing run? What did you need with this old thing for anyway? It's just going to junk up the yard! We don't need our place looking like Old Marmaduke's!"

Runyon answered his mother, "It's good for finding new fishing spots. Do you want to try her out, Ma?"

Ma raised one eyebrow. The one that crosses over both her eyes. "Me? On that thing! Are you stupid or something?!"

"C'mon, Ma, you'll have fun. Just don't go too fast," Runyon replied, pointing to various areas of the machine. "Gas is here, brake down there, headlight switch up here. Don't confuse the headlight switch with the kill switch. Neither works anyway, and no headlight to speak of. Pull the choker here, pull the start cord here, give her some gas there."

Ma's eyes and head were bouncing as Runyon was pointing out all the safety features. "How many gadgets does it take to make it go, anyway?!"

"Don't go too fast in the first gear, Ma, or she'll do a wheely and flip you over."

Ma's eyebrow was frowning. "A what? How the hell do you stop this thing once you get going?" Ma was looking over the machine like it was a sick cow.

"See this reddish wire here?" Runyon pointed to a greasy wire somewhere in the engine block. "Touch it to the engine here and she'll short out."

Ma looked up at Runyon, her eyes squinted and nose crinkled. "Your shittin' me."

"No, really. That's how she stops," Runyon said as if his mother had asked a dumb question. He reached into his truck. "Here, Ma. Puut threw in a helmet. It'll keep your head safe." He handed Ma a brown, vintage leather aviator helmet and goggles. The headpiece looked as if it had been through a war and several aviation accidents. The leather was hard and cracked and the goggles were foggy.

Ma continued to frown and crinkled her nose again as she took the crusty, leather headpiece. "Looks like something that dumb Canuk would wear," she said as she wiggled her head into it, taking her hair out of its bun first and tugging on the leather ear flaps to get it to fit. Once she had it on, she pulled down the thick goggles. She looked at Runyon, who was trying hard not to laugh, and she said sarcastically, "And this is supposed to keep me safe?"

Ma grabbed the rusting handlebars, swung her chunky leg over the machine, and straddled it, bouncing up and down as if she were checking the springs on an old truck. Ma was quite the site standing on the old machine in her faded, floral-pattern dress, shitkicker boots, leather aviator helmet, and goggles.

Runyon tied the ignition wires together and pulled out the choke. Ma reached down and pulled the starter cord. The old crankcase caught the cord and it snapped out of Ma's hand. *"Goddamit!"* Ma exclaimed as she shook her hand off and grabbed it again. After two more pulls the ATV started. Exhaust smoke began emitting from everywhere, the engine and the tailpipe. Exhaust was billowing up around the duct-taped seat. Ma, and the loud machine both began to sputter.

"Let down the choke lever, Ma!" Runyon yelled.

"I did! Thing smokes worse than a dump fire!" she yelled back, even though they were directly beside each other, Ma still standing and straddling the machine, her body shaking to the vibrating of the engine.

Runyon yelled again, "Must run the oil a bit thick! We'll need to adjust it later! She's got an automatic transmission, Ma! Once you shift her down with your left foot and give her the gas, she'll go. Be careful!"

Ma shouted, "Get back, I'm gonna give her some juice!"

"If you get 'er stuck and need to back up you gotta hit that little yellow switch near your left hand and shift her back up with your foot!"

"Screw reverse!" Ma shouted.

"Okay, Ma! Neutral is between the two! Brakes near your right foot!"

Ma was looking straight at Runyon when she yelled out, "Brakes? How fast does this thing go…?!" She was giving the machine just a little too much gas when she shifted into gear and the ATV took off mid-sentence. Ma was forced backward, still standing and holding the handlebars tight as the front tire lifted off the ground and she was operating only its two rear wheels. "Holy *shiiiiit!*" Ma yelled out as she performed a wheely all the way out of the driveway.

El, who was sitting in his favorite easy chair inside the house, watching the snowy-focus television, glanced over as he saw Ma fly by the living room's picture window. He mumbled to himself casually, "That ain't going to end well."

"Down, boy!" Ma yelled as the machine struck the tar curb, shifting her weight back forward and causing the front tire to bounce back down and Ma once again had all three tires on the ground. Ma began speeding uncontrollably down the road, fishtailing a bit and holding onto it hard to keep it under control and in the roadway. *"Wheeeee!"* Ma cried out, settling back down into the seat a bit, crouching near the handlebars with her butt just off the seat and focusing forward. She felt the machine shift to its highest gear as she glanced down at the speedometer. It read forty-five miles per hour. The engine had a high-pitched whine and smoke was billowing out behind her. The leather flaps on her helmet were beating against the back of her head.

El appeared at the front doorway and called out to his boy, "You better take off after her. That ain't going to end well." Runyon looked at his father, then down the road. He snapped back to reality, jumped into his truck, and started to follow the cloud of dust and smoke.

◆ ◆ ◆

Ma was going fifty miles per hour when she turned down Skunk Mountain Road. She nearly didn't make the corner without tipping over sideways. Ma wanted to laugh out loud but she'd determined about a quarter mile earlier that the more her mouth was open, the more bugs she was swallowing and getting caught in her teeth. Ma's dress was flapping in the wind with her butt in the air. It's a good thing I'm wearing britches today, she thought to herself.

As Ma quickly neared the Doody residence, she spotted Mattie in her yard tending to her rock garden near the road's edge. Mattie was wearing a nice, clean white sundress and a new straw hat with a large brim. Ma was still doing about fifty when she leaned to the right and put the ATV into the road shoulder as she went by, kicking up a good bit of roadside dirt and dust. "Up yours, Mattie!" Ma yelled as she roared by. Mattie looked up just in time to see Ma's butt fly by through the flapping dress, and before dust caused her eyes to shut tight and her nice white dress was pelted by tiny rocks and dirt. The wind from the machine going by at high speeds caused her new hat to fly off.

Ma took the corner onto the main road on two wheels again and still going just as fast when a big dragonfly hit her square in the forehead just above the goggles and nearly knocked her off the machine. "Friggin' bugs!" Ma yelled out loud as she fishtailed through the turn and kept on going, "That's going to leave a mark!"

Ma came around the bend near the town hall in the wrong lane, just as she spotted Joshua McIntyre ahead of her. He was in the wrecker truck hauling a broken-down vehicle in tow behind him. It seems that Old Marmaduke's latest jalopy had died roadside nearby and Joshua was helping him retire another one to the Marmaduke homestead.

"Get the hell out of my way, McIntyre!" Ma shouted and waved at him with one hand, the other tight on the throttle as she played chicken with his wrecker. Joshua's eyes ballooned at the site of Ma on the ATV coming straight toward him. Joshua swerved just in time to miss hitting her as Marmaduke's junker fishtailed and broke free of the wrecker's hook. Joshua came to a halt on the wrong side of the road as the old car passed him on the right and went straight to the bend in the road, up onto the curb, and into Mayor Wigglewort's yard, taking out their nice, white picket fence and elderberry bush. The junker finally came to a rest just in front of their picture window, where a wide-eyed mayor and his wife, Eleanor, were watching when the driverless car parked itself on their lawn.

"Serves you right! You were in my lane anyway!" Ma yelled as she glanced back and saw what she'd just caused.

Ma rounded the next bend near McIntyre's garage, where Joshua had come from, and who do you think was sitting in their used car lot in his cruiser? Yes, it was Constable Bob, waiting for speeders that he never intended to pull over to go by. Bob was chewing on a thick stick of beef jerky. Ma spied the cruiser hiding amongst the other used cars as she got halfway around the bend and gunned the throttle as she flew by him. She waved to Bob, but only with one finger which was coincidentally her middle one.

With the jerky sticking out of his mouth, the startled and confused constable slammed the Bonneville into drive and spun his tires getting onto the road to catch up to the strange anomaly. The big, blue bubblegum machine lit up and the wailing siren came on. Not too far behind him was Runyon in his pickup truck, who'd been following the dust and smoke ahead of him.

Ma glanced back and saw Johnson approaching. "Awe, crap!" She cranked on the throttle hard and tried to put some distance between her and the police cruiser.

Bob pushed the gas pedal closer to the floor, and seeing that this was his first vehicle chase ever, he radioed for backup. As he grew nearer the cloud of dust ahead of him, he attempted to determine exactly what he was chasing. He leaned forward as he clutched the steering wheel hard as if it would help him see. What he was able to make out was what appeared to be a large, flowered, and flapping tablecloth with a bug-eyed head and a large ass squatting on an old speeding, smoking three-wheeler. His eyes grew big.

"Jeesus! It can't be! That looks like Ma!"

Ma turned and yelled, "Get off my ass, copper!" Her sanity had apparently left her body on the last corner.

Ma kept on as fast as the machine would go, looking down again and watching the needle go past sixty. She held on tight and looked back to see how close the cruiser was to her. Bob was getting closer and closer to her tail end. Just as she turned her head back forward, she spotted it, and it was too late. Just ahead of her was a skunk in the road. The stinky creature was square in her lane and staring straight at her, paralyzed with fear of what was coming at it. *"Skuuuunk!"* Ma cried out loud as she cranked the handlebars hard to the left, trying to avoid the furry little animal. Just as she zoomed past it, nearly shaving its fur with her front tire, the skunk jumped into the air, turning its tail side towards her, and sprayed. The stink sprayed right up her leg and into her midsection.

"Goddammmit!" she yelled out as she cranked the handlebars back to the right, attempting to not lose control of the machine as it struck the roadside and was heading for the puckerbrush at high speed. Ma flipped the kill switch and then remembered it didn't work, and there was no way to get her hand down to the wire that could ground out the engine, nor would it have stopped the inevitable anyway. She was clutching tight to the handlebars, watching the wood line approach fast and wishing now she'd run over the skunk, seeing that now she smelled like it anyway.

Bob hit the brakes of his cruiser to avoid running into Ma's tail end just as she struck the roadside on the sharp curve. The wheeler's over-inflated front tire and two smaller rear ones bounced up and into the air as she plowed over several small bushes and flew between two tall pines. The front wheel came down in a gopher hole and the two rear tires came over as the machine went end-to-end out into a field. On the first rollover, Ma flew over the handlebars, went straight into the air for about thirty feet, and landed headfirst into a mud hole. She tumbled ass-over-teakettle a few times and finally came to rest on her back, staring up at the sun-filled sky.

Gazing straight up and hearing ringing in her ears, she said incoherently, "Not too many clouds today. That one there looks like a skunk…" as she began to lose consciousness. Just before passing out, her head tilted to the right side and she noticed the ATV had come to rest beside the sign that read, "Foriners Buried Here." Ma had run off the road on her own corner and landed in the field across from the diner.

Bob came to a screeching halt just before the turn and Runyon's truck was right behind him. And being that this was the only chase that Johnson had ever called in, the dispatch center had sent half the county as backup, and it wasn't long before the faint sounds of many sirens could be heard approaching.

The lunch crowd at the diner was light and all that were present, including Cicely Smirnoff who was covering the noontime shift, had seen the fat lady on the three-wheeler go sailing off the turn and into the field. The local patrons began exiting the diner with some gawking and some running towards the field as officers arrived on the scene. There was a long train of cruisers with lights and loud sirens wailing down along the roadway.

Bob and Runyon were kneeling over the dirty, wet, and smelly diner-owner. "Are you all right, Ma? Ain't nothing broken is there?" They both attempted to help Ma sit up as she began to regain consciousness.

Ma looked in a daze, staring off into space, and said in a soft voice, "And grandma says too much fluffernutter in peanut butter fudge makes it stick to your teeth…"

The two assisted Ma to her feet as Johnson exclaimed, "You know, I'd like nothing less than to haul your stupid butt to the slammer, Ma. Except for the fact that you stink like a skunk! You ain't hurt, are you?!"

Ma was wobbly on her feet, and they held onto her arms to steady her. She looked up at Constable Bob, "Aww, what a cute little piggy you are… what are you doing standing up on that whale?" Bob just frowned and shook his head disgustingly.

Runyon gave her a once over, wincing from the smell as he did so. "She looks okay, I don't see nothing broken off or laying around on the ground. I think her bell's just been rung, that's all."

Patrons of the diner, plus the other state and county officers, came running onto the field. Most, if not all, stopping at a safe distance from the smell.

Bob, acting all official, said to the crowd that was forming, "Give her some air. Everything is all right. Nothing to see here." He spoke directly to the other officers, "Sorry, didn't mean to get you all the way up here for nothing."

The crowd, realizing it was just Ma being Ma, all wandered back to finish their lunches. The other officers disgustingly returned to their vehicles and onto other far more important matters.

Ma was beginning to come around, "Who stinks?" she asked as she began to regain her hearing and her eyesight wasn't so blurry anymore. She still had on the leather helmet and goggles.

"That'd be you, Ma," Runyon told her. "You shouldn't have gone so fast on the wheeler and scared that skunk."

"And you shouldn't have given me the finger when you went by!"

"Shut up!" Ma was nearly back to normal now. "That didn't have anything to do with the machine! I just felt like it!" Ma looked over at the mangled ATV as she took the helmet off and threw it to the ground. The machine was now missing even more of its parts than when she began, which were now strewn randomly in the field. "I'm sorry about your new machine, Runyon."

"Don't worry, Puut has plenty of spare parts. I'm sure he can put it back together. Jeez, Ma, you're going to need plenty of tomato paste to get that stink off you."

"Go fetch me some from the diner. I'll get Bob here to drive me home, no need to stink up your truck." Bob frowned a few moments after she said this, having taken him a bit to figure it out.

As they all walked back roadside, Puut came along in his new side-by-side four-wheeler and pulled up beside the three. "What's going on, Ma? Did you shoot another foreigner?" Just then the breeze came his way and he smelled the foul odor and winced, "Nice perfume you have on there, old woman."

"Shut up or I'll come over there and give you a big hug!" Ma blurted out. "And nice machine you sold Runyon. That thing's a death trap!"

"It isn't dangerous unless you drive it that way," Puut replied and glanced out into the field. "I suppose I'm going to need to do some repair work on it for you, Runyon. Looks like she did a good number on the old machine. Oh well, won't take much to get it going again. Not the first time it's been through something like this."

"Let's just leave it there, Puut. If we fix it, she's liable to just do it again," Runyon said as he started towards the diner for a case of tomato paste for Ma's pending bathing and scrubbing.

Bob ended up taking Ma back home. He made her sit in the back seat of his cruiser on two empty trash bags. His cruiser still smelled a bit foul for several days after.

◆ ◆ ◆

Joshua McIntyre would end up getting the ATV out of the field and taking it to Old Marmaduke's house. Runyon gave it to the old man, and to this day, it sits as one of his lawn ornaments somewhere on the property in the tall grass amongst all the other junk.

The actual three-wheeler

Chapter 19

Going to Church

Father Winkin was exiting the diner that spring afternoon as Ma smiled and waved him out the door. From the diner's glass entrance, she watched the preacher as he climbed into his big Cadillac, and then she turned back to Ruby who was seated at the first booth and rolling silverware into clean napkins. "Idiot," Ma remarked in reference to the preacher.

Ruby looked up and quietly chuckled. "Well, I think he's a nice guy. He gives a good sermon on Sundays."

"Good sermon!? That fool doesn't know one single thing about the Bible. He quotes movie lines is all. I doubt he's even ever read the good book." Ma slid down into the booth opposite Ruby. "He does the same thing every Sunday, he starts by reading from the good book, and then he closes it and starts making shit up. Plus, he does that thing where he's talking all quiet and such, makes you feel all comfortable in your seat, and then, wham! He blurts out something stupid and makes everyone jump out of their pew!"

El, who was sitting in the next booth enjoying a cup of coffee and conversation with Puut, turned and chimed in, "You ain't even been to church for weeks, if not longer. It's high time you got back there, Ma. He ain't that bad."

Ma wiggled back up out of the booth and stood between the two, pointing at El, "And for the reason I just told you! Who wants to hear him make up things that have nothing to do with nothing! Everyone thinks he's all high and mighty and takes his word because no one else around here knows better! They all just think what he's saying is gospel because he wears that robe and carries around the Bible! It's crap, that's what it is!"

"Oh, he ain't that bad, Ma," El remarked a bit sarcastically and finished his coffee.

"Ain't that bad?!" Ma frowned and adjusted her glasses, "Two months ago we were sitting in church and the preacher was talking about the Last Supper!" Ma pointed again at El, "You were sitting right there too and heard it! That bubblehead said, and I quote, 'the Lord said unto his apostles not to worry, for I've been told that on my deathbed I will receive total consciousness!' That's a line from the movie Caddyshack!" Ma was on a roll with her ranting and turned to Puut. "I went to confession just after the preacher arrived here in town just to see what he was all about. And no sooner did I get out the words, 'forgive me preacher, for I have sinned,' when he said back to me, 'no worries, you ain't heard nothing yet.' That's a line from The Jazz Singer! I'm telling you, he doesn't know anything from the Bible, and he's been getting worse!"

Puut, sipping his coffee, looked up at Ma over the rim of the cup. "How do you know what he's quoting isn't from the Bible?"

"Because I've read it! Maybe not lately, but I know enough to know that moron isn't quoting it correctly!" Ma noticed that Puut's cup was getting low and walked over to the coffee maker to grab a fresh, full pot. She stopped halfway and turned back, pointing to El. "And do you remember the last time we went to church? When that bubblehead got to the end of his sermon and pretended to give the diner a boost? Like he was doing us a favor? Do you remember when he said that everyone should come here after church because they could get anything they want at my restaurant? Then he told everyone to walk around the back and something about it being a half mile from the railroad tracks? He was practically singing when he said it! We don't have a back entrance, and the train tracks aren't anywhere near here! I don't even know what that means, but I'm pretty sure it was quoted from a movie or something!" Ma turned again to grab the coffee pot as Puut and El looked at each other, eyebrows raised, and Puut began to hum a bar of Alice's Restaurant.

Ma was on her way back with the fresh coffee when Puut stopped humming as he held out his cup, "What version of the good book did you read there, Ma?"

Ma filled his mug with fresh, hot coffee, to which he tipped his head as a thank you. "I don't know, the one that's correct! Certainly not the comic book that moron quotes from."

Puut took a sip of his fresh coffee. "Well, there's plenty of versions you know, old woman. King James, Old English, Eclectic Greek, Modern English. The Septuagint."

El looked confusingly at Puut. "The what?"

Puut placed his hot cup down on the table. "The Septuagint. The Greek Old Testament. There's plenty of versions." He looked back up at Ma, who was glaring. "Maybe he's quoting one of them that you're not familiar with."

El chimed back in, "Could be true there, Ma. Won't know if you don't go, though." El held up his empty cup for Ma to refill, just as she turned and walked away.

"Oh, fine! I'll go this Sunday and show you all that he's full of manure!" Ma put the coffee pot back on the machine and walked into the kitchen. El gave a scowl to his empty coffee cup and just shook his head while looking at Puut, who gave a chuckle and took another sip of his fresh coffee. Ma exited the kitchen a moment later, picked the coffee pot back up, and returned to the dining area. El held his empty cup up again as Ma marched over to an adjacent table where Old Marmaduke had been quietly sitting and listening, and re-filled his cup as she said to the man, "The preacher is almost as bad as you with his tall tales!"

Old Marmaduke gave Ma a befuddled look as he held his cup up for her. "What are you talking about, Ma?"

"I'm talking about how he makes stuff up just like you do! Like that time you tried to tell me how you singlehandedly defeated the entire Venetian army during the Second World War with only a tiny, little miniature handgun while your army buddy Toby, whose life you saved millions of times, stood by and watched! You thought you had me going with that one, didn't you?! Well, poo on you 'cause I checked into it! Venice didn't even have an army, and Italy was on our side during the war! Not to mention you probably weren't even born until three years after the war was over, and I'm guessing you never had a friend in the army! You made that whole thing up just to mess with me, you old fart! Just like the preacher does!"

Marmaduke flashed Ma a cheesy grin from beneath his snowy white beard, winked, and tipped his head as he took a sip from his fresh full cup of coffee. Ma frowned at the old man, turned, and stormed back to the kitchen as El once again lowered his empty coffee cup and shook his head, letting go of any idea that he was getting another fresh cup of coffee this day.

Ruby stretched out her neck and had the last word just before the kitchen door swung closed. "You aren't going to do anything foolish in church this Sunday, now, are you, Ma?"

◆ ◆ ◆

Sunday morning. The church, which sits just down the road a piece from the town office, was semi-full of East Puddleduck's residents. The tiny wooden structure was built in the late 1800s and has a small steeple and bell tower in the center of the tin roof. Inside there are ten rows of pews with a walkway in between each row. At capacity, it can hold a little over a hundred people. This day it had its usual twenty-five or so, all dressed in their Sunday best. Among them was Smirnoff who wore a full suit and tie, with Cicely in a nice yellow dress, sunhat, and gloves right beside him. Mattie was wearing a nice light-purple dress with silk fringe on the cuffs and collar, while her husband and selectperson, Paul, had on a brown corduroy suit. Constable Bob was in a clean uniform, just in case he was called to duty. As usual and out of respect he'd left his gun belt in the cruiser. His wife, Mabel, was all decked out in a nice pink sundress and a large-brimmed hat. Even Ma, who was seated next to El in the third-row pew, had on a nice dress, floral pattern, of course, and flat shoes with her hair all done up nice in a bun under a summer straw hat. Old Marmaduke, seated in the very last pew, even had on a clean white T-shirt, newer-looking blue coveralls, and clean tan work boots.

Myrtle Watson, as usual, was all dressed up nice and off to the side of the altar playing hymns on the electric organ that the townsfolk had pitched in and purchased from the Sears catalog in the early 1970s. It certainly isn't what you'd picture for a church organ but it does the job to the best it can. Myrtle isn't too musically inclined to begin with, so when the musical notes aren't exactly what's called for in the playbook, she blames the equipment.

At 10:00 a.m. the music quieted, and the reverend stood from his sanctuary and walked to the pulpit. Percible was wearing a long, black frock and white collar and carried his Bible with him, opening it and resting it on his podium. The slightly portly; however, statuesque preacher had on his usual driving glasses sitting low on his nose as he looked down through to his parishioners out in front of him. Percible reeked of his usual arrogance as he peered out across his flock, frowning a bit when he spied Ma in the third row looking up at him with a deviant smile on her face. The reverend paused and wondered what she was up to.

The preacher, standing as tall as he could, and straight, placed one hand in the air and began his sermon in a soft but deep voice. "It's so nice to see everyone here today," as he again looked around at the small crowd. "It pleases me to know so many take the time from your busy Sunday schedules to be here to join me on this day of prayer." An endearing although bit arrogant smile crossed the preacher's lips as he spoke and many in the room smiled along with him. He remained silent for a moment or two as he looked out over his parishioners once again.

And then, out of nowhere the reverend scowled and bellowed out loudly, "BLASPHEMY! Sayeth the Lord!" causing everyone in the room to jump in their pews.

"JEESUS!" Ma yelled out as she too was taken by surprise and startled. The reverend stopped and looked down at Ma through his glasses, frowning. He knew she hadn't said it for religious reasons. All others in the room also looked over at Ma. The room remained silent for a moment as Ma peered around at everyone. "Well, what do you expect!" Ma looked up at the reverend. "You nearly made me wet myself!" Ma looked around again and then back up at the reverend and said in a softer voice, "Sorry, didn't mean to curse. Continue on, Preacher."

A fake smile crossed the preacher's lips. "Bless you, my child." The father looked back over the crowd and raised his hand again. Everyone winched, waiting for the preacher to yell out. In a bit softer voice he continued, "Blasphemy, sayeth the Lord! For those of you who have sinned shall be forgiven...!"

Ma was satisfied for the moment that what the preacher was saying was in fact some sort of scripture taken from the good book.

"And the Leviticus twenty-four sayeth, 'bring out of the camp the one who cursed, and let all who heard him lay their hands on his head, and let all the congregation stone him. Whoever blasphemes the name of the Lord shall surely be put to death.'"

"Well, that's a bit harsh," Ma whispered loud enough to be heard by those around her, still believing what the reverend said was at least mostly correct.

"*Shhhh*, Ma," El whispered back softly. Ma frowned at him and adjusted her glasses.

Percible glanced out at Ma, then closed his Bible and continued on, "For he is a swine, a dog, a donkey, a cat, a beast, a filthy one, a mean man and a pariah, who turns his face away from the Guru!"

"Okay, here we go, he's starting to make stuff up," Ma whispered loudly again. This time, Ma heard *"Shhhh!"* from others nearby, to include Smirnoff who was seated directly behind her. Ma turned in the pew and frowned at him. She then turned back and looked up at the reverend, squinting, and crinkled her nose, waiting for the next verse.

"Therefore, to swear vainly or rashly by the glorious and awesome name of God is sinful, and to be regarded with disgust and detestation. For by rash, false, and vain oaths, the Lord is provoked and because of them this land mourns!" the reverend quoted loudly, almost singing the words as his hands were animated out in front of him and he swung his body side to side.

Ma, with a bit confused, a bit disappointed look on her face whispered again, "Crap, that one might be for real. I think he's straying a bit, though." She turned to El, who gave her one of those looks that silently told Ma to be quiet. Ma scowled at El again and shook her head.

The preacher then went silent and looked around the room, seeing that everyone was intently listening, all eyes wide and waiting to hear the next chorus of spirituality and wisdom with even a few leaning forward in their seats in anticipation. Others with their eyes closed in silent prayer. Even Ma was semi-patiently waiting and listening for the next quote.

The preacher then held his head high and while keeping his head straight, looked down through his glasses as his eyes peered all around the room. "BLASPHEMY!" the preacher yelled out again, raising his hands high as he blurted the word loudly, once again startling everyone in the room.

"JEESUS! He did it again!" Ma shouted as her hat flipped backward off her head when she jumped in her seat, landing in Smirnoff's lap. "You sonofabitch!" as Ma began to stand up.

"Sit down, Ma!" El grabbed her arm to pull her back. The reverend had a bit of a smirk on his face, his hands still high in the air as he watched Ma being tugged on by El.

Ma began to sit back down, looking straight at El while she pointed at the preacher, "Well, shit! If he keeps that up, I'm going to piss myself!"

"Shush, Ma! You're causing a scene in church," El pleaded. There was now giggling from a few in the room in response to Ma's outburst, namely the McIntyre boys, Bob Johnson, and the mayor, who got poked in the gut by his wife Eleanor when he chuckled as a warning.

Even Marmaduke couldn't help but smile as he called out, "No cursing in church." Ma snapped around and glared at the old man seated in the last pew, giving him one of those looks that told Marmaduke that he was lucky to be several rows back and out of her reach. Marmaduke blew Ma an air kiss in response, still silently chuckling.

"Excuse me, may I continue?" the reverend asked.

Ma turned back and looked up at him and waived her arm. "Yeah, go ahead. Just quit making me jump! And 'scuse the language." The preacher closed his eyes and nodded at Ma in acknowledgment of her apology. Smirnoff handed Ma back her hat from behind and she angrily plopped it back on her head again and rested back in her pew.

"Yea, as we speak of blasphemous ways, we must remember that we're all sinners!" The preacher continued, "We must ask ourselves what we can do. And yea, we must tell ourselves that we must paddle down that river because it is there…"

Ma frowned, attempting to figure out what the preacher was talking about now, while others in the room were back to listening intently and silently praying.

"…Can't you see sayeth the peasants, oh can't you see, what being blasphemous has been doing to me…"

Ma's eyes widened and she sat up straight. Her eyebrows nearly touched the brim of her hat.

"…And as the gathering of angels appeared above thy head the Lord called to us to come sail away, as he would bring but a storm for forty days and forty nights! And the Lord said unto Noah that you're going to need a bigger boat…"

Ma frowned and looked over at El, who looked back and shrugged his shoulders; however, still putting a finger up to his lips to tell Ma to remain silent as she turned back to the preacher.

"…And Noah did respond to the Lord saying that he would build that bigger boat. And they celebrated thine agreement that day with a great feast of fava beans…and a nice chianti."

Ma's wide stare now turned to one of complete confusion as she crinkled her nose and squinted, pondering hard on what she just heard.

The preacher continued, eyes closed, head tilted back, and speaking loudly, "And even though, sayeth the Lord, that there's no place like home, it is with great reverence that the almighty will make you that offer that thy cannot refuse! For there are times that we cannot handle the truth, but after all, tomorrow is yet but another day. For I'll be back sayeth the Lord!"

Ma turned and looked around the room, a smirk coming over her face. Even though there were those few who were still praying along with the preacher's words, including Mattie who was rocking in her seat and softly chanting "amen" over and over, she noticed that many others had puzzled expressions on their faces. She looked back directly at Smirnoff and Cicely, who returned her glance by shrugging their shoulders in stereo.

Ma turned back around, disgusted, to see the reverend holding his fisted hands high, and with his eyes still closed he yelled out, "And the Lord, who has always relied on the kindness of strangers did sayeth unto his flock, are you talking to me!? I say, are you talking to me?!"

"Hold it!" She couldn't contain herself any longer. Mattie stopped rocking as everyone looked at Ma. She stood up and pointed at the preacher with her stubby finger, who with his hands still held high now opened his eyes and looked down at her. "You just quoted the movie Taxi Driver, there, Preacher!"

Father Winkin began to lower his hands and said to Ma defensively, "That's ridiculous!"

"Not only that," Ma blurted as she began to squeeze her rather large butt past El to get to the center aisle, "You also stole lines from Jaws, the Marshall Tucker Band, Silence of the Lambs, and I think even Deliverance!"

"I did not," the reverend stated, his usual pompous look began to turn to one of a bit of nervousness in his expression.

"Yes, you did!" Ma came back. "All you're doing is quoting movie lines and throwing in an amen here and there!"

"Ludicrous, I tell you!" Percible's arrogance was still trying to show through.

"I heard a Styx song, and I think Kansas too," Joshua McIntyre said softly.

Ma, still looking straight at the preacher, pointed to Joshua and nodded her head quickly in agreement.

"And A Few Good Men…and A Streetcar Named Desire," Cicely Smirnoff said as the preacher's head snapped over to her. The nervous look on his face returned as his arms instinctively and unknowingly began to rise to his chest in defense once again.

"And the Terminator," Wally offered as the preacher swung his head back towards the McIntyre brother.

"And the Wizard of Oz," Ruby said as the preacher looked over at her too, his nervous look now turning to a rather fearful one.

Percible's head then went to the back of the room as Marmaduke spoke, "Don't forget Gone with the Wind."

Ma spoke up again in a sarcastic tone as she stood in the center aisle, "Would you care to try again, there, Preacher? Hmmm?"

"Oh, fine," Percible said, his arrogance returning a bit as he opened up his Bible.

"How about without cheating?" Ma remarked quite casually.

The reverend gave Ma a sarcastic glance and closed the good book. After a moment or two of thought, the preacher grinned arrogantly with one eyebrow cocked upwards. He raised one hand back up in the air he continued in a bit lower tone, "O God, ease our suffering in this, our moment of great despair. Yea, admit this kind and decent woman into thy arms of thine heavenly area, up there. And Moab, he lay us upon the band of the Canaanites, and yea, though the Hindus speak of karma, I implore you, give her a break."

Most everyone, including Ma, froze in place for a moment, each with strange looks on their faces and attempting to figure out where this verse had come from.

Joshua McIntyre slowly raised his hand in the air and Ma took notice, saying softly to him, "This isn't Sunday school, you don't have to put your hand up to speak. Say what's on your mind, boy."

Joshua looked up at the preacher, who was again back in his defensive stance and looking quite nervous, and said to him, "You just quoted Clark Griswold's entire speech from National Lampoon's Vacation after they left Aunt Enda dead on her brother's back porch."

Ma crossed her arms and glared at Percible, as everyone's eyes were on the preacher for a response. Now his hands were fully up against his chest as if he were preparing to deflect an incoming snowball being thrown at him. Instead of his usual standing tall, head back, and looking at everyone down through his glasses, his head and shoulders were drooping down a bit and he was looking out over the top of his spectacles at everyone. His eyebrows were raised, his eyes watered, and he obviously had no answer for his parishioners.

Ma recognized the look and lowered her arms, looking around the room and then back up at the usually confident preacher. Her demeanor eased as the father now looked like a scared, whimpering puppy dog.

"Preacher!" The pastor's head snapped to look at Ma, who now had an unusually endearing expression as she spoke and walked closer to the pulpit. "It's okay. It really is. It seems to reason the fact that everyone here has found something familiar to them in your sermon, right or wrong, it means they're all listening. Truth be told, it may even add a bit of character and I suppose still gets the meaning across."

An equally endearing smile began to cross the reverend's face in response to Ma's kind words as she continued, "You may watch a bit too much television and movies, but your taste in music is just fine." Ma winked at the preacher. "Just try to read a bit more of the good book before you step up there each Sunday and I don't think anyone will mind your style a bit. And try to add in a few more actual quotes from the Bible and I think you'll be okay."

The preacher silently mouthed the words, "Thank you," to Ma and looked out over his flock again; everyone was smiling and nodding.

Ma turned to go back to her seat; however, she stopped to add one last thing and she looked back up at the preacher. "But don't be jumping me with your spontaneous yelling! My bladder can't take much more of it!" The reverend looked back at Ma and smiled as Ma settled back down into her pew.

Father Winkin, with a smile still on his face, raised his hands and began again with confidence in a softer voice, and without startling anyone, "Wherefore I say unto you, all manner of sin and blasphemy shall be forgiven unto men, but the blasphemy against the Holy Ghost shall not be forgiven unto men." The preacher looked down through his glasses at Ma. "And mayeth the force be with all of us, for tomorrow is yet but another day, and the Holy Ghost did say unto all…that this is the stuff that dreams are made of."

Ma simply shook her head and smiled back.

◆ ◆ ◆

Ma began attending church a bit more regularly when time permitted. Primarily to make certain the preacher was doing a better job at quoting the Bible instead of just movie lines and song lyrics.

The actual tiny 4-inch Fommer Lilliput .25 caliber handgun, made in Budapest that the 'Storyteller' used to defeat the Venetians during WWII (supposedly).

Chapter 20

Christmas in East Puddleduck

"I ain't doing it this year!"

"Yes, you are!" Ma yelled out to El, who was dozing on the couch. El had his hand up over his eyes and was listening to the sound of snow on the television as the station was out again due to weather in the east blocking the already poor signal. Fluffbutt was sitting on El's chest, glaring down at Boris who was at his feet, tongue and tail wagging hoping the cat was in the mood to play. She wasn't.

Ma stomped into the family room and pointed at El, "You're playing Santa this year again and I don't want any argument over it!"

El looked up above his arm at Ma with one eye open, "Well, I ain't dying my beard white. You tried that crap last year, remember? You had me down to Ruby's with my head in her sink…" El's thoughts trailed off for a moment as he recalled Ruby's boobs hovering over his face while she was working on his hair, and a smirk came over the old man's face. El quickly shook his head in an effort to return his thoughts to the topic, "When she was done with me, my hair came out bright orange!"

"I remember that," Runyon said as he entered the house, shaking the freshly fallen show off the shoulders of his flannel coat. "You looked like a big, fat candle burning."

Ma interrupted, "Quit your belly-aching! It wasn't that bad. Plus, the kids had a good time painting your beard white! It gave them something to do while their parents all ate supper! Now, look here! Santa has always visited the diner during the season and this year ain't gonna be any different!" Ma was pointing and shaking her stubby finger at El.

Boris stood up as Ma's voice got louder, standing with his head near El's lap. Fluffbutt decided to let out a little growl and swatted the hound on his nose. Boris just wagged his tail faster, enjoying the attention.

El replied back to Ma, "Oh, I remember! It took weeks to get that white acrylic house paint out of my beard! Why don't you get Marmaduke to play Santa? He's got the white hair for it."

"He ain't fat enough. He's jolly enough, but he doesn't look the part. We'd need to duct tape way too many pillows to that toothpick! We don't need a lumpy Santa, we need a fat Santa!"

Fluffbutt continued to swat her hairy puffball of a paw at Boris's nose, each time causing the hound to shake his head and snort, as her hair was tickling his snout.

"Why can't Santa just have a red beard?" El remarked.

"Because, he can't!" Ma barked as she dug into her hutch where she kept her collection of cookbooks and magazines and pulled out an old Reader's Digest. "Now look, there's plenty of home recipes to help us dye your beard white. Bleach, white vinegar, lemon juice, and salt. Maybe hydrogen peroxide and aspirin. Lots of stuff that won't necessarily kill you if we're careful…" Ma trailed off as she walked into the kitchen as El sat up and looked over to Runyon, both wide-eyed and staring at each other at Ma's suggestions on how to make his beard white. Fluffbutt had to re-adjust to keep her hairy tush comfortable in El's lap as she continued to growl and swat at Boris.

Ma emerged from the kitchen and held up a container of Oxy-Clean with bleach. "We can try this stuff. She squinted and crinkled her nose as she checked the label, "Says it's safe as long as you don't drink it." She looked over at El. "We'll add in a little bit of paint thinner and see what happens!" Ma was being serious, which made El and Runyon all the more nervous.

Boris, who'd had enough of the cat's hairy paw on his nose, let out a loud sneeze and blew jowl drool and snot all over Fluffbutt's face, soaking her head and neck fur, staining it brown from the teriyaki beef jerky the dog had gnawed on just a bit earlier when Ma had been cleaning out the fridge. The cat wasn't impressed. Ma looked over at the cat and then back at the Oxy-Clean. As she turned again to continue on into the kitchen, "Looks like we'll need this stuff for something other than you're beard. Good thing the cat's got white fur to begin with."

Fluffbutt the cat jumped down, ran, and hid, and wasn't seen again for three days.

◆ ◆ ◆

Ma, Val, and Cicely were sitting around the center table in the diner late in the evening after closing. Ruby was standing behind the counter bar. On the table and bar top were various magazines and old cookbooks that Ma had dug out. Each had brought their own personal cookbooks along with them as well. Everyone was flipping through pages and seeking something special.

Cicely lowered her book and spoke up first. "What's on your mind, Ma? What are we looking for? Anything in particular?"

"Nope, just something new." Ma's eyes were squinting as she held the magazine up in front of her and tilted it towards the lights above, "I haven't changed the menu in quite a long time." She lowered the magazine and looked at Cicely, "I just figure we need something to break up the monotony. You know, something new and exciting, especially since it's the Christmas season. I don't want things to get stale around here, and even that fancy place in the city…" Ma looked over at Val, "…You know, that place with the upside-down golden buckets? Even they do something special every so often." Ma went back to flipping pages, "I just think we should try something new and out of the ordinary."

"Maybe you should just change the names of the meals up a bit." Val chimed in, "You know, like change the name of the burger and fry plate to something else. Maybe calling it the Puddleduck Beef Burger or something fancy?"

"Naw, that won't work. It'd still be the same meal. We need something new that we only bring out once in a while. Something that'd get people's attention. Make them take notice and realize we ain't just always serving up the same thing over and over all the time."

"You're going at this the wrong way, Ma," Ruby said as she flipped through a magazine on the counter bar, her elbows and boobs all resting on the bar top. "You always decide on the menu. And you always put all the work into it. Why don't you ask others to come up with something new?"

Cicely perked up. "Maybe she's onto something, Ma. Maybe ask others in town to come up with a dish that you'll take on here in the diner. Sort of a friendly competition to see who comes up with the best-tasting new recipe!"

Ma's demeanor perked up as well, "Jeesus, maybe you're right. We'll get others to come up with something new that we'll promise to serve here once in a while. We can even name the dish after the winner! A contest!"

Ruby stood up, her boobs still touching the bar, and said cautiously, "You're not going to do it like you did last one, are you, Ma?"

Ma looked over to Ruby and frowned. "No, there won't be any farting this time." Ma turned back and looked up at the ceiling as if the idea was written across it. "We'll make up flyers and get them out all around town. We'll make it part of the holiday festivities! Be the first to create the diner's new dish and have it named after you! Become part of the menu!"

"I don't know, Ma. What if people can't come up with anything?" Val remarked, "Nobody really knows how to cook, let alone something new. They all eat here every day."

Ma looked back to Val, "Nonsense! People just need to get creative. Put some thought into it. Hell, we thought of this, they can think up a simple new recipe! It's a great idea. It's festive!"

"A great idea. Yeah, right," Ruby whispered to herself sarcastically and leaned back on the counter, continuing to flip through magazine pages.

Ma was still deep in thought, "The flyers should be holiday themed, and we have to make it clear that folks need to be creative. Nothing that we already serve now. It has to be something new."

Ruby bounced back up, literally. "Oh, Ma, let me make the flyers! I'm really good at it! I make all my own advertising for the salon! Let me plan this out for you! You won't be disappointed!"

The three women seated at the table had turned to listen to Ruby, all watching in amazement as Ruby's bouncing boobs settled down. Ma thought for a moment and answered, "Well, all right, but you better not screw this up! And the flyers better look good! And make plenty of them!"

◆ ◆ ◆

The mayor and his two selectpersons were watching the McIntyre boys placing decorations on the town's Christmas tree in front of the municipal building on the snow-dusted front lawn near the gazebo. The boys had brought a front-end loader to assist in the job. Joshua was operating the heavy equipment, while Wally was in the bucket high up in the air, not overly happy about it with his fear of heights. The twenty-foot white pine was again this year generously donated to the town by Ma and El, straight off their homestead. Wally was placing the decorations on the tree, reaching out of the bucket. He began with the Christmas star tree-topper that was placed on the town's tree each year. In the bucket were lights and various decorations for Wally to begin at the top and work his way down. He was having a bit of difficulty keeping his balance while his brother was slowly driving the loader around and around the tree. Constable Bob was also assisting at the base of the tree with a donut in one hand and a hot coffee in the other, warning Wally each time an ornament didn't look straight.

"Star's a bit crooked!" the constable pointed out over the sound of the diesel tractor engine as he took another sip of his coffee.

"Shut up unless you want to come up here and do it!" Wally yelled down to him.

The mayor, all bundled up warm on the early December morning in a plaid flannel jacket over his maroon velvety suit, and a plaid trapper hat with fake fur lining and earmuffs, was supervising the decorating crew while his selectpersons, dressed just as warmly and eerily similar to the mayor, were complaining into his earmuffs.

"We just can't let her do it!" Selectperson Doody whined, "We can't have Ma giving the holiday speech this year on Christmas Eve!"

Daley echoed his counterpart's sentiments, "He's right, Mr. Mayor. Ma always starts out good, talking about the holiday and all, then she gets personal and singles out people to poke fun of and complain about."

"And we're dumb enough to give her an audience, a podium, and microphone right there in the gazebo to do it!" Doody continued his whining, "She takes everyone right out of the Christmas spirit and no one wants to sing the carols."

Constable Bob turned to the three. "It's true, Mayor. Don't you remember last year when she made fun of my police car? She said it looked like an old taxicab and asked how much I charge each prisoner for the rides? And then she made fun of my weight and called me a chunky donut-eating snowman and said the town should put me in front of this here tree for the season, but not to put a carrot on my face in place of my nose 'cause I'd just eat it." Bob stopped talking to take another bite of his jelly cream-filled.

"And two years ago she told Mattie that she couldn't join in the caroling because there weren't any Alvin and the Chipmunks songs in the book of Christmas carols!" Paul Doody reminded, "Do you remember that, Mayor? She said it right in public in front of everyone!"

"I know all that," the mayor responded defensively. "Three years ago she told everyone that my suit coat was so bright that all I had to do was put it on my roof and Santa could home in on its beacon. We all know how nasty Ma can be, but how are we going to say 'no' to her when they donated this nice big tree and all? Not to mention, the free hot cocoa and food she feeds us all on Christmas Eve before we all come up here for the caroling. I don't see how we can. As much as we'd like to tell Ma to shut up, we just can't."

Joshua was coming around the tree with the loader again as the group was talking. Wally was placing silver garland and the lights around the tree and trying his best not to fall out of the bucket as he stretched his arms out, garland in one hand and lights in the other, going in circles and slowly being lowered each time around. Wally was having his challenges balancing and trying not to have the garland and lights become tangled in one another. Bob had completed his snacking and was walking under the loader bucket, feeding the garland up to Wally from the ground, still listening to the conversation as best he could over the diesel engine.

When they came around to the mayor again, Bob stopped and let the shiny silver strand feed itself from his arms up to Wally as he walked back over to the three on the ground, "It's too bad we can't just keep Ma away from the gathering without her knowing about it," Bob remarked.

The mayor's eyes glimmered, and a smirk came over his face. "That's it!" He turned to his two board members, "I've got an idea! Ma's got that food-making contest coming up. She's going to judge everyone's entry in the diner on Christmas Eve before the gathering here at the gazebo. If we just get everyone to make something with alcohol as the main ingredient, without her knowing, she'll get so drunk on the food that she'll pass out before the presentation! We'll schedule her as usual so she don't know, and I'll just stand in after she passes out in the diner!" The mayor's eyes were wide, and he was staring up as if the Wicked Witch of the West were writing instructions across the sky. Neither Daley nor Doody knew what to make of the mayor's idea yet, and it showed on their faces. "It's brilliant, I tell you! We'll just make certain that nobody writes down the food title or ingredient list that there's alcohol in the recipe!" The mayor came back to earth and looked at both of the bewildered men in front of him and pointed, "It's gotta be a real recipe, something that tastes really good so Ma eats a good helping of each! And everyone has got to remain quiet about this!"

Bob was back standing nearer the three wise men, still holding a pile of silver garland in his arms that was feeding itself up to Wally. Having overheard enough of the mayor's plan, "Do you really think it'll work, Mr. Mayor? Do you think Ma won't really know there's alcohol in the food?"

"Well, if everyone makes a good-tasting hot dish chock full of other ingredients and spices and whatnot, then she shouldn't. She's not a big drinker, so if the food tastes really good I don't think she'll be able to tell."

Jacob chimed in, "She's gonna be awful mad when she wakes up with a bad headache."

The mayor had an answer for this too. "If the food's good and strong, she won't wake up until Christmas. And with all the food having booze in it, she won't know which one put her out." He then turned to the constable specifically, "Bob, you find out who's planning to enter a dish into Ma's contest and tell them my…err…our idea. Be sure to be discrete about it! And make sure no one lets on to Ma or we're all in for it!" Bob's head was instinctively and unknowingly nodding in agreement to the mayor's covert operation as silver garland continued to feed out of his arms. The mayor turned to Jacob. "You can't tell Val, she's too apt to tell Ma. And Cicely and Ruby can't know either." He turned back to Bob, "You can probably tell Smirnoff. He'll get a kick out of the whole thing and will probably make something himself without Cicely necessarily knowing about it." The mayor clapped his mitten-covered hands together, "Oh, this is going to be great! Okay, boys, operation Get Ma Tanked is on!"

All three men were nodding in agreement to the mayor's plan, whether they were clear on it or not. It was at that moment that the garland Bob was holding knotted up and went taught, pulling Bob backward towards the tree and yanking Wally from the bucket. He was still halfway up the tree when he fell, pulling the tree lights with him as he tumbled ten feet to the ground, landing on Bob's shoulders and both men went down. The tree shook and several ornaments fell to the snow. Joshua hadn't noticed and was still moving the loader around the tree, slowly dragging the two behind him. The mayor, along with his select board, simply shook their heads as they watched the two fumble on the ground while being dragged by the loader, all twisted up in silver garland and tree lights.

However, it was a bit unclear as to whether Jacob and Paul were shaking their heads from the spectacle before them, or whether it was due to their continued attempts to figure out the logistics of the mayor's plan to keep Ma from giving her speech on Christmas Eve.

◆ ◆ ◆

Ma had the diner all decked out for the holidays with red and green tablecloths and holiday napkins. She had twinkling lights strung around the dining room and counter bar, and a decorated tree in one corner. She'd even put up a Hanukkah menorah on one of the shelves so as not to leave anyone out. The kitchen radio, with its speakers mounted into the dining room that usually had country music playing, now currently had traditional holiday music coming from them. It was just loud enough to be heard over the patron's voices. On this day she'd moved the center tables together to form a long row for all the contestants to place their entries.

Ruby had done a fine job on the holiday flyers. Bob, oddly enough, had also done his part. He'd enjoyed the fact that it had been the first time ever in his career as a police officer that he'd gone undercover for an assignment. He made certain that every chef had put lots of alcohol in the food they'd prepared for Ma's judging, seemingly without her knowing about any of it.

Townsfolk were pouring into the diner, all dressed warmly for the festivities to take place later on that evening outside at the town hall gazebo. It was snowing lightly on this Christmas Eve afternoon, and the diner was toasty warm. Ma was handing out hot chocolate to everyone as they arrived and shed their warm clothing, exposing a multitude of colorful, ugly holiday sweaters. Some folks had battery-powered, multi-colored twinkle-lighted necklaces while others had furry, stuffed antlers rubber-banded to their heads. El was dressed as Santa, just like Ma had told him to do, with his beard bleached semi-white.

The mood was festive and jovial as contestants placed their hand-cooked and very special dishes for Ma to judge on the long center table. Each one had a folded piece of paper with the contestant's name on it without any ingredient list.

The mayor resembled a peppermint candy cane in his specially ordered pink-and-white velvety suit coat and dress pants to match. He was standing with his partners in crime, Daley, Doody, and Constable Bob, who had on one of the aforementioned stuffed antlers on top of his balding head and a big, red clown nose. He was obviously going for the 'Rudolf the Reindeer' look this day.

"You look like an idiot," Daley offered to him. "It's no wonder you want to knock Ma out. She'd crucify you later on for the way you look if she was going to be conscious."

"I'm just trying to get in the spirit of the season," Bob responded and then turned to the mayor and whispered for the two other partners-in-crime to hear, "Do you really think this will work, Mr. Mayor? I tell you, Mable put an awful lot of alcohol in her recipe, a whole bottle full, or at least what she didn't drink herself while she was making it."

"Mattie put real whiskey moonshine in hers!" Paul Doody whispered, "It's over a hundred proof! It might just kill the old woman."

"She'll be fine," the mayor replied softly to all three as he smiled and waved at various people in the diner. "Ain't no one as tough as Ma. It'll just knock her out for the night like we want it to."

Ma banged a pot and pan together to get everyone's attention, which the loud noise certainly achieved in doing. "Folks, quiet down! Plenty of hot cocoa for everyone, help yourself. It's time to do the official tasting while the food's hot and see who'd dish will end up a permanent part of my menu!" The diner crowd broke out in clapping and cheers. Ma walked over to the tables full of alcohol-fueled goodies and looked over the saturated delectables, unsuspecting of what she was about to sample. "My goodness, they all look so good!" she called out as the applauding began to die down, everyone smiling and in the spirit of the season.

The room then went quiet with everyone experiencing the anticipation and waiting for Ma to sample the first dish.

Just then Bob farted.

"Jeesus!" the mayor cried out, as the town leader and two select board members attempted to put space between themselves and the police officer.

"What the hell, Constable?!" Ma blurted, scowling at East Puddleduck's supposedly finest.

"Sorry, Ma. I guess my butt's having a flashback to your last contest. Some things just don't forget, you know."

"Your ass isn't that smart! Even if it does have a mind of its own! It's certainly where your brain is! Open that window behind you and waft that thing out into the air! I've got eating to do!" Bob did what he was told and proceeded to crack the window to air out what his crack had just released. He used a holiday napkin to assist in waving it out of the diner.

Ma's scowl remained as she turned back to the goodies on the table and prepared to sample the first one. It was a nice, big hotplate with Mattie Doody's honey whiskey barbeque pulled pork, heavy on the whiskey moonshine part, which the pork was floating in. Ma bent over the table to admire it and then looked up and found Mattie in the diner crowd. "This yours, Mattie? Well, I suppose it'll taste as good as it looks," remarking a bit sarcastically and smirking.

Mattie responded with a smirk of her own and just as sarcastically, "Oh, you'll like it, Ma. I just know you will."

Ma was a bit dubious of Mattie's tone and expression as she took a fork and put a nice big helping on one of the holiday paper plates and stood back up. She then gobbled a big mouthful of the saturated pork. Her expression turned to a confused frown, and she looked back over at the chef. "Jeesus, Mattie, this is good. It really is." Ma took another forkful and shoveled it in. "Good flavor! What did you season the pork with?"

The mayor, Daley, Doody, and Bob, all terrified and eyes wide, waited for Mattie's response. All three were involuntarily shaking their heads nervously.

"Oh, this and that," Mattie responded. "You know, mother's secret recipe and all."

The four conspirators all took a breath, relieved that the real secret hadn't been revealed.

"Well, it's damn good!" Ma said honestly as the patrons applauded Mattie's surprise dish. Ma took a third bite and then made her way to the second dish; it was Mabel Johnson's champagne risotto with roasted shrimp. Mable had literally drowned the shrimp in the champers and added it to the sauce as well. Ma shoveled a good helping into a plastic bowl and began sampling. She smiled at Mabel. "Once again, very tasty! Very good indeed! What's the secret in the sauce, there, Mabel?"

"Oh, I'll never tell, unless, of course, I win," Mabel smirked and remarked as again the crowd applauded.

The four unwise men in the corner all breathed another sigh of relief. Bob had a bit more trouble than the other three with the breathing part seeing that he had a big red ball on his nose.

Ma poured another big spoonful into her mouth before moving on to the next dish, a hearty warm pot that resembled soup with Smirnoff's name on the folded paper. "What's this?" Ma looked up and inquired of the man.

"It's solyanka. You'll enjoy it, it's a Russian recipe. It's full of sausage, bacon, ham, and beef. It also has vegetables such as cabbage, carrots, onions, and potatoes." What Smirnoff didn't mention was the fact that the broth was made almost completely with vodka.

Ma grabbed a soup spoon, bent over the pot, and shoveled a heaping helping into her mouth. When she stood back up, her eyes were a bit glassy.

"Mmmmm, good! It's very warm going down, more than you'd expect, and the heat tends to linger in your gut." Ma began to visibly wobble a bit and had to grab the tabletop. "Itshh eshtremely tasty," Ma slurred and took her second helping, with lots of broth. She said in a low voice to herself, "That's shom good shhhit." She dropped the spoon back into the pot, splashing solyanka onto the tabletop, and moved on to the next dish.

The mayor's smile widened, causing him to resemble the grinch a bit and he poked Bob in the gut. Pointing to Ma, he whispered, "It's kicking in."

Brazen bourbon meatballs was Myrtle Watson's entry, extremely heavy on the bourbon. Ma, all smiles, stuck her hand in the pot rather than using a spoon and shoved two huge meatballs in her mouth, and closed her eyes. "Mmmm, mmm, good! Tashtes wonderful! Nothing like a mouthful of big, huge meaty balls! Ishh gonna be hard beathing theeshh balls!" Ma reached in and gobbled up a third one before moving on.

The townsfolk all began to take notice, and many were giggling by now at Ma's obvious changing demeanor. Ma wobbled as she looked over at Myrtle and attempted to speak, "Those were very good…Shhhmyrtle. Susha meaty flavor." Ma began to tip sideways and caught herself on the table. "Shhit, almosht fell over. Can't talk very good neisher. Teeshh mushht be a bit loosh."

More giggling emitted from the crowd. The four criminals in the corner were all staring like kids on Christmas morning looking over the wrapped presents under the tree, all waiting for Ma to pass out.

Ma stumbled her way through the next two high-octane dishes, tequila lime shrimp and home brew beer stuffed mushrooms, enjoying each one and becoming more inebriated as she went. Ma finally landed at Puut's homemade dessert, baked banana distilled whiskey pudding. Emphasis on the whiskey that the Frenchman distilled himself. Ma, with great difficulty, grabbed a wooden cooking spoon and scooped up a helping, shoving it all in her pudding hole, much of it dripping down her chin.

She smiled and attempted to stand up straight and speak to the Frenchman, "Ahhh…itshhh…very…delishhhus. So bandana… banana… tashting… ahhhishhhmmm…" Ma's voice trailed, her eyes rolled back in her head and she fell backward. *Thump!* Landing face up on the diner floor, still holding the wooden spoon.

Bob spoke first as the diner crowd had gone quiet and appeared a bit stunned. "What? No winner?"

The mayor backhanded Bob in the gut, "Shut up and help me get her off the floor!"

El and Runyon got to Ma first and began to lift her as the four conspirators approached, one on each arm, and sat Ma down into a booth. El looked over at the mayor, "You better hope she doesn't remember this in the morning."

All four conspirators looked quite surprised and the mayor quipped, "You know?"

"Everyone knows! What'd you think was going to happen when you put the constable in charge of your ridiculous plan? The first thing he did that evening was broadcast it over his two-way police radio, telling anyone planning to enter her competition to drown it all in alcohol! Then he did the same on his CB radio…and then on a ham radio! The entire county knew! You're all just lucky Ma doesn't pay attention to any of those things."

El and Runyon sat Ma up straight. El wiped her face with a napkin and Runyon stuck a candy cane in each of her hands and propped them both on the booth table. El adjusted her glasses, Ma still had a grin on her unconscious face.

The mayor looked over at the constable, "You idiot! I said to be discrete and what do you do?! You had to go and broadcast it to the entire world!"

Bob shrugged his shoulders and approached the booth, taking the fake red nose off himself and putting it on Ma, as well as the fuzzy antlers rubber-banded to her head. Ma looked like Rudolph's homely mother-in-law.

El shook his head and repeated himself to the mayor, "You really better hope she don't remember any of this. Or at least doesn't figure out who was behind it."

The mayor responded a bit nervously, "Well, let's all have another cup of cocoa and head to the gazebo for the festivities."

♦ ♦ ♦

The microphone squeaked loudly as the mayor stood at the podium inside the tiny gazebo just outside of the town hall. "I'd like to start the evening by thanking the McIntyre brothers for the good job they did on the tree!" Pointing to the tree as the onlookers admired the lights and decorations on it this year. Bob, standing behind the mayor with Daley and Doody, led the townsfolk in clapping to the mayor's words, and the crowd joined in.

Everyone had left Ma sitting in her booth and they'd all gathered at the gazebo for the evening's holiday festivities, which would normally consist of Ma's verbal abuse followed by caroling to the children's choir, led by Myrtle Watson. Off to the side of the gazebo, Myrtle was preparing the children for when it was time and after Reverend Winkin was to be done with his annual Christmas blessing. The townsfolk each had a book of Christmas carols to sing along with the children, and many were holding lit candles. The snow was still coming down lightly and glimmering off the lights on the tree.

The mayor continued, "And a special thanks to…" The mayor stopped mid-sentence and looked up the roadway. "…Oh shit…" the mayor said softly and with a bit of fear as Bob, Paul, and Jacob also looked up and saw her coming. The townsfolk all began to turn around and see what they were gazing at. The preacher, Myrtle, and the children's choir off to the side all stretched their necks out to also determine what the anomaly was that everyone was looking at.

Under the dim streetlights and through the lightly falling snow Ma was seen staggering up the road towards them, and certainly not in a straight line. Ma's hair was down out of its bun and dangling in her face, the antlers and her reading glasses cocked off sideways in opposite directions. And, a big red ball stuck on her nose. For every two steps she took to the left going forward, she'd take three to the right, and with great difficulty in her balance. Ma didn't have on a jacket over her Christmas sundress. Instead, it appeared she had one of her green tablecloths draped over her shoulders and a red one tied loosely around her waist and dragging behind her.

"We're all dead men," Paul Doody whispered. All four in the gazebo were terrified and their wide eyes stared as Ma staggered closer. At one point she strayed so far to the right that she walked off the roadway and into a small, snow-covered pine bush. However, that didn't stop her as she got right back up and continued staggering forward, slurring a curse word, or possibly several.

When Ma finally walked up to the rear of the crowd, she stopped, swaying as she stood with a frown on her red-nosed face. The townsfolk remained silent and cautious, waiting to see what wrath their intoxicated matriarch was about to unleash. Ma's glassy eyes scanned the crowd through her crooked glasses. She looked up at the gazebo's occupants and pointed at them with the one hand that didn't have a mitten on it, and all four winced as if Ma's finger had shot lightning from it. Ma proceeded forward and the crowd parted to give her way, all relieved that they weren't the brunt of whatever was to come. Ma staggered to the podium and tripped on the steps, catching herself and managing to remain upright. The four conspirators backed up as Ma approached. Unfortunately for them, they had nowhere to go with Ma blocking the gazebo's entrance. Ma approached the mayor and stood, swaying and frowning, facing the petrified town leader. He winced, waiting for Ma's vengeance.

"Merry Chrishtmas, Mishtor Mayor!" Ma yelled out, smiled, and threw her arms around the man. The mayor's eyes widened as the drunken woman fell into him and hugged him tightly. The crowd remained stunned and silent. Ma then pushed Rupert away and grabbed both selectpersons, each in one arm, and pulled them in tight to her. "Poopy and Ukulele! You two scallywags! Happy Hanukah!" Both men were in shock, each literally holding Ma upright as she hugged them, looking confusingly at each other behind her back. People in the crowd began to chuckle at the inebriated women's actions. Ma then pushed the two select board members away and turned to the constable, facing him and swaying as she looked up at the fat man. Bob looked down at Ma, his eyes still wide. He cautiously put his arms out in wait for his hug.

Ma looked the constable up and down, swaying and nearly losing her balance. "Holy shit, Krish Krinkle, you're taller than I thought you'd be. And a lot fatter, too!" Bob's expression frowned. "Jusht kidding, conshtable. I think I love you mosht of all! Feline Navidash!" Ma fell into Bob and wrapped her drunken arms around the man. Bob smiled and returned the hug. Ma then pushed Bob away and turned, falling into the podium, and began her drunken holiday speech, yelling her slurring voice into the microphone. "I jusht want to say to everyone that I love you all! Even you, Mattie, you old warthog!"

Ma was all smiles as she lost her footing again when she raised a hand above her head. Bob reached out and caught her, preventing her from falling to the gazebo floor. Ma then pointed at the town's tree while keeping her other hand on the podium to steady herself. "And look at that beautiful shree! It's just gorgeoush! It brings out the holiday shhpirit in all of ushh! You're all sushh wonderful people, even Shhhmirnoff…" Ma looked around the crowd, what she could clearly see of them. "Where is that big, Russshian bear? Ah, there you are!"

Smirnoff was chuckling at Ma's comments. He blew her an air kiss and called out over the crowd's laughing, "We love you too, old woman!"

"Aff coursh you do! Ha, ha! Who wouldn't love thish?!" Ma yelled back and attempted to strike a pose, nearly falling sideways.

The crowd was laughing and a few applauded at the spectacle in the gazebo. El leaned to Runyon, "They all better hope she doesn't remember this tomorrow." Runyon nodded back in agreement.

Ma squinted and crinkled her nose seeking out her next target, causing the red ball to pop off and bounce out of the gazebo. "Whoopsies, losht my nosesh…heh, heh, heh!" Ma spotted her next victim, "Marmadick…dink… duke, Marmaduke! Yeah, that's it. Marmaduke, my friend! I love you, you schnowy white candlshtick, you!"

Marmaduke, seemingly unimpressed, just shook his head as he made his way closer to El and Runyon through the crowd of chuckling onlookers. He poked his head between the two, "You need to get her out of that gazebo," he told them both.

"Let's shing!" Ma cried out and turned to the four behind her. "Whose got the mushic book?" All four shook their heads slowly at Ma and she turned back around, grabbing the podium to assist her balance. "Shcrew it! We'll make the shhhit up! Shing along with me!" She cried out to the townsfolk and then turned to the children's choir, "You too, you lovely little sherubs!

Sching along! …Jingle bellshh, Voisine schmells, Mattie laid an egg..!" Ma sang out loud into the microphone, blaring her drunken voice through the speakers.

The laughing from the onlookers grew louder as the mayor, Bob, Paul, and Jacob all backed up against the wooden side rails, all unsure of what to do. Marmaduke repeated to El and Runyon that they needed to get the drunken woman out of the gazebo.

"C'mon! Itsha holiday conshert!" Ma slurred loudly, "Wait, I'll prove it and take my bra off and toshh it at the band!" Pointing as best she could towards the children who were all waiting off to the side of the gazebo, wide-eyed in their holiday best. Each child wondered what to make of the disheveled, drunken woman. Father Winkin was standing with them, more than a bit stunned himself, his head instinctively shaking slowly and not knowing what to do as Ma tugged at her tablecloths in an attempt to remove her brazier.

"Oh, Jeesus!" El cried out. El, Runyon, and Marmaduke all rushed toward the gazebo. They each grabbed onto Ma before she could yank her sundress up and expose herself to the children's choir, and quickly began to escort her out of the gazebo.

"Wait," Ma said to them, "I want to shhing with everyone, it's Chrishtmoushh!"

As the three carried Ma out of the gazebo, quite literally, she passed out in their arms. "Let's get her back to the diner and put the coffee to her," El said as the three waded through the crowd that had gone mostly silent and stared as they carried the unconscious woman back up the road to the diner.

The mayor approached the podium as everyone watched Ma being hauled away. A few in the crowd were still giggling, while others were a bit stunned, not really knowing what to think. When they turned back to focus their attention on the mayor, Rupert opened his mouth to speak. He intended to announce that the caroling would begin; however, he hesitated at the microphone and changed his mind after thinking for a moment or two while staring up the road. "Folks," he began as he looked over the crowd, "I think we should all go back to the diner for the caroling and blessing." A sincere tone overtook the mayor, "It wouldn't be right to leave anyone out." The mayor glanced over to the preacher, who nodded and closed his eyes in agreement. He then looked back to the three behind him, all looking down with their shoulders slumped a bit, and nodding silently in agreement. The mayor turned his attention back to the townsfolk, "Let's all carol our way back to the diner! Father Winkin, if you'd please have the children's choir lead us there."

And so, the townsfolk who were led by the children's choir all walked back to the diner singing carols along the way under the lightly falling snow.

When they arrived, they found Ma had been returned to her booth, this time without the candy canes, furry antlers, or big red nose. Ruby took a moment to put Ma's hair back up in its usual bun, and El put the Santa jacket over her shoulders. Runyon made some fresh coffee, and Cicely and Val brewed up more hot chocolate and reheated all the food, although dispensing it sparingly so that no one got tipsy from eating meatballs and such. They all remained in the diner, eating good food, drinking hot drinks, and singing Christmas carols. All except for that one that Father Winkin held off on having the children sing just yet.

◆ ◆ ◆

It was about two hours later that Ma began to come around. The mayor noticed and motioned for everyone to gather around the booth. Father Winkin and Myrtle Watson readied the children. Ma woke up with El sitting beside her and everyone in the diner, at the preacher's signal, quietly began singing "Silent Night."

Ma opened her eyes and looked at El. "What happened?" she asked.

"How you feel, Ma?" Runyon inquired as he set a hot cup of coffee in front of her.

"Fine. Never better. Bit of a headache."

"You did good, Ma," El said, "you declared Mattie the winner of the contest and gave a fine speech at the gazebo."

"I did? Can't seem to remember it," Ma replied as the singing softly continued around her.

Old Marmaduke sat down in the booth in front of Ma. "And you had everyone come back here to sing in the warmth of the diner and eat some good food."

"I did? Why can't I remember any of this?" She looked up and located Smirnoff standing nearby, who was looking down at Ma and smiling. "You put something in that soup, didn't you?" Pointing up at the man, "You poisoned me with that weird Russian food."

Smirnoff just winked and blew Ma an air kiss, and then sipped more hot chocolate. Ma simply smiled back at him through her slight headache.

El put the Santa suit back on and handed out gifts to the choir, and the townsfolk sang and drank hot cocoa to the stroke of midnight when Father Winkin gave the blessing, welcoming Christmas once again to the little town of East Puddleduck.

It would be a holiday season that the townsfolk would reminisce about often in the years to come. However, when doing so in front of Ma, they'd purposely leave out a few details.

And Ma honored her contest rules and added Mattie's pulled pork as a holiday menu item. The only thing was, Ma just couldn't exactly make it taste the same as Mattie's did on that Christmas Eve no matter how hard she tried…

…for some strange reason.

Chapter 21

The Krona

The month was March. Constable Bob rushed into Mayor Wiggleswort's office, panting and sweating, and this time not simply from his self-induced condition of obesity. He nearly caused the wooden legs on the mayor's desk to crack and break as he fell against it with exhaustion. The mayor's candy dish which was full of peppermint snowflake balls tipped over from the impact, which annoyed the mayor immensely. The mayor had been seated in conference with first and second selectpersons, Daley and Doody, which basically translated to they were all having coffee together and talking about the weather with nothing better to do.

"Mayor, we have a serious problem!" The constable blurted out, "I just heard from the town manager in Skunksquirt! It's the Krona!"

The mayor, obviously quite annoyed with Bob as he was plucking up snowflakes to put them back in their dish, checking each one carefully for dust, looked up at Bob over his reading glasses that were perched on the bridge of his nose. With one eyebrow raised, "And what, may I ask, is the Krona?"

"It's a bad virus, Mayor! It's everywhere and spreading! They said it's a global panda-demic!" And, as if the mispronounced word had stuck everyone in the office in their behinds with a long needle, they all sprang up from their chairs and began caterwauling in a panic.

"A pandemic?!" the mayor exclaimed. "That's worse than a virus!" As the mayor pointed at Bob, who was already nodding his head uncontrollably, "We haven't had a pandemic for nearly over one hundred years! Are you certain?!"

"They said it's everywhere and spreading fast!"

"How do you catch it?!" Daley squawked and asked with a terrified look on his face.

"How do we prevent it?!" Came from Doody directly to the constable, as if he was a professional on the subject.

Bob spoke up again, "They say it's spreading fast! It makes you real sick! They said it can put you in the hospital, or worse, can even kill you! They say to prevent it you gotta put on a mask and buy toilet paper!"

"Put on a mask? What kind of a mask?" the mayor asked with a puzzled look, crinkling his nose as he asked the question and adjusted his eyeglasses upwards.

Doody blurted out and asked, "You have to buy toilet paper? Why? Does it give you the shits?!"

Bob answered, still panting but now having enough energy to stand up from the mayor's desk, sweat pouring off his pudgy brow, "I don't know, but they said you have to wear an approved mask, and toilet paper's running out fast everywhere, they said! They also said it lasts for fourteen days if it don't kill you first!"

"You get the shits for fourteen days?!" Doody cried out with his eyes wide, "There'll be nothing left of anyone after fourteen days!"

Daley turned to the mayor, "It must be true, Mayor! This explains why Smirnoff said yesterday that he couldn't find any toilet paper to restock the store! I was in the store when he said it! He said he's never seen it happen before!"

"Jeesus, it must be bad if the toilet paper's running out," Doody exclaimed to the others and then turned to the mayor. "We gotta do something! I can't have the shits for fourteen days!"

"Did they say what's causing it?" Mayor Wiggleswort inquired of Bob, putting one hand on the lawman's shoulder and looking a bit scared.

"They said a Chinese vampire bat bit someone! That's what started it all. And, they said you gotta stay back away from everyone or you'll catch it!"

The mayor jerked his hand back, and the four in the room looked at each other cautiously. Everyone took a step back from one another.

"They said you have to put the masks to keep from catching it and the mask has gotta cover your mouth and nose. And they have to be approved by someone!" Constable Bob blurted out with a more-than-terrified expression on his perspiring face.

"Approved? Why do they need to be approved? Who approves the masks?" Doody asked, his head bouncing back and forth between everyone in the room.

The mayor quickly answered, "Well, I suppose I do, being at the top of the decision tree for the town and all," looking around the room as if seeking acknowledgment from the other three, who were all unconsciously nodding to his words.

Doody, who was now a wreck and shaking at the thought that he might have the runs for two weeks straight looked to the mayor for guidance. "We have to do something! We have to let people know! We have to find more toilet paper! What do we do, Mayor?!"

"We'll call an emergency town meeting!" the mayor declared. "We can't let this…," turning to Constable Bob, "what did you call it? Krona?"

"Yes, sir." As Bob popped a peppermint snowflake in his mouth, which seemed to calm his nerves considerably.

"We can't let this Krona thing get into town and spread. We can't have everyone having the shits all at once, that'd be disastrous! The wastewater system just can't handle a surge like that!" The mayor looked around the room at the other three. "Make sure you all find a mask of some sort and we'll meet tonight! And don't tell your better halves yet, we don't want this getting out before the meeting and we end up with a panic on our hands!" The mayor turned to Bob, "You go out and find us all some masks to pass out later on!"

Everyone in the room nodded in confusing, terrified agreement as the mayor directed Constable Bob to make the necessary notifications to the residents by putting up flyers around town that there would be a town meeting in the council chambers later that same evening, and that all residents should be urged to attend. And, seeing that emergency town meetings weren't common in the tiny town and rumors were certain to spread quickly about what the meeting may be about, it was expected that all of the residents, or at least a majority, would be in attendance. Not to mention, the flyer Bob came up with read like this:

EMERGENCY TOWN MEETING
TONIGHT IN THE COUNCIL CHAMBERS
AT 7:00 P.M.
ALL RESIDENTS URGED TO ATTEND!
MAYOR NEEDS TO ALERT THE TOWN ABOUT
POSSIBLE TOILET PAPER SHORTAGE

◆ ◆ ◆

Later that evening the first to arrive at the meeting was Ma, with El dragging behind. Ma waddled into the council chambers, squawking as soon as she entered the building and even before opening the swinging double doors to the meeting room. She was looking straight down at the floor as if the floor could understand her complaining. "Town's wasting my time! Making us all meet and talk about toilet paper!" What the hell is this all…?!" She ceased mid-sentence as she swung the doors open and entered the room. Standing up straight, she immediately saw the three board members sitting far apart from each other at three folding tables that were set up in a semi-horseshoe fashion. Seated to the far left was Councilperson Doody, sporting an old hockey mask that was dirty and cracked, causing the man to resemble Jason Voorhees from the Friday the 13th movie franchise. She looked to the far right at Daley who was wearing a Woody Woodpecker Halloween mask with a long, limp rubber beak. In the middle was the mayor, wearing a furry gorilla mask he'd once worn to an office party several years back. In fact, to be extra cautious, the mayor had on the entire furry gorilla suit, which was somewhat tattered and smelled heavily of mothballs from years of storage in his attic.

"As I live and breath! Did I miss something?" Ma exclaimed and then burst out in laughter, one hand on her belly and the other pointing at the mayor, "Did I miss the memo about this being a costume party, or have all three of you finally gone mad?" She continued her uncontrollable laughter.

"Just sit down, Ma, and quit your fun-making," the gorilla exclaimed, waving his furry arm and motioning to Ma to take a seat. "This is serious business!"

"I'm sure it is, King Kong," Ma said as she took a seat in the front of three rows of metal chairs, which were all spaced apart. "If I would've known I would've brought you some bananas from the diner," she said in a lower voice to herself but loud enough to be overheard. She settled into her uncomfortable metal chair, still giggling to herself.

One by one, many, if not most of the residents of East Puddleduck sauntered into the meeting, each eager to know what the problem was with the town's toilet paper supply. Each giggled or all-out laughter as they entered and viewed the spectacle sitting at the board tables. The chuckling and chatter in the audience all surrounding what sort of drugs the three board members may have taken with their dinner to cause the donning of ridiculous costumes. Even the three wives, who hadn't been told in advance by their spouses what the meeting would be about, sat together all with their arms folded in a bit of a foul mood. Each wondered what stupidity their husbands were going to cause them, which was certain to result in great embarrassment, if it hadn't already.

The last to stroll into the chambers was Marmaduke. As he entered, he looked at the three and simply shook his head as if it was not a surprise to him that the town's decision-makers were dressed up like they were going trick-or-treating in March. He pointed at the mayor and said, "You know, I really loved you in Every Which Way But Loose." Marmaduke sat down in the last row. After a few moments, and after the mayor quieted the crowd by banging his gavel, Marmaduke began singing softly the "Banana Boat Song," otherwise affectionately known as "Day-O," made famous by Harry Belafonte. Others began joining in, because, as you know, it's one of those jingles that you just can't help but sing along to. Soon, the entire room, minus the three costumed selectpersons, were singing:

♬ "Come, mister tally man, tally me banana…
…Daylight come and me wan' go home"♬

The gorilla gaveled down and attempted to yell over the crowd, "Stop that! Stop that now!"

♬ "Lift six foot, seven foot, eight foot bunch…
…Daylight come and me wan' go home"♬

"Stop that now!" the ape yelled louder as he banged the gavel to the point that it finally broke into two pieces and the head flew backward and bounced off the wall. Just as it hit the floor, Contestable Bob rushed into the room wearing a Richard Nixon full-head mask and carrying a large box. The gorilla pointed the broken end of the gavel he was still holding at him. "You're late!"

"I had a hard time finding more masks!" the former president exclaimed as he shuffled up to the board table and placed the box near the gorilla, then took a spot standing nearer to Jason Voorhees at the end of his table. "We didn't have a whole lot left over from that party you threw in ninety-nine. I found these in the attic upstairs. Do you remember that party, Mayor? That one where you wore that same gorilla suit and was drinking vodka martinis? Remember, you tried to stick those three bananas…"

The furry mayor cut the president short, "All right! No one needs to reminisce about that! Let's get this meeting started. We have a serious situation on our hands. We are here to discuss the Krona!"

"What's a Krona?" a question came from Marmaduke in the last row.

Ma turned around as best she could, swiveling her butt cheeks on the metal chair, and said in the most serious tone as if she knew what she was talking about, "It's a beer. You put a lime in it. It isn't bad. We had a few at camp once." Ma swung back around towards the board and pointed. "Is that what you got us down here for?! You want me to start serving liquor at the diner, don't you?!" She had a serious scowl on her face as she pointed straight at the gorilla.

"No, Ma, shush up!" The mayor continued, "It's a pandemic! A big one! People are getting sick everywhere! All over the world and everywhere else too! Folks are getting sick, and some are even dying."

The crowd gasped in awe at the news. Whispering immediately began amongst the crowd. Questions were asked. Confusion took over the room quickly. "What do we do?!" came the first question out loud from the audience, quickly followed by the second, "How do we stop it?!"

Joshua turned to his brother, "It must make you turn stupid and put on costumes!" Joshua then stood and addressed the board, "You three got it already?!"

Woody Woodpecker replied, sternly, which caused his rubber beak to flap up and down uncontrollably, "No! You have to wear a mask and buy toilet paper to keep from catching it!"

"Toilet paper?! Why?! Does it give you the shits?!" Runyon stood up and inquired loudly.

"We don't know, but it's spreading and you have to do it! There ain't no shot for it yet! It's a new virus, nothing like anyone's ever seen! And it's bad!" Jason Voorhees attempted to explain to everyone.

"What caused it…this pan-de-mic?" El asked, being careful to pronounce the word correctly.

President Nixon spoke up, "A Chinese bat bit a vampire and started it all!"

"Shut up, you idiot, you got it wrong," came the response from Jason Voorhees, turning towards the ex-president.

Ma's turn, "And Corona cures it? No problem! I'll order several cases right away and have them ready in the diner! You're going to need to take a vote to give me a temporary liquor license!" Ma directed her comments to the three unwise men before turning to speak to the audience. "Wait! If it's that bad and causes the shits, maybe we should go stronger!" She turned back towards the cartoon characters at the head of the room and pointed, "Maybe we get a good supply of the Boone's Farm Tickled Pink instead! That'll do the trick! We'll even add some Pepto to it to stop the flow!" Unfortunately, Ma was being dead serious at this point, not wanting to see everyone get the shits and all. If it kept the residents healthy, she'd be willing to do her duty and temporarily serve alcohol.

"No, no, no!" The hairy mayor exclaimed, "It's called Krona! It ain't cured by Corona! Nor Boone's Farm neither! There ain't no cure yet. We have to be careful and wear masks. And they said the masks need to be approved. Now, I'm the only one here important enough to approve them…" The mayor now dug into the box as he continued, "Now, I've approved these masks here…" The first one the mayor pulled out was an old rubber Frankenstein mask and he flopped it onto the table, with the second being an equally aging and cracking plastic clown mask, complete with a tiny rubber string.

"You mean we have to wear those old, ugly things all the time?!" Marmaduke exclaimed loudly and sarcastically, "I ain't putting one of those stupid things on my head! I'll take my chances, I just dug a new hole for the outhouse anyway last week and I got lots of toilet paper! If that runs out, I got plenty of maple leaves!"

Another voice spoke up from the audience; it was Smirnoff's, "What's a pandemic?!"

Woody Woodpecker answered him, "It's a bad bug that gives you the shits! You don't want it! I had the shits a few years back from that virus those birds caused. I couldn't stop going for a week, and I chaffed something awful! And this one must be way worse if all the toilet paper's running out everywhere!"

Smirnoff agreed, addressing the audience, "It's true. I can't get any туалетная бумага from any of my suppliers now, it's all gone."

"English, you asshole! Speak English!" Ma yelled as she squirmed around in her chair to face Smirnoff, causing the metal chair legs to scrape on the floor. It made a noise similar to running one's fingernails across a chalkboard, causing everyone in the room to cringe. "It's called toilet paper! Butt wipes! Ass napkins! Tush towels! Not whatever you just said!"

Smirnoff just responded with an air kiss to Ma as she scowled and turned back around, fixing her chair by bouncing it back into place and facing forward.

The former President Nixon chimed in, "I heard that we all need to stock up on canned food too!"

"It makes canned food disappear?! What kind of God-awful disease is this?!" The panicked voice was from Eleanor Wiggleswort, who cried out as her furry husband pulled from the box a rubber alligator mask, complete with a long floppy snout in one hand, and a rubber donkey mask with an equally floppy snout in the other. He gazed at both of them with peculiar interest.

Just then the instigator of the Watergate scandal spoke up, "Wait, Mayor! You can't use that gator mask!"

The gorilla turned to him, "What, why? Who says so?"

President Nixon continued, "I don't know exactly, but they said to me you can't use a gator mask. Something about they don't protect you as well! They said they ain't approved!"

Mayor Kong gazed at the mask, "That doesn't make any sense! What's the difference between this gator mask and this donkey mask?" Shoving both into the air as he spoke, "I'm making the decisions on what's approved and what isn't! And we don't have a lot of masks to go around! I say this here gator mask is fine!" Throwing both on the table as he said this.

"How does it spread?" Another question from the audience. "Do we have to be bitten by the Chinese bat too? I got bats in my barn, how do I know if they're Chinese? What does a mask have to do with getting bit by a bat?!"

"You don't catch it from a Chinese bat, nor any other! You just catch it if you're too close to someone that's got it!" The furry mayor pulled another mask from the box, this one being a full rubber werewolf head with half of its fur missing. The gorilla just shook his head and put it on the table with the others.

A voice from the second row, "I got an old Phantom of the Opera mask at home in the attic somewhere! Would that be okay?!"

The mayor looked up. "Does it cover your whole face? It has to cover your whole face!"

"How about Wild Turkey? Eighty proof!" Ma shouted.

"I told you, alcohol doesn't cure it!" Still digging through the box and removing a green-colored, stringy clown wig, "This won't do…" Throwing it back in the box.

"Don't hurt none, either. I vote for the Boone's Farm!" Another voice responded.

"Right turn, Clyde." Obviously from Marmaduke.

Still, another voice, "What about a costume without the mask? I've got an old Saturday Night Fever disco costume I think in my basement somewhere. It might still fit!"

"Doubtful." And yet another. If nothing else, the meeting was getting plenty of citizen involvement like never before.

The fur-covered mayor stopped pawing through the box and looked up, pointing his hairy gorilla-gloved finger at the townsfolk. "Now, look, I'm not telling you all again. Plus, I'm starting to sweat in this monkey suit! I told you all, masks that cover your whole face! The rest of the costume is optional! And toilet paper, don't forget the toilet paper!" The mayor attempted to end the meeting by banging his gavel, only to swing a broken stick, having forgotten that he'd lost the rest of it at the beginning of the meeting. He scowled through his mask and simply waved the broken handle in the air in front of him. "Meeting adjourned! Grab a mask on your way out!"

◆ ◆ ◆

And so, for nearly two weeks following the meeting, the townsfolk went about their daily business. As a result, anytime they were out in the community they donned their "approved" costume masks. The town looked as if Halloween had come too early, or possibly too late that year. They also bought up all of Smirnoff's stock of toilet paper and canned food, at least what he had left. Along with the rest of the country, everyone began to panic more about the diminishing supply of butt wipes rather than the virus itself.

Ma began serving up complimentary shots of Wild Turkey with every meal she served at the diner, just in case, wanting to do her all for the cause. She still didn't have a liquor license but, as usual, she wasn't a bit concerned about that.

Two weeks later the next local paper finally arrived in town explaining just what the pandemic was all about, what an "approved mask" actually was, and the other recommendations that came along with it. Needless to say, it certainly didn't explain the whole thing about toilet paper and canned food.

You would have thought that the townsfolk, at that point, would have felt rather silly having worn Halloween costumes daily for the better part of two weeks, but they really didn't. It was comical to see the diner filled with characters of all sorts. There remained a bit of a challenge, though, in attempting to eat a meal through a mask. A bit of quick thinking from Ma resulted in a run on berry smoothies that could be consumed through a straw during that time Not to mention you could drink your shot of Wild Turkey in the same manner.

Wild Turkey and strawberry smoothies became the preventative measure for the residents of East Puddleduck during the COVID pandemic. Well, except for Ma's own rule of no alcohol shots for anyone under the age of eighteen. And for once the townsfolk didn't mind Ma's sign over the road at the town border. They didn't want any outsiders bringing the mysterious virus that devoured toilet paper and caused canned food to disappear to their tiny town.

Chapter 22

The Last Chapter

Well, just like with every beginning, there must be an ending. At least for the time being, anyway.

Life today is still mostly the same in East Puddleduck. Things here don't seem to change much, even with concerns like a pandemic causing changes everywhere else. Ma and Mattie are still feuding over everyday things, and El's still asleep on the couch most of the time. Dreaming of his weather lady while Fluffbutt continues to wag her tail in his face, Boris lays at his feet, and Ma yells at him to get up and do something.

Runyon does, in fact, have a girlfriend who's from Skunksquirt that he's dating, and he's started bringing her to the homestead more often. He's still trying to figure out how to explain to Ma the minor detail about where she's from as their relationship becomes more serious.

Puut continues to fawn over Ruby and has even proposed marriage to her at least once that we know of. Who knows, she just might say yes. Wouldn't that be a sight? Ruby living off-grid on Puut's homestead, taking showers in his backyard pond water and peek-a-boo shower stall. They'd be certain to be spontaneously visited more often by the menfolk from town if that happens. Chances are, though, it won't, and Ruby will just continue to enjoy his attention.

There is one thing that might just confirm the mystery of whether or not Puut and Ruby are dating. The McIntyre brothers now claim that Puut confirmed that the pin-up photo in their garage is, in fact, Ruby in her younger days. I don't necessarily believe it, though. I think they're just bragging amongst themselves.

Constable Bob keeps things quiet and continues to have his supper, as well as most other meals in the diner every day. And, it's not always just the free chili that he won. Ma limits him on that and has sternly warned him against any unexpected flatulence within her establishment unless it's during the annual 'Bucksnort' competition.

It's also a good bet that the mayor is certain to win the next election again, assuming that no cartoon characters run against him.

And Ma is still, "Ma." She has no intention of changing for anyone. She still dislikes both moose and foreigners. In fact, Ma says her next gimmick, when she finally shoots her moose, will be to have the entire animal stuffed with its head mounted inside the diner and the rest of the body outside of the establishment. She wants it to look as if the moose just poked its head through the diner wall. She said she got the idea from Runyon who, when he was a child, would sit in the diner and admire the deer head mounted to the wall, always asking Ma where the rest of the animal was. I think this idea just might get Ma's Diner into the papers this time like she so desperately has been attempting to achieve.

One other thing; the powers-that-be did, in fact, vote to have a new sign made up for the over the road at the edge of town that still reads, "Welcome to East Puddleduck." Only this time without Ma's "Except for Foriners!" added to it. Now, Ma has those exact words on a huge, embroidered banner that hangs just beneath the town sign, outlined in bright, flashing neon lights that are constantly powered by two solar panels and seven batteries.

THE END

ABOUT THE AUTHOR

David Wilson is a native Mainer, both living and working in the central and northern regions of the pine tree state. Over the years, he's enjoyed many adventures with friends and family, many haven taken place at their family camp in the northern Maine woods.

Growing up at camp, David experienced what it was like to live life without electricity, running water and other creature comforts. He learned how to utilize nature, the lake, and the woods of Maine as his forms of enjoyment rather than more modern forms of amusement such as cellphones, video games or even indoor plumbing.

Along his journey, David has met many unique characters each with amusing stories to tell which David enjoys incorporating into his books. David uses these, and his adventures as the inspiration for his novels.